ROBIN HOBB

DRAGON KEEPER

Volume One of the *Rain Wilds Chronicles*

HARPER Voyager

An Imprint of HarperCollinsPublishers

HARPER Voyager

An Imprint of HarperCollins*Publishers*
195 Broadway
New York, NY 10007

First Harper Voyager mass market printing: February 2011
First Eos hardcover printing: February 2010

Harper Voyager and ⟩ is a trademark of HCP LLC.

Printed in the U.S.A.

20 19 18 17 16 15

*To the memory of Spot and Smokey, Brownie-butt
and Rainbow, Rag-bag and Sinbad.
Fine pigeons, one and all.*

CONTENTS

Cast of Characters

The Rain Wilds Chronicles

Keepers and Dragons

ALUM: Pale skin, silvery gray eyes. Very small ears. Nose almost flat. His dragon is ARBUC, a silver-green male.

BOXTER: Cousin to Kase. Coppery-eyed, short, stoutly built. His dragon is orange male SKRIM.

COPPER: An unclaimed, sickly brown dragon.

GREFT: Eldest of the keepers, and most heavily marked by the Rain Wilds. His dragon is blue-black KALO, the largest male.

GRESOK: Large red dragon, first to leave the cocooning grounds.

HARRIKIN: Long and slim as a lizard, at twenty, he is older than most of the other keepers. Lecter is his foster brother. His dragon is RANCULOS, a red male with silver eyes.

JERD: A blond female keeper, heavily marked by the Rain Wilds. Her dragon is VERAS, a queen, dark green with gold stippling.

KASE: Boxter's cousin. He has copper eyes and is short, wide, and muscular. His dragon is orange male DORTEAN.

LECTER: Orphaned at seven, raised by Harrikin's family. His dragon is SESTICAN, a large blue male with orange scaling and small spikes on his neck.

NORTEL: A competent and ambitious keeper. His dragon is lavender male TINDER.

RAPSKAL: A heavily marked keeper. His dragon is the small red queen HEEBY.

SILVER: Has an injured tail and no keeper.

SYLVE: A twelve-year-old girl, youngest of the keepers. Her dragon is golden MERCOR.

TATS: The only keeper to have been born a slave. He is tattooed on the face with a small horse and a spider web. His dragon is the smallest queen, green FENTE.

THYMARA: Sixteen years old; has black claws instead of nails and is at home in the trees. Her dragon is a blue queen, SINTARA, also known as SKYMAW.

TINTAGLIA: An adult queen dragon, she assisted the serpents on their journey up the river to cocoon. It has been years since she has been seen in the Rain Wilds.

WARKEN: A tall, long-limbed keeper. He is devoted to his dragon BALIPER, a scarlet male.

THE BINGTOWNERS

ALISE KINCARRON FINBOK: Comes from a poor but respectable Bingtown Trader family. The dragon expert. Married to Hest Finbok. Gray eyes, red hair, many freckles.

HEST FINBOK: A handsome, well-established, and wealthy Bingtown Trader.

SEDRIC MELDAR: Secretary to Hest Finbok, and friends with Alise since childhood.

THE CREW OF THE *TARMAN*

BELLIN: Deckhand. Married to Swarge.

BIG EIDER: Deckhand.

CARSON LUPSKIP: Hunter for the expedition. Leftrin's old friend.

DAVVIE: Apprentice hunter to Carson Lupskip. About fifteen years old.

GRIGSBY: Ship's cat. Orange.

HENNESEY: First mate.

JESS: Hired hunter for the expedition.

LEFTRIN: Captain. Robust build, gray eyes, brown hair.

SKELLY: Deckhand. Leftrin's niece.

SWARGE: Tillerman. He has been with the *Tarman* for more than fifteen years.

TARMAN: A river barge, long and low. Oldest existing liveship. Home port Trehaug.

MISCELLANEOUS CHARACTERS

ALTHEA VESTRIT: First mate, *Paragon* out of Bingtown. Aunt to Malta Khuprus.

BEGASTI CORED: Chalcedean merchant; bald, rich, trading partner of Hest Finbok.

BRASHEN TRELL: Captain of the *Paragon* out of Bingtown.

CLEF: Ship's boy on the *Paragon,* former slave.

DETOZI: Keeper of the messenger birds at Trehaug.

DUKE OF CHALCED: Chalced's dictator, elderly and ailing.

EREK: Keeper of the messenger birds at Bingtown.

MALTA KHUPRUS: The Elderling "queen," resides in Trehaug. Married to Reyn Khuprus.

PARAGON: A liveship. Helped escort the sea serpents up the river to the cocooning grounds.

SELDEN VESTRIT: A young Elderling; Malta's brother and Althea's nephew.

SINAD ARICH: Chalcedean merchant who strikes a deal with Leftrin.

DRAGON KEEPER

Day the 2nd of the Plough Moon

*Year the 6th of the Reign of the Most Noble
and Magnificent Satrap Cosgo*

From Erek, Keeper of the Birds, Bingtown
To Detozi, Keeper of the Birds, Trehaug

This night have dispatched to you four birds, bearing in two parts our agreement with the dragon Tintaglia, to be ratified by the Rain Wild Council. Trader Devouchet, leader of the Bingtown Traders' Council, suggested that duplicates be sent. They sum up the formal agreement between the Traders and the dragon. We are to aid her serpents in traveling up the Rain Wild River in exchange for her assistance with defending the Trader cities and waterways against the Chalcedean invaders.

*PLEASE DISPATCH A BIRD AS SOON AS POSSIBLE
TO CONFIRM RECEIPT OF THIS MESSAGE.*

Detozi,

A brief message of my own, penned in haste in a very small space. All is chaos here. My bird coop scorched in the fires the invaders set, many of my birds dead from smoke. I'm sending Kingsly as one of the messenger birds tonight. You know I raised him from a squab by hand after his parents died. Please keep him safe there and do not return him until we know that all is well. If Bingtown falls, treat him well and keep him as your own. Pray for us here. I do not know that Bingtown will survive this invasion, dragon or no.

Erek

SERPENTS' END

They had come so far, yet now that she was here, the years of journeying were already fading in her mind, giving way to the desperate needs of the present. Sisarqua opened her jaws and bent her neck. It was hard for the sea serpent to focus her thoughts. It had been years since she had been completely out of the water. She had not felt dry land under her body since she had hatched on Others' Island. She was far from Others' Island's hot dry sand and balmy waters now. Winter was closing in on this densely forested land beside the chill river. The mudbank under her coiled length was hard and abrasive. The air was too cold, and her gills were drying out too quickly. There was nothing she could do about that except to work more swiftly. She scooped her jaws into the immense trough and came up with a mouthful of silver-streaked clay and river water. She threw her great head back and gulped it down. It was gritty and cold and strangely delicious. Another mouthful, another swallow. And again.

She had lost count of how many gulps of the grainy soup she had ingested when finally she felt the ancient reflex trigger. Working the muscles in her throat, she felt her poison sacs swell. Her fleshy mane stood out all around her throat in a toxic, quivering ruff. Shuddering down her full length, she opened her jaws wide, strained, gagged, and then met with success. She clamped and locked her jaws to contain the liquid, releasing it only as a thin, powerful stream of clay, bile, and saliva tinged with venom. With difficulty, she turned her head and then coiled her tail closer to her body. The extrusion was like a silvery thread, thick and heavy. Her head wove as she layered the wet winding over herself.

She felt a heavy tread nearby, and then the shadow of the walking dragon passed over her. Tintaglia paused and spoke to her. "Good. Good, that's right. A nice even layer to begin with, one with no gaps. That's right."

Sisarqua could not spare a glance for the blue-and-silver queen who praised her. Creating the case that would shelter her during the remaining months of winter took all her attention. She focused on it with a desperation born of weariness. She needed sleep. She longed to sleep; but she knew that if she slept now, she would never wake again in any form. *Finish it,* she thought. *Finish it, and then I can rest.*

All around her on the riverbank other serpents labored at the same task, with varying degrees of success. Between and among them, humans toiled. Some carried buckets of water from the river. Others mined chunks of silvery clay from a nearby bank and loaded them into barrows. Youngsters trundled the barrows to a hastily constructed log enclosure. Water and clay were dumped into the immense trough; other workers used shovels and paddles to break up the lumps of clay and render the water and clay into a loose porridge. It was this slurry that Sisarqua had consumed as the major ingredients for manufacturing her case. The lesser ingredients were just as essential. Her body added the toxins that would plunge her into a sleep half a breath above death. Her saliva contributed her memories to the keeping of her case. Not just her own memories of her time as a serpent, but all the memories of those of her bloodline spooled around her as she wove her case.

Missing were the memories she should have received from watchful dragons tending the serpents as they made their cases. She had enough memories to recall that there should have been at least a score of dragons present, encouraging them, chewing the memory sand and clay and contributing their own regurgitated saliva and history to the process. But there weren't, and she was too tired to wonder how that lack might affect her.

A great weariness washed over her as she reached the neck of her case. It had to be constructed in a way that would eventually allow her to draw her head in and then seal it behind her. It came to her, slowly, that in previous generations, the dragons who had tended the serpents had sometimes helped them seal their cases. But Sisarqua knew better than to hope for that help. Only 129 serpents had massed at the mouth of the Serpent River to begin the desperate upriver migration to the traditional cocooning grounds. Maulkin, their leader, had been gravely concerned that so few of them were female: less than a third. In any cocooning year, there should have been hundreds of serpents, and at least as many females as males. They had waited so long in the sea, and then come so far in the hope of restoring their species. It was hard to hear that they might be too few and too late.

The difficulties of the river journey had reduced the number still further. Sisarqua was not certain how many had reached the cocooning beach. About ninety, she thought, but the graver news was that fewer than twenty of the survivors were female. And all around her, exhausted serpents continued to die. Even as she thought of it, she heard Tintaglia speak to a human worker. "He is dead. Bring your hammers and break up his case. Work it back into the troughs of memory clay. Let the others keep alive the memories of his ancestors." She could not see, but she heard the sounds of Tintaglia dragging the dead serpent from his unfinished

cocoon. She smelled his flesh and blood as the dragon devoured his carcass. Hunger and weariness cramped her. She
wished she could share Tintaglia's meal but knew that it was
too late for eating now. The clay was in her gut and must be
processed.

And Tintaglia needed the food. She was the sole dragon
left alive to shepherd all of them through this process. Sisarqua did not know where Tintaglia got her strength. The
dragon had been flying without rest for days to shepherd
them up the river, so unfamiliar to them after decades of
change. She could not have many reserves left. Tintaglia
could offer them little more than encouragement. What
could one dragon do when faced with the needs of so many
sea serpents?

Like the gossamer recollection of a dream, an ancestral memory wafted briefly through her mind. *Not right,*
she thought. *None of this is right; none of it is as it should
be.* This was the river, but where were the broad meadows
and the oak forests that had once edged it? The lands that
bounded the river now were swamp and boggy forest, with
scarcely a bit of firm ground to be seen. If the humans had
not labored to reinforce the bank of this beach with stone
before the serpents arrived, they would have churned it to
mud. Her ancestral serpent memories told her of broad,
sunny meadows and a rich bank of clay near an Elderling
city. Dragons should have been clawing chunks of clay free
and churning the clay and water to slurry, dragons should
have been putting the final seals on the serpents' cases.
And all of this should have been happening under a bright
summer sun in the heat of the day.

She gave a shudder of weariness, and the memory faded
beyond her recall. She was only a single serpent, struggling
to weave the case that would protect her from winter's cold
while her body underwent its transformation. A single serpent, cold and weary, finally come home after an eternity of
roaming. Her mind drifted back over the last few months.

The final leg of her journey had seemed an endless battle
against the river current and the rocky shallows. She was a
newcomer to Maulkin's tangle and astonished by it. Usually

a tangle numbered twenty to forty serpents. But Maulkin had gathered every serpent he could find and led them north. It had made foraging for food along the way far more difficult, but he had deemed it necessary. Never had she seen so many serpents traveling together as a single tangle. Some, it was true, had degenerated to little more than animals, and others were more than half mad with confusion and fear. Forgetfulness shrouded the minds of too many. Yet as they had followed the prophet-serpent with the gleaming gold false-eyes in a long row down his flanks, she had almost recalled the ancient migration route. All around her, both spirits and intelligence had rallied in the embattled serpents. This arduous journey had felt right, more right than anything had for a very long time.

Yet even so, she had known moments of doubt. Her ancestral memories of the river told her that the waterway they sought flowed steady and deep, and it teemed with fish. Her ancient dreams told her of rolling hills and meadows edged with open forests abounding with game for hungry dragons. This river had a deep channel that a ship could follow, but it threaded a wandering way inland through towering forest thick with creepers and brush. It could not be the way to their ancient cocooning grounds. Yet Maulkin had doggedly insisted that it was.

Her doubt had been so strong that she had nearly turned back. She had almost fled the icy river of milky water and retreated to the warmer waters of the oceans to the south. But when she lagged or started to turn aside from the path, others of the serpents came after her and drove her back into the tangle. She had had to follow.

But though she might doubt Maulkin's visions, Tintaglia's authority she had never questioned. The blue-and-silver dragon had recognized Maulkin as their leader and assisted the strange vessel that guided his tangle. The dragon had flown above them, trumpeting her encouragement, as she shepherded the tangle of serpents north, and then up this river. The swimming had been good as far as the two-legs city of Trehaug. Wearily but without excessive difficulty, they had followed the ship that led the way.

But past that city, the river had changed. The guiding ship had halted there, unable to traverse the shallows beyond. Past Trehaug, the river spread and widened and splintered into tributaries. Wide belts of gravel and sand invaded it, and dangling vines and reaching roots choked its edges. The river they followed became shallow and meandering, toothed with rocks in some places and then choked with reeds in the next stretch. Again Sisarqua had wanted to turn back, but like the other serpents, she had allowed herself to be bullied and driven by the dragon. Up the river they had gone. With more than one hundred of her kind, she had flopped and floundered through the inadequate ladder of log corrals that the humans had built in an attempt to provide deeper water for their progress through the final, killing shallows.

Many had died on that part of their journey. Small injuries that would have healed quickly in the caressing salt water of the sea became festering ulcers in the river's harsh flow. After their long banishment at sea, many of the great serpents were feeble both in mind and spirit. So many things were wrong. Too many years had passed since they had hatched. They should have made this journey decades ago, as healthy young serpents, and they should have migrated up the river in the warmth of summer, when their bodies were sleek with fat. Instead they came in the rains and misery of winter, thin and battered and speckled with barnacles, but mostly old, far older than any serpents had ever been before.

The single dragon who watched over them was less than a year's turning out of her own cocoon. Tintaglia flew overhead, glinting silver whenever the winter sunlight broke through the clouds to touch her. "Not far!" she kept calling down to them. "Beyond the ladder the waters deepen again and you can once more swim freely. Keep moving."

Some were simply too battered, too weary, too thin for such a journey. One big orange serpent died draped across the log wall of the penned water, unable to drag himself any farther. Sisarqua was close to him when his great wedge-shaped head dropped suddenly beneath the water. Impatiently, she waited for him to move on. Then his spiky mane of tendrils suddenly spasmed and released a final rush of toxins. They were faint and feeble, the last reflexive defenses of his body, yet they clearly signaled to any serpents within range that he was dead. The smell and taste of them in the water summoned her to the feast.

Sisarqua had not hesitated. She had been the first to tear into his body, filling her mouth with his flesh, gulping it down and tearing another chunk free before the rest of the tangle even realized the opportunity. The sudden nourishment dizzied her almost as much as the rush of his memories. This was the way of her kind, not to waste the bodies of the dead but to take from them both nourishment and knowledge. Just as every dragon carried within him the memories of his entire line, so every serpent retained the memories of those who had gone before. Or was supposed to. Sisarqua and every other serpent wallowing dismally alongside her had remained in serpent form too long. Memories had faded and with them, intelligence. Even some of those who now strove to complete the migration and become dragons were reduced to brutish shadows of what they should have been. What sort of dragons would they become?

Her head had darted in, mane abristle, to seize another sizable chunk of the orange serpent's flesh. Her brain whirled with memories of rich fishing and of nights spent singing with his tangle under the jewel-bright skies. That memory was very old. She suspected it had been scores of years since any tangle had risen from the Plenty to the Lack to lift their voices in praise of the star-speckled sky above them.

Others had crowded her then, hissing and lifting their manes in threat to one another as they strove to share the feast. She tore a final piece of flesh free and then wallowed over the log that had stopped the orange. She had tossed the hunk of warm meat down whole and felt it distend her gullet pleasantly. *The sky,* she thought, and in response felt a brief stir of the orange serpent's dim dragon memories. The sky, open and wide as the sea. Soon she would sail it again. Not much farther, Tintaglia had promised.

But distance is measured one way by a dragon a-wing

and quite another way by a battered serpent wallowing up
a shallow river. They did not see the clay banks that afternoon. Night fell upon them, sudden as a blow, the short day
spent almost before it had begun. For yet another night,
Sisarqua endured the cold of the air that the shallow river
did not allow her to escape. The water that flowed past was
barely sufficient to keep her gills wet; the skin on her back
felt as if it would crack from the dry cold that scoured her.
And in the late morning, the sun that found its way down
onto the wide river between the jungled banks revealed
more serpents who would never complete the migration.
Again, she was fortunate enough to feed from one of the
corpses before the rest of the horde drove her away from it.
Again, Tintaglia circled overhead, calling down the promise
that it was not far to Cassarick and rest, the long peaceful
rest of the transformation.

The day had been chill, and the skin of her back was
dried by a long night spent above water. She could feel the
skin cracking beneath her scales, and when the river deepened enough to allow her to submerge and soak her gills,
the milky river water stung her split skin. She felt the acidic
water eat at her. If she did not reach the cocooning beach
soon, she would not make it.

The afternoon was both horribly short and painfully
long. In the deeper stretches where she could swim, the
water stung her breached skin. But that was preferable to the
places where she crawled on her belly like a snake, fighting
for purchase on the slimy rocks at the bottom of the riverbed. All around her, other immense sea serpents squirmed
and coiled and flexed, trying to make their way upriver.

When she arrived, she did not know it. The sun was already westering behind the tall banks of trees that fronted
the river. Creatures that were not Elderlings had kindled
torches and stuck them in a great circle on a muddy riverbank. She peered at them. Humans. Ordinary two-legs, little
more than prey. They scampered about, apparently in service to Tintaglia, serving her as once Elderlings would have
done. It was oddly humiliating; was this how low dragons
had fallen, to be reduced to consorting with humans?

Sisarqua lifted her maned head high, tasting the night air. It was not right. It was not right at all. She could find no certainty in her hearts that this was the cocooning place. Yet on the shore she could see some of the serpents who had preceded her. A few were already encapsulated in cases spun from the silver-streaked clay and their own saliva. Others still struggled, wearily, to complete the task.

Complete the task. Yes. Her mind jolted back to the present. There was no more time for these memories. With a final heave, she brought up the last of the clay and bile that remained to her and completed the thick lip of her case's neck. But she was empty now; she had misjudged. She had nothing left to seal her case. If she tried to reach the slurry, she would break the coiled cocoon she had made, and she knew with painful certainty that she would not have the strength to weave it again. So close she had come, so close, and yet here she would die, never to rise.

A wave of panic and fury washed through her. In one instant of conflict, she decided to wrest herself free of the cocoon, and to remain absolutely still. The stillness won, bolstered by a flood of memories. That was the virtue of having the memories of one's ancestors; sometimes the wisdom of old prevailed over the terrors of the present. In the stillness, her mind cleared. She had memories to draw on, memories of serpents who had survived such an error, and dying memories of ones who had not. The corpses of the failed serpents had been devoured by those who survived. Thus even the memories of fatal errors lived on to serve the needs of survivors.

She clearly saw three paths. Stay within her case and call for a dragon to help her finish sealing her case. Well, that was of no use to her. Tintaglia was already overwhelmed. Break free of her case and demand that the dragon bring her food, so that she might eat and regain her strength to spin a new case. Another impossible solution. Panic threatened again. This time it was an act of her own will that pushed it aside. She was not going to die here. She had come too far and struggled through too many dangers to let death claim her now. No. She was going to live, she was going to emerge in spring as a dragon and take back her mastery of the skies. She would fly again. Somehow.

How?

She would live to rise as a queen. Demand that which was owed to a queen dragon now. The right of first survival in hard times. She drew what breath she could and trumpeted out a name. "Tintaglia!"

Her gills were too dry, her throat nearly destroyed from the spinning of the coarse clay into thread. Her cry for aid, her demand, was barely a whisper. And even her strength to break free of her case was gone, fading beyond recall. She was going to die.

"Are you in trouble, beautiful one? I feel your distress. Can I help you?"

Inside the restrictive casing she could not turn her head. But she could roll her eyes and see the one who addressed her. An Elderling. He was very small and very young, but in the touch of his mind against hers, there was no mistaking him. This was no mere human, even if his shape still resembled one.

Her gills were so dry. Serpents could rise above the water for a time, could even sing, but this long exposure to the cold, dry air was pushing her to the edges of her ability to survive in the Lack. She drew in a labored breath. Yes. The scent was there, and she knew without any doubt that Tintaglia had imprinted him. He brimmed with her glamour. Slowly she lidded her eyes and unlidded them again. She still could not see him clearly. She was drying out too quickly. "I can't," she said. They were the only words she could manage.

She felt him swell with distress. An instant later, his small voice raised the alarm. "Tintaglia! This one is in trouble! She cannot finish her case. What should we do?"

The dragon's voice boomed back to him from across the cocooning grounds. "The clay slurry, very wet! Pour it in. Do not hesitate. Cover her head with it and smooth it over the open end of her casing. Seal her in, but be sure that the first layer is very wet." Even as she spoke, the dragon herself hastened to Sisarqua's side. "A female! Be strong, little sister. There are few who will hatch to be queens. You must be among them."

The workers had come running, some trundling barrows, others bearing slopping buckets of silvery-gray clay. She had drawn her head in as far as it would go and lidded her eyes. The young Elderling outside her case shouted his orders, bidding them, "Now! Don't wait for Tintaglia! Now, her skin and eyes are drying too fast. Pour it in. That's it! And more! Another bucket! Fill that barrow again. Hurry, man!"

The stuff sloshed over her, drenching and sealing her. Her own toxins, present in the sections of the case she had woven, were affecting her now. She felt herself sinking into something that was not sleep. It was rest, however. Blessed, blessed rest.

She sensed Tintaglia standing close by her. She felt the sudden weight of warm, regurgitated slurry and knew with gratitude that the dragon had sealed her case for her. For a moment, toxins rich with memories stung her skin. Not just dragon memories from Tintaglia, but a share of serpent lore from the one Tintaglia had recently devoured enriched her case. Dimly she heard Tintaglia directing the scurrying workers. "Her case is thin here. And over here. Bring clay and smooth it on in layers. Then bank her case with leaves and sticks. Cover it well from the light and the cold. They cocoon late. They must not feel the sun until summer is full upon them, for I fear they will not have fully developed when spring comes. And when you are finished here, come to the east end of the grounds. There is another one struggling there."

The Elderling's voice reached into Sisarqua's fading consciousness. "Did we seal it in time? Will she survive to hatch?"

"I do not know," Tintaglia replied gravely. "The year is late, the serpents old and tired, and half of them are next to starved. Some from the first wave have already died in their cases. Others still struggle in the river or struggle to pass the ladder. Many of them will die before they even reach the shore. That is for the best; their bodies will nourish the others and increase their chances of survival. But there is small good to be had from those who die in their cocoons, only waste and disappointment."

Darkness was wrapping Sisarqua. She could not decide if she was chilled to her bones or cozily warm. She sank deeper, yet still felt the uneasy silence of the young Elderling. When he finally spoke, his words came to her more from his thoughts than from his lips. "The Rain Wild people would like to have the cases of the ones who die. They call such material 'wizardwood' and have many valuable uses for—"

"NO!" The emphatic denial by the dragon shocked Sisarqua back to a moment of awareness. But her depleted body could not long sustain it, and she almost immediately began to sink again. Tintaglia's words followed her down into a place below dreams. "No, little brother! All that is of dragons belongs only to dragons. When spring comes, some of these cases will hatch. The dragons who emerge will devour the cases and bodies of those who do not hatch. Such is our way, and in such a way is our lore preserved. Those who die will give strength to those who live on."

Sisarqua had but a moment to wonder which she would be. Then blackness claimed her.

Day the 17th of the Hope Moon

*Year the 7th of the Reign of the Most Noble and
Magnificent Satrap Cosgo*

Year the 1st of the Independent Alliance of Traders

From Detozi, Keeper of the Birds, Trehaug
To Erek, Keeper of the Birds, Bingtown

Attached you will find a formal appeal from the Rain
Wild Council for a just and fair payment of the additional and unexpected expenses incurred by us in the
care of the serpent cases for the dragon Tintaglia. A
swift reply is requested by the Council.

Erek,

*A spring flash flood has hit us hard. Tremendous
damage to some of the dragon cases, and some are
missing entirely. Small barge overturned on the river,
and I fear it was the one carrying the young pigeons
I was sending you to replenish the Bingtown flock. All
were lost. I will allow my birds to set more eggs, and
send you the offspring as soon as they are fledged.
Trehaug does not seem like Trehaug anymore, there are
so many Tattooed faces! My master has said that I must
not date things according to our Independence, but I
defy him. Rumor will become a reality, I am sure!*

Detozi

CHAPTER ONE

THE RIVERMAN

It was supposed to be spring. Damn cold for spring. Damn cold to be sleeping out on the deck instead of inside the deckhouse. Last night, with the rum in him and a belt of distant stars twinkling through an opening in the rain forest canopy, it had seemed like a fine idea. The night hadn't seemed so chilly, and the insects had been chirring in the treetops and the night birds calling to one another while the bats squeaked and darted out in the open air over the river. It had seemed a fine night to lie back on the deck of his barge and look up at the wide world all around him and savor the river and the Rain Wilds and his proper place in the world. Tarman had rocked him gently and all had been right.

In the iron-gray dawn, with dew settled on his skin and clothes and every joint in his body stiff, it seemed a damn-fool prank more suited to a boy of twelve than a riverman of close to thirty years. He sat up slowly and blew out a long breath that steamed in the chill dawn air. He followed it with a heartfelt belch of last night's rum. Then, grumbling under his breath, he lurched to his feet and looked around. Morning. Yes. He walked to the railing and made water over the side as he considered the day. Far above his head, in the treetops of the forest canopy, day birds were awake and calling to one another. But under the trees at the edge of the river, dawn and daylight were tenuous things. Light seeped down, filtered by thousands of new leaves and divested of its warmth before it reached him. As the sun traveled higher, it would shine down on the open river and send fingers under the trees and through the canopy. But not yet. Not for hours.

Leftrin stretched, rolling his shoulders. His shirt clung to his skin unpleasantly. Well, he deserved to be uncomfortable. If any of his crew had been so stupid as to fall asleep out on the deck, that's what he would have told them. But they hadn't been. All eleven of his men slumbered on in the narrow, tiered bunks that lined the aft wall of the deckhouse. His own more spacious bunk had gone empty. Stupid.

It was too early to be awake. The fire in the galley stove was still banked; no hot water simmered for tea, no flatcakes bubbled on the grill. And yet here he was, wide awake, and of a mind to take a walk back under the trees. It was a strange impulse, one he had no conscious rationale for, and yet he recognized it for the kind of itch it was. It came, he knew, from the unremembered dreams of the night before. He reached for them, but the tattered shreds became threads of cobweb in his mind's grasp, and then were gone. Still, he'd follow their lingering inspiration. He'd never lost out by paying attention to those impulses, and almost inevitably regretted it the few times he'd ignored them.

He went into the deckhouse, past his sleeping crew and through the little galley and forward to his cabin. He exchanged his deck shoes for his shore boots. The knee boots of greased bullhide were nearly worn through; the acidic waters of the Rain Wild River were not kind to footwear, clothing, wood, or skin. But his boots would survive another trip or two ashore, and as a result, his skin would, too. He caught up his jacket from its hook and slung it about his shoulders and walked aft past the crew. He kicked the foot of the tillerman's bunk. Swarge's head jolted up and the man stared at him blearily.

"I'm going ashore, going to stretch my legs. Probably be back by breakfast."

"Aye," Swarge said, the only acceptable reply and close to the full extent of Swarge's conversational skills. Leftrin grunted an affirmation and left the deckhouse.

The evening before, they had nosed the barge up onto a marshy bank and tied it off to a big leaning tree there. Leftrin swung down from the blunt-nosed bow of the barge onto mud-coated reeds. The barge's painted eyes stared off into the dimness under the trees. Ten days ago, a warm wind and massive rainstorms had swelled the Rain Wild River, sending the waters rushing up above their normal banks and over the low shores. In the last two days, the waters had receded, but the plant life along the river was still recovering from being underwater for several days of silt-laden flooding. The reeds were coated with filth, and most of the grasses were flattened beneath their burdens of mud. Isolated pockets of water dotted the low bank. As Leftrin strode along, his feet sank and water seeped up to fill in his tracks.

He wasn't sure where he was going or why. He let his whim guide him as he ventured away from the riverbank into the deeper shade beneath the vine-draped trees. There, the signs of the recent flooding were even more apparent. Driftwood snags were wedged among the tree trunks. Tangles of muddy foliage and torn webs of vines were festooned about the trees and bushes. Fresh deposits of river silt covered the deep moss and low-growing plants. The gigantic trunks of the enormous trees that held up the roof of the Rain Wilds were impervious to most floods, but the undergrowth that rioted in their shade was not. In some places, the current had carved a path through the underbrush; in others, the slime and sludge of the flood burdened the foliage so heavily that the brush bent in muddied hummocks.

Where he could, Leftrin slogged in the paths that the river current had gouged through the brush. When the mud became too soft, he pushed through the grimy undergrowth. He was soon wet and filthy. A branch he pushed aside sprang back, slapping him across the brow and spattering his face with mud. He hastily wiped the stinging stuff from his skin. Like many a riverman, his arms and face had been toughened by exposure to the acidic waters of the Rain Wild River. It gave his face a leathery, weathered look, a startling contrast to his gray eyes. He privately believed that this was why he had so few of the growths and less of the scaliness that afflicted most of his Rain Wild brethren. Not that he considered himself a thing of beauty or even a handsome man. The wandering thought made him grin ruefully. He pushed it from his mind and a dangling branch away from his face and forced his way deeper.

There came a moment when he stopped suddenly. Some sensory clue he could not pin down, some scent on the air or some glimpse he had not consciously registered told him he was near. He stood very still and slowly scanned the area all around him. His eyes went past it, and then the hair on the back of his neck stood up as he swiveled his gaze back suddenly. There. Mud-laden vegetation draped over it, and the river's raging flood had coated it in muck, but a single streak of gray showed through. A wizardwood log.

It was not a huge one, not as big as he had heard that they could be. Its diameter was perhaps two-thirds of his height, and he was not a tall man. But it was big enough, he thought. Big enough to make him very wealthy. He glanced back over his shoulder, but the undergrowth that blocked his view of the river and his moored barge would also shield him from spying eyes. He doubted that any of his crew would be curious enough to follow him. They'd been asleep when he left, and no doubt were still abed. The secret trove was his alone.

He pushed his way through the vegetation until he could touch the log. It was dead. He had known that even before he had touched it. When he was a boy, he'd been down to the Crowned Rooster chamber. He'd seen Tintaglia's log before she had hatched from it, and he had known the crawly sensation it had wakened in him. The dragon in this log had died and would never hatch. It didn't much matter to him if it had died while the log still rested on the banks of the cocooning beach, or if the tumbling it had taken in the flood had killed it. The dragon inside it was dead, the wizardwood was salvageable, and he was the only one who knew where it was. And by his great good fortune, he was one of the few who knew how best to use it.

Back in the days when the Khuprus family had made part of its vast fortune from working wizardwood, back before anyone had ever known or admitted what the "wood" really was, his mother's brothers had been wizardwood workers. He'd been just a lad, wandering in and out of the low building where his uncles' saws bit slowly through the iron-hard stuff. He'd been nine when his father had decided he was old enough to come and work on the barge with him. He'd taken up his rightful trade as a bargeman, and he learned his trade from the deck up. And then, when he had just turned twenty-two, his father had died and the barge had come to him. He'd been a riverman for most of his life. But from his mother's side, he had the tools of the wizardwood trade, and the knowledge of how to use them.

He made a circuit of the log. It was heavy going. The floodwaters had wedged it between two trees. One end of it had been jammed deep into mud while the other pointed up at an angle and was wreathed in forest-flood debris. He thought of tearing the stuff clear so he could have a good look at it and then decided to leave it camouflaged. He made a quick trip back to the barge, moving stealthily as he took a coil of line from the locker, and then returned hastily to secure his find. It was dirty work but when he had finished he was satisfied that even if the river rose again, his treasure would stay put.

As he slogged back to his barge, he noticed the heavy felt sock inside his boot becoming damp. His foot began to sting. He increased his pace, cursing to himself. He'd have to buy new boots at the next stop. Parroton was one of the smallest and newest settlements on the Rain Wild River. Everything there was expensive, and bullhide boots imported from Chalced would be difficult to find. He'd be at the mercy of whoever had a pair to sell. A moment later, a sour smile twisted his mouth. Here he had discovered a log worth more than ten years of barge work, and he was quibbling with himself over how much he was going to have to pay for a new pair of boots. Once the log was sawn into lengths and discreetly sold off, he'd never have to worry about money again.

His mind was busy with logistics. Sooner or later, he'd have to decide who he would trust to share his secret. He'd need someone else on the other end of the crosscut saw, and men to help carry the heavy planks from the log to the barge. His cousins? Probably. Blood was thicker than water, even the silty water of the Rain Wild River.

Could they be that discreet? He thought so. They'd have to be careful. There was no mistaking fresh-cut wizardwood; it had a silvery sheen to it, and an unmistakable scent. When the Rain Wild Traders had first discovered it, they had valued it solely for its ability to resist the acid water of the river. His own vessel, the *Tarman,* had been one of the first wizardwood ships built, its hull sheathed with wizardwood planks. Little had the Rain Wild builders suspected the magical properties the wood possessed. They had merely been using what seemed to be a trove of well-aged timber from the buried city they had discovered.

It was only when they had built large and elaborate ships, ships that could ply not just the river but the salt waters of the coast, that they had discovered the full powers of the stuff. The figureheads of those ships had startled everyone when, generations after the ships had been built, they had begun to come to life. The speaking and moving figureheads were a wonder to all. There were not many liveships, and they were jealously guarded possessions. None of them was ever sold outside the Traders' alliance. Only a Bingtown Trader could buy a liveship, and only liveships could travel safely up the Rain Wild River. The hulls of ordinary ships gave way quickly to the acid waters of the river. What better way could exist to protect the secret cities of the Rain Wilds and their inhabitants?

Then had come the far more recent discovery of exactly what wizardwood was. The immense logs in the Crowned

Rooster chamber had not been wood; rather, they had been the protective cocoons of dragons, dragged into the shelter of the city to preserve them during an ancient volcanic eruption. No one liked to speak of what that really meant. Tintaglia the dragon had emerged alive from her cocoon. Of those other "logs" that had been sawed into timber for ships, how many had contained viable dragons? No one spoke of that. Not even the liveships willingly discussed the dragons that they might have been. On that topic, even the dragon Tintaglia had been silent. Nonetheless, Leftrin suspected that if anyone learned of the log he had found, it would be confiscated. He couldn't allow it to become common knowledge in Trehaug or Bingtown, and Sa save him if the dragon herself heard of it. So, he would do all that he could to keep the discovery private.

It galled him that a treasure that he once could have auctioned to the highest bidder must now be disposed of quietly and privately. But there would be markets for it. Good markets. In a place as competitive as Bingtown, there were always Traders who were willing to buy goods quietly without being too curious about the source, an aspiring Trader willing to barter in illegal goods for the chance to win favor with the Satrap of Jamaillia.

But the real money, the best offers, would come from Chalcedean traders. The uneasy peace between Bingtown and Chalced was still very young. Small treaties had been signed, but major decisions regarding boundaries and trades and tariffs and rights of passage were still being negotiated. The health of the ruler of Chalced, it was rumored, was failing. Chalcedean emissaries had already attempted to book passage up the Rain Wild River. They had been turned back, but everyone knew what their mission had been: they wished to buy dragon parts—dragon blood for elixirs, dragon flesh for rejuvenation, dragon teeth for daggers, dragon scales for light and flexible armor, dragon's pizzle for virility. Every old wives' tale about the medicinal and magical powers of dragon parts seemed to have reached the ears of the Chalcedean nobility. And each noble seemed more eager than the last to win his duke's favor by supplying him with an antidote to whatever debilitating disease was slowly whittling him away. They had no way of knowing that Tintaglia had hatched from the last wizardwood log the Rain Wilders possessed; there were no embryonic dragons to be slaughtered and shipped off to Chalced. Just as well. Personally, Leftrin shared the opinion of most Traders: that the sooner the Duke of Chalced was in his grave, the better for trade and humanity. But he also shared the pragmatic view that, until then, one might as well make a profit off the diseased old warmonger.

If Leftrin chose that path, he need do no more than find a way to get the ponderously heavy log intact to Chalced. Surely the remains of the half-formed dragon inside it would fetch an amazing price there. Just get the cocoon to Chalced. If he said it quickly, it almost sounded simple, as if it would not involve hoists and pulleys just to move it from where it was wedged and load it on his barge. To say nothing of keeping such a cargo hidden, and also arranging secret transport from the mouth of the Rain Wild River north to Chalced. His river barge could never make such a trip. But if he could arrange it, and if he was neither robbed nor murdered on the trip north or on his way home, then he could emerge from his adventure as a very wealthy man.

He limped faster. The stinging inside his boot had become a burning. A few blisters he could live with; an open wound would quickly ulcerate and hobble him for weeks.

As he emerged from the undergrowth into the relatively open space alongside the river, he smelled the smoke of the galley stove and heard the voices of his crew. He could smell flatcakes cooking and coffee brewing. Time to be aboard and away before any of them wondered what their captain had been up to on his morning stroll. Some thoughtful soul had tossed a rope ladder down the bow for him. Probably Swarge. The tillerman always was two thoughts ahead of the rest of the crew. On the bow, silent, hulking Eider was perched on the railing, smoking his morning pipe. He nodded to his captain and blew a smoke ring by way of greeting. If he was curious as to where Leftrin had been or why, he gave no sign of it.

Leftrin was still pondering the best way to convert the wizardwood log into wealth as he set his muddy foot on the first rung of the ladder. The painted gaze of Tarman's gleaming black eyes met his own, and he froze. A radical new thought was born in his mind. *Keep it. Keep it, and use it for myself and my ship.* For several long moments, as he paused on the ladder, the possibilities unfolded in his mind like flowers opening to the early dawn light.

He patted the side of his barge. "I might, old man. I just might." Then he climbed the rest of the way up to his deck, pulled off his leaking boot, and flung it back into the river for it to devour.

$\diamond \ \diamond \ \diamond$

Day the 15th of the Fish Moon

*Year the 7th of the Reign of the Most Noble and
Magnificent Satrap Cosgo*

Year the 1st of the Independent Alliance of Traders

From Detozi, Keeper of the Birds, Trehaug
To Erek, Keeper of the Birds, Bingtown

Within the sealed scroll, a message of Great Importance from the Rain Wild Traders' Council at Trehaug to the Bingtown Traders' Council. You are invited to send whatever representatives you wish to be present on the occasion of the Rain Wild dragons emerging from their cases. At the direction of the most exalted and queenly dragon Tintaglia, the cases will be exposed to sunlight on the 15th day of the Greening Moon, forty-five days hence. The Rain Wild Traders' Council looks forward with pleasure to your attendance as our dragons emerge.

Erek!

Clean your nesting boxes and paint the walls of your coop with fresh limewash. The last two birds I received from you were infested with lice and spread it to one of my coops.

Detozi

CHAPTER TWO

THE HATCH

Luck brought Thymara to the right place at the right time. It was the best good luck that had ever favored her, she thought, as she clung to the lowest branch of a tree at the edge of the serpents' beach. She did not usually accompany her father down to the lower levels of Trehaug, let alone make the journey to Cassarick. Yet here she was, and on the very day that Tintaglia had decreed that the dragon cocoons be uncovered. She glanced at her father, and he grinned at her. No. Not luck, she suddenly knew. He had known how much she would enjoy being here, and he scheduled their jaunt accordingly. She grinned back at her father with all the confidence of her eleven years and then returned her gaze to the scene below her. Her father's cautioning voice reached her from where he perched like a bird on a thicker branch closer to the trunk of the immense tree that they shared.

"Thymara. Be careful. They're newly hatched. And hungry. If you fell down there, they might mistake you for just another piece of meat."

The scrawny girl dug her black claws deeper into the bark. She knew he was only half teasing. "Don't worry, Da. I was made for the canopy. I won't fall." She was stretched out along a drooping branch that no other experienced limbsman would have trusted. But she knew it would hold her. Her belly was pressed to it as if she were one of the slender brown tree lizards that shared her perch. And like them, she clung with the full length of her body, fingers and toes dug into the wide cracks in the bark, thighs hugging the limb. Her glossy black hair was confined to a dozen tight braids that were knotted at the back of her neck. Her head was much lower than her feet. Her cheek was pressed tight to the rough skin of the tree as her gaze devoured the drama unfolding below her.

Thymara's tree was one of uncounted thousands that made up the Rain Wild Forest. For days and days in all directions, the forest spread out on either side of the wide gray Rain Wild River. Close to Cassarick and for several days upriver, picket trees predominated. The wide-spread horizontal branches were excellent for home building. Mature picket trees dropped questing roots from their branches down to the earth far below, so that each tree established its own "picket fence" around its root structure, anchoring the tree securely in the muddy soil. The forest that surrounded Cassarick was much denser than that around Trehaug. The horizontal branches of the picket trees were far more stable than those Thymara was accustomed to. They made climbing and moving from tree to tree almost ridiculously easy. Today she had ventured out onto the unsupported end branch of one, to gain an unobstructed view of the spectacle below her.

Before her, on the other side of the mudflats, the panorama of moving water stretched flat and milky. She had a foggy glimpse of the distant, dense forest on the opposite side of the river. Summer had awakened a million shades of green there. The sound of the river's rush, of gravel churning beneath its opaque waters, was the constant music of her life. Closer to the shore, on Thymara's side of the river, the waters were shallow, and strips of exposed gravel and clay broke up the current's access to the flat clay banks below her tree. Last winter, this section of the riverbank had been hastily reinforced with timber bulkheads; the floods of winter had not been kind to them, but most of the logs remained.

For several acres, the bare riverbank was littered with serpent cases like drift logs. Once the area had been covered with tufts of coarse grass and prickly brush, but all that had been destroyed with the wave of sea serpents that had arrived last winter. She had not seen that migration, but she had heard about it. No one who lived in the tree cities of the Rain Wilds had escaped the telling of that tale. A herd, a tangle of more than one hundred immense serpents, had come up the Rain Wild River, escorted by a liveship and shepherded by a glorious blue-and-silver dragon. The young Elderling Selden Vestrit had been there to greet the serpents and welcome them back to their ancestral home. He had supervised the ranks of Rain Wilders who had turned out to assist the serpents in forming their cases. For most of that winter, he had remained in Cassarick, checking on the dormant serpents, seeing that the cases were kept well covered with leaves and mud to insulate them from cold and rain and even sunlight. And today, she had heard, he was here again, to witness the hatch.

She hadn't seen him, much as she would have liked to. Chances were good that he was over at the central part of the hatching grounds, on the raised dais that had been set up for the Rain Wild Council members and other important dignitaries. It was crowded over there, with robed Traders mobbed around the dais, and many of the general population festooning the trees like a flock of migratory birds. She was glad her father had brought her here, to the far end of the hatching area, where there might be fewer cases but also fewer people to block her view. Still, it would have been nice to be close enough to the dais to hear the music and hear the speeches, and to see a real Elderling.

Just to think of Selden Vestrit swelled her heart with

pride. He was Bingtown stock, of Trader descent, just like her, but the dragon Tintaglia had touched him and he had begun to change into an Elderling, the first Elderling that any living person had ever seen. There were two other Elderlings now, Selden's sister Malta and Reyn Khuprus, himself of the Rain Wilds. She sighed. It was all like a fairy tale, come true. Sea serpents and dragons and Elderlings had returned to the Cursed Shores. And in her lifetime, she would see the first hatch of dragons within anyone's memory. By this afternoon, the young dragons would have emerged and taken flight.

The dull gray cases that now littered the riverbank for as far as Thymara could see each held what had been a serpent. The layers of leaves, twigs, and mulch that had covered them all winter and spring had been cleared away from them. Some of the cases were immense, as long as a river barge. Others were smaller, like log sections. Some of the cases gleamed fat and silvery. Others, however, had collapsed or sagged in on themselves. They were a dull gray color and to Thymara's sensitive nose, they stank of dead reptile. The serpents that had entered those cases would never emerge as young dragons.

As the Rain Wild Traders had promised Tintaglia, they had done their best to tend the cocooned serpents under Selden's supervision. Additional layers of clay had been smoothed over any case that seemed thin, and then leaves and branches had been heaped protectively over them. Tintaglia had decreed that the cases had to be protected not just from winter storms, but from the early spring sunlight, too. The dragons had cocooned late in the year. Light and warmth would stimulate them to hatch, and so she had wished them to remain covered until high summer, to give the dragons more time to develop. The Rain Wild guardians and the Tattooed—former Jamaillian slaves, now freed—had done their best. That had been part of the bargain the Rain Wild Traders had struck with the dragon Tintaglia. She had agreed to guard the mouth of the Rain Wild River against incursions by the Chalcedeans; in return, the Traders had promised to help the serpents reach their old cocooning grounds and tend them while they matured inside the cases. Both sides had kept their bargains. Today would see the fruit of that agreement as a new generation of dragons, dragons allied with Bingtown and the Rain Wilds, rose in their first flight.

The winter had not been kind to the dragon cases. Tearing winds and pounding rains had taken their toll on them. Worst, once the storm-swollen river had swept through the cocooning grounds, damaging many of the cases as it rolled them up against others or ate away at the protective clay. The count taken after the flood had subsided showed that a full score of the cocoons had been swept away. Of the seventy-nine cocooned dragons, only fifty-nine remained, and some were so battered that it was doubtful the occupants had survived. Flooding was a familiar hazard of living in the Rain Wilds, but it grieved Thymara all the same. What, she wondered, had become of those missing cases and the half-formed dragons within them? Had they been eaten by the river? Washed all the way to the salt sea?

The river ruled this forested world. Wide and gray, its current and depth fluctuated wildly. No real banks confined it. It flowed where it wished, and nowhere in Thymara's world was "dry ground" a meaningful phrase. What was forest floor today might be swamp or slough tomorrow. The great trees alone seemed impervious to the river's shifting flow, but even that was not a certainty. The Rain Wilders built only in the largest and stoutest trees; their homes and walkways bedecked the middle branches and trunks of the forest trees like sturdy garlands. Their swaying bridges spanned from tree to tree, and closer to the ground, where the trunks and limbs were thickest, sturdy structures housed the most important markets and provided dwelling space for the wealthiest families. The higher one went in the trees, the smaller and more lightweight the structures became. Rope-and-vine bridges joined the neighborhoods, and staircases spiraled up the main trunks of the huge trees. As one ascended, the bridges and walkways became flimsier. All Rain Wilders had to have some level of limbsman skills to move throughout their settlement. But few had Thymara's skill.

Thymara had no trepidations about her precarious roost.

Her mind was occupied and her silver-gray eyes filled with the wonders unfolding below her.

The sun had risen high enough that its slanting rays could reach over the tall branches of the forest and rest on the serpent cocoons littering the beach. It was not an exceedingly warm day for summer, but some of the cases had begun to steam and smoke as the sun warmed them. Thymara focused her attention on the large case directly below her. The rising steam reached her, carrying a reptilian stink with it. She narrowed her nostrils and gazed in rapture. Below her, the wizardwood of the log was losing it solidity.

Thymara was familiar with wizardwood; for years her people had used it as exceptionally strong timber. It was hard, far beyond what other people called "hardwood." Working it could blunt an ax or dull a saw in less than a morning. But now the silvery-gray "wood" of the dragon case below was softening, steaming and bubbling, sagging to mold around the still form within it.

As she watched, the form twitched and then gave a lively wriggle. The wizardwood tore like a membrane. The liquefied cocoon was being absorbed by the skeletal creature inside the log. As Thymara watched, the dragon's meager flesh plumped and color washed through it. It was smaller than she had expected it to be, given the size of the case and what she had heard of Tintaglia. A cloud of stink and moisture wafted up, and then the blunt-nosed head of a dragon thrust clear of the sagging log.

Outside!

Thymara felt a wave of vertigo as the dragon-speak touched her mind. Her heart leaped like a bird bursting into upward flight. She could hear dragons! Ever since Tintaglia had appeared, it had become clear that some folk could "hear" what a dragon said, while others heard only roaring, hissing, and a sinister rattling. When Tintaglia had first appeared in Trehaug and spoken to the crowd, some had heard her words right away. Others had shared nothing of her thoughts. It thrilled Thymara beyond telling to know that if a dragon ever deigned to speak to her, she would hear it. She edged lower on the branch.

"Thymara!" her father warned her.

"I'm careful!" she responded without even looking at him.

Below her, the young dragon had opened a wide red maw and was tearing at the decaying fibers of the log that bound her. *Her*. Thymara could not say how she knew that. For a newly hatched thing, her teeth were certainly impressive. Then the creature ripped a mouthful of the sodden wizard-wood free, tossed her head back, and swallowed visibly. "She's eating the wizardwood!" she called to her father.

"I've heard they do that," he called back. "Selden the Elderling said that when he witnessed Tintaglia's emergence, her cocoon melted right into her skin. I think they derive strength from it."

Thymara didn't reply. Her father was obviously right. It did not seem possible that an enclosure that had held a dragon would now fit inside the belly of one, but the dragon below her seemed intent on trying to consume it all. She continued to struggle free of the confining case as she ate her way out of it, ripping off fibrous chunks and swallowing them whole. Thymara grimaced in sympathy. It seemed tragic that something so newly born could be so ravenously hungry. Thank Sa she had something she could eat.

A collective gasp from the watching crowd warned Thymara. She clutched her tree limb more tightly just in time. The gush of pushed air that swept past her nearly tore her loose and left her branch swaying wildly. An instant later, there was a huge thump that vibrated through her tree as Tintaglia landed.

The queen dragon was blue and silver and blue again, depending on how the sunlight struck her. She was easily three times the size of the young dragons who were hatching. Watching her fold her wings was like watching a ship lower its sails. She tucked them neatly to her body, then folded them tight to fit as closely against her as a bird's wings so that her scaled feathers seemed a seamless part of her skin. She dropped the limp deer that hung from her jaws. "Eat," she instructed the young dragons. She did not pause to watch them, but moved off to the river. She lowered her great head and drank the milky water. Sated, she raised her head and partially opened her wings. Her powerful hind-quarters flexed; she sprang high, and two battering beats of her wide wings caught her before she could plummet back to earth. Wings beating heavily, she rose slowly from the riverbank and flew off, upriver, hunting again.

"Oh." Her father's deep voice was heavy with pity. "What a shame."

The dragon below Thymara was still tearing sticky strips of wizardwood free from her case and devouring them. A gray swathe of it stuck to her muzzle. She pawed at it with the small claws on her stubby front leg. To Thymara, she looked like a baby with porridge smeared on its cheeks and hair. The dragon was smaller than she had expected, and less developed, but surely she would grow to fulfill her promise. Thymara glanced at her father in puzzlement, and then followed his gaze.

While she had been focused on the hatchling right beneath her tree, other dragons had been breaking free of their cases. The fallen deer and the reek of its fresh blood now summoned them. Two dragons, one a drab yellow and the other a muddy green, had staggered and tottered over to the carcass. They did not fight over it, being too intent on their feeding. The fighting, Thymara suspected, would come when it was time to seize the last morsel. For now, both squatted over the deer, front feet braced on the carcass, tearing chunks of hide and flesh free and then throwing their heads back to gulp the warm meat down. One had torn into the soft belly; entrails dangled from the yellow dragon's jaws and painted stripes of red and brown on his throat. It was a savage scene, but no more so than the feeding of any predator.

Thymara glanced at her father again, and this time she caught the true focus of his gaze. The feeding dragons, hunched over the rapidly diminishing carcass, had blocked her view. The young dragon her father was watching could not stand upright. It wallowed and crawled on its belly. Its hindquarters were unfinished stubs. Its head wobbled on a thin neck. It gave a sudden shudder and surged upright,

where it teetered. Even its color seemed wrong; it was the
same pale gray as the clay, but its hide was so thin that she
could glimpse the coil of white intestines pushing against
the skin of its belly. Plainly it was unfinished, hatched too
soon to survive. Yet still it crawled toward the beckoning
meat. As she watched, it gave too strong a push with one of
its malformed hind legs and crashed over on its side. Foolishly, or perhaps in an effort to catch itself, it opened its
flimsy wings. It landed on one, which bent the wrong way
and then snapped audibly. The cry the creature gave was not
as loud as the bright burst of pain that splashed against Thymara's mind. She flinched wildly and nearly lost her grip.
Clinging to her tree branch, eyes tightly shut, she fought a
pain-induced wave of nausea.

Understanding slowly came to her; this was what Tintaglia had feared. The dragon had sought to keep the cocoons
shielded from light, hoping to give the forming dragons a
normal dormancy period. But although they had waited
until summer, they had still emerged too soon, or perhaps
had been too worn and thin when they went in. Whatever
the reason for their deformities, they were wrong, all wrong.
These creatures could scarcely move their own bodies. She
felt the confusion of the young dragon mixed with its physical pain. With difficulty, she tore her mind free of the dragon's bafflement.

When she opened her eyes, a new horror froze her. Her
father had left the tree. He was on the ground, threading his
way among the hatching cases, heading directly toward the
downed creature. From her vantage, she knew it was dead.
An instant later, she realized it was not that she could see it
was dead so much as that she had felt it die. Her father, however, did not know that. His face was full of both trepidation
and anxiety for the creature. She knew him. He would help
it if he could. It was how he was.

Thymara was not the only one who had felt it die. The
two young dragons had reduced the deer to a smear of blood
and dung on the trodden, sodden clay. They lifted their
heads now and turned toward the fallen dragon. A newly
hatched red dragon, his tail unnaturally short, was also

making his tottering way toward it. The yellow let out a low
hiss and increased his pace. The green opened its maw wide
and let out a sound that was neither a roar nor a hiss. Feeble
globs of spittle rode the sound and fell to the clay at his feet.
The target had been her father. Thank Sa that the creature
was not mature enough to release a cloud of burning toxin.
Thymara knew that adult dragons could do that. She had
heard about Tintaglia using her dragon's breath against the
Chalcedeans during the battle for Bingtown. Dragon venom
ate right through flesh and bone.

But if the green did not have the power to scald her father
with his breath, his act of aggression had directed the short-
tailed red dragon's attention to her father. Without hesitation, both yellow and green dragons closed in on the dead
hatchling and began snarling threats at each other over its
fallen body. The red began his stalk.

She had thought that her father would realize that the
hatchling had died and was beyond his help. She had expected him to retreat sensibly from the danger the young
dragons presented. A hundred times, a thousand times, her
father had counseled her to wariness where predators were
concerned. "If you have meat and a tree cat wants it, leave
the meat and retreat. You can get more meat. You cannot get
another life." So surely, when he saw the red dragon lurching toward him, its stubby tail stuck straight out behind him,
he would retreat sensibly.

But he wasn't watching the red. He had eyes only for the
downed hatchling, and as the other two dragons closed on
it, he shouted, "No! Leave it alone, give it a chance! Give it
a chance!" He waved his arms as if he were shooing carrion birds away from his kill and began to run toward it.
To do what? she wanted to demand of him. Either of the
hatchlings was bigger than he was. They might not be able
to spit fire yet, but they already knew how to use their teeth
and claws.

"Da! No! It's dead, it's already dead! Da, run, get out of
there!"

He heard her. He halted at her words and even looked up
at her.

"Da, it's dead, you can't help it. Get out of there. To your left! Da, to your left, the red one! Get clear of it!"

The yellow and the green were already preoccupied with their dead fellow. They dove on it with the same abandon they had showed toward the deer. Strengthened by their earlier feast, they seemed more inclined to quarrel with each other over the choicest parts. Thymara had no interest in them, except that they kept each other busy. It was the red she cared about, the one who was lurching unevenly but swiftly toward her father. He saw his danger now. He did what she had feared he would do, a trick that often worked with tree cats. He opened his shirt and spread it, holding the fabric wide of his body. "Be large when something threatens you," he had often told her. "Take on a shape it doesn't recognize and it will become cautious. Present a larger aspect and sometimes it will back down. But never turn away. Keep an eye on it, be large, and move back slowly. Most cats love a chase. Don't ever give them one."

But this was not a cat. It was a dragon. Its jaws were wide open and its teeth showed white and sharp. Its hunger was the strongest thing in it. Although her father became visually larger, it showed no fear. Instead, she heard, no, *felt* its joyful interest in him. *Meat. Big meat. Food!* Hunger ripped through it as it staggered after the retreating man.

"Not meat!" Thymara shouted down at it. "Not food. Not food! Run, Da, turn and run! Run!"

The two miracles happened simultaneously. The first was that the young dragon heard her. Its blunt-nosed head swiveled toward her, startled. It threw itself off balance when it turned to look at her and staggered foolishly in a small circle. She saw then what had eluded her before. It was deformed. One of its hind legs was substantially smaller than the other. *Not food?* She felt a plaintive echo of her words. *Not meat? No meat?* Her heart broke for the young red. No meat. Only hunger. For that moment of oneness with it, she felt its hunger and its frustration.

But the second miracle tore her from that joining. Her father had listened to her. He had lowered his arms, turned away, and was fleeing back to the trees. She saw him dodge away from a small blue dragon who reached after him with yearning claws. Then her father reached the tree trunk and with the experience of years, ascended it almost as swiftly as he had run across the ground. In a few moments he was safely out of any dragon's reach. A good thing, for the small blue had trotted hopefully after him. Now it stood at the foot of the tree, snorting and sniffing at the place where her father had climbed up. It took an experimental nip at the tree trunk, and then backed away shaking its head. *Not meat!* it decided emphatically, and it wobbled off, charting a weaving path through the hatching grounds where more and more young dragons were emerging from their wizard-wood logs. Thymara didn't watch the blue go. She had already slithered up onto the top of her branch. She came to one knee, then stood and ran up the branch to the trunk of the tree. She met her father as he came up. She grabbed his arm and buried her face against his shoulder. He smelled of fear sweat.

"Da, what were you thinking?" she demanded, and was shocked to hear the anger in her voice. An instant later, she knew that she had every right to be angry. "If I had done that, you'd be furious with me! Why did you go down there, what did you think you could do?"

"Up higher!" her father panted, and she was glad to follow him as he led the way to a higher branch. It was a good branch, thick and almost horizontal. They both sat down on it, side by side. He was still panting, from fear or exertion or perhaps both. She pulled her water skin from her satchel and offered it to him. He took it gratefully and drank deeply.

"They could have killed you."

He took his mouth from the bag's nozzle, capped it, and gave it back to her. "They're babies still. Clumsy babies. I would have got away. I did get away."

"They're not babies! They weren't babies when they went into their cocoons and they're full dragons now. Tintaglia could fly within hours of hatching. Fly, and make a kill." As she spoke, she pointed up through the foliage to a passing glint of blue and silver. It suddenly plummeted as the dragon dived. The wind of wildly beating wings assaulted both tree and Rain Wilders as the dragon halted her descent. A deer's carcass fell from her claws to land with a thump on the clay, and without a pause her wings carried her up and away, back to her hunt. Squealing dragon hatchlings immediately scampered toward it. They fell on the food, tearing chunks of meat free and gulping them down.

"That could have been you," Thymara pointed out to her father. "They may look like clumsy babies now. But they're predators. Predators that are just as smart as we are. And bigger than we are, and better at killing." The charm of the hatching dragons was fading rapidly. Her wonder at them was being replaced with something between fear and hate. That creature would have killed her father.

"Not all of them," her father observed sadly. "Look down there, Thymara. Tell me what you see."

From this higher vantage point, she had a wider view of the hatching grounds. She estimated that a fourth of the wizardwood logs would never release young dragons. The dragons who had hatched were already sniffing at the failed cases. As she watched, one young red dragon hissed at a dull case. A moment later, it began to smoke, thin tendrils of fog rising from it. The red set its teeth to a wizardwood log and tore off a long strip. That surprised Thymara. Wizardwood was hard and fine-grained. Ships were built from it. But now the wood seemed to be decaying into long fibrous strands that the young dragons were tearing free and eating greedily. "They are killing their own kind," she said, thinking that was what her father wished her to see.

"I doubt it. I think that in those logs, the dragons died before they could break free of their cases. The other dragons know that. They can smell it, probably. I think something in their saliva triggers a reaction to soften the logs and make them edible. Probably the same reaction that makes the logs break down as the youngsters are hatching. Or maybe it's the sunlight. No, that wasn't what I was talking about."

She looked again. Young dragons wandered unsteadily on the clay beach. Some had ventured down to the water's edge. Others clustered around the sagging cases of the failed dragons, tearing and eating. Of the deer that Tintaglia had brought and of the dead hatchling, scarcely a smear of blood remained. Thymara watched a dragon with stubby forelegs sniffing at the sand where it had been. "He's badly formed." She looked at her father. "Why are so *many* of them badly formed?"

"Perhaps . . ." her father began, but before he could speak on, Rogon dropped down from a higher branch to join them. Her father's sometime hunting partner was scowling.

"Jerup! You're unharmed then! What were you thinking? I saw you down there and saw that thing go for you. From where I was, I couldn't see if you'd made it up the trunk or not! What were you trying to do down there?"

Her father looked down, half smiling, but perhaps a bit angry as well. "I thought I could help the one that was being attacked. I didn't realize it was already dead."

Rogon shook his head contemptuously. "Even if it wasn't, there would be no point. Any fool could see it wasn't fit to live. Look at them. Half of them will be dead before the day is out, I should think. I had heard rumors that the Elderling boy was concerned something like this might happen. I was just over at the dais; no one knows how to react. Selden Vestrit is visibly devastated. He's watching, but not saying a word. No music playing now, you can bet. And half of those important folks clutching scrolls with speeches on them won't give them now. You never saw so many important people with so little to say. This was supposed to be the big day, dragons taking to the skies, our agreement with Tintaglia fulfilled. And instead, there's this fiasco."

"Does anyone know what went wrong?" Her father asked his question reluctantly.

His friend tossed his wide shoulders in a shrug. "Something about not enough time in the cocoons, and not enough dragon spit to go around. Bad legs, crooked backs—look, look at that one there. It can't even lift its head. The sooner the others kill it and eat it, the kinder for it."

"They won't kill it." Thymara's father spoke with certainty. She wondered how he knew it. "Dragons don't kill their own kind, except in mating battles. When a dragon dies, the others eat it. But they don't kill one another for food."

Rogon had sat down on the tree limb next to her father. He swung his bare calloused feet lazily. "Well, there's no problem that doesn't benefit someone. That's what I was coming to talk to you about. Did you see how quickly they ate that deer?" He snorted. "Obviously they can't hunt for themselves. And not even a dragon like Tintaglia can possibly hunt enough to feed them all. So I'm seeing an opportunity for us here, old friend. Before this day is out, it's going to dawn on the Council that someone has to keep those beasties fed. Can't very well leave a hungry little herd of dragonlings running wild at the base of the city, especially not with the excavation crews going back and forth all the time. That's where we come in. If we approach the Rain Wild Council to hire us to hunt to feed the dragons, there'll be no end of work for us. Not that we could keep up with the demand, but while we can, the pay should be good. Even with the big dragon helping us kill for them, we'll quickly run short of meat animals for them. But for a while, we should do well." He shook his head and grinned. "I don't like to think of what will happen when the meat runs out. If they don't turn on one another and eat their kin, well, I fear that we'll be the closest prey. These dragons were a bad bargain."

Thymara spoke. "But we made a deal with Tintaglia. And a Trader's word is his bond. We said we'd help Tintaglia take care of them if she kept the Chalcedeans away from our shores. And she has done that."

Rogon ignored her. Rogon always ignored her. He never treated her as badly as some of the others did, but he never looked directly at her or replied to her words. She was accustomed to that. It wasn't personal. She glanced away from the men, caught herself cleaning her claws on the tree's bark, and stopped. She looked back at them. Her father had black nails. So did Rogon. Sometimes it seemed such a small difference to her, that her father had been born with black nails on his hands and feet and that she had been born with claws, like a lizard. Such a small difference on which to base a life-or-death decision.

"My daughter speaks the truth," her father said. "Our Council agreed to the bargain; they have no choice but to live up to it. They thought their promise to aid the dragons would end with the hatching. Obviously, it isn't going to."

Thymara resisted the impulse to squirm. She hated it when Da forced his comrades to acknowledge her existence. It was better when he allowed them to ignore her. Because then she could ignore them as well. She looked aside and tried not to listen to the men as they discussed the difficulties of hunting enough meat to feed that many dragons, and the impossibility of simply ignoring the newly hatched dragons at the base of the city. There were ruins beneath the swampy grounds of Cassarick. If the Rain Wilders wanted to excavate them for Elderling treasure, then they'd have to find some way to keep these young dragons fed.

Thymara yawned. The politics of the Rain Wild Traders and the dragons would never have anything to do with her and her life. Her father had told her that she should still care about things like that, but it was hard to force herself to be interested in situations she would never have a say in. Her life was apart from such things. When she considered her future, she knew she was the only one she could ever rely on.

She looked down at the dragons and suddenly felt queasy. Her father had been right. And Rogon was right. Below her, young dragons were dying. Their fellows were not killing them, though they did not hesitate to ring the ones who had collapsed, eagerly waiting for them to shudder out a final breath. So many of them, she thought, so many of the hatched dragons had emerged unfit to face the harsh conditions of the Rain Wilds. What had gone wrong? Was Rogon right?

Tintaglia paid another swooping visit. Another carcass plummeted from above, narrowly missing the young dragons who had gathered at her approach. Thymara didn't recognize the beast Tintaglia had dropped. It was larger than any deer she had ever seen and had a rounded body with coarse hair. She glimpsed a thick leg with a split hoof

before the mob of dragons hid it from her view. She didn't
think that was a deer; not that she had seen many deer. The
swampy tussocks that characterized the forest floor of the
Rain Wilds were not friendly to deer. One had to journey
days and days to get to the beginning of the foothills that
edged the wide river valley. Only a fool hunted that far from
home. Such hunters consumed food on the way there and
had to eat from their kill on the way back. Often the meat
that survived the journey was half spoiled, or so little of it
remained that the hunter would have been better off to settle
for a dozen birds or a good fat ground lizard closer to home.
The dropped creature had a glossy black hide, a big hump of
flesh on its shoulders, and wide sweeping horns. She wondered what it was called, and then a brief touch of dragon
mind told her. *Food!*

A rising note of anger in Rogon's voice drew her unwilling attention back to the men's conversation. "All I'm
saying, Jerup, is that if those creatures don't get up on their
legs and learn to fly and hunt for themselves within the year,
they'll either die or become menaces to folk. Bargain or no,
we can't be responsible for them. Any creature that can't
feed itself doesn't deserve to live."

"That wasn't the bargain we struck with Tintaglia, Rogon.
We didn't barter for the right to decide if those creatures
would live or die. We said we'd protect them in return for
Tintaglia protecting the river mouth from Chalcedean ships.
The way I see it, we'd be wise to keep our end of the bargain
and give those youngsters a chance to grow and survive."

"A chance." Rogon pursed his mouth. "You've always
cared too much about giving chances to things, Jerup. One
day it will be the death of you. It nearly was today! Did
that creature think about giving you 'a chance' to live? No.
And we won't even speak of what sort of fortune you bought
for yourself eleven years ago with the last thing you gave 'a
chance' to live. "

"No. We won't," her father agreed abruptly, in a voice
that was anything but agreeable.

Thymara hunched her shoulders, wishing she could
make herself smaller, or suddenly take on the colors of the

bark like some of the tree lizards could. Rogon meant her. And he was speaking loud and clear because he wanted her to hear. She shouldn't have tried to speak to him, and her father should not have tried to force him to acknowledge her. Camouflage was always better than fighting.

Despite his harsh words about her, she knew Rogon was her father's friend. They had grown up together, had learned their hunting and limbsman skills together, had been friends and companions throughout most of their lives. She had seen them together in the hunt, moving as if they were two fingers on the same hand, closing in on whatever prey they stalked. She had seen them laughing and smoking together. When Rogon injured his wrist and couldn't hunt or harvest for a season, her father had hunted for both families. She had helped him, though she had never gone with him to deliver the food they gathered. No sense rubbing Rogon's nose in the fact that he was accepting aid from someone who should never have been born.

Their friendship was what had made Rogon come down the tree so swiftly to check on her father's safety. It was what had made him angry at her father for risking himself. And ultimately, it was why he wished that she didn't exist. He was her father's friend, and he hated to see what her existence had done to her father's life. She was a burden to him, a mouth to feed, with no hope that she would ever be an asset.

"I don't regret my decision, Rogon. And make no mistake about it. It was *my* decision, not Thymara's. So if you want to blame anyone, blame me, not her. Ignore and exclude me, not her! I was the one who followed the midwife. I was the one who went down and picked up my child and brought her home again. Because I looked at her, and from the moment she was born, I knew she deserved a chance. I didn't care about her toenails, or if there was a line of scales up her spine. I didn't care how long her feet were. I knew she deserved a chance. And I was right, wasn't I? Look at her. Ever since she was old enough to follow me up into the canopy or along the branchways, she has proved her worth. She brings home more than she eats, Rogon. Isn't that the measure of a hunter or gatherer's value to the people? Just what is it that makes you uncomfortable when you look at her? Is it that I broke some silly set of rules and wouldn't let my child be carried off and eaten? Or is it that you look at her and see that those rules were wrong, and wonder how many other babies could have grown up to be Rain Wilders?"

"I don't want to have this conversation," Rogon said suddenly. He stood up so abruptly that he nearly lost his balance. Something her father had said had hit a nerve with him. Rogon was among the best of the limbsmen. Nothing ever rattled him. Sudden cold crept through her. Rogon had children. Two of them, both boys. One was seventeen and the other was twelve. Thymara wondered if his wife had never been pregnant in the years between the two. Or if she had miscarried. Or if the midwife had carried a squalling bundle or two away from his home and off into the Rain Wild night.

She turned her gaze back to the riverbank below and kept it there. She wondered if her father had just ended a lifelong friendship with his harsh words. *Don't think about it,* she counseled herself, and stared down at the dragons. There were fewer than there had been, and almost nothing remained of the logs that hadn't hatched. Some people would be disappointed by that. Wizardwood was a very valuable substance, and there had been speculation that when the dragons did emerge, the log husks that were left might be salvageable. Of the folks who had gathered to watch the dragons emerge, some would have been hoping for a profit rather than coming to witness an amazing event. Thymara tried to count the dragons who remained. She knew there had been seventy-nine wizardwood logs to start with. How many had yielded viable dragons? But the creatures kept milling around, and when Tintaglia made another pass and dropped a freshly killed buck, it created a chaos that destroyed her effort at counting. She felt her father move to crouch on the limb beside her. She spoke before he could. "I make it at least thirty-five," she said, as if she had never heard his words to Rogon.

"Thirty-two. It's easier if you count them by color groups and then add them up."

"Oh."

A little silence fell before he spoke again. His voice was deeper and serious.

"I meant what I said to him, Thymara. It was my decision. And I've never regretted it."

She was silent. What could she say to that? Thank him? Somehow that seemed cold. Should a child ever have to thank a parent for being alive, thank her father that he hadn't allowed her to be exposed? She scratched the back of her neck, digging her claws along the line of scales there to calm an itch, and then clumsily changed the subject. "How many of them do you think will survive?"

"I don't know. I suppose a great deal will depend on how much Tintaglia brings them to eat, and how well we keep our promise to the big dragon. Look over there."

The strongest of the young dragons had already converged on the fallen meat. It was not that they deliberately deprived their weaker brethren; it was simply that only so many could cluster around the kill, and the first ones there were not giving way. But that was not what her father was pointing to. At the edge of the hatching ground, a group of men were approaching carrying baskets. Many of them had Tattooed faces. They were recent immigrants to the Rain Wilds, former slaves trying to build a new life here. As she watched, the foremost man darted out, dumped his basket, and hastily retreated. A silver heap of fish spilled out, skidding against one another to spread over the dull gray of the riverbank. The second man added his load to the slithering pile, and then the third.

The crowded-out dragons had noticed. Slowly they turned, staring, and then as if animated by a single will, they left the huddle of feeding dragons and raced toward the food, their wedge-shaped heads extended on their serpentine necks. The fourth man looked up, gave a yell, and dropped his load. The rolling basket spilled fish as it went. The man made no pretense; he spun and fled at a dead run. Three more men behind him dumped their loads where they stood and ran. Before the fleeing men had reached the line of trees, the dragons were on the fish. They reminded Thymara of birds as each dragon seized a fish and then flung its head back to swallow. Behind the first rank of dragons, others came. This rank of dragons lurched and stumbled. They were the lame and the halt, the blind, and, Thymara thought, the simply stupid. They tottered over, giving shrill roars as they came. A pale blue one fell suddenly on its side and just lay there, kicking its feet as if it were still moving toward the feed. For now, the others ignored it. Soon, Thymara knew, it would become food for the rest.

"They seem to like fish," she said, to avoid saying anything else.

"They probably like any form of meat. But look. It's already gone. That was a morning's catch, and it's gone in just a few heartbeats. How can we keep up with appetites like those? When we made our bargain with Tintaglia, we thought the hatchlings would be like her, independent hunters within a few days of hatching. But unless I'm mistaken, not a one of those can use its wings yet."

The young dragons were licking and snuffing at the clay. One green one lifted up his head and let out a long cry, but Thymara could not decide if it was a complaint or a threat. He lowered his head and became aware that the blue dragon had stopped kicking its feet. The green lurched toward it. The others, noting his sudden interest, also began to hasten in that direction. The green broke into a rocking trot. Thymara looked away from them. She didn't want to see them eat the blue.

"If we can't feed them, I suppose that the weak ones will starve. After a time, there will be few enough dragons that we can feed them." She tried to speak calmly and maturely, voicing the fatality that underpinned the philosophy of most Rain Wild Traders.

"Do you think so?" her father asked. His voice was cool. Did he rebuke her? "Or do you think they might find other meat?"

BLOOD, SO COPPERY and warm. That was what she wanted. She snaked out her long tongue and licked her own face, not just to clean it, but to gather in any smear of food that might be left there. The deer had been excellent, unstiffened and warm. The entrails had steamed their delightful aroma when her jaws closed on the deer's belly. Delicious, delicate . . . but there had been so little of it. Or so her stomach told her. She had eaten almost a quarter of a deer. And all of the cocoon that she had not absorbed during her hatch, she had devoured. She should feel, if not satiated, at least comfortable. She knew that was so, just as she knew so much else about being a dragon. After all, she had generation after generation of memories at her beck and call. She had only to cast her mind back to know the ways of her kind.

And to take a name, she suddenly remembered. A name. Something fitting, something appropriate to one of the Lords of the Three Realms. She pushed her hunger from her mind for the moment. First a name, and then a good grooming. And then, after preening her wings, to hunt. To a hunt and a kill that she would share with no one! The thought of that flushed through her. She lifted her folded wings from her back and gently waved them. The action would pump her blood more swiftly through the tough membranes. The wind they generated nearly pushed her off her feet. She gave a challenging caw, just to let anyone who might think of mocking her know that she had intended that sudden sideways step. She'd caught her balance now. What color was she, in this life? She limbered her neck and then turned to inspect herself. Blue. Blue? The most common color for a dragon? She knew a moment's disappointment but then pushed it aside. Blue. Blue as the sky, all the better to conceal herself during flight. Blue as Tintaglia. Blue was nothing to be modest about. Blue . . . was . . . Blue was . . . No. Blue *is.* "Sintara!" She hissed her name, trying it on the air. Sintara. Sintara of the clear blue morning skies of summer. She lifted her head, drew in a breath, and then threw her head back. "Sintara!" she trumpeted, proud to be the first of this summer's hatch to name herself.

It did not come out well. She had not taken a deep enough breath, perhaps. She threw her head back again, drew the wind into her lungs. "Sintara!" she trumpeted again, and as she did, she reared onto her hind legs and then sprang upward, stretching her wings.

A dragon carries within her the memories of all her

dragon lineage. They are not always in the forefront of her mind, but they are there to draw on, sometimes deliberately when seeking information, sometimes welling up unobtrusively in times of need. Perhaps that was why what happened next was so terrible. She lifted unevenly from the ground; one of her hind legs was stronger than the other. That was bad enough. But when she tried to correct it with her wings, only one opened. The other clung to itself, tangled and feeble, and unable to catch herself, she crashed to the muddy riverbank and lay there, bewildered, on her side. The physical impact was debilitating, but she was just as stunned by the certainty that, for as far back as her memories could reach, nothing like this had ever happened to any dragon in her lineage. She could not assimilate the experience at first; she had no guide to tell her what to expect next. She pushed with her stronger wing, but only succeeded in rolling onto her back, a most uncomfortable position for a dragon. Within moments, she felt the discomfort in the greater effort it took to breathe. She was also aware in a panicky way that she was extremely vulnerable in such a posture. Her long throat and her finely scaled belly were exposed. She had to get back on her feet.

She kicked her hind feet experimentally, but felt no contact. Her smaller forelegs scrabbled uselessly at air. Her folded wing was partially pinned under her. She struggled, trying to use her wing to roll herself over, but the muscles did not answer her. Finally it was her lashing tail that propelled her onto her belly. She scrabbled to get her hind legs under her and then to surge upright. Sticky clay covered half her body. Anger fought with shame that any of her fellows had seen her in such a distressing position. She shuddered her hide, trying to rid it of the clinging mud as she glared all around herself.

Only two other dragons had looked her way. As she recovered her footing and stared menacingly at them, they lost interest in her and diverted to another sprawled figure on the ground. That dragon had ceased moving. For a brief time the twain regarded him quizzically and then, comfortable that he was dead, they bent their heads to the feast. Sintara

took two steps toward them and then halted, confused. Her
instincts bade her go and feed. There was meat there, meat
that could make her stronger, and in the meat there were
memories. If she devoured him, she would gain strength for
her body and the priceless experiences of a different dragon's lineage. She could not be dissuaded because she herself
had come so close to being that meat. All the more reason to
feed and grow stronger.

It was the right of the strong to feed on the weaker.

But which was she?

She lurched a step on her unevenly muscled legs, and
then halted. She willed her wings to open. Only the good
one unfurled. She felt the other twitch. She turned her head
on her long neck, thinking to groom her wing into a better
position. She stared. *That* was her wing, that stunted thing?
It looked like a hairless deer hide draped over a winter-kill's
bones. It was not a dragon's wing. It would never take her
weight, never lift her in flight. She nudged at it with her
nose, scarcely believing it could be part of her body. Her
warm breath touched the flimsy, useless thing. She drew her
nose back from it, horrified at the wrongness of it. Her mind
spun, trying to make sense of it. She was Sintara, a dragon,
a queen dragon, born to rule the skies. This deformity could
not be a part of her. She riffled through her memories, pushing back and back, trying to find some thought, some recall
of an ancestor who had had to deal with a disaster such as
this. There were none.

She looked again at the two feasters. Little was left of the
weakling who had died. Some red glazed ribs, a sodden pile
of entrails, and a section of tail. The weak had gone to sustain the strong. One of the feeding dragons became aware
of her. He lifted his bloody red muzzle to bare his teeth and
arch his crimson neck. "Ranculos!" he named himself, and
with his name, he threatened her. His silver eyes seemed to
shoot sparks at her.

She should have withdrawn. She was crippled, a weakling. But the way he bared his teeth at her woke something
in her. He had no right to challenge her. None at all. "Sintara!" she hissed back at him. "Sintara!"

She took a step toward him and the remains of the carcass, and then a gust of wind slapped against her back. She spun about, lowering her head defensively, but it was Tintaglia returning, laden with new meat. The doe she dropped landed almost at Sintara's feet. It was a very fresh kill, its eyes still clear and brown, and the blood still running from the deep wounds on its back. Sintara forgot Ranculos and the pitiful remains he guarded. She sprang toward the fallen doe.

She had once more forgotten her uneven strength. She landed badly, but this time she caught herself in a crouch before she fell. With a lunge, she spread her forelegs over the kill. "Sintara!" she hissed. She hunched over the dead doe and roared a warning to any who would challenge her. It came out shrill and squawkish. Another humiliation. No matter. She had the meat, she and no other. She bent her head and savaged the doe, tearing angrily at its soft belly. Blood, meat, and intestines filled her jaws, comforting her. She clamped down on the carcass and worried it, as if to kill it again. When the flesh tore free, she threw her head back and gulped the mouthful down. Meat and blood. She lowered her head and tore another mouthful free. She fed. She would live.

Day the 1st of the Greening Moon

Year the 7th of the Reign of the Most Noble and Magnificent Satrap Cosgo

Year the 1st of the Independent Alliance of Traders

From Erek, Keeper of the Birds, Bingtown
To Detozi, Keeper of the Birds, Trehaug

Detozi,

Please release a flock of at least twenty-five of my birds even if you currently have no messages for them to carry. Message traffic to Trehaug was so heavy with Traders anxious to say they would attend the dragon hatch that my flocks are sorely depleted of carriers.

Erek

CHAPTER THREE

AN ADVANTAGEOUS OFFER

Alise. You have a guest."

Alise lifted her eyes slowly. Her sketching charcoal hovered over the heavy paper on her desk. "Now?" she asked reluctantly.

Her mother sighed. "Yes. Now. As in the 'now' that I have been telling you to expect all day. You knew that Hest Finbok was coming. You have known it since his last visit, last week at this same hour. Alise, his courtship honors you and our family. You should always receive him graciously. Yet whenever he calls, I have to come and ferret you out of hiding. I wish you would remember that when a young man comes to call on you, it is only polite to treat him respectfully."

Alise set down her charcoal. Her mother winced as Alise wiped her smudged fingers clean on a dainty kerchief embroidered with Sevian lace. It was a tiny act of vindictiveness. The kerchief had been a gift from Hest. "Not to mention that we must all remember that he is my only suitor, and therefore my only chance of wedding." Her comment was almost too soft for her mother to hear. With a sigh, she added, "I'm coming, Mother. And I will be gracious."

Her mother was silent for a moment. "That is wise of you," she said finally, adding in a voice that was cool but still gentle. "I am relieved to see that you have finally stopped sulking."

Alise could not tell if her mother was stating something she believed was true or was demanding that she accede to a dictation of deportment. She closed her eyes for an instant. Today, to the north, in the depths of the Rain Wilds, the dragons were emerging from their cases. Well, she amended to herself, today was the day appointed by Tintaglia for the leaves and debris to be swept away from them, so that the sunlight might touch them and stir them to wakefulness. Perhaps even now, as she sat at her tidy little desk in her pale room, surrounded by her tattered scrolls and feeble efforts at notes and sketching, dragons were tearing and shouldering their way out of the cocoons.

For a moment, she could imagine the whole scene: the verdant riverbank warmed by summer sunshine, the brilliantly hued dragons trumpeting joyously as they emerged into daylight. The Rain Wild Traders were probably heralding the hatching with all sorts of festivities. She imagined a dais decorated with garlands of exotic flowers. There would be speeches of welcome to the emerging dragons, song, and feasting. No doubt each dragon would parade before the dais, be joyously introduced, and then would open wide its glittering wings and lift off into the sky. These would be the first dragons to hatch in Sa knew how many years. Dragons had come back into the world . . . and here she was, trapped in Bingtown, shackled to a docile existence and subject to a courtship that baffled and annoyed her.

Disappointment suddenly smothered her. She had dreamed of making the trip to witness the dragons' hatching since she had first heard of the serpents encasing themselves. Alise had begged it of her father, and when he had said it might be improper for her to travel on her own, she had flattered and bribed her younger brother's wife until she had persuaded Alise's younger brother to promise to accompany her. She had secretly sold off items from her hope chest to amass the passage money she needed and pretended to her parents that she had been saving from the small monthly allowance they gave her. The precious billet for the trip was still wedged in the corner of her vanity mirror. For weeks, she had seen it every day, a stiff rectangle of cream-colored paper scribbled over with a clerk's spidery handwriting attesting that she had paid full price for two round-trips. That bit of paper had represented a promise to herself. It had meant that she would see what she had read of; she would witness an event that would, that *must* change the course of history. She would sketch the scene and she would write of it authoritatively, tying all she witnessed to her years of scholarly research. Then everyone would have to recognize her knowledge and ability and concede that although she might be self-educated on the matter, she was certainly far more than an eccentric old maid obsessed with dragons and their Elderling companions. She was a scholar.

She would have something that belonged to her, something salvaged out of the miserable existence that life in Bingtown had become. Even before war had descended, her family's fortune had been scraping bottom. They lived simply, in a modest manor house on the unfashionable edges of Bingtown. No grand park surrounded their home, only a humble rose garden tended by her sisters. Her father made his living by expediting trades between wealthier families. When war came and trading faltered, there was little profit for a go-between. She was, she knew, a plain, solid girl, from a plain, solid family ensconced firmly toward the lower end of the Bingtown Traders' social ladder. She had never been anyone's idea of a "good catch." It had not brightened her forecast when her mother had delayed her debut into society until her eighteenth year. She'd understood the reasons: her family had been arranging and financing her older sister's wedding. They'd had nothing to spare to launch yet another daughter. When, finally, she had been presented to Trader society three years ago, no man had raced to claim her from the butterfly mob of young girls. Three crops of Bingtown femininity had been released into the pool of eligible maidens since then, and with every passing year, her prospects of courtship and marriage had dimmed.

The war with Chalced had obscured them entirely. Her mind shied from recalling those nights of fire and smoke and screams. Chalcedean vessels had invaded the harbor and burned the warehouses and half the market square to the ground. Bingtown, the fabled and fabulous trade town where "if a man could imagine it, he could find it for sale," had become a city of stinking ruins and sodden ash. If the dragon Tintaglia had not come to their aid, like as not, Alise and her entire family would be tattooed slaves somewhere in Chalced by now. As it was, the invaders had been repelled, and the Traders had formed a rough alliance with the Pirate Isles. Jamaillia, their motherland, had come to its senses and seen that Chalced was not an ally but a plundering nation of thieves. Today, Bingtown Harbor was clear of invaders, the city had begun to rebuild, and life had begun a hesitant return to routine. She knew she should have been grateful that her family's home had escaped burning, and that their holdings, several farms that grew mostly root crops, were now producing food that was greatly in demand.

But the truth was, she wasn't. Oh, not that she wished to be living in a half-burned hovel or sleeping in a ditch. No. But for a few frightening, exhilarating weeks, she had thought she might escape from her role as the third daughter in a lesser Bingtown family. The night Tintaglia had landed outside the burned shell of the Traders' Concourse and struck her bargain with the Traders, offering her protection of their city in exchange for the Traders' pledge to aid the serpents and the young dragons when they hatched, Alise's heart had soared. She had been there. She had stood, shawl clutched about her shoulders, shivering in the dark, and listened to the dragon's words. She had seen the great creature's gleaming hide, her spinning eyes, and yes, she had fallen under the spell of Tintaglia's voice and glamour. She had fallen gladly. She loved the dragon and all that she stood for. Alise could think of no higher calling than to spend the rest of her life chronicling the history of dragons and Elderlings. She would combine what she knew of their history with her recording of their glorious return to the world. On that night, in that moment, Alise had suddenly perceived she had a place and a mission in the world. In that time of flames and strife, anything had seemed possible, even that someday the dragon Tintaglia would look at her and address her directly and, perhaps, even thank her for dedicating herself to such a work.

Even in the weeks that followed, as Bingtown pieced itself back together and struggled to find a new normalcy, Alise had continued to believe that the horizons of her life had widened. The Tattooed, the freed slaves, had begun to mingle with the Three Ships folk and with the Traders as all united to rebuild Bingtown's economy and physical structures. People — even women — had left their usual safe orbits and pitched in, doing whatever they must to rebuild. She knew that war was a terrible, destructive thing and that she should hate it, but the war had been the only really exciting thing that had ever happened in her life.

She should have known her dreams would come to naught. As homes and businesses were rebuilt, as trade took on a new shape despite war and piracy, everyone else had tried desperately to make things go back as they were before. Everyone except Alise. Having glimpsed a possible future for herself, she had struggled wildly to escape from the suffocating destiny that sought to reclaim her.

Even when Hest Finbok had first begun to insinuate himself into her life, she had kept her focus on her dream. Her mother's enthusiasm and her father's quiet pride that the family's wallflower had finally attracted not only a suitor but such a rare prize of a suitor had not distracted her from her plan. Let her mother flutter and her father beam. She knew Hest's interest in her would come to nothing, and thus she had paid little mind to it. She was past pinning her hopes on such silly, girlish dreams.

The Traders' Summer Ball was only two days away now.

It would be the first event to be held in the newly rebuilt Traders' Concourse. All of Bingtown was in a stir about it. Representatives and guests from the Tattooed and the Three Ships folk would join the Bingtown Traders in commemorating the rejuvenation of their city. Despite the ongoing war, it was expected to be a celebration beyond anything Bingtown had ever experienced, the first time that the general population of Bingtown had been invited to the traditional event. Alise had given it little thought, for she had not expected to attend it. She had her ticket for her trip to the Rain Wilds. While other eligible women fluttered their fans and spun gaily on the dance floor, she would be in Cassarick, watching a new generation of dragons emerge from their cocoons.

But two weeks ago Hest Finbok had asked her father's permission to escort her to the ball. Her father had given it. "And having given it, my girl, I can scarcely withdraw it! How could I imagine that you would want to go up the Rain Wild River to see some big lizards hatch rather than go to the Summer Ball on the arm of one of Bingtown's most eligible bachelors?" He had smiled proudly the day he had dashed her dream to pieces, so sure he had known what was truly in her heart. Her mother had said that she had never even imagined that her father should consult her on such a matter. Didn't she trust her parents to do what was in her best interest?

If she had not been strangling on her dismay and disappointment, Alise might have given her father and her mother a response to that. Instead she had turned and fled the room. For days afterward she had mourned the lost opportunity. Sulked, as her mother put it. It hadn't deterred her mother from calling in seamstresses, and buying up every measure of rose silk and pink ribbon that remained in Bingtown. No expense would be spared for her dress. What did it matter that Alise's dream had died in the egg, if they had theirs of finally marrying off their useless and eccentric second younger daughter? Even in this time of war and tightened budgets, they would spend feverishly in hopes of being not only rid of her but also gaining an important trade alliance. Alise had been sick with disappointment. Sulking, her mother called it. Was she finished with it?

Yes.

For an instant, she was surprised. Then she sighed and felt herself let go of something that she hadn't even known she was clutching. She almost felt her spirit sink back to a level of ordinary expectations, back to accepting the quiet, restrained life of a proper Trader's daughter who would become a Trader's wife.

It was over, it was past, it was finished. Let it go. It wasn't meant to be. She had turned her eyes to the window during her brief reverie. She had been staring sightlessly out at the little rose garden that was now in full blossom. It looked, she thought dully, just as it had every summer of her life. Nothing ever really changed. She forced the words out past the gravel in her throat. "I'm not sulking, Mother."

"I'm glad. For both of us." Her mother cleared her throat. "He's a fine man, Alise. Even if he were not such a good catch, I'd still say that about him."

"Better than you expected for me. Better than I deserve."

A pause of three heartbeats. Then her mother said brusquely, "Don't make him wait, Alise." Her long skirts swished gently against the hardwood floor as she left the room.

She had not, Alise noticed, contradicted her. Alise was aware of it, her parents were aware of it, her siblings were aware of it. No one had ever spoken it aloud, until now. Hest Finbok was too good for her. It made no sense that the wealthy heir of a major Bingtown family would wish to wed the plain middle child of the Kincarron Traders. Alise felt strangely freed that her mother had not denied her words. And she was proud that she had spoken her words without resentment. *A bit sad,* she thought as she resmudged her fingers by neatly restoring her charcoal to its little silver box. A bit sad that her mother had not even tried to claim she deserved such a fine man. Even if it was a lie, it seemed to her that a dutiful mother would have said it, just to be polite to her least attractive daughter.

Alise had tried to think of a way to explain her lack of

interest in Hest to her mother. But she knew that if she said to her mother, "It's too late. My girlhood dreams are dead, and I like the ones I have now better," her mother would have been horrified. But it was the truth. Like any young woman, she had once dreamed of roses and stolen kisses and a romantic suitor who would not care about the size of her dowry. Those dreams had died slowly, drowned in tears and humiliation. She had no desire to revive them.

A year past her emergence into society, with no suitors in sight, Alise had resigned herself to her fate and begun grooming herself for the role of maiden aunt. She played the harp, tatted excellent lace, was very good at puddings, and even had selected a suitably whimsical hobby. Long before Tintaglia had jolted her dreams, she'd become a student of dragon lore, with a strong secondary knowledge of Elderlings. If a scroll existed in Bingtown that dealt with either topic, Alise had found a way to read, buy, or borrow it long enough to copy it. She believed she now had the most extensive library of information on the two ancient races that anyone in the town possessed, much of it painstakingly copied over in her own hand.

Along with that hard-earned knowledge, she had earned a reputation for eccentricity that not even a large dowry would have mitigated. In a middle daughter from a less affluent Trader family, it was an unforgivable flaw. She didn't care. Her studies, begun on a whim, had seized her imagination. Her dragon knowledge was no longer an eccentric hobby; she was a scholar, a self-taught historian, collecting, organizing, and comparing every scrap of information she could garner about dragons and the ancient Elderlings rumored to have lived alongside the great beasts. So little was known of them, and yet their history was woven through the ancient underground cities of the Rain Wilds and hence into the history of Bingtown. The oldest scrolls were antiquities from those cities, written in letters and a language that no one could read or speak. Many of the newer scrolls and writings were haphazard attempts at translations, and the worst ones were merely wild speculation. Those that were illustrated were often stained or tattered, or the inks and vellum had become food for vermin. One had to guess what had originally been there. But with her studies, Alise had begun to be able to do more than guess, and her careful cross-referencing of surviving scrolls had yielded up to her a full score of words. She felt confident that with time, she could force all their secrets from the ancient writings. And time, she knew, was one thing an old maid had in abundance. Time to study and ponder, time to unlock all these tantalizing mysteries.

If only Hest Finbok had not stepped into her life! Five years her senior, the heir son of a Trader family that was very well-to-do, even by Bingtown standards, he was the answer to a dream. Unfortunately, the dream was her mother's, not Alise's. Her mother had near fainted with joy the first time Hest had asked Alise to dance. When, during the same evening, he had danced with her four more times, her mother had scarcely been able to contain her excitement. On the way home in the coach she had been unable to speak of anything else. "He is so handsome, and always so well dressed. Did you see the look on Trader Meldar's face when Hest asked you to dance? For years, his wife has been throwing her daughters at him; I've heard she has asked Hest to dinner at her home as many as seven times in a month! The poor man. All know the Meldar girls are nervous as fleas. Can you imagine sitting at a table with all four of them at once? Twitchy as cats, the lot of them, their mother included. I believe he only goes there for the sake of the younger son. What was his name? Sedric? He and Hest have been friends for years. I hear that Trader Meldar was offended when Hest offered Sedric a position in his household. But what other prospect does the man have? The war has taken most of the Meldar family fortune. His brother will inherit what is left, and they'll either have to dower the girls well to marry them off, or keep them all and feed them! I doubt Sedric will see so much as an allowance."

"Mother, please! You know that Sophie Meldar is my friend. And Sedric has always been kind to me. He's a very nice young man, with prospects of his own."

Her mother had scarcely heard her words. "Oh, Alise,

you looked so lovely together. Hest Finbok is the perfect height for you, and when I saw the pale blue of your gown against the royal blue of his jacket, well! It was as if you'd both just stepped out of a painting. Did he speak to you while you danced?"

"Only a few words. He's a very charming man," Alise had admitted to her mother. "Very charming indeed."

And he was. Charming. Intelligent. More than handsome enough for all ordinary purposes. And wealthy. On that night, Alise had been unable to divine what on earth Hest wanted of her. She had been unable to think of a single thing to say to him while they danced. When he had asked her what she did to pass the time, she told him that she enjoyed reading. "An unusual occupation for a young lady! What sorts of things do you read?" he had pressed her. She had, in that moment, hated him for asking but she had answered truthfully.

"I read about dragons. And Elderlings. They fascinate me. Now that Tintaglia has allied with us, and a new generation of dragons will soon grace our skies, someone must become knowledgeable about them. I believe that is my destiny." There. That should betray to him how hopelessly unsuitable a dance partner she was.

"Do you?" he had asked her, quite seriously. His hand pressed the small of her back, easing her into a turn that seemed almost graceful.

"Yes, I do," she had replied, effectively ending his small talk. Yet, inexplicably, he had asked her to dance yet again, and he smiled silently at her as he deftly led her through that evening's final measures. As the last notes of the music died away, he had held her hand perhaps a moment too long before releasing her fingers. She had been the one to turn and walk away from him, back to the table where her mother waited, pink cheeked and breathless with excitement.

All the way home in the carriage, she had listened, baffled, while her mother gloated. The next day, when the flowers arrived with a note thanking her for dancing with him, she had thought he was mocking her. And now, three months later, after ninety days of being besieged by his deliberate and carefully waged courtship of her, she still had no answer. What did Hest Finbok, one of the most eligible bachelors in Bingtown, see in her?

Alise forced herself to admit she was deliberately dawdling. She tidied away her sketches and notes with a scowl. She had been working with information from three separate scrolls, trying to divine what an Elderling had truly looked like. She knew she would not be able to get back to her work again this afternoon. With a sigh, she went to her mirror, to be sure that no errant smudge of charcoal remained on her face or hands. No. She was fine. She wasted just a moment looking into her own eyes. Gray eyes. Not snapping black eyes, nor yet placid blue nor jade green. Gray as granite, with short lashes, above a short, straight nose and a wide, full-lipped mouth. Her ordinary features she could have tolerated, were they not dotted everywhere with freckles. The freckles were not a gentle sprinkling across her nose like some girls had. No. She was evenly dotted, like a speckled egg, all over her face and on her arms as well. Lemon juice did not fade them and the slightest kiss of the sun turned them darker. She thought of powdering her face to obscure them and then decided against it. She was what she was, and she wasn't going to deceive the man or herself by dabbing on paint and powder. She patted at her upswept red hair, pushing a few dangling tendrils back from her face, and spent a moment making the lace of her collar lie flat before she left her room to descend the stairs.

Hest was waiting for her in the morning room. Her mother was chatting with him about how promising the roses looked this year. A silver tray set with a pale blue porcelain pot and cups rested on a low table near him. Steam from the pot flavored the air with the delicate scent of mint tea. Alise wrinkled her nose slightly; she did not care for mint tea at all. Then she controlled her face with a pleasant smile, lifted her chin, and swept into the room with a gracious, "Good morning, Hest! How pleasant to have you come calling."

He rose as she approached, moving with the languid grace of a big cat. The eyes he turned toward her were green, a startling contrast to his well-behaved black hair, which, in defiance of current fashion, he wore pulled back from his face and fastened at the nape of his neck with a simple leather tie. Its sheen reminded her of a crow's folded wings. He was attired in his dark blue jacket today, but the simple scarf at his throat echoed the green of his eyes. He smiled with white teeth in a wind-weathered face as he bowed to her, and for just that moment, her heart gave a lurch. The man was beautiful, simply beautiful. In the next moment, she recalled herself to the truth. He was far too beautiful a man to be interested in her.

As soon as she had taken a chair, he resumed his own seat. Her mother muttered an excuse that neither one paid any attention to. It was her pattern, to leave them in each other's company as often as she decently could. Alise smiled to herself. She was certain her mother's vicarious imaginings of what she and Hest said and did in her absence were far more interesting than the reality of their quiet and rather dull conversations. "May I offer you more tea?" she asked him politely, and when he demurred, she filled her own cup. Mint. Why would her mother have chosen mint when she knew that Alise disdained it? As he raised his own cup to drink from it, she knew. So that her mouth and breath would be fresh, if Hest should decide to steal a kiss.

She inadvertently gave a tiny snort of skepticism. The man had never even tried to take her hand. His courtship had been painfully free of any attempts at romance.

Abruptly, Hest set his cup down on its saucer with a tiny clink. Alise was startled when he met her eyes with something of a challenge in his glance. "Something amuses you. It is me?"

"No! No, of course not. That is, well, of course, you are amusing when you choose to be, but I was not laughing at you. Of course not." She took a sip of the tea.

"Of course not," he echoed her, but his tone said that he doubted her words. His voice was rich and deep, so deep that when he spoke softly, it was sometimes hard to understand him. But he wasn't speaking softly now. "For you've never laughed, or truly favored me with a smile. Oh, you bend your mouth when you know you should smile, but it isn't real. Is it, Alise?"

She had never foreseen this. Was this a quarrel? They'd scarcely ever had a real conversation, so how could they have a quarrel? And, given her complete lack of interest in the man, why should his displeasure with her make her heart beat so fast? She was blushing; she could feel the heat in her cheeks. So silly. What would have been fine and appropriate in a girl of sixteen scarcely was fitting for a woman of twenty-one. She tried to speak plainly in an effort to calm herself but found herself falling over the words. "I've always tried to be polite to you—well, I always am polite, to everyone. I am not a giggling girl, to simper and smirk at every jest you make." She found a sudden curb for her tongue and forced herself to claim the higher ground. "Sir, I do not think you have any grounds to complain of my behavior toward you."

"Nor any grounds to rejoice at it," he replied easily. He leaned back in his chair with a sigh. "Alise, I've a confession to make to you. I listen to gossip. Or rather, I should say that my man Sedric has a positive knack of hearing every rumor and scrap of scandal that Bingtown ever breeds. And from him I hear the tale that you are not happy with the courtship, nor pleased at the prospect of attending the Summer Ball with me. According to what Sedric has heard, you would rather be in the Rain Wilds, watching the sea serpent eggs hatch into dragons."

"The serpents hatch from dragon eggs," she corrected him before she could stop herself. "The serpents weave cases that some folk call 'cocoons,' and in the spring the new dragons emerge from them, fully formed." Her mind darted frantically. What had she said, and to whom, that he had come to know of her other plans? Ah, yes. Her brother's wife. She had commiserated with her over the wasted ticket money, and Alise had carelessly replied that she wished she were going on her journey rather than to the ball. Why on earth had that stupid woman repeated such a thing; and why had Alise ever been so careless as to utter it aloud?

Hest leaned forward in his seat. "And you would rather witness that than attend the Summer Ball on my arm?"

It was a blunt question and suddenly it seemed to deserve the bluntest possible answer. She thought she had accepted her fate, but now a final spark of regret blazed up as defiance. "Yes. Yes, I would. Such was my intent when I purchased a ticket on a liveship bound up the river. But for you and the Summer Ball, I would be there right now, sketching them and taking notes, hearing their first utterances and watching Tintaglia as she ushered them into the world and up into the sky. I'd witness dragons come back into our world."

He was silent for a time, watching her very intently. She felt her blush deepen. Well, he had asked. If he didn't want the answer, he shouldn't have asked the question. He steepled his fingers for a moment and looked at them. She fully expected him to rise and stalk, insulted, out of the door. It would be a great relief, she told herself, for this mockery of a courtship to be over. Why, then, did she feel her throat tightening and her eyes begin to prickle with tears? He kept his gaze on his hands as he asked his final question. "Dare I hope that the chill of your displeasure over the last few weeks has been a result of your disappointment in missing your trip rather than a disappointment in me as a suitor?"

The question was so unexpected that she couldn't think of an answer for it. He continued to regard her with a direct and inquiring glance. His lashes were long, his brows perfectly shaped. "Well?" he prompted her again, and her thoughts suddenly snapped back to his question. She looked away. "I was very disappointed not to go," she started huskily. Then she amended it, "I *am* very disappointed not to be there now. It is not just a once-in-a-lifetime occurrence; it is something that will never ever happen again! Oh, there may be other hatches—I fervently hope there will be other hatches. But none like this, none like the first hatch of dragons after generations of absence!" Abruptly she set the cup of horrid mint tea down with a clatter on the saucer. She rose from her chair and went to stand at the window, looking out over her mother's cherished roses. She didn't see them.

"Others will be there. I just know it. And they will sketch it and write of what they see, at first hand. Their knowledge will not come from musty bits of calfskin with faded letters in a language no one knows. They will study what happens there, and they will become known for their learning. The respect and the fame will go to them. And all of my studies, all of my years of puzzle-piecing will be for naught. No one will ever think of me as a scholar of dragons. If anything, they will think only that I am the dotty old woman who mutters over her tatty old scrolls, rather like Mama's aunt Jorinda who collected boxes and boxes of clamshells, all of the same size and color."

She halted her tongue, horrified that she had just revealed such a thing about her family. Then she clamped her jaws tightly. What did she care what he thought? She was sure that sooner or later, he would realize that she was an unsuitable bride and be done with her. He would have trifled with her just long enough for her to lose her single opportunity to make something of herself, to be something besides the old maiden aunt living off her brother's charity. Outside the window, the world basked in a summer that was full of promise for everyone else. To her, it was a season of opportunity lost.

Behind her, she heard Hest give a heavy sigh. Then he took a deep breath and spoke. "I . . . well, I am sorry. I did know of your interest in dragons. You told me of it, yourself, the first night I danced with you. And I did take it seriously, Alise, I did. I just didn't realize how important it was to you, that you actually wanted to study the creatures. I'm afraid that I *have* been thinking it was just some eccentricity of yours, just an amusing hobby perhaps that you had taken up to occupy hours that I, well, that I hoped I might soon fill for you."

She listened, caught between amazement and horror. She had wanted someone to recognize her studies as more than an amusement, but now that he did, she felt humiliated that he knew how serious she was about them. It suddenly seemed a foolish, no, an almost insane fixation rather than a legitimate study. Was it any better than letting oneself obsess about clamshells? What had she to do with dragons, what were they to her, really, other than an excuse not to engage with the life fate had given her? She felt first hot, then faint. How could she have ever imagined that anyone would consider her an expert on dragons? How foolish she must appear to him.

She had not turned to him nor made any reply. She heard him sigh again. "I should have known that you were not an idle dilettante, waiting for someone else to come give shape and purpose to your life. Alise, I apologize. I've treated you badly in this regard. My intentions were good, or so I thought them. Now I perceive that I have been only serving my own ends, and trying to fit you into a space in my life where I thought you best should go. I've experienced the same sort of treatment from my own family, so I know what it is to have one's dreams trampled."

There was so much emotion in his voice that she felt shamed by it. "Please," she said in a small voice. "Please, don't let it concern you. It was an idle fancy, a cobweb dream that I have built too large. I shall be fine."

He seemed not to hear her. "I came here with a gift today, thinking that perhaps I might persuade you to think better of me. But now I fear you can only see it as a mockery of your true dreams. Still, I pray you will accept it, as small reparation for what you have lost."

A gift. The last thing she wanted from him was a gift. He'd brought her gifts before, the expensive lacy handkerchief, a tiny glass vial of fine perfume, fancy candies from the market, and a bracelet of seed pearls. Gifts that were all the dearer, procured as they were in a time of war. Gifts fit for a young maiden, gifts that had seemed to mock her, a woman on the verge of spinsterhood. She found her tongue and made it move to say the right things. "You are too kind to me." If only he could understand that she meant the words with her whole heart.

"Please, come back and sit down. And let me give it to you. I fear you will find it more bitter than sweet."

Alise turned away from the window. After staring out at the bright day, the room seemed dim and uninviting. Until her eyes adjusted, Hest was just a darker silhouette in the gloomy room. She didn't want to sit down near him, didn't want to take the chance of his reading on her face what she truly felt. She could make her voice obey her; it was harder to keep the truth from her eyes. She took a deep breath. She hadn't cried, not a single tear. There was that to be proud of. And the man in the chair might represent the only other path fate was now offering her. She didn't, she couldn't believe in him.

But for now, the dictates of society directed that she must feign that she did. She would not make herself any more of a fool before him than she already had. She fixed her mind on the thought that whatever she might do or say to him now might become the humorous little tale that he told at a dinner years from now, when he had a true and appropriate wife at his side to laugh sweetly at his story of a foolish courtship before he'd met her. She schooled her face to a calm expression; she knew she could not manage to smile pleasantly yet, and she walked with a measured step back to her chair. She sat down and took up her cooling cup of tea. "Are you certain that you would not like me to freshen your tea for you?"

"Absolutely certain," he replied brusquely. The beast. He wasn't going to let her find refuge in polite small talk. She took a sip from her own cup to cover the flash of anger she felt toward him.

He twisted in his seat, retrieving a leather satchel from behind it. "I have a contact in the Rain Wilds. He's a liveship captain who sails up there frequently. You know about the excavations at Cassarick. When they first found the buried city there, they were quite elated. They thought it would be like Trehaug was, with miles of tunnels to excavate and treasures to be found in chamber after chamber. But whatever disaster buried the Elderling cities was far harsher to Cassarick. The chambers had collapsed rather than merely filling with sand or mud. As of yet, little of anything has been found intact. But a few items were."

He opened the satchel. His brief introduction had focused all her attention on the satchel. Trehaug was the major city of the Rain Wilds, built high in the trees in the swampland. But below it the Rain Wild Traders had found and plundered an ancient buried Elderling city. Similar mound formations at Cassarick near the serpents' cocooning beach had seemed to promise a similar buried treasure city. Little had been heard since the trumpeting of the discovery, but that was not unexpected or unusual. The Rain Wild Traders were a short-spoken lot, keeping their secrets close even from their Bingtown kin. Her heart sank at Hest's news. She had dreamed of them uncovering a library or at least a trove of scrolls and art. In her dreams, she had been there, lingering after the dragon hatch, and she had imagined herself saying, "Well, I've studied everything I could lay my hands on from Trehaug. I can't translate all of this, but there are words I can pick out. Give me six months, and perhaps I'll have something for you." They would have been dazzled by her knowledge and grateful to her. The Rain Wild Traders would have recognized her worth; a translated scroll was worth hundreds of times the value of an undeciphered one, not just in terms of knowledge but in trade appraisal. She would have stayed on in the Rain Wilds, and been valued there. So she had imagined it a hundred times in her darkened room at night. On a summer afternoon, here in the parlor, her dream faded to a child's self-indulgent imagining. It had, she thought again, all been a dream built of vanity and cobwebs.

"How sad," she managed to say in an appropriate voice. "I knew there were such high hopes when rumors of a second buried city first surfaced."

He nodded, his dark head bent over the buckles of the satchel. She watched his fingers work the strap through the metal and at last pull it free. "They did find one room with scrolls and such in it. The lower half of the room had silted in; I understand they are making efforts to salvage what they can of the scrolls that were buried, but the river water can be acid. However, there was one tall case in there, and six of the scrolls on the upper shelves were behind glass, in tubes made perhaps from horn and tightly stoppered. They were not perfectly preserved, but they did survive. Two seem to be plans for a ship. One has many illustrations of plants. Two others are possibly plans for a building. And the last one is here. For you."

She could not speak. He had taken from the satchel a fat horn cylinder and she found herself wondering what sort of a beast had furnished such an immense and gleaming black horn. With a twist, he freed a wooden stopper from it, and then coaxed forth the contents. The scroll he drew out was pale tan, a thick roll of fine parchment wrapped around a dowel of polished black wood. The edges looked a bit frayed, but there were no outward signs of water damage or insect attacks or mildew. He offered it to her. She lifted her hands and then let them fall back in her lap. Her voice quavered when she spoke. "What . . . what does it concern?"

"No one is exactly sure. But there are illustrations of an Elderling woman with black hair and golden eyes. And a dragon with similar coloring."

"She was a queen," Alise breathed. "I don't know how to translate her name. But images of a crowned woman with dark hair and golden eyes occur in four of the scrolls I've studied. And in one, she is shown being carried in a sort of basket by a black dragon. He flew with her in the basket."

"Extraordinary," Hest muttered. He sat very still, holding the scroll out to her. Alise discovered that her hands were gripping each other tightly. After a moment he said, "Don't you want to look at it?"

She drew a ragged breath. "I know how much a scroll like that is worth; I know how much you must have paid for it." She swallowed. "I can't accept such an expensive gift. It's not . . . that is . . ."

"It wouldn't be proper. Unless we were engaged." His voice had gone very deep. Was it a plea or a taunt?

"I don't understand why you court me!" she burst out suddenly. "I'm not pretty. My family is not wealthy or powerful. My dowry is pitiful. I'm not even young. I'm past twenty! And you, you have everything, you are handsome, wealthy, intelligent, charming . . . why are you doing this? Why do you court me?"

He had drawn back from her a little bit, but he didn't seem flustered. On the contrary, a small smile bent his mouth.

"Do you think this is funny? Is it some sort of joke, some wager, perhaps?" she demanded wildly.

At those words, the smile fled his face. He rose abruptly, the scroll still clasped in his hand. "Alise, that is . . . beyond insult! That you could accuse me of such a thing! Is that what you truly think of me?"

"I don't know what to think of you!" she responded. Her heart was beating somewhere in her throat. "I don't know why you asked me to dance that first time. I don't know why you court me. I fear it can only end in disappointment and . . . and humiliation when you finally realize I am unsuitable and walk away from me. I had become accustomed to the idea that I would never wed. I had found a new purpose for my life. And now I fear that I will lose both my resignation to my spinsterhood and my opportunity to be something besides a withered old maid in the back rooms of my brother's house."

Hest slowly sank back into his seat. He held the precious scroll loosely in his hands as if he had forgotten it, or at least forgotten how valuable an object it was. She tried not to stare at it. When he spoke, his words came slowly. "Again, Alise, you make me see I have been unfair to you. Truly, you are no ordinary woman." He paused and it seemed to Alise that it was a century before he spoke again. "I could lie to you now. I could flatter you with sweet words and pretend to be infatuated with you. But I perceive now that you would soon see through such a ruse, and would disdain me all the more for attempting it." He pressed his lips together for a long moment before he spoke again.

"Alise, you say you are not young. Neither am I. I am five years older than you are. I am, as you bluntly say, wealthy. The war has greatly affected our fortune, to be sure, as it has the fortune of every Bingtown Trader. And yet, as our trading has been diverse as are our holdings, we have been less damaged than many. I trust that we shall weather this war and emerge as a powerful family in the new Bingtown. And when my father dies, I will be the Trader for my family. I have been blessed, or sometimes I think, cursed, with a pleasing appearance. I have schooled myself to a charming manner, for we know that honey sweetens a bargain more than vinegar. I appear a social, convivial man, for that best suits the business I must do. Yet I do not think you will be surprised if I tell you that there is another Hest, a private and restrained one who, like you, enjoys being left in peace to pursue his own interests.

"I will tell you plainly that for several years now, my parents have been urging me to wed. I spent my youth in being educated and in traveling, the better to understand my father's trading partners. Balls and festivals and indeed"—he gestured at the tray and cups—"polite tea parties bore me. And yet, according to my parents, I must court and wed a woman if I am to have children to follow me. I must have a wife who will keep track of our social duties, entertain lavishly when it is required, and move easily within Bingtown society. In short, I must marry a woman who is Trader born and raised. I admit that I would enjoy a quiet home of my own, and undemanding companionship from a woman who respected my foibles. So, when my parents told me, quite seriously, that I must either wed or begin to train my cousin to be my heir, I sighed at first. Then I looked about for a woman who would be calm, sensible, and able to be independent of me for her own amusements. I needed someone capable of running my household without my constant attention. A woman who would not feel neglected if left alone for an evening, or even for months, when business forces me to travel. You were suggested to me by one of my friends who had, indeed, heard of your interest in dragons and Elderlings. I believe you rather boldly went to his family home to borrow scrolls from his father's library. He was very impressed with your forthrightness and your scholarship."

His words froze her. She suddenly knew who had recommended her to him. Sedric Meldar, Sophie's brother. He had been the one to help her find the scrolls in his father's study on the day she had borrowed them. She had always felt friendly toward Sedric; she'd even been infatuated with him when she was a girl. Yet it still shocked her to think he had urged his friend to consider her as a bride. Unaware of her confusion, Hest continued his tale.

"So, when I was lamenting my situation, he told me that I should find no better bride than a woman who already had a life and an interest of her own. And so I have found you to be. Indeed, you have such a life and interest of your own that I begin to wonder if a husband is something you could fit into your schedule." He suddenly lifted his dark gaze to her. Did a spark of amusement twinkle in those depths?

"This is not a romantic proposal, Alise. I suspect that you deserve far better than I am offering you. Yet, bluntly speaking, I do not think you will be offered better. I am a wealthy man. I am intelligent and well mannered, and I think myself kind. I think we shall get on well enough, me with my business and you with your scholarly pursuits. In fact, I think that after we are wed, we shall both be greatly relieved to leave behind the nagging of our parents. So. Can you give me an answer today, Alise? Will you marry me?"

He paused. She could find no breath to answer his outrageous proposal. He thought, perhaps, that she hesitated. He repeated what, to another woman, might have seemed insult most foul, but to her was simply an acknowledgment of their positions. "I do not think you will get a better offer. I am rich. Servants will do all the drudgery. You may hire whatever housekeepers and butlers you wish. Hire a secretary and a cook to plan our dinners and entertainments. Whatever staff you need to preserve our façade, you shall have. You will have not only the time to pursue your studies, but an income sufficient to acquire the scrolls and books you require. And if you must travel to follow your studies, I will provide you with the proper companionship to allow you to do so. I do, sincerely, regret that I have made you lose the opportunity to see the dragons hatch. I promise you that if you accept my proposal, you will be allowed to journey up the Rain Wild River and take whatever time you think you need to study the creatures for yourself. Come now. You cannot hope for a better bargain than that!"

Alise spoke slowly. "You would buy me, in the hopes of a simpler life for yourself. You would buy me, with scrolls and time for scholarship."

"You put it a bit crudely, but—"

"I accept," she said quickly. She held out her hand to him, thinking perhaps he would lift it to his lips and kiss it. Thinking, perhaps, he might even draw her into an embrace. Instead, he took it with a smile, shook it firmly as if they were two men sealing an agreement, and then turned it palm up. He set the treasured scroll into it. It was heavy, preserved by oil rubbed into it perhaps. The smell of its secrets rose to entice her. She hastily raised her other hand to cradle the precious thing. Hest was speaking, his deep voice rich with satisfaction.

"With your permission, I will announce our nuptials at the Summer Ball. After, of course, I have begged your father's leave."

"I scarcely think you will have to beg it," she murmured. She clasped the scroll to her breast as if it were her firstborn and wondered what she had agreed to do.

THE HEELS OF Hest's boots clacked sharply against each stone step as he descended from the entry of the Kincarrons' modest manor house. Sedric straightened up from where he had been lounging against the tall red wheel of the pony trap. He brushed his brown hair back from his eyes and smiled as his tall friend approached. The broad grin on Hest's face promised good tidings. The little horse lifted his head and whickered softly as Sedric greeted him with, "And so?"

"Both so impatient, are you?" Hest asked them affably as he approached.

"Well, you were a bit longer than we thought you'd be," Sedric agreed as he clambered to the seat and took up the reins. "I thought it might mean things weren't going so well. The signs lately have not been encouraging."

Long-legged Hest easily mounted to the passenger side of the cramped vehicle and sat down with a sigh. "I hate this contraption. The top of the seat hits me just above the small of my back, and the wheels find every bump in the road. I'll be grateful when father lets me put the carriage back into service."

Sedric clucked to the horse and he leaned into his harness. "I expect that won't be soon. While the roads are so bad, this is a much more sensible mode of transport. We can thread our way around and through the blockages in the streets. Half of Gold Drive is blocked with stacked timber this week, and that's because they're rebuilding. There is still so much of Bingtown that needs to be demolished and hauled away before new structures can be erected. Half the shops in the Grand Market are still burned husks."

"And the summer only makes the reek of the burned-out buildings worse. I know. I tried to find an open tea shop there yesterday, and the stench drove me away. I know the pony trap is more sensible. Just as wedding Alise Kincarron is the sensible thing to do. I don't have to like either one, only endure them. I tell you, Sedric, I've only been sensible for a few months now, and I'm already heartily sick of it." With a groan, Hest leaned his lanky frame back on the low-backed seat, then sat up with an exclamation of disgust and rubbed his back. "This is the most uncomfortable mode of transport ever invented. Why on earth did the Kincarrons build their manor so far from the center of town?"

"Possibly because it was the piece of land they were originally granted by the Satrap. It's had one benefit for them. The raiders and the looters didn't want to come out this far."

"Keeping an ugly house intact is small recompense for living in such a forsaken location. Didn't they ever consider moving to a better part of town?"

"I doubt they've had the financial option."

"Seems like poor planning. A few less daughters to dower and they'd have had a better estate for their sons."

Sedric chose to ignore his friend's complaint. He held the reins lightly in his browned hands, guiding the horse around a washed-out bit of the road. "So. Must I drag the details from you? How did your courting go? Have you divined why the lady has seemed to scorn such an eminently fine catch as yourself?"

"It was as you surmised. It shocks me to admit this, but your penchant for knowing the gossip and peculiarities of Bingtown has paid off yet again. Alise would genuinely rather travel up the Rain Wild River and watch dragons hatch than accompany me to the ball. She herself admitted that her dragon fixation is a bit of an obsession; apparently she had resigned herself to being an old maid and deliberately chosen an eccentric pursuit to occupy her lonely days. And then I not only dashed her dreams of spinsterhood all to splinters, but spoiled her chance of watching dragons hatch by viciously begging that she accompany me to the ball. So. I'm a beast. Naturally, that devastates me."

Sedric cast a glance over at his usually devil-may-care friend. Hest looked solemn. "So, I will have to drag it out of you, won't I? Did you salvage anything? Will she accompany you to the ball?"

"Oh, she'll do better than that." Hest stretched casually, and then turned and gave Sedric the full benefit of his perfect grin. His green eyes sparked in conspiratorial glee. "Your gift suggestion worked perfectly. One glimpse of it and she accepted my proposal. Asking her father for her hand will be a mere formality, as she herself noted. Congratulate me, my friend. I'm to be wed." As he made that final announcement, his voice flattened, his tone suddenly at odds with his words.

Sedric bit his lower lip for a moment, quelling his own dismay. Quietly, he offered, "Congratulations. I wish you both every happiness."

Hest scowled at him. "Well, I don't know about her, but I intend to be happy. Because I don't intend that this should change any aspect of my life. And if she's wise, she'll choose to be happy, too. She won't get a better offer. Oh, don't give me that rebuking look, Sedric. You're the one who suggested that the best way for me to make my family happy was to find a woman who wouldn't expect much of me. You even suggested that Alise Kincarron would perfectly fill the requirement. I met her, I agreed with you, and now she's to be mine. In time, she'll grace my home, provide me with a fat baby to inherit my name and fortune, and guarantee to me that my father doesn't choose my cousin as heir over me. All very practical and wise, and at a minimum of inconvenience to myself."

"But sad, nonetheless," Sedric said quietly.

"Why sad? We'll all be getting what we want."

"Not precisely," Sedric muttered. "And not honestly." He sighed. "And Alise deserves better. She's a good person. A kind person."

"You, my friend, are too prone to sentiment. And honesty is vastly overrated. Why, if we imposed honesty on Bingtown in general, all the Traders would be paupers by next week."

Sedric found he could not frame a reply to that. After a moment, Hest asked defensively, "Why did you put the idea in my head, if you didn't intend me to act on it?"

Sedric gave a small shrug. He hadn't, truly, expected that Hest would follow up on his cynical suggestion. That he had done so slightly undercut his admiration for the man. "It's an old saying. If you want to be happy, marry an ugly woman and live with a grateful wife." Then he admitted uncomfortably, "I was in my cups when I made the suggestion to you and feeling a bit morose about my own situation. Alise isn't a bad person. And she's certainly not ugly. Just not, well, not beautiful. Not by Bingtown standards. But she's kind. She used to come visit my sisters when we were younger. She was kind to me during a time when most girls treated me as if I had some sort of a disease."

"Oh, yes. I'd forgotten that spotty phase you went through," Hest needled him merrily. "She probably thought you'd keep your spots and they'd match her freckles." His green eyes danced mischievously.

Sedric resisted a smile. "My 'spots' were more than a phase; they seemed to last a lifetime! So her kindness, her willingness to be my partner at cards or to sit beside me at the table when she stayed for luncheon was important to me. She was my friend then. Not that I know her well now—I don't—just well enough to know that she was nice and had a good mind, if not a pretty face or a fortune." Sedric shook his head unhappily, and then pushed his unruly hair back from his eyes. "I would never wish ill on her. When I suggested she'd make you a fine, undemanding wife, I never thought you would actually propose to her."

"Oh, of course you did!" Hest was heartless in his accusation. "You've been by my side for most of my courtship of her. And you've been instrumental to the whole plan! You picked her out, you even told me what gift, exactly, might warm her toward me. And I should let you know that you were precisely correct on that! I thought the whole game was lost, until I trotted out that scroll. Turned the whole situation around for me, it did."

"You're welcome," Sedric replied sourly. He tried not to think of his role in Hest's scheme; he felt sullied by it now. Alise had been his friend. What had he been thinking, the night her name had rolled off his drunken tongue? He knew the guilty answer to that. He'd been thinking of himself, and how pleasant life was at the side of Hest Finbok. He'd been thinking of how he could keep that life intact and still advance his friend's ambitions for himself.

He pushed the thought aside and busied himself guiding the horse around the worst of the potholes. Bingtown had focused its efforts on rebuilding burned and vandalized buildings and neglected maintenance of the existing roads. By the time they got around to them again, there would be a whole season of repairs to be done. Sedric shook his head. Lately he felt as if the whole city was eroding away; everything that had made him so proud to be the son of a Bingtown Trader was now broken or tarnished or changed.

In the aftermath of the Chalcedean raids, the various factions of Bingtown had turned on one another to settle old scores. When those had finally been resolved, the rebuilding had seemed slow and dispirited. It was better now, for the Traders' Council had finally resumed its authority and enforced the laws. People felt it was safe now to rebuild, and with limited trade resuming, some had the resources to do so. But the new buildings going up seemed to have less character than the old ones, for they were built with haste rather than deliberation, and many looked almost identical. And Sedric was still not sure he agreed with the Council's decision to allow so many non-Traders to share power and decisions in the rebuilding process. Former slaves, fishermen, and newcomers were mingling with the Traders now. It was all changing too fast. Bingtown would never be restored to what it was. Last night, when he had lamented the situation to his father, the man had been singularly unsympathetic to his view.

"Don't be an idiot, Sedric. You're so dramatic about these things. Bingtown will go on. But it will never be what it was before, because Bingtown never was 'what it was before.' Bingtown thrives on change. Bingtown is change. And those of us who can change will prosper right along with our town as it changes. A little change won't hurt any of us. Wherever there is change, a clever man can find a profit. That's what you should be turning your wits toward. How can you make this change benefit your family?" And then his father had taken his short-stemmed pipe from his mouth, pointed it at his son, and demanded, "Have *you* thought that maybe a bit of personal change would do you good? This arrangement you have as secretary for Hest and his right-hand man, well, it's a good connection for you. You'll meet many of his trading partners. You need to think how you can use those connections. You can't spend your entire life playing second fiddle to your friend, no matter how deep the friendship or how pleasant a lifestyle it offers. And you should make the best of what you have, since you've thrown away all the opportunities I won for you."

Sedric sighed at the memory. His father always turned any conversation back onto his failures as a son.

"Are those heartfelt sighs for me, my friend?" Hest gave an indulgent laugh. "Seddy, you always think the worst of me, don't you? You're fearing that the poor woman is deceived, her head turned by sweet words and my charming smile, aren't you?"

"Isn't she?" Sedric asked tightly. He already felt bad enough that he'd suggested Alise to his friend. Hest's mockery of his regret stung.

"Not at all. You're chastising yourself over nothing. It's all for the best, my friend!" Hest clapped him genially on the shoulder and left his hand there as he leaned toward Sedric and confided, "She understands the arrangement completely. Oh, not at first. Initially, she stung me enough to make me nearly lose my aplomb, for she asked me, very bluntly, if my courtship were a jest or perhaps the result of a bet! That jolted me a bit, I'll tell you. And then I recalled that you had said she was nobody's fool, but a woman with an intellect. Scary little creatures, aren't they?

"So, I hastily reconsidered my strategy. I turned the tide of battle when I put all my cards on the table for her to see. I admitted to her that I was intent on making a marriage of convenience, and I even told her that I had specially selected her as the female most likely to cause me the least disruption to my life. Oh, don't give me that baleful look! Of course, I put it a great deal more tactfully than that! But I made no avowals of love and affection. Instead, I offered her the chance to hire a staff for my house to keep all her housewifely duties at bay, and the budget to pursue her own eccentric little hobby."

"And she accepted that? She accepted your marriage proposal on those terms?"

Hest laughed again. "Ah, Sedric, not all of us are idealistic romantics. The woman knew a good bargain when she was offered one. We shook hands on it, like good Traders, and that was the end of it. Or rather, I should say, this is the beginning of it. She'll marry me, I'll get an heir from her, and my father will stop lecturing me on how important it is to him to see the family robe and vote have a worthy heir before he dies. He's all but threatened to make my cousin his heir, and all on the basis of him being so infernally fecund. Two sons and a daughter, and Chet's a year younger than I am. The man has no moderation at all. It pleases me unreasonably that when I get myself a son off Alise, he may come to regret how generously he's plowed and planted that wife of his. Wait until Chet realizes he's going to have to find a way to provide for all of them, without my family's fortune to sustain them!" He lifted his hand, slapped his own knee, and leaned back, well pleased with himself. A moment later, he had straightened up again and nudged his friend.

"Well, say something, Sedric! Isn't this what we both wanted? Life goes on for us. We're free to travel, to entertain, to go out with our friends—nothing has to change. All is well in my world."

Sedric was silent for a time. Hest crossed his arms on

his chest and chuckled contentedly. The wheels of the cart jolted across a rutted crossroads, and then Sedric asked quietly, "And getting yourself a son with her?"

Hest shrugged his shoulders. "I'll blow out the candles and pursue my goal manfully." He laughed heartlessly. "Sometimes the dark is a man's best friend, Sedric. In the dark, I can pretend she's anyone. Even you!" He laughed uproariously at Sedric's horrified expression.

When Sedric managed a reply, his voice was low. "Alise deserves better. Anyone does."

Hest feigned an offended look. "Better than me? Doesn't exist, my friend, as you well know. Better than me doesn't exist." His laughter rang out on the summer day.

✦ ✦ ✦

Day the 2nd of the Growing Moon

Year the 7th of the Reign of the Most Noble and Magnificent Satrap Cosgo

Year the 1st of the Independent Alliance of Traders

**From Detozi, Keeper of the Birds, Trehaug
To Erek, Keeper of the Birds, Bingtown**

Erek,

This is my fourth bird bearing a copy of this request. Please send a bird back confirming receipt as soon as possible. I fear hawks are taking my birds before they reach you. In the enclosed sealed case is a message for the Bingtown Traders' Council. It is the fourth copy of the Rain Wild Traders' Council's request for advice on how best to deal with the young dragons. I believe this one also contains a request for additional funds to aid in the hiring of hunters. I hope you will reply that my birds are safe with you and that it is only your council that is so slow to respond to ours in this matter.

Detozi

✦ ✦ ✦

CHAPTER FOUR

VOWS

J ust one more dusting," her mother pleaded.

Alise shook her head. "There is more flour on my face now than we used for the wedding cake. And as tight and heavy as this gown is, I'm already starting to perspire. Hest knows I have freckles, Mother. I'm sure he would rather see them than have our guests see cracks in the powder layer on my face."

"I tried to keep her out of the sun. I warned her to wear a hat and veil." Her mother turned away from her as she muttered the words, but Alise knew that she intended them to be heard. She would not, she suddenly realized, miss her mother's softly voiced comments and rebukes.

Would she miss anything about her old home?

She glanced around her small bedchamber. No. She wouldn't. Not the bedstead that had once belonged to her great-aunt, not the worn curtains or the threadbare rug. She was ready to leave her father's home, ready to begin something new. With Hest.

At the thought of him, her heart gave a small surge. She shook her head at herself. It was not time to think of her wedding night. Right now, she had to focus on getting through the ceremony. She and her father had worked carefully on the promises she would make to Hest. They had exchanged their list of proposed vows, negotiated changes, and discussed wording for several months now. A marriage contract in Bingtown was to be as carefully scrutinized as any other contract. Today, in the Traders' Concourse, before families and guests, the terms of the marriage contract would be spoken aloud before either one of them set a signature to the final document. All would witness the agreement between Hest and her. The demands of Hest's family had been precise, and some had made her father scowl. But at the last, he had recommended she accept them. Today she would formalize the agreement before witnesses.

And afterward, when the business was done, they would celebrate as a newly wed couple.

And consummate their agreement tonight.

Anticipation and dread roiled and fought in her. Some of her married friends had warned her of the pain of surrendering her virginity. Others had smiled conspiratorially, whispered of envy for her handsome mate, and gifted her with perfumes and lotions and lacily beribboned nightdresses. Many a comment had been made about how handsome Hest was, and how well he danced and what a fine figure he cut when he went out riding. One less reserved friend had even giggled as she said, "Competence in one saddle sometimes bespeaks competence in another!" So, even though their courtship had been bereft of stolen kisses or whispered endearments, she dared to hope that their first night alone might break his reserve and reveal a concealed passion for her.

She snapped open a lacy little fan and cooled her face with it. A subtle fragrance rode the small breeze from the perfumed lace of the fan. She looked a final time into her vanity mirror. Her eyes were sparkling, her cheeks pink. *As infatuated as a silly little girl,* she thought, and smiled forgiveness at her own image. What woman would not have given way to Hest's charms? He was handsome, witty, intelligent, and a delightful conversationalist. The small gifts he showered upon her were thoughtful and apt. He'd not only accepted her ambition to be a scholar; his bridal gifts to her revealed that he would support her in her studies. Two excellent pens with silver tips, and ink in five different hues. A glass ground to magnify the fading letters of old manuscripts. A shawl embroidered with serpents and dragons. Earrings made from tinted flaked glass to mimic dragon scales. Every gift had been tailored to her interests. She suspected that his gifts said what he was too reserved to put into words. In response, she, too, had remained correct and formal, but despite her quiet manner, warmth for him had begun to grow in her heart. The restraint she practiced daily only fueled her fantasies at night.

Even the homeliest girl secretly dreams that a man might fall in love with her inner spirit. He had told her, plainly, that their marriage was one of convenience. But did it have to be, she wondered? If she devoted herself to him, could she not make it something more than that, for both of them? In the months that had slowly passed since the announcement of their engagement, she had become ever more aware of Hest. She learned the shape of his mouth as he spoke to her, studied his elegant hands as he lifted a cup of tea, admired his wide shoulders that pulled at the seams of his jacket. She stopped asking why and disbelieving that love could find her and drowned joyously in her infatuation.

War had ravaged Bingtown, and even if her parents had had money to fling into the wind, there were many items that simply could not be bought. For all that, this day still seemed like something out of a tale to her. It did not matter to her that her dress had been made from her grandmother's gown; it only made it seem more significant. The flowers that decorated the Traders' Concourse came not from hothouses or the Rain Wilds, but from the gardens of her family and friends. Two of her cousins would sing while their father played his fiddle. It would all be simple, and honest, and very real.

In the previous weeks, she had imagined their wedding night a hundred ways. She had dreamed him bold, and then boyishly shy, gentle, and hesitant, or perhaps rakishly bawdy or even demanding of her. Every possibility had warmed her with desire and chased sleep from her bed. Well. It was only a matter of hours now before she would find out. She caught a glimpse of herself in the mirror. The smile on her face surprised her. She tilted her head and studied her own reflection. Alise Kincarron, smiling on her wedding day—who would ever have imagined it?

"Alise?" Her father stood at the door. She turned to him in surprise and felt an odd lurch of her heart at the soft, sad smile he wore. "Darling, it's time to come downstairs. The carriage is waiting for us."

SWARGE STOOD STIFFLY in the small galley. At a nod from his captain, he sat down. His big, rough hands rested lightly on the edge of the table. Leftrin sat down opposite him with a sigh. It had been a long day; no, it had been a long three months.

The secrecy the project demanded had tripled the work involved. Leftrin had not dared to move the log; towing it down the river to a better place to work on it was not an option. Any passing vessel would have recognized what he had. So the work of cutting the log into usable lengths and sections had all had to be done right there, in the mud and brush of the riverbank.

Tonight it was finished. The wizardwood log was gone; the small scraps that remained had been stowed as dunnage in Tarman's holds. Outside on the deck, the rest of the crew was celebrating. And in light of what they'd conspired to do, Leftrin had decided it would be best if all of them made a fresh commitment to Tarman. All the rest of them had signed the ship's papers. Only Swarge remained. Tomorrow, they'd relaunch Tarman and return to Trehaug to drop off the carefully selected and discreet woodworkers who had served them so well. And afterward, they would go back to their regular run on the river. But for now, they celebrated the completion of a massive project. It was finished, and Leftrin found he had no regrets.

A bottle of rum and several small glasses occupied the center of the table. Two of them weighted down a scroll. A bottle of ink and a quill rested beside it. One more signature, and Tarman would be secure. Leftrin nodded to himself as he studied the riverman opposite him. Streaks of dried mud and tar clung to the tillerman's rough shirt. His thick fingernails were packed with silvery sawdust, and there was a stripe of dirt on his jaw where he'd probably scratched his face earlier.

Leftrin smiled to himself. He was probably just as grubby as the tillerman. It had been a long, hard day's work, and it was labor of a kind neither one of them was accustomed to. It was coming to a close now, and Swarge had more than proven himself. He had been willing to join Leftrin's little conspiracy and had done more than his share without complaint. It was one of the things that Leftrin liked about the man. Time to let him know that. "You don't complain. You don't whine, and you don't find fault when something just plain goes wrong. You jump in and do your best to fix the situation. You're loyal and you're discreet. And that's why I want to keep you on board."

Swarge glanced at the small glasses and Leftrin got the message. He uncorked the bottle and dolloped out small measures for both of them. "Best clean your hands before you eat or drink. That stuff can be poisonous," he advised his tillerman. Swarge nodded and carefully wiped his hands down the front of his shirt. Then they both drank before Swarge responded.

"Forever. I heard from the others that's what this is about. You're asking me to sign on and stay aboard Tarman forever. Until I die."

"That's right," Leftrin confirmed. "And I hoped they mentioned that your wages will go up as well. With our new hull design we're not going to need as large a crew as we've shipped in the past. But I'll budget the same for pay, and every sailor aboard will get an equal share of it. That has to sound good, doesn't it?"

Swarge bobbed a nod at him, but didn't meet his eyes. "Rest of my life is a long time, Cap."

Leftrin laughed aloud. "Sa's blood, Swarge, you been with Tarman for ten years already. For a Rain Wild man, that's half of forever already. So what's the problem with signing on permanent? Benefits us both. I know I got a good tillerman for as long as Tarman floats. And you know that no one is ever going to decide you're too old to work and put you ashore without a penny. You sign this, it binds my heir as well as me. You give me your word on this, you sign the paper with me, and I promise that as long as you live, Tarman and I will take care of you. Swarge, what else you got besides this boat?"

Swarge answered the question with one of his own. "Why has it got to be forever, Cap? What's changed so much that I got to promise to sail with you forever now or clear off the ship?"

Leftrin concealed a small sigh. Swarge was a good man and great on the tiller. He could read the river as few men could. Tarman felt comfortable in his hands. With all the changes the ship had undergone recently, Leftrin didn't want to break in a new tillerman. He met Swarge's look squarely. "You know that my claiming that wizardwood and what we've done with it is forbidden. It's got to stay a secret. Best way to keep a secret, I think, is to make sure it benefits every man who knows it. And to keep those who share the secret in one place.

"Before we started, I let go any man I didn't think was mine, heart and soul. I've got a plum little crew here now, handpicked, and I want to keep you all. It comes down to trust, Swarge. I kept you on because I knew you'd done some boatbuilding back when you were a youngster. I knew you'd help us do what Tarman needed doing, and keep it quiet. Well, now it's done, and I want you to stay on as his tillerman. Permanently. If I bring a new man aboard, he's going to know immediately that something about this ship is very unusual, even for a liveship. And I won't know if he's someone I can trust with a secret that big. He might just have a big mouth, or he might be the type that thinks he could squeeze some money out of me for silence. And then I'd have to take steps I'd rather not take. Instead, I'd rather keep you, as long as I can. For the rest of your life, if you'll sign on for that."

"And if I don't?"

Leftrin was silent for a moment. He hadn't bargained on this. He thought he'd chosen carefully. He'd never imagined that Swarge would be the one to hesitate. He said the first thing that came into his mind. "Why wouldn't you? What's stopping you?"

Swarge shifted from side to side on his chair. He glanced at the bottle and away again. Leftrin waited. The man wasn't known for being talkative. Leftrin poured another jot of rum for both of them and waited, almost patiently.

"There's a woman," Swarge said at last. And there he stopped. He looked at the table, at his captain, and then back at the table.

"What about her?" Leftrin asked at last.

"Been thinking to ask her to marry me."

Leftrin's heart sank. It would not be the first time he'd lost a good crewman to a wife and a home.

THE RECENTLY REPAIRED and renovated Traders' Concourse still smelled of new timber and oiled wood. For the ceremony, the seating benches had been removed to the sides of the room, leaving a large open space. The afternoon sun slanted in through the windows; fading squares of light fell on the polished floor and broke into fragments against those who had gathered to witness their promises to each other. Most of the guests were attired in their formal Trader robes in the colors of their families. There were a few Three Ships folk there, probably trading partners of Hest's families, and even one Tattooed woman in a long gown of yellow silk.

Hest had not arrived yet.

Alise told herself that did not matter. He would come. He was the one who had arranged all this; he would scarcely back out of it now. She wished devoutly that her gown did not fit her so snugly, and that it was not such a warm afternoon. "You look so pale," her father whispered to her. "Are you all right?"

She thought of all the white powder her mother had dusted on her face and had to smile. "I'm fine, Father. Just a bit nervous. Shall we walk about a bit?"

They moved slowly through the room, her hand resting lightly on his forearm. Guest after guest greeted her and wished her well. Some were already availing themselves of the punch. Others were unabashedly scanning the terms of their marriage contract. The dual scrolls of their agreement were pegged down to the wood of a long central table. Silver candelabra held white tapers; the light was needed for anyone who wished to read the finely written words. Matching black quills and a pot of red ink awaited Hest and her.

It was a peculiarly Bingtown tradition. The marriage contract would be scrutinized, read aloud, and signed by both families before the far briefer blessing invocation. It made sense to Alise. They were a nation of traders; of course their nuptials would be as carefully negotiated as any other bargain.

She had not realized how anxious she was until she heard the wheels of a carriage in the drive outside. "That must be him," she whispered nervously to her father.

"It had better be him," he replied ominously. "We may not be so rich as the Finboks, but the Kincarrons are just as much Traders as they are. We are not to be trifled with. Nor insulted."

For the first time, she realized how much her father had feared Hest would leave her standing unclaimed, their promises unsigned. She looked deep into his eyes and saw the anger that mingled with his fear. Fear that he'd be humiliated, fear that he'd have to take his unclaimed daughter home. She looked away from him, and some of the shine went off the day. Not even her own father could believe that Hest was truly in love with her and would want to marry her.

She drew as deep a breath as the tightly sewn dress would allow her. She stiffened her spine and with it her resolve. She was not going back to live in her father's house as his failed daughter. Never again. No matter what.

Then the door of the Concourse was flung wide, and Hest's men poured in dressed in the formal robes of their family lineages. They cascaded down the steps, an unruly laughing mob of his friends and business associates. Hest was carried down in their midst. Her first glimpse of him sent her heart racing. His dark hair was tousled boyishly, and his cheeks were reddened. He was grinning good-naturedly as they hurried him along. His wide shoulders were emphasized by his closely tailored jacket of dark green Jamaillian silk. He wore a white neckcloth pinned with an emerald stickpin that was not greener than his eyes.

When his eyes found her, his face went suddenly still. His smile faded. She held his gaze, challenging him to change his mind now. Instead, as he regarded her solemnly, he nodded slowly, as if confirming something to himself. Dozens of well-wishers had moved forward to greet him when he had entered. He moved through them as a ship cuts through waves, not rudely, but refusing to be delayed or distracted by them. When he reached Alise and her father, he bowed formally to both of them. Alise, startled, managed a hasty curtsy. As she rose from it, Hest held out a hand to her. But it was her father he smiled at as he said, "I believe this is mine now, isn't it?"

She put her hand in his.

"I believe that there is a contract to be signed first," her father said, but he spoke jovially. With that one gesture, Hest had changed his anxiety to good nature. Her father was beaming proudly to see his daughter claimed so confidently by such a handsome and wealthy man.

"That there is!" Hest exclaimed. "And I propose that we get to it immediately. I have no patience with lengthy formalities. The lady has made me wait quite long enough!"

A thrill shot through Alise at his words while a murmur of approving amusement and some small laughter rippled through the gathered guests. Hest, ever charming and charismatic, literally hurried her across the Concourse to the waiting contracts.

As tradition demanded, they moved to their positions on opposite sides of the long table. Sedric Meldar came forward to hold the inkwell for Hest. Alise's elder sister Rose had demanded the honor of being her attendant. Hest and Alise would move in unison down the long table, each reading aloud a term from their wedding contract. As each term was agreed to, both would sign. At the end of the table, the couple would finally stand together, to be blessed by their parents. Each contract scroll would be carefully sanded and dried, and then rolled up and stored in the Concourse archives. It was rare that the terms of a dowry or the subject of a child's inheritance came into question, but the written records often served to prevent such strife.

There was nothing of romance in these written words. Alise read aloud that in the event of Hest's untimely death before he sired an heir, she would relinquish all claim to his estate in favor of his cousin. Hest countered that by reading and then signing the clause that stipulated his widow would be granted a private residence of her own on his family's land. In the event of Alise's death with no heir, the little vineyard that was her sole dowry would revert to her younger sister.

There were standard pledges expected in all Bingtown marriage contracts. Once they were wed, each would have a say in the financial decisions of the household. The amount of each one's personal allowance was agreed to, and provisions were made either to increase or decrease such allowances as their fortunes prospered or faded. Each agreed to be faithful to the other, and each attested that neither had already produced a child. Alise had requested the old form of agreement, in which the firstborn child of either sex was to be recognized as the full heir. It had warmed her that Hest had not objected at all to that, and when she read aloud the clause that she had insisted on, that she be allowed to travel to the Rain Wilds to continue her study of the dragons, at a date to be agreed upon in the future, he signed his name with a flourish. She blinked away tears of joy, willing that they not spill and make tracks down her powdered face. What had she done to deserve such a man? She vowed to be worthy of his generosity.

The provisions of the contract were precise, not vague,

and recognized that no marriage was perfect. Term after endless term was delineated. Every detail was considered; nothing was too intimate to be mentioned. If Hest sired a child outside of the marital bed, such a child would be ineligible to inherit anything, and Alise could, if she chose, terminate their marriage agreement immediately, while claiming 15 percent of Hest's current estate. If Alise were found to have committed an infidelity, Hest could not only turn her out of his home but could dispute the parentage of any child born after the date of the transgression; such children became the financial responsibility of Alise's father.

It went on and on. There were provisions by which they could mutually end their agreement, and stipulations on transgressions that rendered the contract null and void. Each had to be read aloud and formally signed by both of them. It was not unusual for the process to take hours. But Hest was having none of that. With each phrase he read, he increased the tempo of his reading, plainly anxious to be done with this part of the ceremony. Alise found herself caught up in play, and matched the speed of her words to his. Some of the guests seemed affronted at first. Then, as they noticed Alise's pink cheeks and the sly smile that wafted across Hest's face periodically, they, too, began to smile.

In a remarkably short time, they reached the end of the table. Alise was out of breath as she babbled through the last stipulation from her family. She spoke the final proviso aloud, the standard one. "I will keep myself, my body and my affections, my heart and my loyalty, solely to you." As he repeated it, it seemed a redundancy to her, after all they had already promised to each other. They signed. The quills were handed back to their attendants. Finally freed of such tedious formality, they joined hands and stepped to where the table no longer divided them. Together they turned to face their waiting parents. Hest's hands were as warm as Alise's were cold; he held her fingers gently, as if afraid he might harm her with a firmer grip. She closed her hands on his; let him know now that all her hesitations were gone. She was his, and she gave her well-being into his hands.

First their mothers and then their fathers joined in bless-

ing the couple. Hest's parents spoke a much longer blessing
than Alise's did, imploring Sa for prosperity, many children, a happy home, longevity with health for both of them,
healthy dutiful children—the list went on and on. Alise felt
her smile grow fixed.

When the blessings were finally finished, they turned to
face each other. The kiss. It would be their first kiss, and
suddenly she appreciated that he had reserved it for this
moment. She took as deep a breath as her gown would allow
her and turned her face up to him. He looked down on her.
His green eyes were unreadable. As he bent to her, she
closed her eyes and let her lips relax. Let him take charge of
this moment. She felt his breath as his mouth hovered over
hers. Then he kissed her, the lightest brushing touch of his
mouth against hers. As if the wing of a hummingbird had
just brushed her lips.

A small shiver passed over her, and she caught her breath
as he stepped back from her. Her heart was thundering. *He
teases me,* she thought, and could not keep a smile from
her face. He would not meet her eyes, but a sly smile stole
across his face as well. Cruel man. He would make her
admit to herself that she was as eager as he was. *Let the
night come,* she thought and stole a sideways glance at her
husband's handsome face.

"So. TELL ME about her," Leftrin ventured when the silence
had grown long.

Swarge sighed and then looked up at him and smiled. It
transformed his face. Years dropped away, and the bluish
glints behind his blue eyes seemed almost kindly. "Her
name is Bellin. She's, well, she likes me. She can play the
pipes. We met a couple of years ago, in a tavern in Trehaug.
You know the one. Jona's place."

"I know it. River folk trade there." He cocked his head
and looked at his tillerman, reluctant to ask the question that
came to his mind. Most of the women he'd met at Jona's
were whores. Some of them were nice enough, but most
were good at their trade and unlikely to give it up for one
man. He wondered if Swarge were dim-witted in that area

and was being deceived. He almost asked if he'd been giving her money to save up for a house for them. Leftrin had seen that trick played on a gullible sailor more than once.

But before he could ask Swarge anything, the tillerman must have seen his captain's doubts in his eyes. "Bellin's river folk. In there with the rest of her crew for a drink and a hot meal. She works on that little barge, the *Sacha,* that goes back and forth between Trehaug and Cassarick."

"What does she do?"

"Poleman. That's part of what makes it hard for us. When I'm in port, she's out; when she's in port, I'm out."

"Marrying her won't change that," Leftrin pointed out.

Swarge looked down at the table. "Captain on the *Sacha* offered me a job last time Bellin and I were in port at the same time. Said if I wanted to jump boats, he'd take me on as tillerman for the *Sacha.*"

After a moment, Leftrin unknotted his fists and spoke in a controlled voice. "And you said yes? Without even telling me you might go?"

Swarge drummed his fingers on the edge of the table and then, without invitation, poured more rum for both of them. "I didn't say anything," he said after he'd tossed off his shot. "Like you said, Cap, I been with Tarman over ten years. And Tarman's a liveship. I know I'm not family, but we got a bond, even so. I like the feel of him on the water. Like how I get that little shiver of knowing right before I see something to watch out for. *Sacha*'s a good little barge, but she's just a piece of wood to push around on the river. Would be hard to leave Tarman for that. But . . ."

"But for a woman, you would," Leftrin said heavily.

"We'd like to marry. Have children, if we can. You just said it yourself, Cap. Ten years is half of forever for a Rain Wild man. I'm not getting any younger and neither is Bellin. If we're going to do this, we've got to do it soon."

Leftrin was quiet, weighing his choices. He couldn't let Swarge go. Not now. Things were going to be strange enough for a time on the liveship without making Tarman get used to a new tillerman as well. Did he need another crewman? He had Hennesey to run the deck and man a pole, skinny little Skelly, Big Eider, and himself. Swarge on the tiller, he hoped. It wouldn't be bad to have another crew member. It might even make Tarman's momentum more believable. Yes, he decided. That charade might work. He stifled the grin that passed over his face. He totted up his finances and made his decision.

"She any good?" he demanded of Swarge, and then, at the offended look on the man's face, he clarified, "As a pole-man. Does she do her share? Could she handle duties on a barge the size of Tarman if things got tricky?"

Swarge just stared at him for a moment. Hope flickered in his eyes. He looked hastily down at the table, as if to conceal it from his captain. "She's good. She's not some flimsy little girl. She's a woman with meat and muscle on her frame. She knows the river and she knows her business." He scratched his head. "Tarman's a much bigger vessel and a liveship to boot."

"So you think she wouldn't be up to it?" Leftrin baited him.

"Of course she would." Swarge hesitated, then demanded almost angrily, "Are you saying she could join Tarman's crew? That we could be together on Tarman?"

"Would you rather be with her on *Sacha*?"

"No. Of course not."

"Then ask her. I won't ask you to sign your papers until she agrees to sign as well. But the deal is the same. It's for a lifetime."

"You ain't even met her yet."

"I know you, Swarge. You think you can stand her for a lifetime, then I'm pretty sure I can, too. So ask her."

Swarge reached for the pen and the paper. "Don't need to," he said as he dipped the quill. "She's always wanted to serve on a liveship. What sailor doesn't?" And with a smooth and legible hand, he signed his life over to Tarman.

MORE THAN ONE guest commented on the pink of her cheeks at their wedding ceremony at the Traders' Hall. And when the guests had followed them to their new home to share a wedding dinner, she had scarcely been able to taste the honeycake or follow the conversations around her. The dinner was endless, and she could hardly remember a word said to her long enough to make intelligent conversation. She watched only Hest at the other end of the long table. His long-fingered hands cupping a wineglass, his tongue moving to moisten his lip, the soft fall of his hair on his brow. Would the dinner never end, would all these people never leave?

As tradition dictated, when Hest and his men retired for brandy in his new study, she bid her guests a formal farewell and then retreated to her new marital chambers. Sophie and her mother accompanied her, to help her remove her heavy gown and underskirts. It had been a few years since she and Sophie had been truly close, but as Sedric was serving as Hest's man, it had seemed appropriate that his sister serve as her attendant. Her mother had left her, with many fond wishes, to assist Alise's father in bidding farewell to the departing guests. Sophie lingered, helping her tie the dozens of tiny bows that secured the lacy wrapper over her gauzy, beribboned nightdress. Then, as Alise sat, she had helped her take down her red hair and brush it smooth and loose upon her shoulders.

"Do I look silly?" she'd demanded of her old friend. "I'm such a plain girl. Is this nightgown too fancy for me?"

"You look like a bride," Sophie had replied. There was a trace of sadness in her eyes. Alise understood. Today, with Alise's wedding, they left the last remnant of their girlhood behind. They were both wedded women now. Despite her anticipation, Alise felt a brief moment of regret for the life she left behind. *Never a girl again,* she thought. Never another night in her father's house as his daughter. And that, she abruptly recognized as relief.

"Are you worried at all?" Sophie asked her as their eyes met in the elaborately framed vanity mirror.

"I'll be fine," she replied and tried to control her smile.

"Will it be strange, the three of you sharing a home?"

"You mean Sedric? Of course not! He was ever my friend, and I'm only too glad to see that he and Hest get along so well. I know so few of the other Traders in Hest's circle. I shall be very glad to have an old friend at my side as I move into my new life."

Sophie met her gaze in the mirror; she looked surprised. Then she cocked her head at her friend and said, "Well, you were ever the one for making the best of things! And I think that my brother will be happy to have such a staunch ally as you've always been to him! And I can make you no more beautiful than you already are. You seem so happy with all this. Are you, truly?"

"Truly, I am," she assured her friend.

"Then I shall leave you, with my very best wishes. Good night, Alise!"

"Good night, Sophie."

Alone, she sat before her mirror. She picked up her brush and ran it again through her auburn hair. She scarcely knew the woman in the lacy peignoir. Her mother had expertly applied her powder earlier in the day; her freckles had been subdued, not just on her face but on her bosom and arms. She was, she'd thought, about to step into a life that she hadn't even tried to imagine since she was a little girl and full of dreams. Downstairs, the musicians played a final song that bid her guests good night. Her bedchamber window was open. She heard the sounds of carriage wheels on the drive as guest after guest left. She tried to be patient, knowing that Hest must remain downstairs until the last one was gone. Eventually, she heard the door close a final time, and she recognized through the open window the voices of her parents bidding Hest's father good night. They would be the last, she was sure. She freshened her perfume. Two carriages departed. She blew out half the scented candles, dimming the room. Downstairs in the house, all was still. In the candlelit bedchamber filled with elegant vases of fragrant flowers, she anticipated her husband's arrival. Heart thundering, she waited, ears straining for the sounds of his boots on the stair.

And waited. The night deepened. And chilled. She donned a soft lambswool shawl and settled into a chair by the hearth. The evening insects stopped their chirring. A lonely night bird called and received no response. Slowly her mood sank from expectant to nervous to anxious and then foundered in bewilderment. The hearth fire that had warmed the room burned down. She added another log to it, blew out the guttering candles in the ornate silver stands, and relit the other ones. She sat, legs curled beneath her, in the cushioned armchair beside the hearth, waiting for her groom to come and claim his right to her.

When the tears came, she could not stem them. After they passed, she could not repair the damage to her powdered face. So she washed her face clean of all pretense, confronted her dappled self in the mirror, and asked herself when she had become such a fool. Hest had stated his terms clearly, from the beginning. She was the one who had made up a foolish fairy tale about love and draped it over the cold iron trellis of their bargain. She could not blame him. Only herself.

She should simply disrobe and go to bed.

Instead, she sat down again by the fire and watched the flames devour the log and then subside.

Long past the deep of night, in the shallows of early morning, when the last of her candles were burning low, her drunken husband came in. His hair was rumpled, his step unsteady, and his collar already loosened. He seemed startled to find her awaiting him by the dying fire. His gaze walked up and down her, and suddenly she felt embarrassed for him to see her in a nightgown that was virginally white and elaborately embroidered. His mouth twitched, and for a second she saw a flash of his teeth. Then he looked aside from her and said in a slurred voice, "Well, let's get to it, then."

He didn't come to her. He walked toward the bed, loosening his clothing as he crossed the room. His jacket and then his shirt fell to the thick rug before he stopped by the four remaining candles. He bent at the waist and with a single harsh whoosh of breath, he extinguished them, plunging the room into darkness. She could smell the liquor on his breath.

She heard the bed give to his weight as he sat down on it. There was one thump and then another as he tugged off his boots and dropped them to the floor. A rustle of fabric told her that his trousers had followed them. The bed sighed as he dropped back onto it. She had remained where she was, frozen by shock tinged with fear. All her sexual anticipation, all her silly romantic dreams were gone. She listened to his breathing. After a moment, he spoke, and there was a note of sour amusement in his voice. "This would be much easier for both of us if you also were in the bed."

Somehow she arose from her chair and crossed to him, even as she wondered why she was doing it. It seemed inevitable. She wondered if it was her lack of experience in these areas that had raised her expectations so high. As she left the hearth's warmth, she felt as if she swam a cold river to cross the cool room. She reached the bedside. He had not said another word to her; the room was so dark, he could not have been watching her approach. Awkwardly, she seated herself on the edge of the bed. After a time had passed, Hest pointed out heavily, "You'll have to take that off and lie on the bed if we're to accomplish anything."

The front of her nightgown was secured with a dozen tiny bows of silky ribbons. As she undid each one, terrible disappointment rose in her. What a fool she had been, to tease herself with thoughts of how his fingers would pull each ribbon free of its partner. What a silly anticipation she had felt as she had donned this garment; only a handful of hours ago, its extravagance had seemed feminine and seductive. Now she felt she had chosen some silly costume and assayed to play a role she could never fulfill. Hest had seen through it. A woman like her had no right to these silky fabrics and feminine ribbons. This was not to be romance for her, not even lust. This was duty on his part. Nothing more. She sighed as she stood and let the nightgown slide from her body to the floor. She opened the bedclothes and lay down on her half of the bed. She felt Hest roll to face her.

"So," he said, and the spirits on his breath now brushed her face. "So." He sighed. A moment later he took a deep breath. "Are you ready?"

"I suppose so," she managed to say.

He shifted in the bed, coming closer to her. She rolled

to face him, and then froze, suddenly dreading his touch. It shamed her that despite her fear, she felt a flush of warmth as well. Dread and desire mingled in her. It reminded her with disgust of two of her friends who had endlessly nattered on about the dangers of being raped by Chalcedean raiders. It had been all too apparent to Alise that they were as titillated as they were frightened by the prospect. Stupid, she had thought them then, making breathless fantasy of lust and violence.

Yet now, as Hest's hand settled on her hip, she gave a small involuntary gasp. No man had ever touched her bared flesh before. The thought sent a shiver over her skin. Then, as his touch turned hard, as his fingers gripped her flesh to pull her close, she gave a low cry of fear. She had heard it might hurt, the first time, but had never feared he would be cruel about it. Now she did.

Hest abruptly gave a small huff of breath as if something were suddenly more to his liking. "Not so different," he muttered, or perhaps his words were, "Not so difficult." She scarcely had time to think of them, for with a suddenness that drove the breath from her, he pushed her onto her back and he shifted his body onto hers. His knee parted her thighs and pushed her legs open. "Ready indeed," he said, and thrust against her that which she had never seen.

She managed to accommodate him. She gripped the bedsheets; she could not bring herself to embrace him. The pain she had been told to expect was not as great as she had feared, but the pleasure she had heard of in whispers and had gullibly anticipated never arrived. She was not even certain that he enjoyed it. He rode her quickly to a finish she didn't share, and then drew his body apart from hers immediately afterward. His trailing member smeared warmth and wet across her thigh. She felt soiled by it. When he fell back onto his half of the bed, she wondered if he would now drop off to sleep, or would rest and then approach the matter again, perhaps in a more leisurely way.

He did neither. He lay there long enough to catch his breath, then rolled from the bed and found, at last, the soft warm robe that had been lain out for him. She more heard than saw him don it, and then there was a brief flash of dim light from the hooded candles in the hall. Then the door shut behind him and her wedding night was over.

For a time she remained as she was on the bed. A shiver ran over her. It became a quivering that developed into a shuddering. She didn't weep. She wanted to vomit. Instead, she scrubbed her leg and her crotch with the sheets on his side of the bed, and then rolled over to a clean spot. She worked at pulling air into her lungs and then pushing it out again. Deliberately, she made her breathing slow. She counted, holding each inhalation for a count of three and then breathing it out as slowly.

"I'm calm," she said aloud. "I'm not hurt. Nothing is wrong. I've lived up to the terms of my marriage contract." A moment later, she added aloud, "So has he."

She got up from the bed. There was another log for the fire. She put it on the coals and watched it catch while she thought. In the remainder of the predawn hours she contemplated the folly of the bargain she had struck. She'd shed her tears. For a time, she choked on her disappointment and humiliation and regretted her foolish choice. Briefly, she entertained the idea of storming out of Hest's house and going home.

"Home" to what? To her father's house? To questions and scandals and her mother demanding to know every detail of what had upset her? She imagined her father's face. There would be whispers in the market if she went to shop, muted conversation at the next table if she stopped for a cup of tea. No. She had no home to go to.

Before the sun rose, she set aside her girlish fancies and her anguish. Neither could save her from her fate. Instead, she summoned to the forefront of her mind the practical old maid she had rehearsed to be. No tenderhearted maiden could endure what had befallen her. Best set her aside. But the dedicated spinster could accept her fate with resignation and begin to weigh the advantages of it.

As the sun kissed the sky, she rose and summoned a maid. Her own maid, as a matter of fact; her own *personal* maid, a pretty girl with only a small tattoo of a cat by her nose to mark that once she had been a slave. The girl brought her hot tea and an herbal wash to bathe her eyes. Then, at Alise's request, she had fetched a hot breakfast of Alise's choosing, on a lovely enameled tray. While Alise ate, the girl set out a selection of pretty new dresses for Alise to choose from.

That afternoon, Alise sailed into the first of several reception teas in their honor, attired in a demure gown of pale green with white lace. The simplicity of the dress belied how expensive it had been. She smiled cheerily and colored prettily when some of her mother's friends whispered to her that marriage seemed to agree with her. The gem of her satisfaction was when Hest appeared, nattily attired, but hollow eyed and pale.

He stood in the door of the drawing room, late for the gathering and obviously looking for her. When his gaze found her, she smiled and waved her fingers at him. He had seemed astonished both at her air of well-being and how little she seemed to care for his quickly whispered apology for his "condition" the night before. She merely nodded and gave all her attention to her hostess and the guests assembled to honor them. She did her best to be charming, even witty.

Strange to discover it was not that difficult. Like any decision, once she had reached it, the world suddenly seemed simpler. Her decision, cemented as dawn rosed the sky, was that she would meticulously live up to her end of the bargain. And that she would see that Hest did, too.

The very next day, she summoned the carpenters who transformed the dainty sewing room next to her bedchamber into her personal library. The tiny desk, all white and gilt, she replaced with a large one of heavy dark wood with numerous drawers and pigeonholes. And in the weeks that followed, the booksellers and antiquity dealers quickly learned to bring their freshest inventory for her to peruse before offering it to the general public. Before six months passed, the shelves and scroll racks of her little library were well populated. She judged that if she had sold herself, at least she'd demanded a high price.

✧ ✧ ✧

Day the 17th of the Rain Moon

*Year the 8th of the Reign of the Most Noble
and Magnificent Satrap Cosgo*

Year the 2nd of the Independent Alliance of Traders

From Detozi, Keeper of the Birds, Trehaug
To Erek, Keeper of the Birds, Bingtown

In the enclosed scroll case, two queries. The first, to
be posted generally, asking if any mariner or farmer
has had any sighting of the dragon Tintaglia, who has
been absent some months from the Rain Wilds. The
second, a message for the Bingtown Traders' Council,
a reminder that funds are due to assist in paying those
who tend and hunt for the young dragons. A swift
reply is desired and expected.

Erek,

*My deepest condolences on your loss. I know how
joyously you anticipated wedding Fari. To hear of her
untimely death saddens me beyond words. These are
hard times for all of us.*

Detozi

✧ ✧ ✧

Day the 10th of the Greening Moon

*Year the 8th of the Reign of the Most Noble
and Magnificent Satrap Cosgo*

Year the 2nd of the Independent Alliance of Traders

*From Erek, Keeper of the Birds, Bingtown
To Detozi, Keeper of the Birds, Trehaug*

Sealed scroll is a message for the Rain Wild Councils at Trehaug and Cassarick, from the Bingtown Traders' Council, requesting a complete accounting of funds already sent for the upkeep of the young dragons. No more funds will be gathered or released to the Council at Cassarick without such an accounting.

Detozi,

I'm getting a curled foot defect in almost half the young pigeons I've hatched here in the last month. Have you ever seen this in your flock or heard of a remedy? I fear that poor feed is at the root of my problem, yet the damned Council here will not give me sufficient funds to buy a good variety of grain and the dried peas that are so essential to bird health. They will tax us to death to rebuild the roads and raise the wrecks in the harbor, but turn a deaf ear to my plea for decent food for my birds!

Erek

Day the 23rd of the Fish Moon

*Year the 9th of the Reign of the Most Noble
and Magnificent Satrap Cosgo*

Year the 3rd of the Independent Alliance of Traders

From Detozi, Keeper of the Birds, Trehaug
To Erek, Keeper of the Birds, Bingtown

In the sealed scroll, this month's accounting of funds expended by the Rain Wild Councils of Trehaug and Cassarick, with an invoice for the Bingtown Traders' Council's share of the expenses. By separate bird you will receive the text of a post that we request all outbound ships carry, which is a reward offered for substantial news about the dragon Tintaglia.

Erek,

My cousin Sethin is seeking an apprentice position for her son Reyall. He is a responsible lad of fourteen, already experienced in the care and feeding of messenger birds. I commend him to you without reservation. Although I am confident you are not one to make much of this, I assure you he is but lightly marked and can go about his tasks unveiled without causing distress or inciting curiosity in any who may visit your coops. If you have a position for an apprentice, we would gladly send him to you, at our expense, with the next shipment of young birds to freshen the blood of the Bingtown flock. He had been expecting to be taken on at Cassarick when they decided to coop a flock of their own, but the Cassarick Council hired two Tattooed instead. The Rain Wilds are not what they used to be! Please let me hear back from you on this matter by a separate bird addressed only to me.

Detozi

Day the 17th of the Change Moon

Year the 4th of the Independent Alliance of Traders

From Erek, Keeper of the Birds, Bingtown
To Detozi, Keeper of the Birds, Trehaug

In a sealed scroll case, a warning of danger from the Bingtown Traders' Council to the Rain Wild Traders' Councils at Cassarick and Trehaug. A forgery ring has been discovered operating in Bingtown, creating false trading credentials and licenses to travel on the Rain Wild River. Caution is advised in creating new trade partnerships, especially with those foreign to the Cursed Shores. Scrutinize credentials closely.

Detozi,

I am writing with a small concern about your nephew and my apprentice, Reyall. For the last year, he has been in all ways admirably devoted to the birds, steady, reliable, and conscientious. But recently he has formed friendships with several youths who spend much of their time gambling and carousing, much to the detriment of his work. The mingling of Trader, Three Ships, and Tattooed youth in our city is not always beneficial to building a solid work ethic. I have given him a stern warning, but I think a similar chastisement from his family might have a greater effect. If he does not settle to his work again, I fear I must send him home without his journeyman papers.

Regretfully, Erek

$\diamond$ $\diamond$ $\diamond$

Day the 14th of the Hope Moon

Year the 5th of the Independent Alliance of Traders

From Detozi, Keeper of the Birds, Trehaug
To Erek, Keeper of the Birds, Bingtown

A sealed missive from Trader Goshen to Derren
Sawyer, Three Ships Town, concerning a shipment of
hardwood that is late for delivery.

Erek,

*Apologies to both you and Reyall that his allowance has
been delayed. Thank you so much for helping him with
his finances. The storms have been terrible, delaying
shipments on the river and causing much misery for
man and bird. Let my Kitta rest well before you return
her to me. Reyall's funds should arrive as soon as the
Hardy makes port in Bingtown. Again, our gratitude.*

Detozi

$\diamond$ $\diamond$ $\diamond$

CHAPTER FIVE

BLACKMAIL AND LIES

Leftrin stood on the deck, watching the Chalcedean ship's boat draw near. The skiff rode low in the water, burdened by the portly merchant, the rowing crew, and a heap of grain sacks. The tall three-masted ship they were coming from dwarfed his barge. It was one reason that he declined to approach it. If the Chalcedeans wished to trade with him, let them come to him, where he could look down on them before they boarded. None of them appeared to be carrying weapons.

"Aren't you going to go look at their cargo before they start delivering to us?" Swarge asked him. The well-muscled tillerman slowly pulled on the long handle of the sweep.

Leftrin, leaning on the railing, shook his head. "If they want my gold, let them do the work of delivering to me." Leftrin had no love for Chalcedeans, and no trust in them.

He wouldn't venture onto their deck where any sort of treachery might befall an honest man. Swarge made a slow sweep with the steering oar, effortlessly holding the barge in place against the river's spreading current. All around them, the pale waters of the Rain Wild River were dispersing into the brack of the shallow bay. This was as far as Leftrin ever brought Tarman and farther than he usually did. He made most of his living trading up and down the river among the Rain Wilder settlements, just as his father and grandfather had before him. Not for him the open seas and foreign shores. No. He made only a few yearly forays to the river's mouth, usually when a reliable go-between contacted him. Then he went only to trade for the foodstuffs that the Rain Wild residents needed to survive. He couldn't be as fussy about whom he dealt with at the river mouth, but Leftrin kept his guard up. A wise trader knew the difference between making a deal and making a friend. When dealing with a Chalcedean, there was only business, never friendship, and the trader who bartered with them had best have eyes in the back of his head. Technically, the two countries were at peace now, but peace with Chalced never lasted.

So Leftrin watched them come with narrowed eyes and a suspicious set to his mouth. The fellows on the oars looked to be ordinary sailors, and the sacks of grain no more than sacks of grain. Nonetheless, as the small boat pulled alongside his barge and tossed a line, he let Skelly, their youngest crew member, catch it and make it fast. He kept his place by the railing and watched the men in the boat. Big Eider ghosted up alongside him and stood, quietly scratching his black beard and watching the boat come. "Watch the sailors," Leftrin told him softly. "I'll keep an eye on the merchant."

Eider nodded.

Ladder cleats were built right onto Tarman's sides. The Chalcedean merchant climbed them easily, and Leftrin revised his estimate of the man; he might be on the heavy side, but he looked physically able enough. He wore a heavy sealskin cloak, trimmed and lined with scarlet. A wide leather belt decorated with silver secured his woolen tunic.

The sea wind caught at the man's cloak and sent it billowing, but the merchant appeared unfazed by it. *As much sailor as merchant,* Leftrin thought. Once aboard, the merchant nodded gravely to Leftrin and received a curt bow in return. The merchant leaned over the side and barked several commands in Chalcedean to his oarsmen before turning back to Leftrin.

"Greetings, Captain. I will have my crewmen bring aboard samples of both my wheat and my barley. I trust the quality of my goods will meet your approval."

"That is yet to be seen, Merchant." Leftrin spoke affably but firmly, smiling all the while.

The man glanced around at his bare deck. "And your trade goods? I expected to find them set out for my inspection."

"Coin needs little inspection. When the time comes, you'll find the scale set up in my stateroom. I go by weight rather than coinage."

"And to that, I have no objection. Kings and their mints may rise and fall, but gold is gold and silver is silver. Still"—and here the man dropped his voice—"when one comes to the mouth of the Rain Wild River, one does not expect gold and silver. I had hoped for a chance to purchase Rain Wild goods from you."

"If you're after Rain Wild goods, then you'll have to take yourself to Bingtown. Everyone knows that is the only place to obtain them." Leftrin watched past the Chalcedean's shoulder as one of his men gained the deck. Eider was ready to meet the man, but he didn't offer to take his sack from him. Bellin stood nearby, her heavy pole ready to hand. Without even intending to, she looked more formidable than Eider.

The foreign oarsman lugged a heavy sack of grain slung across his shoulder. He took two steps from the rail, let his sack thud to Leftrin's deck, and then turned back to fetch another one. The sack looked good, tightly woven hemp, unmarked by salt or damp. But that didn't mean the grain inside was good, or that all the bags would be of like quality. Leftrin kept his face neutral.

The Chalcedean trader came a half step closer. "That is, indeed, what men say and what many men hear. But a few men hear of other goods, and other bargains, quietly struck and to the great benefit of both parties. Our go-between mentioned that you were a man well known as both a shrewd captain and a savvy trader, owner of the most efficient barge ever seen. He said that if there was anyone who might have the sort of special goods I seek, it would be you. Or that you would know to whom I should speak."

"Did he?" Leftrin asked affably as the oarsman deposited another bag on his deck. It looked as tightly woven and well kept as the first one. He nodded to Hennesey, and the mate opened the deckhouse door. Grigsby, the ship's yellow cat, sauntered out onto the deck.

"He did," the merchant asserted in a bold yet quiet voice.

Past the merchant's shoulder, Leftrin watched the cat. The sassy little bastard stuck his claws in the *Tarman*'s deck, stretched, and then pulled his claws in toward himself, leaving tiny scratches on the wood. He strolled toward the captain, making a leisurely tour of the deck before settling to his task. He went to the unfamiliar sacks, sniffed them casually, and then butted his head against one, marking it as worthy of being his possession. Then he moved on toward the galley door. Leftrin pursed his mouth and gave a small nod of approval. If there'd been any scent of rodent on the sacks at all, the cat would have shown more interest. So this grain merchant came from a clean ship. Remarkable.

"Special goods," the man repeated quietly. "He said it was known to him that you had access."

Leftrin turned his head sharply to meet the merchant's intense gray gaze. His brow furrowed. The man misinterpreted his look.

"Of all kinds. Even the smallest scale. A piece of skin." He lowered his voice more. "A piece of cocoon wood."

"If that's what you want to trade for, you've come to the wrong man," Leftrin said bluntly. He turned away from the merchant and crossed the deck to the sacks of grain. He went down on one knee, drawing his belt knife as he did so. He cut the twine that stitched the sack's mouth and pulled it free, then plunged his hand into the grain and rolled the kernels in the palm of his hand. It was good grain, clean and free of chaff and straw. He spilled it back into the sack and pulled a handful from the depths of the bag. When he brought it out into the light, it was just as pleasing as the first handful. With his free hand, he picked up some of the wheat and put it into his mouth. He chewed it.

"Dried in sunlight, to keep well, but not dried so much that it has no flavor or virtue," the merchant informed him.

Leftrin nodded abruptly. He poured what he held back into the bag, dusted his hands, and turned his attention to the next bag. He cut the knot, unlaced the sack, and continued his sampling process. When he was finished, he sat back on his heels, swallowed the mouthful of barley, and conceded, "The quality is good. If the rest of the shipment matches the samples in these bags, I'll be a happy buyer. Once we've set the price per bag, you can start transferring the cargo. I'll reserve the right to refuse any bag, and I'll inspect each one as it comes onto my deck."

The merchant favored him with a slow nod that made his agreement formal. "Your terms are easy to accept. Now. Shall we retire to your quarters to set the price per bag and perhaps discuss other transactions?"

"Or we could negotiate here," Leftrin observed evenly.

"If you please, your quarters would be more private," the merchant replied.

"As you will." Once or twice, Leftrin had trafficked in forbidden goods. He had no such goods that he wished to trade now, but he'd let the man make an incriminating offer. Possibly an offended reaction and a suggestion that the merchant's offer might be reported to the Rain Wild authorities, thus curtailing his trading permit, would bring the price of his grain down. Leftrin was not above such tactics. The man was, after all, a Chalcedean. No fairness was owed to any of them. He gestured toward the door of his small stateroom, certain that this well-garbed merchant would be appalled at his tiny quarters.

"And while we talk, I will have my workers ferry the grain to your barge."

"Before we have set a price?" Leftrin was surprised. It gave him too much of an advantage. If he delayed the bargaining until most of the cargo was on board his vessel, and then refused to meet the merchant's demands, the Chalcedean would have to have his crew unload the entire barge again.

"I am very certain that we shall agree upon a price we both find fair," the man said quietly.

So be it, Leftrin thought. Never turn down an advantage in bargaining. Over his shoulder, he called to the mate, "Hennesey! You and Grigsby watch the grain sacks as they bring them. Keep a count of each. Don't be shy about checking any that look light or water stained or rat gnawed. Tap on my door when we've got a load."

When they had entered the stateroom and seated themselves, Leftrin on his bunk and the merchant on the room's sole chair at the small table, the man lost none of his aplomb. He looked about the humble room and then again made his formal nod and said, "I wish you to know my name. I am Sinad of the Arich heritage. The sons of my family have been traders for longer than Bingtown has existed. We have not favored the wars that have put our countries at odds with each other and restricted our traffic and our profits. So, now that the hostilities have subsided, we hasten to make contact directly with the traders of the Rain Wild River. We wish to establish custom that will eventually, we hope, be very profitable to both of us. In fact, exclusive custom with a small circle of reputable traders would make us rejoice."

Despite his reservations about all Chalcedeans, the man's directness impressed Leftrin favorably. He brought out the bottle of rum and the two small glasses he kept in his room for trading negotiations. The glasses were ancient, heavy and a very dark blue. As he poured the rum, silver stars suddenly sparkled in a band around the rim of each glass. The display had the desired effect on the merchant. He gave a small gasp of amazement and then leaned forward avariciously. He took up his glass without being invited to do so and held it up to the cabin's small window. Leftrin spoke while he was still admiring the priceless article.

"I'm Leftrin, captain and owner of the river barge *Tarman*. And I don't know what my family did for a living before we left Jamaillia, and I expect it doesn't much matter. What I do now is run this barge. I trade. If you're an honest man with clean goods, we'll strike a bargain, and the next time I see you, I'll be even more prone to bargain. But I don't trade exclusively with anyone. The man who gets my coins is the man with the best bargain. So. Let's settle to our task. How much per sack for the wheat, and how much for the barley?"

The Chalcedean lowered his glass back to the table. He had not tasted it. "What are you offering? For goods such as these," and he tapped the glass before him with the back of his forefinger's nail. "I'd be willing to give you an excellent exchange."

"I'm offering only coin, this trip. Coins of silver and gold, by weight value rather than minting. Nothing else." The glasses were of Elderling make. He had a few treasures of that nature. A woman's shawl that seemed to generate warmth. A strong box that emitted chimes and a bright light whenever the lid was opened. There were other items as well, mostly things his grandfather had bought for his grandmother many years ago. He kept them all beneath a secret hatch under his bunk. It pleased him to use glasses worth a fortune to serve a Chalcedean merchant rum in the confines of his seemingly humble stateroom.

Sinad Arich leaned back on the small chair. It creaked as it took his weight. He lifted his wide shoulders and then let them fall. "Coin is good, for grain. I can use coin, of any minting. With coin, a man can traffic in any goods he chooses. Grain on this trip, for example. But on my last journey I visited Bingtown, with coin of my own. And there what I bought for my coin was information."

Chill uncertainty rose in Leftrin. The man had not made a threatening move, but his earlier comment about his "efficient barge" now took on an ominous meaning. Leftrin continued to lean back in his chair and to smile. But the smile didn't reach his pale eyes. "Let's set a price for the grain and be done. I'd like to be heading back up the river by the turn of the tide."

"As would I," Sinad concurred.

Leftrin took a swig from his glass. The rum went down warm, but the glass seemed unusually cold against his fingers. "Surely you mean that by the turn of the tide, you hope to be back to sea."

Sinad took a gentlemanly sip from his own glass. "Oh, no. I am most careful to say exactly what I mean, especially when I am speaking in a tongue once foreign to me. I am hoping that by the time the tide turns, my grain and my personal effects will be loaded on your barge. I expect that we will have settled a price for my grain and for your services, and that you will then take me up your river."

"I can't. You must know our rules and laws in this matter. You are not only a foreigner, you are a Chalcedean. To visit the Rain Wilds, you must have a permit from the Bingtown Traders' Council. To trade with us, you must have the proper licenses from the Rain Wild Council. You cannot even travel up the river without the proper travel papers."

"Which, as I am not a fool, I have. Stamped, sealed, and signed in purple ink. I also carry letters of recommendation from several Bingtown Traders, attesting that I am a most honest and honorable trader. Even if I am a Chalcedean."

A drop of sweat had begun to trickle down Leftrin's spine. If the man actually possessed the paperwork he claimed to have, then he was either a miracle worker or a most adept blackmailer. Leftrin could not recall a time in his life when he had seen a Chalcedean visiting the Rain Wilds legally. They had come as raiders, as warriors, and occasionally as spies, but not as legitimate traders. He doubted that a Chalcedean would know how to be a legitimate trader. No. This man was trouble and danger. And he had deliberately chosen to approach Leftrin and the *Tarman*. Not good.

Sinad set his glass carefully back on the small table. It remained half full. He smiled at it and then observed blandly, "This vessel of yours fascinates me. For instance, it interests me that propelling it once demanded a dozen oarsmen. Now, it is said, you crew it with only six men, counting yourself. For a barge of this size, I find that startling. Almost as surprising that your tillerman can hold his place here at the river's mouth with apparent ease." He lifted the glass again and held it to the light as if admiring the small stars.

"I redesigned the hull to make the barge more efficient." A second drop of sweat joined the first in its journey down his back. Who had talked? Genrod, of course. He'd heard, a few years ago, that the man had moved from Trehaug to Bingtown. At the time Leftrin had suspected that the money he had paid him for his work on Tarman had financed the man's move. Genrod was an amazing artisan, a master in the working of wood, even wizardwood, and four years ago Leftrin had paid him well, very well indeed, for both his skill and his silence. The results of his efforts had far surpassed Leftrin's wildest hopes, and he recalled now, with a sinking heart, that more than once Genrod had mourned that his "greatest work must remain secret and submerged forever." Not money, but Genrod's egotistical need to brag was what had betrayed Leftrin's trust. If he ever saw the skinny little wretch again, he'd tie a knot in him.

The Chalcedean was regarding him closely. "Surely I am not the only one who has noticed this? I imagine that many of your fellow Traders envy your newfound efficiency, and doubtless they have importuned you to know the secret of your new hull design. For if you have modified a ship as old as yours, one that, I am told, is among the oldest of the Trading vessels built from the marvelous dragon wood, then surely they will wish to do the same with theirs."

Leftrin hoped he had not gone pale. He abruptly doubted that Genrod was the source of *all* this information. The carver might have bragged of working on Tarman, but Genrod was Trader through and through. He would not have spoken openly of Tarman's pedigree as the eldest liveship. This trader had more than one source of gossip. He tried to bait a name out of him. "Traders respect one another's secrets" was all he said.

"Do they? Then they are like no other traders I have ever known. Every trader I know is always eager to discover whatever advantage his fellow has. Gold is sometimes offered for such secrets. And when gold does not buy the desired item, well, I have heard tales of violence done."

"Neither gold nor violence will buy what you seek from me."

Sinad shook his head. "You mistake me. I will not go into whether it was gold or violence, but I will tell you that the exchange has already been made, and all that I need to know about you and your ship, I know. Let us speak plainly. The High Duke of Chalced is not a young man. With every year, nay, with almost every week, that passes some new ailment frets him. Some of the most experienced and respected healers in all of Chalced have attempted to treat him. Many have died for their failures. So, perhaps, it is expediency that now makes so many of them say that his only hope for improved health and long life will come from medicines made from dragon parts. They are so apologetic to him that they do not have the required ingredients. They promise him that as soon as the required ingredients are procured, they will concoct the elixirs that will restore his youth, beauty, and vigor." The merchant sighed. He turned his gaze to the cabin's small window and stared off into the distance. "And thus, his anger and frustration passes over his healers and settles instead on the trading families of Chalced. Why, he demands, can they not procure what he needs? Are they traitors? Do they desire his death? At first, he offered us gold for our efforts. And when gold did not suffice, he turned to that always effective coin: blood." His gaze came back to Leftrin. "Do you understand what I am telling you? Do you understand that no matter how much you may despise Chalcedeans, they, too, love their families? Cherish their elderly parents and tender young sons? Understand, my friend, that I will do whatever I must to protect my family."

Desperation vied with cold ruthlessness in the Chalcedean's eyes. This was a dangerous man. He had come, empty-handed, to Leftrin's vessel, but the Rain Wild Trader now perceived he had not come without weapons. Leftrin cleared his throat and said, "We will now set a reasonable price for the grain, and then I think our trading will be done."

Sinad smiled at him. "The price of my grain, trading partner, is my passage up the river and that you speak well of me to your fellows. If you cannot procure what I need, then you will see that I am introduced to those who can.

"And in return, I will give you my grain *and* my silence about your secrets. Now what could be a better trade than that?"

BREAKFAST HAD BEEN delicious and perfectly prepared. The generous remains of a meal intended for three still graced the white-clothed table. The serving dishes were covered now in what would be a vain attempt to keep the food at serving temperature. Alise sat alone at the table. Her dishes had already been efficiently and swiftly cleared away. She lifted the teapot and poured herself another cup of tea and waited.

She felt like a spider crouched at the edge of her web, waiting for the fly to blunder into her trap. She never lingered over meals. Hest knew that. She suspected it was why he was so frequently late to the table when he was home. She hoped that if she sat here long enough, he'd come in to eat and she'd finally have the chance to confront him.

He deliberately avoided her these days, not just at the table but anywhere that they might be alone. She did not agonize about it. She was glad enough to be left to eat in peace, and even gladder when he did not disturb her in her bed at night. Unfortunately, that had not been the case last night. Hest had stridden into her room in the small hours of the morning, shutting the door with a firm thump that had wakened her from a sound sleep. He'd smelled of strong tobacco and expensive wine. He'd taken off his robe, tossed it across the foot of the bed, and then clambered in beside her. In the dark room, she saw him only as a deeper shadow.

"Come here," he'd said, as if commanding a dog. She'd stayed where she was, on the edge of the bed.

"I was sound asleep," she'd protested.

"And now you're not, and we're both here, so let's make a fine fat baby to make my father's heart rejoice, shall we?" His tone was bitter. "One is all we need, darling Alise. So cooperate with me. This won't take long, and then you can go back to sleep. And wake up in the morning and spend the day giving my money to scroll dealers."

It had all fallen into place. He'd been to see his father, and been chided yet again for his lack of an heir. And yesterday Alise had bought not one but two rather expensive old scrolls. Both were from the Spice Islands. She couldn't read a word of either of them, but the illustrations looked as if they were intended to depict Elderlings. It made sense to her; if the Elderlings had occupied the Cursed Shores in ancient days, they would have had trading partners, and those trading partners might have made some written record of their dealings. Lately she had turned her efforts to seeking out such old records. The Spice Island scrolls had been her first real find. Even she had blanched at the cost of them. But she'd had to have them, and so she had paid.

And tonight she would pay again, both for their childless state and for daring to expand her research library. If she had not stayed up so late poring over her latest acquisitions, she might have simply accommodated him. But she was tired and suddenly very weary of how he treated this portion of their married life.

She said something she'd never said before. "No. Perhaps tomorrow night."

He'd stared at her. In the darkness she'd felt the anger of his gaze. "That's not your decision," he said bluntly.

"It's not your sole decision either," she'd retorted and started to leave the bed.

"Tonight, it is," he said. With no warning, he lunged across the bed, seized her by the arm, and dragged her back. With the length of his body, he pinned her down.

She struggled briefly but as he dug his fingers into her upper arms and held her down, it was quickly apparent that she could not escape him. "Let me go!" she whisper-shrieked at him.

"In a moment," he replied tightly. And a moment later, "If you don't struggle, I won't hurt you."

He lied. Even after she had acquiesced, her head turned to one side, her eyes fixed on the wall, he'd held her arms tightly and thrust hard against her. It hurt. The pain and the humiliation made it seem as if it took him forever to accomplish his task. She didn't weep. When he rolled away from her and then sat up on the edge of her bed, she was dry-eyed and silent.

He sat in the quiet dark for a time, and then she felt him stand and heard the whisper of fabric as he donned his robe again. "If we are fortunate, neither of us will have to go through that again," he said dryly. What had stayed with her the rest of the night was that she had never heard him sound more sincere. He'd left her bed and her room.

Unable to sleep, she'd spent the rest of the night thinking about him and their sham of a marriage. He'd seldom been so rough with her. Sex with Hest was usually perfunctory and efficient. He entered her room, announced his intention, mated with her, and left. In the four years they'd been together, he'd never slept in her bed. He had never kissed her with passion, never touched any part of her body with interest.

She'd made humiliating efforts to please him. She'd anointed herself with perfumes and acquired and discarded various forms of nightdress. She had even tried to instigate romance with him, coming to his study late one evening and attempting to embrace him. He had not thrust her aside. He'd risen from his chair, told her that he was quite busy just now, and walked her to the door of the room, and shut her out of it. She'd fled, weeping, to her room.

Later that month, when he'd come to her bed, she had shamed herself again. She'd embraced him when he mounted her, and strained to kiss him. He'd held his face away from her. Nonetheless, her hungry body had tried to take whatever pleasure it could from his touch. He hadn't responded to her willingness. When he had finished, he had rolled away from her, ignoring her attempt to hold him. "Alise. Please. In the future, don't embarrass us both," he'd said quietly before he shut the door behind him.

Even now, her face reddened as she recalled her failed attempts to seduce him. Indifference was bad enough; but last night, when he had proven that he not only could but would force her if he wished to, she'd had to recognize the ugly truth. Hest was changing. Over the last year, he'd become ever more abrupt with her. He had begun to deploy his little barbed comments against her in public as well as in private. The small courtesies that any woman could expect from her husband were vanishing from her life. In the beginning, he had taken pains to be attentive to her in public, to offer his arm when they walked together, to hand her up into her carriage. Those small graces had vanished now. But last night was the first time that cruelty had replaced them.

Not even the precious Spice Island scrolls were worth what he had done to her. It was time to end this charade. She had the evidence of his infidelity. It was time to use it to render her marriage contract void.

The clues were small but plain. The first had come as an invoice mistakenly placed on her desk instead of his. It was for a very expensive lotion, one she knew she had never bought. When she had queried the merchant about it, he had produced a receipt for its delivery, signed in Hest's hand. She had paid the bill, but kept the papers. In a similar fashion, she had come to discover that Hest was paying the rent on a cottage half a day's ride from their home in an area of small farms, mostly settled by Three Ships immigrants. And the last was the item she had noticed last night; he wore a ring she had never seen before; she had felt the bite of it as he had gripped her arms so cruelly tight last night. Hest enjoyed jewelry and often wore rings. But his taste ran to massive worked silver; this ring had been gold, with a tiny stone set in it. She knew with certainty that it was nothing Hest would ever have bought for himself.

So now she understood. He'd married her only to keep his family content, so that they might show to the world their son's proper Trader wife. The Finboks would never accept a Three Ships girl into their family, let alone recognize her child as their heir. The lotion, she was sure, had been a gift for his mistress. The ring he now wore was her pledge to him. He was unfaithful. He had broken their contract, and she would use his broken vow as a way to free herself from him.

She would be poor. There would be a settlement from his

family, of course, but she didn't deceive herself that she could live on it as she did under his roof. She would have to retreat to the little piece of land that had been her dowry. She'd have to live simply. She'd have her work, of course, and—

The door opened. Sedric entered, laughing about something and speaking over his shoulder to Hest. He turned and saw her and smiled. "Alise, good morning!"

"Good morning, Sedric." The words came out of her mouth, a reflexive pleasantry.

Then, as Hest glared at her, annoyed at still finding her at the breakfast table, she heard herself blurt out, "You've been unfaithful to me. That voids our marriage contract. You can let me go quietly, or I can take this to the Traders' Council and present my evidence."

Sedric had been in the act of seating himself. He dropped abruptly into his chair and stared at her in white-faced horror. She was suddenly ashamed that he had to witness this. "You don't have to stay, Sedric. I'm sorry to make you a party to this." She chose formal words, but her shaking voice ruined them.

"A party to what?" Hest demanded. He raised one eyebrow at her. "Alise, this is the first I've heard of this nonsense, and if you are wise, it will be the last! I see you've finished eating. Why don't you go and leave me in peace!"

"As you left me in peace last night?" she asked bitterly, pushing the hard words out. "I know everything, Hest. I've put it all together. Expensive palat lotion. A little cottage in the Three Ships district. That ring you're wearing. It all fits together." She took a breath. "You have a Three Ships mistress, don't you?"

Sedric made a small scandalized sound as if he gasped for air. But Hest was unfazed. "What ring?" he demanded. "Alise, this is all nonsense! You insult us both with these wild accusations."

His hands were bare. No matter. "The one you wore last night. The little stone on it scratched me. I can show you the mark, if you'd like."

"I can't think of anything I'd like less!" he retorted. He flung himself into a chair at the table and began lifting the covers on the dishes. He scooped up a spoonful of eggs, glared at them, and then splatted them back into the dish. He leaned back in the chair and regarded her. "Are you sure you are well?" He almost sounded concerned for her. "You've taken an odd collection of small facts and made them lead in a very insulting direction. The ring you saw last night belongs to Sedric. How could you imagine it was mine? He'd left it on the table at the inn. I put it on my hand so it wouldn't be lost. And I gave it back to him this morning. Are you satisfied? Ask him if you wish." He lifted the cover on another dish, muttering, "Of all the idiocy. Before breakfast, too." He speared several small sausages and shook them off on his plate. Sedric hadn't moved or spoken. "Sedric!" Hest snapped at him abruptly.

He startled, gaped at Hest, and then turned hastily to Alise. "Yes. I bought the ring. And Hest gave it back to me. Yes." He looked acutely miserable.

Hest suddenly relaxed. Nonchalantly, he rang the bell for a servant. When a maid came to the door, he gestured at the table. "Bring some hot food. This is disgusting. And make a fresh pot of tea. Sedric, will you have tea?"

When Sedric just stared at him, Hest snorted in exasperation. "Sedric will have tea, also." As soon as the door closed behind the maid, Hest spoke to his secretary. "Explain the lotion, if you would, Sedric. And my supposed 'love cottage.'"

Sedric looked ill. "The palat lotion was a gift."

"For my mother," Hest cut in. "And the cottage is a place that Sedric uses, not I. He said he needed some privacy, and I agreed. It seemed a small accommodation to make for him, as well as he has served me. And if he chooses to entertain there, and who he has in to visit him, I consider none of my business. Nor yours, Alise. He's a man, and a man has needs." He bit off a piece of a sausage and chewed and swallowed it. "Frankly, I'm shocked at all this. You are my wife. To imagine you shuffling through my papers, digging in the hope of discovering some nasty secret; well, it's dismaying. What ails you, woman, to even think of such a thing?"

She found she was trembling. Was it all so easily explained away? Could she be that wrong? "You're a man, too." She pointed out in a shaking voice. "With needs. Yet you seldom visit me. You ignore me."

"I'm a busy man, Alise. With concerns much more profound than, well, your carnal desires. Must we speak of this in front of Sedric? If you cannot spare my feelings, can you at least consider his?"

"You have to have someone else. I know you do!" The words came out of her as a quavering cry.

"You know nothing," Hest retorted in sudden disgust. "But you shall. Sedric. As Alise has made you a party to our nasty little squabble, I shall avail myself of you. Sit up and tell the truth." Hest turned suddenly back to her. "You will believe Sedric, won't you? Even if you consider your wedded husband a lying adulterer."

She locked eyes with Sedric. The man was pale. He was breathing audibly, his mouth half ajar. What had ever possessed her to speak out in front of him that way? What would he think of her now? He had ever been her friend. Could she salvage at least that? "He has never lied to me," she said. "I'll believe him."

"Alise, I . . ."

"Now, quiet, Sedric, until you hear the question." Hest put his forearms on the table and leaned on them thoughtfully. His voice was as measured as if he were stating the terms of a contract. "Answer my wife truthfully and fully. You are with me almost every hour of my working day and sometimes far into the night. If anyone knows my habits, it's you. Look at Alise and tell her true: Do I have another woman in my life?"

"I . . . that is, no. No."

"Have I ever shown any interest, here in Bingtown or on our trading journeys, in any woman?"

Sedric's voice had grown a little stronger. "No. Never."

"There. You see." Hest leaned forward to help himself to a slice of fruit bread. "Your foul accusations had no foundation at all."

"Sedric?" She was almost pleading with him. She had been so sure. "You are telling me the truth?"

Sedric took a ragged breath. "There are no other women in Hest's life, Alise. None at all."

He looked down at his hands, embarrassed, and she saw that the ring she had seen on Hest's hand last night was now on Sedric's. Shame scalded her. "I'm sorry," she whispered.

Hest thought she spoke to him. "Sorry? You insult me and humiliate me in front of Sedric, and 'sorry' is the best you can manage? I think I'm owed substantially more than that, Alise."

She had come to her feet, but she felt unstable. Suddenly she just wished to be out of the room and away from this horrible man who had somehow come to dominate her life. All she wanted now was the quiet of her room, and to lose herself in ancient scrolls from another world and time. "I don't know what else I can say."

"Well. There's isn't much you can say, after such a grave insult. You've apologized, but it scarcely mends the matter."

"I'm sorry," she said again, surrendering to him. "I'm sorry I ever brought it up."

"That makes two of us. Now let this be an end of this. Don't ever accuse me of something like that again. It's beneath you. It's beneath both of us to have conversations like this."

"I won't. I promise." She nearly knocked her chair over as she left the table and hurried toward the door.

"I will hold you to that promise!" Hest called after her.

"I promise," she repeated dully and fled from the room.

NIGHT WAS CLOSING in. Even in summer, the days seemed short. The towering trees of the rain forest carpeted the wide flat valley and gave way only to the river's gray swathe. Daylight trickled down only when the sun was high enough for its light to strike the narrow alley of water and land between the brooding walls of trees that hemmed the river. Evening began its slow creep when the sun moved past it. Bright daylight was short, and twilight dominated their lives. Four years had passed since the summer she had emerged from her case. Four years of thwarted hopes, poor food, and neglect. Four summers of too much shade, four winters of rainy gray days. Four years of no life save eating and then sleeping, sleeping far too many hours of every day. Instead of feeling as if she slept too much, Sintara always felt vaguely weary. Swampy land and dimness was the province of newts, not dragons. *Dragons,* she thought, *were creatures of strong sunlight, dry sand, and long, hot days.* And flight. How she longed to fly. Fly away from the mud and the crowded conditions and the gloomy riverbank.

She craned her neck to nuzzle at a patch of gritty mud that had dried behind her wing. She rubbed at it, then stretched her stunted wing and slapped it several times against her body in an attempt to dislodge the irritation. Most of it went trickling down her side in a cascade of dust. It was a minor relief. She longed to bathe herself in a pool of hot, still water, to emerge into strong sunlight to dry, and then to roll and scratch in abrasive sand until her scales gleamed. None of those things existed in her current life. Only her ancestral dreams informed her of them.

It was not the only dragon memory that taunted her. She had many dreams. Dreams of flight, of hunting, of mating. Memories of a city with a well of liquid silver where a dragon could slake that thirst no water could quench. Many memories of gorging on hot, freshly killed meat. Memories of mating in flight, of hollowing out a sandy beach nest for her eggs. Many, many frustrating memories. Yet for all that, she knew she did not have a full complement of memories. It was maddening that she knew enough to know she was missing whole areas of knowledge, but could not reconstruct for herself exactly what that missing knowledge was. It was an additional cruelty that the dragon memories she did have showed her so clearly all her physical body lacked.

The memories were a heritage denied her. It was the way of her kind. In the serpent stage of their lives, they retained access to an ancestral hoard of serpent memories. Migration routes, warm currents, and fish runs were not the only information; there was also the knowledge of the gathering places and the songs and the structure of their society as serpents. When a serpent entered the cocoon, such memories faded until by the time the dragon emerged from its case, its life as a serpent was only a hazy recollection. Replacing those memories was the hereditary wealth of a dragon's proper knowledge. How to fly by the stars, and where the best hunting was to be found in each season, the traditional challenges for a mating duel, and what beach was best for the laying of eggs were some of those memories. But each dragon also could claim the more distant but personal memories of a dragon's particular ancestry. The memories came, not just from the serpent's changing body, but from the saliva of the dragons who helped the serpents shape their cocoons. There had been precious little of that when this generation of serpents cocooned. Perhaps that was what they were all lacking now. Perhaps that was why some of their number were as dull-witted as cattle.

The sun must have reached the unseen horizon. The stars were beginning to show in the narrow stripe of sky over the river. She looked up at the band of night and thought it a good metaphor for her truncated and restricted existence. This muddy beach by the river bounded by the immense forest behind her was the only existence she had known since she hatched into this life. The dragons could not retreat into the forest. The picket trees fenced them onto the shore as effectively as their namesake. Although the immense trees had been well spaced out by nature, their supplementary roots and all manner of underbrush, vines, and plants grew in the swampy spaces between them. Not even the much smaller humans could travel easily on the rain forest floor. Paths pushed through the brush soon became sodden trails and eventually swampy fingers of mud. No. The only way out of this forest for a dragon was up. She flapped her useless wings again and then folded them onto her back. Then she lowered her head from her stargazing and looked around her. The others were huddled together beneath the trees. She despised them. They were stunted and misshapen things, sickly, quarrelsome, weak, and unworthy.

Just as she was.

She plodded through the mud to join them. She was hungry, but she scarcely noticed that anymore. She had been constantly hungry since the day she hatched from her case.

Today she'd been fed seven fish, large if not fresh, and one bird. The bird had been stiff. Sometimes she dreamed of meat that was warm and limp with the blood still running. It was only a dream now. The hunters were seldom able to find large game close by; when they did get a marsh elk or a riverpig, the creatures had to be chopped into pieces before they could be transported back to the dragons. And the dragons seldom got the best parts of the beasts. Bones and guts and hide, tough shanks and horned heads, but seldom the hump from a riverpig's back or the meat-rich hind haunch of a marsh elk. Those parts went to the humans' tables. The dragons were left with the scraps and offal like stray dogs begging outside a city's gate.

The boggy ground sucked at her feet each time she lifted them and her tail seemed permanently caked with mud. The land here suffered as much as the dragons did; it never had a chance to harden and heal. All the trees that bordered the clearing were showing the effects of the dragons' residence. The lower trunks were scarred and scraped. Dragons scratching vermin from their skin had eroded bark from some of the trees, and the roots of others had been exposed by the traffic of clawed feet. She had overheard the humans worrying that even trees with trunks the size of towers would eventually die from such treatment. And what would happen when such a tree fell? The humans had somewhat wisely moved their homes out of the treetops of the affected trees. But didn't they realize that if one of the trees fell, it would doubtless crash through the branches of neighboring trees? Humans were stupider than squirrels in that regard.

Only in the summer months did the muddy beach approach a level of firmness that made walking less strenuous. In winter, the smaller dragons struggled to lift their feet high enough to walk. At least they had struggled. Most of them had died off last winter. She thought of that with regret. She had anticipated each of the weaklings dying and had been swift enough, twice, to fill her belly with their meat and her mind with their memories. But they were all gone now, and barring accidents or disease, her mates looked as if they would survive the summer.

She approached the huddled mass of dragons. That was not right. Serpents slept so, tangled and knotted together beneath the waves lest the currents of the ocean sweep them apart and scatter them. Most of her serpent memories now were dimmed, as was appropriate. She had no need of them in this incarnation. She had been Sisarqua in that life. But that was not who she was now. Now she was Sintara, a dragon, and dragons did not sleep huddled together like prey.

Not unless they were crippled, useless, weakling things, little better than moving meat. She approached the sleeping creatures and shouldered her way into them. She stepped on Fente's tale, and the little green wretch snapped at her. At her, but not scoring her skin. Fente was vicious, but not stupidly so. She knew that the first time she actually bit Sintara was the last time she'd bite anything. "You're in my spot," Sintara warned her, and Fente clapped her tail close to her side.

"You're clumsy. Or blind," Fente retorted, but quietly, as if she hadn't meant Sintara to hear her. In casual vengeance, Sintara shouldered Fente into Ranculos. The red had already been asleep. Without so much as opening his silver eyes, he kicked Fente in rebuke and resettled his bulk.

"What were you doing?" Sestican, the second-largest blue male asked her as she settled against him. It was her place. She always slept between him and the dour Mercor. It did not indicate friendliness or any sort of alliance. She had chosen the place because they were two of the largest males, and sheltering between them was the wisest place to sleep.

She didn't mind his question. He was one of the few she considered capable of intelligent conversation. "Looking at the sky."

"Dreaming," he surmised.

"Hating," she corrected him.

"Dreaming and hating are the same for us, in this life."

"If this is to be the last life, if all my memories must die with me, why must it be so dreary?"

"If you keep up your useless talk and disturb my sleep, I might make your last life end much faster than you expected." This from Kalo. His blue-black scaling made him nearly invisible in the dark. Sintara felt the small venom sacs in her throat swell with her hatred of him, but she kept her silence. He was the largest of them all. And the meanest. If she had been capable of producing enough venom to damage him, she would probably have spit it at him, regardless of the consequences. But even on days when she had fed well, her sacs produced barely enough venom to stun a large fish. If she spat at Kalo, he would kill her with his teeth and eat her. Useless. Useless anger from an impotent dragon. She wrapped her tail around herself and folded her stumpy wings on her back. She closed her eyes.

There were only fifteen of them left now. She cast her mind back. More than one hundred serpents had massed at the mouth of the river and migrated up it. How many had actually cocooned? Fewer than eighty. She didn't know how many had initially emerged, nor how many had survived the first day. It scarcely mattered now. Disease had taken some, and a few had fallen prey to a flash flood. The disease had been the most terrifying to her. She could not recall anything similar, and those others who were capable of intelligent speech had likewise been baffled by it. It had begun with a dry barking cough at night, one that disturbed the whole gathering of dragons. It had continued and spread until almost all of the dragons suffered from it to various degrees.

Then one of the smaller dragons had awakened them all by squawking hoarsely. It had been a small orange dragon with stumpy legs and wings that were only stubs. If he had ever had a name, Sintara couldn't recall it now. He had been trying to paw at his eyes that were crusted shut with mucus. His truncated front legs would not reach. With every distressed squawk he gave, he sprayed thick tendrils of phlegm. All the dragons had moved aside from him in disgust. By midmorning he was dead, and a few moments later, all that remained of him was a smear of blood on the damp earth and a couple of fellow dragons with full bellies. By then, two of the others were wheezing and drooling mucus from their mouths and nostrils.

Drier weather brought an end to the malaise. All had suffered from it to some degree. Sintara suspected that the constantly wet riverbank and the mud they had to live in, combined with the dense population, had caused the sickness. If any of them had been able to fly, they would have left and, she suspected, in doing so outflown the contagion.

One dragon actually had left. Gresok had been the largest red, a male who was physically among the healthiest but mentally among the dullest. One afternoon, he had simply announced that he was leaving to find a better place, a city he'd seen in his dreams. Then he walked away, crashing through underbrush until they could no longer hear his passage. They'd let him go. Why not? He seemed to know what he wanted, and it would mean slightly more food for the rest of them when the human hunters meted out what they'd killed.

But no more than half a day had passed before they'd felt his dying thoughts. He cried out, not to them, but simply shouting his fury to himself. Humans had attacked him. That much was clear. And as they felt him die, two of the other dragons, Kalo and Ranculos, had charged off to follow his trail. They went, not to assist or avenge him, but only to claim his carcass as their rightful food. That night, they had returned to the riverbank. Neither had spoken of what they had done, but Sintara had her suspicions. Both had smelled of human blood as well as Gresok's flesh. She suspected they'd come upon humans butchering the fallen Gresok, and included them in their feasting. She saw nothing wrong in that. Any human who dared to attack a dragon deserved to die himself. And dead, of what use was he, unless someone ate him? She didn't see why leaving a human to be eaten by worms was more acceptable.

All of the dragons were well aware that it was better to cover all traces of such encounters. The humans were very poor at concealing their thoughts. The dragons were well aware of the anger and resentment that some felt toward them. Illogical as it was, it seemed that they preferred to have their dead eaten by fish rather than let a dragon have the use of the meat. Only a few afternoons ago, a group of humans had been putting the body of a dead relative into the river. She had waded out into the water and followed the weighted canvas packet as the current carried it until it sank under the water. She had retrieved it and dragged it ashore, well away from human eyes. She had eaten it, canvas covering and all. When she returned and realized how distressed the humans were, she had sought to save their feelings by denying she had eaten the corpse. They hadn't believed her.

Their reaction made no sense to her. If the body had sunk to the bottom, fish and worms would have devoured it, tearing it to insignificant pieces. But because she had eaten the body, the human's tiny store of memories had been preserved in her. True, most of the memories made little sense to her, and the woman had lived but a breath of time, only some fifty turnings of the seasons. Even so, something of her would go on. Did humans think it better that the woman's body do no more than nourish another generation of sucker fish? Humans were so stupid.

Her dragon memories included a few scattered recollections of Elderlings. She wished they were clearer; they slipped and slid through her mind like a fish seen through murky water. The flavor of those memories offered tolerance, even fondness of such beings. They were useful and respectful creatures, willing to groom and greet dragons, to build their cities to accommodate them; they acknowledged the intelligence of dragons. How could sophisticated creatures such as Elderlings possibly be related to humans?

The soft-bodied little sacks of seawater that were supposed to tend the dragons now chattered and complained constantly about their simple tasks. They performed those duties so poorly that she and her fellows lived in abject misery. They deceived no one. They took no pleasure in tending the dragons. All the hairless tree monkeys truly thought about was despoiling Cassarick. The remains of the ancient Elderling city were buried nearly under the hatching grounds. They would plunder it as they had the buried city at Trehaug. Not only had they stripped it of its ornaments and carried off objects that they could not possibly comprehend, they had slain all but one of the dragons that the Elderlings had dragged into the dubious safety of their city right before that ancient catastrophe. Anger burned through her afresh as she thought of it.

Even now, some of the "liveships" built from "wizard-wood logs" still existed, still served humans as dragon spirits incarnated into ship bodies. Even now, the humans pleaded ignorance as an excuse for the terrible slaughter they had wrought. When Sintara thought of the dragons who had waited so many years to hatch, only to be tumbled half formed from their cases onto the cold stone floor, she swelled with anger. She felt her poison sacs fill and harden in her throat, and agitation swept through her. The humans deserved to die for what they had done, every one of them.

From beside her, Mercor spoke. Despite his size and apparent physical strength, he seldom spoke or asserted himself in any way. A terrible sadness seemed to enervate him, draining him of all ambition and drive. When he did speak, the others found themselves pausing in whatever they were doing to listen to him. Sintara could not know what the others felt, but it annoyed her that she felt both drawn toward him and guilty about his great sadness. His voice made her memory itch, as if when he spoke, she should recall wonderful things but could not. Tonight he said only, in his deep and sonorous voice, "Sintara. Let it go. Your anger is useless without a proper focus."

It was another thing he did that bothered her. He spoke as if he could know her thoughts. "You know nothing of my anger," she hissed at him.

"Don't I?" He shifted miserably in the muddy wallow where they slept. "I can smell your fury, and I know that your sacs swell with poison."

"I want to *sleep*!" Kalo rumbled. His words were sharp with irritation, but not even he dared to confront Mercor directly.

On the edge of the huddled group of dragons, one of the small dim-witted ones, probably the green who could barely drag himself around, squeaked in his sleep. "Kelsingra! Kelsingra! There, in the distance!"

Kalo lifted his head on his long neck and roared in the green's direction, "Be silent! I wish to sleep!"

"You do sleep, already," Mercor replied, impervious to the big blue's anger. "You sleep so deeply that you no longer dream." He lifted his head. He was not bigger than Kalo, but it was still a challenge. "Kelsingra!" he suddenly trumpeted into the night.

All the dragons stirred. "Kelsingra!" he bellowed again, and Sintara's keen hearing picked up the distant fluting cries of humans disturbed from their evening slumber. "Kelsingra!"

Mercor threw the name of the ancient city up to the distant stars. "Kelsingra, I remember you! We all do, even those who wish we did not! Kelsingra, home of the Elderlings, home of the well of the silver waters and the wide stone plazas baking in the summer heat. The hillsides above the city teemed with game. Do not mock that one who dreams of you still. Kelsingra!"

"I want to go to Kelsingra. I want to lift my wings and fly again." A voice rose from somewhere in the night.

"Wings. Fly! Fly!" The words were muffled and ill formed, but the longing of the dim-witted dragon who uttered them filled them with feeling.

"Kelsingra," someone else groaned.

Sintara lowered her head, tucking it in close to her chest. She was shamed for them and shamed for herself. They sounded like penned cattle lowing before the slaughter begins. "Then go there," she muttered in disgust. "Just leave and go there."

"Would that we could." Mercor spoke the words with true longing. "But the way is long, even if we had wings that would bear us. And the path is uncertain. As serpents, we could barely find our way home. How much stranger must the land be now that lies between us and the place where Kelsingra used to be?"

"Used to be," Kalo repeated. "So much used to be, and no longer is. It is useless to speak or think of any of it. I want to go back to sleep."

"Useless, perhaps, but nonetheless, we do speak of it.

And some of us still dream of it. Just as some of us still dream of flying, and killing our own meat and battling for mates. Some of us still dream of living. You do not want to sleep, Kalo. You want to die."

Kalo twitched as if struck by an arrow. Sintara felt the big dragon stiffen, sensed how his poison sacs suddenly swelled. A few moments ago, she had thought that resting between the two large males had been a place of safety. Now she perceived that she was in the thick of the danger, trapped between Sestican and Mercor. Kalo lifted his head high and glared down on Mercor. If he spat acid now, Mercor would be helpless to avoid it. And she would also be caught in the spray. She hunched her shoulders uselessly.

But Kalo spoke rather than exhaled poison. "Do not speak to me, Mercor. You know nothing of what I think or feel."

"Don't I? I know more of you than you recall yourself, Kalo." Mercor suddenly threw his head back and bellowed. "I know you all! All of you! And I mourn what you are because I remember what you were and I know what you were meant to be!"

"Quiet! We're trying to sleep!" This was no bellow of an outraged dragon, but the shrill cry of a frustrated human. Kalo turned his head toward the source of the sound and gave a roar of fury. Sestican, Ranculos, and Mercor suddenly echoed him. When that blast of sound died away, a few of the dimmer dragons on the edge of the herd imitated it.

"You be silent!" Kalo trumpeted up at the human dwellings. "Dragons speak when they wish to speak! You have no control over us!"

"Ah, but they do," Mercor said quietly. The very softness of his words seemed to bring all attention to him.

Kalo turned his head sharply. "You, perhaps, are controlled by humans. I am not."

"You do not, then, eat when they feed you? You do not remain here, where they have corralled us? You do not accept the future they plan for us, that we will remain here, dependent upon them, until we slowly die off and stop being a nuisance to them?"

Sintara found that, against her will, she was listening raptly to his words. They were frightening and challenging at the same time. When his voice stopped, the quieter sounds of the evening flowed in. She listened to the river lapping at the muddy shore, to the distant noises of humans and birds settling in the trees for the night, and to the sounds of dragons breathing. "What should we do then?" she heard herself ask.

All heads turned toward her. She did not look at anyone except Mercor. The night had stolen the colors from his scales, but she could make out his gleaming black eyes. "We should leave," he said quietly. "We should leave here and try to find our way to Kelsingra. Or to anywhere that is better than this."

"How?" Sestican abruptly demanded. "Shall we knock down the trees that hem us in? Humans can slip between their trunks and find pathways through the swamp. But if you have not noticed, we are slightly larger than humans. Gresok went blundering off, going not where he willed but only where the trees would permit him passage. There is no escape that way, only swamp and dimness and starvation. And poorly fed as we are, at least the humans bring us something to eat each day. If we left here, we'd starve."

"There's no need for us to starve at all. We should eat the humans," someone on the edge of the herd suggested.

"Be quiet if you cannot make sense," Sestican retorted. "If we eat the humans, once they are gone, we are still trapped here, with no food."

"They want us to leave." Kalo spoke suddenly, startling everyone.

"Who does?" Mercor demanded.

"The humans. Their Rain Wild Council sent a man to speak. One of the feeders asked me to talk with him. He told the Council man that I am the biggest of the dragons and therefore the leader. So he spoke to me. He wanted to know if I knew when or even if Tintaglia would return. I told him I did not. Then he said that they were very upset that someone had eaten a corpse out of the river, and that someone else had chased a worker down into the tunnels

that go to the buried city. And he said they were running out
of ways to feed us. He said that his hunters have hunted out
all the large meat for miles around, and that the fish runs are
nearly over for the year. He said the Council wishes us to
call Tintaglia, to let her know that the Council demands that
she return to help them solve this difficulty."

In the darkness, several of the dragons snorted with contempt for such foolishness.

Mercor spoke with disdain. "Call Tintaglia. As if she
would respond to us. Kalo, why did you not speak of this
before?"

"They told me nothing that we do not all know already.
Why bother repeating it? They are the ones who refuse
to accept what they already know. Tintaglia's not coming
back," Kalo confirmed bitterly. "She has no reason to. She
has found a mate. Together they are free to fly and hunt
wherever they will. In a decade or two, when her time is
ripe, she will lay her eggs and when they hatch, there will be
a new generation of serpents growing. She has no need of us
any longer. She only helped us stay alive because we were
her last resort. And now we are not. If Tintaglia had had a
mate at the time we emerged from our cases, she would
have despised us. She knows as well as we all do that we are
not fit to live."

"But live we do!" Mercor broke in angrily on Kalo's rant.
"And dragons we are. Not slaves, not pets. Nor are we cattle,
for humans to slaughter and butcher and sell off to the highest bidder."

Sestican flared the diminutive spikes on his neck. "Who
even dares think of such a thing!"

"Oh, let us not be fools as well as cripples," Mercor returned sarcastically. "There are plenty of humans who are
unable to comprehend us when we speak to them. And some
of them judge us little more than beasts, and unhealthy
ones at that. I've overheard their words; there are those who
would buy our flesh, our scales, our teeth, any parts of our
bodies for their elixirs and potions. What do you think happened to that poor fool Gresok? Kalo and Ranculos know,
even if Kalo chooses to pretend ignorance. Humans killed

him, thinking to butcher him for trophies. They did not know we would be able to sense him dying. How many of them were there, Kalo? Enough humans to make you a good meal even after you'd devoured Gresok?"

"There were three." Ranculos was the one who spoke. "Three we caught, and one who fled."

"Were they Rain Wilders?" Mercor demanded.

Ranculos blew out a snort of disdain. "I did not ask them. They were guilty of slaying a dragon, and I saw that they paid for it."

"A pity we do not know. We might have a better idea of how much we can trust the Rain Wilders if we knew. Because we are going to need their help, much as it distresses me to say so."

"Their help? Their help is next to worthless. They bring us food that is half rotted or merely the scraps of their kill. And there is never enough of it. What can humans help us with?"

Mercor's reply was deceptively placid. "They can help us go to Kelsingra."

A chorus of dragons replied all at once.

"Kelsingra may not even exist anymore."

"We don't know where it is. Our memories are of small use in finding our way there. We could not have found our way here to the cocooning grounds unassisted. Everything is changed."

"Why would humans help us go to Kelsingra?"

"Kelsingra! Kelsingra! Kelsingra!" prattled the depraved dragon at the edge of the huddle.

"Make that fool be silent!" Kalo roared, and there was a sudden yelp of pain as someone did just that. "Why would humans help us go to Kelsingra?" he repeated.

"Because we would make them think it was their own idea. Because we would make them want to take us there."

"How? Why?"

It was full dark now. Even Sintara's keen eyes could not see Mercor's face, but his amusement filled his voice. "We would make them greedy. You have seen how willingly they dig and delve here in the hopes of unearthing Elderling treasure. We would tell them that Kelsingra was three times the size of Cassarick and that the Elderling treasury was there."

"Elderling treasury?" Kalo asked.

"We would *lie* to them," Mercor explained patiently. "To make them want to take us there. We know they want to be rid of us. If we leave it to them, they will let us slowly starve to death or leave us living in our own filth until disease claims us. This way, we offer them the chance to be rid of us, and to profit at the same time. They will be willing to help us, because they will think we are guiding them to riches."

"But we don't know the way," Kalo bellowed in frustration. "And if they knew of an Elderling city to plunder, they would have done so by now. So they don't know where Kelsingra is either." He lowered his voice and added dismally, "Everything is changed, Mercor. Kelsingra may be buried under mud and trees just as Trehaug and Cassarick are now. Even if we could find our way back to it, what good would it do us?"

"Kelsingra was at a much higher elevation than either Trehaug or Cassarick. Do not you recall the view from the mountain cliffs behind the city? Perhaps the mud that flowed and buried these cities did not cover Kelsingra. Or perhaps it was upstream of the mudflow. Anything is possible. It is even conceivable that Elderlings survived there. Not dragons, no, for if any of the dragons had lived, we would have heard them by now. But the city may still be there, and the fertile croplands, and the plain beyond teeming with antelope and other herd beasts. It may all be there, just waiting for us to return."

"Or nothing might be there," Kalo replied sourly.

"Well, nothing is what we have here, so what do we have to lose?" Mercor demanded stolidly.

"Why do we need the humans' help at all?" Sintara asked into the quiet. "If we wish to go to Kelsingra, why don't we just go?"

"As humiliating as it is to admit it, we will require their help. Some of us are barely able to limp about this mudflat. None of us can hunt enough to sustain ourselves. We are dragons, and we are meant to be free to the land and the sky. Without healthy bodies and the use of our wings, we cannot hunt. Some fish we can catch for ourselves, when the runs are thick. But we need humans to hunt for us, and to help those of us who are feeble of body or mind."

"Why not just leave the weaklings behind?" Kalo asked.

Mercor snorted his disgust for such an idea. "And let the humans butcher them and sell off their parts? Let them discover that, yes, dragon liver does have amazing healing powers when dried and fed to a human? Let them discover the elixir in our blood? Let them discover what wondrous sharp tools they can make from our claws? Let them find that, yes, those myths have a sound basis in reality? And then, in no time at all, they would come after us. No, Kalo. No dragon, no matter how feeble, is prey for a human. And we are too few to discard so casually any of our race. Nor can we afford to abandon them as meat or as a source of memories for the rest of us. On that we must be united. So when we go, we must take every dragon with us. And we must demand that humans accompany us, to help provide meat for us until we reach a place where we can provide for ourselves."

"And where might that be?" Sestican demanded sourly.

"Kelsingra. At best. A place more congenial to dragons, with better hunting, at worst."

"We don't know the way."

"We know it isn't here," Mercor replied tranquilly. "We know Kelsingra was along the river and upstream of Cassarick. So, we begin by going up the river."

"The river has shifted and changed. Where once it flowed narrow and swift between plains rich with game, now it is wide and meanders through a bogland of trees and brush. Humans, light as they are, still cannot move easily through this region. And who knows what has become of the lands between here and the mountains. A score of rivers and streams once fed into this river. Do they still exist? Have they, too, shifted in their courses? It is hopeless. In all the time that these humans have lived here, they haven't explored the upper reaches of the river. They want to find dry, open land as badly as we do. If humans *could* travel in that direction, they would have trekked up the river long ago, and if Kelsingra still existed for them to find, they would have discovered it by now. You want us to leave what little safety and food we have, journey through a bogland in the hopes of eventually finding solid land and Kelsingra. It's a foolish dream, Mercor. We'll all just die on the way to a mirage."

"So, Kalo, you would prefer to just die here?"

"Why not?" the big dragon challenged him sarcastically.

"Because I, for one, would prefer to die as a free creature rather than as cattle. I'd like a chance to hunt again, to feel hot sand against my scales again. I'd like to drink deeply of the silvery wells of Kelsingra. If I must die, I'd like to die as a dragon rather than whatever pathetic thing it is that we've become."

"And I'd like to sleep!" Kalo snapped.

"Sleep, then," Mercor replied quietly. "It's good practice for death."

His final words seemed to end all conversation. The dragons shifted and settled and shifted again, each looking, Sintara thought, for a comfortable spot that no longer existed. It was not just that the cold, damp earth was uncomfortable; it was that Mercor's words had destroyed the small amount of acceptance that the dragons had built for their situation. The anger and her stubborn endurance now seemed more like cowardice and resignation.

Since Sintara had emerged from her case, she had known that everything in her life was wrong. Mercor's proposal filled her thoughts with possibilities. Cautiously, unwilling to wake the others, she extended her puny wings and stretched her neck to allow herself to groom them. Had they grown at all? Nightly she waited for dark and performed this senseless ritual. Night after night, she pretended to herself that they had grown and would continue to grow. They were laughable things, scarcely a third of the size they should have been. Flapping them scarcely stirred a breeze, let alone lifted her bulk off the ground. Carefully, quietly, she folded them back to her body.

Wings made a dragon, she thought. Without wings, she could not hunt successfully, and she could never hope to mate. Indignation roiled suddenly through her. Only a few weeks ago, stretched out to sleep in a small band of sunlight, she had been rudely awakened when Dortean had tried to mount her. She had wakened with a roar of outrage. He was an orange, with stumpy legs and a thin tail. That he had even attempted to mate with her was humiliation enough. He was stupid and pathetic. To awaken to his muddy legs straddling her back as he hunched hopefully at her was a disgusting contrast to all her stored memories of dragons mating in flight.

Usually males fought for a female once she had indicated she was willing. And when the strongest male defeated his rivals and rose to join her in flight, he usually had to face the final challenge of dominating the female. Dragon queens did not mate with weaklings. Nor would a drake accept as a mate a docile female. Why mingle one's bloodline with that of a bovine female, whose offspring might lack the true fire of a dragon? So to be straddled and humped by a dim-witted and deformed creature was an insult beyond bearing. She had rounded on him, snapping and slapping at him ineffectually with her dwarfed wings. At first, it had more inflamed than deterred him. He had continued to come at her, muddy necked and with his small eyes blazing with febrile lust. He had tried to clutch her to him, but a desperate swipe of her tail had knocked him off his feet and into the ever-present mud. Misshapen as he was, he could not easily right himself, and she had stormed away from him, down to the river, to wash his muddy paw prints from her back and haunches. She wished the acid waters of the river could have washed the humiliation from her as well.

She settled herself for sleep, but it did not come to her. Instead, memories flickered in her mind, filling her with sadness—memories of flight, of mating, of the distant beaches where her ancestors had laid their eggs and then basked on the hot sand. Terrible longings replaced her sadness. "Kelsingra," she said softly to herself, and to her surprise, memories of the place flooded her. To describe it as a city by the river could not begin to do it justice. It had been a place constructed as much with the mind and heart as with stone and beam. The entire city had been laid out to reflect that both Elderling and dragon lived amicably there. The streets had been wide, the doors to the public buildings ample, and the art on those walls and around the fountains had celebrated the companionship enjoyed by both dragons and Elderlings.

And there was something else, she recalled slowly. There was a well there, a well deeper than the river that bordered the city. A bucket dropped into its depths sank past ordinary water to a deeper river of a most extraordinary substance. Even a tiny amount of it was dangerously intoxicating for an Elderling and possibly fatal for a human. But dragons could drink from it. She closed her eyes and let the old memories of other dragons rise to the forefront of her mind. An Elderling woman, gowned in green and gold, turned the crank on the windlass of a well and brought up a bucket full of gleaming silver drink. It was emptied into a polished trough, and another brought up, and another, until the vessel of polished stone brimmed with silver. In her dreams Sintara drank of it, the silver running through her veins, filling her heart with song and her mind with poetry. She allowed herself to float on the exhilarating memories, leaving the reality of her present life behind.

In this other remembered life, she was a queen dragon who preened herself, her silver-dripping muzzle spreading the fine sheen over her feathery scales. The green-and-gold robed woman rejoiced in letting her drink her fill of the silvery stuff. Together they left the well and strolled through the bright sunlit streets of the city. They passed lavish squares where fountains leaped and played, and brightly robed denizens of the city greeted her with bows and curtsies. The market was in full voice, filled with the songs of minstrels and the dickering of merchants and customers. Scents of cooking meat and sacks of spices, rare perfumes, and pungent herbs filled her nostrils. When she and her companion reached the river's edge, they bid each other the fond farewells that old friends share. And then the queen dragon spread and limbered her gleaming scarlet wings.

She crouched low on her powerful hindquarters and then sprang effortlessly into the air. Three, four, five beats of her wings and the wind off the river captured her and flung her aloft. She caught the current of warm summer air and soared on it.

The crimson queen blinked transparent lids over her whirling gold eyes. The wind slapped her, but the blow changed to a caress as she banked into it and rode it ever higher. Warm summer sunlight kissed her back, and the wide world spread out below her. It was a golden land, a wide river valley that gave, on both sides, to rolling hills dotted with oak groves and then to steeper cliffs and finally craggy mountains. On the flat lands along the river, cultivated fields of grain alternated with pastures where kine and sheep grazed. A fine road of smooth black stone bordered one side of the river, with tributary paths and byways wandering out to the more rural districts. Beyond the settlements of humanity, in the foothills and the narrow valleys that threaded back into the mountains, game was plentiful.

On the updrafts over the hills, other dragons soared, their glistening hides winking like jewels in the summer sunlight. One, a pale-green dragon with gold mottling on his haunches and shoulders, trumpeted to her. A thrill ran through her as she recognized her most recent mate. She answered his greeting and saw him bank to meet her. As soon as he had committed to his turn, she mocked him with a shrill call and beat her own wings powerfully to gain altitude. He gave a deep cry of challenge to her in response and came after her.

Rain. Cold sleeting rain suddenly spattered on her back with the force of a shower of pebbles. Sintara's eyes flew open, the dream and the respite it had brought her shattered. In the next moment, the cold water was coursing down her flanks and sides. All around her in the darkness, dragons shifted and reluctantly huddled closer to one another. Sorrow vied with fury in her. "Kelsingra," she promised herself aloud. "Kelsingra."

In the darkness, the voices of the other dragons echoed hers.

Day the 17th of the Greening Moon

Year the 5th of the Independent Alliance of Traders

From Erek, Keeper of the Birds, Bingtown
To Detozi, Keeper of the Birds, Trehaug

In the sealed scroll case, a letter from the Bingtown Traders' Council to the Rain Wild Traders' Councils of Trehaug and Cassarick, suggesting that the Elderling Selden might go on a journey to discover the whereabouts of Tintaglia and persuade her to return and once more engage in the care of the young dragons.

Detozi,

I take up pen on behalf of your nephew Reyall to assure you that the Three Ships girl Karlin is indeed of good character, being industrious, dutiful to her parents, and able to both read and write. Although he is young to form such an attachment, I am willing to consent to my apprentice becoming engaged to her, so long as he pledges to me that they will not marry before he reaches his journeyman standing. I am pleased to give this testimonial to Karlin's character and truly believe that in every way she can be as good a wife to him as any girl that is Trader born and bred. It is not, of course, a trivial decision, but I will remark that she comes from a family of five healthy children, and that both her sisters have wed and produced fine healthy offspring. In these times, a lad could do far worse than Karlin.

Erek

CHAPTER SIX

THYMARA'S
DECISION

It was unusual for her mother to greet them with a smile on their return from their daily gathering. Even more unusual was for her to be fairly bursting with enthusiasm to speak to them. Thymara and her father were scarcely inside the door with their baskets before her mother spoke. Her eyes were bright with hope. "We've had an offer for Thymara."

For an instant, both the young woman and her father froze as they were. Thymara could barely make sense of the words. An offer? For her? At sixteen years of age, she was long past the age when most Rain Wild girls were engaged. She knew that in some places in the world she would still be considered little more than a child. In others, she would be seen as just ripening for marriage. But in the Rain Wilds, folk did not live as long as other people. They knew that if a family bloodline was to continue, they'd best have their offspring spoken for as children, wed young as soon as they were fecund, and with child within the year. Even if a girl came from a poor family, if her looks were passable, she'd be spoken for by ten. Even the ugly girls had prospects by twelve.

Unless they were like Thymara, never meant to survive at all, let alone wed and produce children. Invisible to some folk, barely tolerated by others. Yet, here was her mother, eyes shining, saying there had been an offer for her. It was too strange. To accept a marriage offer when children were forbidden to her? It made no sense. Who would make such an offer and why would her mother even consider it?

"A marriage offer for Thymara? From whom?" Her father's voice was thick with disbelief. Foreboding grew in Thymara's heart as she studied her mother's face. Her smile was thin. She did not look at either of them as she crouched by the baskets and began to select which items in them would become their evening meal. She spoke to the food they had gathered. "I said we'd had an offer for Thymara, Jerup. Not a *marriage* offer."

"What sort of an offer, then? From whom?" her father demanded. A storm cloud of anger threatened in his words.

Her mother kept her aplomb. She didn't look up from her task. "An offer of useful employment and a life of her own, apart from us in our declining years. As for 'from whom,' it comes directly from the Rain Wild Traders' Council. So it's nothing to sniff at, Jerup. It's a wonderful opportunity for Thymara."

Her father shifted his glance to Thymara and waited for her to speak. It was no secret in their little family that her mother worried constantly about her "declining years." Plainly she believed that if they could shed responsibility for Thymara's upkeep, they could save more for their old age. Thymara wasn't certain that were so; she toiled every day alongside her father. Much of what he carried home, Thymara had harvested from the highest reaches of the tallest branches, sunny places where no one else dared climb. Would her mother think it such a relief when her father's baskets were lighter each day? And if she were gone, who would do the day-to-day chores for them as their bodies aged and grew feeble?

Thymara didn't voice any of that. "What sort of 'useful employment' did they offer?" she asked quietly. Thymara kept her voice unaccusing, or tried to. She dreaded what her mother might answer. There were all sorts of "useful employment" in Trehaug. There was always the most hazardous digging in the buried Elderling city. It was backbreaking labor, shovel- and barrow-work, often done in near darkness, and always with the possibility that a door or wall in the ancient buried city might suddenly give way and release an avalanche of mud. Usually, they chose boys for that task because they were stronger. "Unproductive" girls like her were most often given the task of maintaining the bridges that traversed the highest and lightest branches. There had been recent talk of a major expansion of the network of footbridges that connected the widely scattered settlements on both sides of the Rain Wild River and a lot of debate as to how far a bridge of chain and wood could successfully be stretched. With a sinking heart, Thymara suspected she would be part of the team that would find out. Yes. That was probably it. Everyone in their neighborhood knew of her prowess at climbing. And such work would require her to leave her home and live close to the project. It would take her far from her parents, and perhaps even promise a swift end to her existence. Her mother might welcome that.

Her mother's voice was falsely cheery as she began her tale. "Well. There was a Trader in the trunk market today, dressed very fine in an embroidered robe, and with a scroll from the Rain Wild Council. He said he had come looking for strong young people, for people without spouses or children, to undertake a special task in service to Trehaug and to all the Rain Wilders. The pay would be very good, he said, and an advance would be given immediately, even before the task was begun, and at the end, when the workers returned to Trehaug, they would be well rewarded for their efforts. He said he expected many people would wish to be chosen, but that the candidates must be exceptionally hardy and tough."

Thymara stifled her impatience. Her mother could never simply state something. She told a story or a piece of news by talking all around it. Asking her questions would simply take her down yet another side track. Thymara pressed her teeth together and held her tongue.

Her father didn't have her patience. "So it's not a marriage offer; it's an offer of work. Thymara already has work. She helps me gather. And why should she wish for 'a life of her own,' as you put it, away from us? We are not getting any younger, and if there is a time when I would want her by my side, it is, as you put it, during our 'declining years.' Who else do you think will take care of us? The Rain Wild Council?"

Her mother pressed her lips together tightly, and the lines in her brow deepened. "Oh, very well, then," she said bitterly. "I'll say no more. I see I was foolish to listen to the man at all, or to think that Thymara might wish to have a bit of adventure in her life." Almost quivering with indignation, she gave them a sour look and radiated silence and anger.

The main room of their house was tiny, but as her mother set the food on the woven pads onto the table mat, she pretended to ignore them. Thymara and her father both kept silent. Asking for more information would only increase her mother's pleasure at withholding it from them. Feigning disinterest would win it more quickly. So her father filled the washbasin, used it, flung the dirty water out the window, and then refilled it for her. He passed it to her, saying casually, "I think that instead of harvesting tomorrow, we should make an expedition to bring back some new plants. Shall we rise early?"

"I suppose that would be wisest," Thymara replied cautiously.

Her mother couldn't stand that they appeared to be having a simple conversation. She spoke to the kura nuts she was grinding into paste. "I suppose I know nothing at all about my daughter. I thought she would be thrilled to work with the dragons. She seemed so interested in them when she was younger."

Her father made a tiny hand motion at Thymara, cautioning her to keep silent so her mother would keep talking. Thymara couldn't. "The dragons? The dragons I saw hatch, the abandoned dragons? I'd be working with them?"

Her mother gave a small, satisfied sniff. "Apparently not. Your father thinks it better that you remain here, to live with us until we shrivel up and die, and then for you to be alone for the rest of your life." She set the bowl of mashed kura nuts on the food mat and placed a plate of weddle stalks beside it. She had baked flatbread at the community oven earlier in the day. There were six flats, two for each of them. It was not a plentiful or elaborate meal, but it would "fill the belly" as her father would say. Hungry as Thymara had been but a few seconds ago, she didn't even want to look at it now.

But her father had been right. Thymara had fed her mother's fury, not slaked it with her question, and now the woman burned with a cold and righteous fire. She smiled and made small talk during the meal, as if all were well and she were merely a subservient wife conceding to her husband's demands. Thymara asked about the offer twice more, unable to resist the bait her mother had dangled, and each time her mother told her that surely Thymara would not want to leave home and family and she would say no more on such a silly topic.

All Thymara could do was simmer in her seething curiosity.

As soon as the meal was ended, Jerup announced he had errands and left the house. Thymara tidied away the remains of the meal, trying not to meet her mother's resentful stare. As soon as she could, she left the house and the little walkways that connected it to its neighbors. She clambered higher in the canopy. She needed to think, and she'd do that best if she were alone. Dragons. What could the dragons possibly have to do with an offer for her?

Thymara had seen the dragons twice in her life. The first time had been five years ago, when Thymara had been almost eleven. Her father had taken her down the trunk and across the Necklace Bridges and then down, down, all the way to the earth. The trail that led to the hatchery by the riverbank had been trodden into muck by the passage of so many feet. That had been Thymara's first visit to Cassarick.

The memory of watching them emerge haunted her still. Their wings had been weak, and their flesh was thin on their bones. Tintaglia had come and gone, bringing fresh meat to feed them. Her father had felt sympathy for the poor misshapen creatures. A rueful smile twisted her mouth as she recalled his scrambling flight from one newly hatched dragon.

In the early days following the hatch, everyone had hoped that the dragons who survived would grow and prosper. Her father had been employed for a time as a hunter to help feed the dragons. But the densely forested Rain Wilds could not long support such large and ravenous carnivores. The best efforts of the hunters could not create more game than there was. The Council had become more and more penurious about paying for the hunters' work. Her father soon quit that occupation and returned to their home in Trehaug. He told a sad tale of the sickly dragons quickly dying off. Those who remained grew larger, but not heartier or more self-sufficient. "Sometimes Tintaglia comes, bringing meat, but one dragon cannot feed so many. And her shame for those poor creatures radiates from her. It will come to a bad end for all of us, I fear."

For the earthbound dragons, it had grown worse. For against all odds, Tintaglia had found a mate. All had believed that Tintaglia was the last true dragon in the world. To discover it was not so was shocking, and the tale of the black dragon who had risen from the ice was almost too farfetched to believe.

Some prince of the far Six Duchies had unearthed the dragon, digging him out of an icy grave for reasons of his own, ones that did not matter to her. The black drake had not been dead after all; he had risen from his long and icy sleep and taken Tintaglia as his mate. They had flown off together to hunt and feed and mate. Wild as the tale was, one thing was unmistakably true: since that time, the queen dragon had returned to the Rain Wilds only sporadically.

There were reports from some Rain Wilders that they had seen the two great dragons flying in the distance. Some said bitterly that now that she had no need of humans for companionship or aid, she had parted from them, not only abandoning to their care the ravenous young dragons but ceasing to cast her protective shadow over the waters of the Rain Wild River.

Even though Tintaglia had ceased to observe her end of their bargain, the Rain Wilders had little choice but to continue to care for the young dragons. As many had pointed out, the only thing worse than a herd of dragons living at the foot of your city was a herd of hungry, angry dragons living at the foot of your city. Although the cocooning grounds were substantially upriver of Trehaug, they were almost on top of the buried city of Cassarick. The most accessible parts of the ancient Elderling city beneath Trehaug had been mined of Elderling treasure long ago. Cassarick now seemed to offer the same potential, but only if the young dragons were kept in a frame of mind to allow the humans access to it.

Thymara wondered how many of the young dragons now remained alive. Not all of the serpents who entered their cocoons had emerged as dragons. The last time her father had journeyed to Cassarick, Thymara had gone with him. That had been a little more than two years ago. If she recalled correctly, there had been eighteen surviving creatures then. Disease, lack of fresh food, and battles among themselves had taken a heavy toll on them. She had watched from the trees, not venturing near. The dirty hulking creatures seemed tragic, almost obscene when she recalled the glittering newness of the freshly emerged dragons. They were large, ill-formed hulks, smeared with mud, living in a trampled mucky area by the river. They stank. They stalked about listlessly, wading through their own droppings and nosing through the offal of old meals. None of the dragons had ever achieved the ability to fly. Some of them could hunt for their own food, in a very limited way. Their efforts consisted of wading out into the river and snatching at the migratory fish runs. A sensation of suppressed strife rose to her, thicker than their reptilian stench. She had turned away from them, unable to bear looking at the bony, ill-tempered creatures.

Thymara shook her head to clear it of memories and focus on her climb. She dug in her claws and moved up, into the branches that arched over the roof of her home. It was among the highest in Trehaug. From here, she looked down over most of the tree-top city.

She drew her knees up under her chin and pondered as she sat watching nightfall devour the city and forest. She liked this particular perch. If she leaned out and angled herself just right, she had a tiny window up through all the intersecting branches, through which she could glimpse the night sky and the myriad stars that filled it. No one else, she thought, knew that such a view existed. It belonged to her alone.

For a short time, she had peace. Then she felt the small vibrations of the branch that told her that someone was coming to join her in her precarious perch. Not her father. No. This person moved more swiftly than her father did. She did not turn to look at him, but spoke as if she had seen him. "Hello, Tats. What brings you up to the canopy tonight?"

She felt him shrug. He'd been standing up on the branch. Now he dropped to all fours to creep along the narrow limb to join her. When he reached her, he sat up but locked his wiry legs around the branch beneath him. "Just felt like visiting," the Tattooed boy said quietly. She finally turned her head to look at him.

Tats met her gaze without comment. She knew that recently her eyes had taken on the pale blue glow that some Rain Wilders had. He'd never commented on it, nor on her black claws. But then, she'd never asked any questions about the tattoos that sprawled across his face beside his nose. The one closest to his nose was a little horse symbol. The one that spread across most of his left cheek was a spider's web. They marked that he had been born into slavery. She knew the bones of his tale. Six years ago, with the return of the serpents, the Rain Wild Council had invited the Tattooed of Bingtown to emigrate there. Many of the recently freed slaves had few other prospects. Some had been criminals, others had been debtors, but the tattoos of slavery had reduced them all to a near equal footing. The Council had invited them to journey up the Rain Wild River, to settle and intermarry, to begin new lives. In exchange, the Tattooed had offered their labor in dredging out the river shoals and building the water ladders that had allowed the serpents to complete their migration. Many of the Tattooed had gone on to become valued citizens of the Rain Wilds. Those who had been debtors were often skilled artisans or craftsmen, and they brought their talents to the Rain Wilds.

Unfortunately, some of them had been thieves, murderers, and pickpockets. And some of them brought those skills to the Rain Wilds as well. Despite the chance to make a new life, they had fallen back on what they knew. Tats's mother had been one of them. Thymara had heard that she was a thief, and no more than that, until a burglary had gone wrong and turned into a murder. Tats's mother had fled; no one knew where, least of all Tats, a boy of about ten at the time. Abandoned to his own devices, he had been fostered among the other Tattooed. Thymara had the impression that he had lived everywhere, and nowhere, picking up what food he could as it was offered to him, wearing castoffs, and doing whatever menial tasks he could to earn a coin or two for himself. She and her father had met him at one of the trunk markets, the large market days held closest to the huge trunks of the five main trees of central Trehaug. They had birds to sell that day, and he'd offered to do anything they needed, if only they'd give him the smallest one. He hadn't had meat in months. Her father, as always, had been too kindhearted. He'd put the boy to hawking their wares, a task he usually did himself, and much better, for his voice was louder and more melodious. Still, Tats had been willing, no, eager to earn a meal for himself.

Since that day, two years ago, they'd seen him often. When her father could make work for him, he did, and Tats was always grateful for whatever they could spare. He was a handy fellow, even here in the high canopy where folk who had been born on the ground never ventured. Often enough,

Thymara welcomed his company. She had few friends. The children who had socialized with her when she was small had long grown up, wedded, and commenced new lives as parents and partners. Thymara had been left behind in her strangely extended adolescence. It was oddly comforting to have found a friend who was as single as she was. She wondered why he wasn't married or at least courting by now.

Her thoughts had wandered. She only realized that her silence had grown long when he asked her, "Did you want to be alone tonight? I don't intend to bother you."

"No, you're no bother, Tats. I was just taking some time to myself to think."

"About what?" He settled himself more firmly on the branch.

"I'm considering my options for my future. Not that there are many." She managed a laugh.

"No? Why not?"

She looked at him, wondering if he were teasing. "Well, I'm sixteen years old and still living with my parents. No one's ever made an offer for me and no one ever will. So, either I live with my parents until the end of my days, or I strike out on my own. I know something about hunting, and I know something about gathering. But what I mostly know about both of them is that if I try to go it alone with those as my only skills, I'm going to lead a skimpy life. In the Rain Wilds, it always seems to take at least two people in partnership, working hard, to keep skin and bone together. And I'm always going to be just one."

Tats looked startled at her flood of words and a bit uncomfortable. He cleared his throat. "Why you think you're always going to have to make it on your own?" More quietly he added, "You talk about living with your parents like it's terrible. Me, I'd love to have a mother or a father to stay with." He gave a short laugh. "I can't even imagine having both."

"Living with my parents isn't terrible," she admitted. "Though sometimes, I know my mother wishes I weren't around. Da is always good to me; he lets me know I'm welcome to stay for always. I suppose that when he brought me back home, he knew then that I'd probably be underfoot for the rest of my life."

Tats knit his brows. His confused scowl made the spiderweb across his cheek crawl strangely. "Brought you back home? Where had you gone?"

It was Thymara's turn to feel awkward. She'd always supposed that everyone knew what she was and the story behind it. Any Rain Wilder would be able to tell just by looking at her. But Tats wasn't Rain Wilds born, and she and her kind were not something the Rain Wilders spoke about to outsiders. Just as some of them never spoke to her or looked directly at her, so her existence was not a topic for casual conversation with outsiders. That Tats didn't know meant that most people still considered him an outsider. He truly didn't know. The newness of that thought stung her. She gritted her teeth in a strange smile and held up her hand to him. "Notice anything?"

He leaned closer and peered at her hand. "You cracked one of your claws?"

She choked on a laugh, and suddenly understood something about him that she never had before. He'd acted friendly toward her because he truly didn't know better.

"Tats, what you should notice is that I *have* claws. Not fingernails. Claws like a toad. Or a lizard." She sank them into the branch and drew them back toward her, leaving four stripes of torn bark. "Claws make me what I am."

"I've seen lots of Rain Wild folk with claws."

She stared at him. Then she said, "No, you haven't. You've seen lots of folk with black nails. Even thick black nails. But not claws. Because when a baby is born with claws instead of fingernails, the parents and the midwife know what they have to do. And they do it."

He hitched closer to her on the branch. "Do what?" he asked hoarsely.

She looked away from his intent stare, into the interlacing branches that webbed the night. "Get rid of it. Put it somewhere, away from where people go. And leave it there."

"To die?" He was shocked.

"Yes, to die. Or be eaten by something, a tree cat or a

big snake." She glanced back at him and found she couldn't meet his horrified stare. It seemed accusing, and it made her feel ungrateful, as if she were being disloyal to talk about what happened to deformed children. "Sometimes they strangle the baby or smother it so it doesn't suffer too long. And then they drop it in the river. It depends on the midwife, I guess. My midwife just put me out of the way; wedged me into a forking branch away from any path and hurried back to my mother, who was bleeding more than she should." She cleared her throat. Tats was staring at her, his mouth slightly ajar. For the first time, she noticed that one of his middle bottom teeth slightly leaned past its neighbor. She glanced away from her rapt listener.

"The midwife didn't know my father had followed her. I was not their first child, but I was the first one to be born alive. Da says he just couldn't stand to let go of me, that he felt I deserved a chance. So he followed the midwife and he brought me back home, even though he knew a lot of people would say he was doing wrong."

"Doing wrong? Why?"

She looked back at him, wondering if he were teasing her. He had pale eyes, blue or gray depending on the time of day. But they never glowed. Not like hers. They looked at her without guile. His earnest look almost exasperated her. "Tats, how can you not know these things? You've lived in the Rain Wilds for, what, six years? A lot of Rain Wild children are born, well, touched by the Wilds. And as they grow, they become even more different. So, well, people had to draw the line somewhere. Because, if you're too different when you're first born, if you already have scales and claws, then who knows what you'll grow to be? And if the ones like me married and had children, well, those children would likely be even less close to human when they were born, and might grow to be Sa knows what."

Tats took a deep breath and blew it out, shaking his head. "Thymara, you talk like you don't think you're human."

"Well," she said, and then stopped. For a time, she chased words around inside her mind. *Maybe I'm not.* Did she believe that? Of course not. Well, maybe not. What was she then, if not human? But if she was human, how could she have claws?

Tats spoke again before she could find words. "You don't look that much stranger to me than most of the folk in the Rain Wilds. I've seen people here with a lot more scales and fringe than you have. Not that it bothers me now. When I was little, when I first came here, you were a pretty scary bunch. Not anymore. Now you're just, well, people who are marked. Just like Tattooed were marked."

"Your owners marked you. To say you were a slave."

He flashed white teeth at her in a grin that denied her words. "No. They marked me to try to make people believe they owned me."

"I know, I know," she said quickly. It was a difference that many of the former slaves insisted on. She didn't understand why it was so important to them, but it obviously was. She was willing to let him explain it however he liked. "But my point is that someone did it to you. Before then, you were just like everyone else. But me, I was born this way." She turned her hand over and regarded her black claws curving in toward her palm. "Always different. Not fit for marriage." She lowered her voice and looked away from him as she added, "Not even fit to live."

He didn't reply to her words. Instead he said quietly, "Your ma just came out and looked up here at us. She's still down there, staring at me." He shifted a tiny bit, ducking his shaggy head and bowing his shoulders in toward his narrow chest as if that would make him invisible. "She doesn't like me, does she?"

Thymara shrugged. "Right now, it's me that she really doesn't like. We had a, well, a family disagreement earlier. My da and I came home from gathering, and my mother said that someone had made an offer for me. Not a marriage offer, but a work offer. So Da said I had work already and, well, she got angry and wouldn't even say what the offer had been." She sprawled back on the branch and sighed. The Rain Wild night was deepening around them. Lamps were being kindled in the little dangling houses. As far as she could see, the scattered sparks of the upper reaches of Trehaug sparkled through the network of branches and leaves. She shifted onto her belly and looked down; there, the lights were thicker and brighter in the more prosperous sections of the tree-built city. The lamplighters were at work now, illuminating the bridges that spanned the trees like glittering necklaces strung through the forest. Almost every evening it seemed there were more lights. Six years ago there had been a flood of Tattooed to swell the populations of Trehaug and Cassarick. And since then more and more outsiders had come. She'd heard that the little trading villages downriver had grown as well.

The light-sprinkled forest below was beautiful. And it was hers, yet it would never be hers. She gritted her teeth and spoke through them. "It's frustrating. I've got few enough choices, and my mother is holding one back from me." She glanced up at the skinny boy who shared the branch with her.

Tats's grin, always startling in how it changed his face, suddenly broke through. "I know what your offer is. I think."

"You know what?"

"I know what the offer was. Because I heard about it, too. That was one of the reasons I came up here tonight, to ask you and your da what you both thought of it. Because you've seen more of the dragons than I have."

She sat up so suddenly that Tats gasped. But Thymara knew she was in no danger of falling. "What was the offer?" she demanded.

His face lit with enthusiasm. "Well, there was a fellow who was posting notices at every trunk market. He tacked one up and then read it to me. According to him, the Rain Wild Council is looking for workers, young, healthy workers, 'with few attachments.' Meaning no family, he said." Tats paused suddenly in his excited telling. "So I guess that couldn't be your offer, could it? Because you've got family."

"Just tell," Thymara demanded brusquely.

"Well, here is the gist of it. The dragons are getting to be too much trouble over at Cassarick. They've done some bad stuff, scaring people and acting up, and the Council has decided they have to be moved. So they're looking for people to move them away from Cassarick. They need people to herd them along and get food for them, that sort of thing. And resettle them, and keep them from coming back."

"Dragon keepers," Thymara said softly. She looked away from Tats and tried to imagine what it would be like. From what she had seen of the dragons, they were not easily managed creatures. "I think it would be dangerous work. And that's why they're looking for orphans or people without family. So that no one complains when a dragon eats you."

Tats squinted at her. "Seriously?"

"Well . . ."

"Thymara!" Her mother's sharp call broke the night. "It's getting late. Come in."

She was startled. Her mother seldom called her name in public, let alone desired her presence. "Why?" she called down to her. Perhaps her father had come home and wanted her. She couldn't recall that her mother had ever called her back into the house.

"Because it's late. And I said so. Come inside."

Tats eyes had widened. He spoke in a whisper. "I knew she didn't like me. I'd better go, before I get you in trouble."

"Tats, it's nothing to do with you. I'm sure of it. You don't have to go. She probably just has some chores for me." In truth, she had no idea why her mother would suddenly summon her back to the house. She knew she should probably go down to where their small dwelling swung gently from the branches that supported it. But she wasn't inclined to go. When her father wasn't home, the little rooms seemed uncomfortably small, filled with her mother's disapproval. A sudden obstinacy, very unlike her usual subservience to her mother, suddenly filled her. She'd go, but not right away. After all, what could her mother do? She'd never come up on the flimsy branches where Thymara and Tats now perched. Her mother disdained even the tree-ways in this part of Trehaug. The Cricket Cages, as this district of tiny homes perched high in the upper reaches of the canopy was called, relied on lightweight bridges and fine trolley lines to ferry its populace from branch to branch. Her mother hated living in such a poor section of Trehaug, but the dangling cottages were affordable. Almost everything was cheaper up here in the higher reaches of the canopy.

"Aren't you going in?" Tats asked her quietly.

"No," she said decisively. "Not just yet."

"What were you thinking about, just then?"

She shrugged. "About how much everything has changed." She looked over the branch and down at the glittering lights of Trehaug. Their gleams were scattered and broken by the massive trunks and wide-reaching branches of the rain forest. "My family wasn't always poor. Before I was born, when my parents were first married, they lived down there. Way down there. My father was the third son of a Rain Wild Trader. His family had a share of a claim in the old buried city, and they were fairly well-to-do. But then my grandfather died. My father has two older brothers. The eldest inherited the claim, and the next son had the knowledge of how best to manage it. But there really wasn't enough there to support three families, and my father had to strike out on his own. Sometimes I think that made my mother bitter, even before I was born. I think she'd expected to live an easy life with pretty things and have handsome children who married well."

A strange smile twisted her face. "One little detail, and it might have been different for everyone. I think that if my father had been the eldest son and inherited, someone would have offered to marry me by now, even if I had a tail like a monkey and squeaked like a tree rat."

A bubble of laughter burst from Tats, startling her. After a moment, she joined in.

"Would you have liked that life better than what you have now?" His question seemed genuine.

She snorted at how silly he was. "Well, I liked it better when I was younger and we weren't as poor as we are now."

"Poor?"

"You know. Hand to mouth. Living in the highest reaches of Trehaug where the branches are thin and the paths so narrow; we didn't always live up here."

"You don't seem poor to me," Tats protested.

"Well. We've been richer. That's for sure." Thymara's

mind roved back over her early childhood. They had lived well enough, then. "My da was a hunter back then, and a pretty good one. He did that for a time. And he hunted meat for the dragons for a while, until the Council stopped paying decent wages. That was when he decided to try being a grower."

"A grower? Where? There's no land you can plant in the Rain Wilds."

"Not all food plants grow on land. That's what he always says. Lots of the plants that we harvest for food actually grow in the canopy, in pockets of soil in the bends of the trunk, or with air roots, or as parasites on the trees." She tried to explain it to Tats, even though the idea of it always made her weary. Instead of wandering the branches, tree-tops, and byways of the Rain Wilds, taking meat as he saw it and gathering whatever the canopy offered, her father began to attempt to cultivate a section of the canopy. It was an old idea, but no one had ever been able to make the forest yield predictably for any length of time. But every now and then, someone like her father would think he had it figured out. He had brought together the various food plants and tried to persuade them to grow in the locations he had chosen rather than where Sa had sown them.

Her father was not the first to attempt it. Others had failed before him. He was merely more dogged, more determined than those who had previously failed. Some folks said that determination was a good thing. Her mother had once told her that it just meant that their family had lived in poverty for more years than the others who had tried and failed at the same experiment and quickly gone back to hunting and gathering. Their "gardening" took up a good amount of their time and yielded them less than their gathering, but her father persisted in it because he believed that one day it would pay off for them.

"I could see that could be true about your da," Tats said quietly.

"My mother said that everything she cherished had been sacrificed for my father's dream. Maybe it's true. I don't know. When I was little, and he was a gatherer all the time, we lived in four rooms, built so close to a trunk that they scarcely swayed even in storm winds."

Those were the best houses in the Rain Wilds. The closer one lived to a trunk, the sturdier everything was, and the less wind and rain found them. The trunk markets were closer, and if one went down the trunks, there were taverns and playhouses. It was also true that there was less sunlight close to the trunk, but Thymara had always thought that a body could climb if she had a mind to feel sunlight and wind. The bridges and walkways that spanned the trees near their first home had been stoutly built, their guard walls tightly woven and kept in excellent repair. If she had to climb to find the sunlight, she also had the ability to go down and feel solid earth beneath her feet sometimes. She was never that enthused about those visits to the ground, but her mother had enjoyed them.

"Why didn't you like the ground? Seems the most natural place to live to me. I miss the ground. I miss just being able to run or walk and not be afraid of falling."

Thymara shook her head. "I don't think I could ever trust the ground. Here in the Rain Wilds, if you're close to the ground, then you're close to the river. And sooner or later, the river always rises. Sometimes so suddenly that there is no warning. Anything we build on the ground, we know it won't last. Once, the river rose high enough to flood the old city. That was awful. A lot of workers were trapped and drowned." The wide relentless river frightened Thymara. She knew that seasonally it rose and flooded and that sometimes there had been sudden floods. The water was mildly acidic at the best of times; after quakes, it sometimes turned a deathly gray-white, and when it ran that color, it could mean a man's death to fall into it, and those who had boats knew to hoist them from the water until the river returned to its usual color. Every moment she was on the ground, she dreaded that suddenly the river would rush up and devour her. Only when she was in the sturdy trees, high above the vagaries of the river and surrounding swamplands did she feel safe. It was a foolish fear, a child's fear, but one that many Rain Wilders shared.

Tats dismissed her fears with a shrug. He glanced around at the leafy branches that screened her from their neighbors and from a clear view of either sky above or earth below. "You never seemed poor to me," he said quietly. "I always thought you had it pretty good, living up here."

"It's not so bad, for me. It's harder for my mother. She was used to a fancier way of life, with parties and pretty clothes and fine things. But there are other things I miss about where we used to live. Maybe it was just the age I was. But back then, down there, I had a lot more friends. When we were little, I guess no one cared so much about claws or nails. We just all played on the landings between levels. My father paid for me to be schooled; he bought my books, even though most of the other children paid by the week to borrow them. People thought he really spoiled me, and it made my mother furious about the wasted money. And we used to go places. I remember that once we traveled way down trunk to a play put on by actors from Jamaillia. I couldn't understand what it was about, but the costumes were beautiful. Once we went to a grand entertainment, music, and a play, and jugglers and singers! I loved that. The stage was suspended in an opening among several trees, with the platform that supported it and the seating cross-roped and netted for sturdiness. That was the first time I realized just how big a city Trehaug really was. Leaves and branches hid most of the ground below us, but there was one vista of the river, and overhead, through the hole in the canopy, I could see a huge patch of black sky and all sorts of stars. But the lights of thousands of homes twinkled, too, in the trees surrounding us, and the lantern-lit walkways reminded me of jeweled necklaces reaching from tree to tree." Thymara closed her eyes and turned her face up, recalling that sight.

"And back then, once a month, as a family, we'd go out for an evening meal in Grassara's Spice Bazaar, and we'd have meat as our main course. A whole piece of meat to eat myself, and one for my mother and one for my father." She shook her head. "My mother was discontented even then. But I guess she always was and always will be. No matter how much we have, she wants more."

"Sounds pretty normal to me," Tats said quietly. She opened her eyes and was surprised to see that he had edged closer to her perch without her even feeling it. He was getting better at moving through the branches. Before she could compliment him on it, he asked, "So when did it all change?"

"It changed when my father started putting more of his time into trying to grow things. Seems like every year we had to move a bit higher and farther out." She glanced at Tats. He sat astride the limb, with one ankle locked around his other leg. He looked secure if a bit uncomfortable. His attention to her face made her self-conscious. Was he staring at her scaling? At the tiny scales that outlined her lips, at the nub of fringe that ran along her jawline? She turned her face away from him and spoke to the trees. "The last place we lived before we came to the Cricket Cages was the Bird Nests. Those used to be the poorest part of Trehaug. But then the Tattooed came and then other newcomers, and we got pushed out of there."

The houses in the Bird Nests had consisted of small rooms, woven of vine and lath, with airy narrow pathways that led down several levels before one reached the good wide walkways and branch paths. "We lived in the Bird Nests for only a couple of years before we saw a flood of artists and artisans moving in. A lot of them were Tattooed, new to the Rain Wilds and needing cheaper rents and neighborhoods where their neighbors would not complain about noise and parties and strange lifestyles." Thymara smiled to herself. She had loved living in the Bird Nests as much as her mother had despised it. Artists displayed their creations on every branch. The poorest section of the city became rich in beauty. Wind chimes hung at every crossroads, the safety walls along the paths were tapestries of colored string and beads, and faces were painted on the rough bark of the tree branches that supported the flimsy homes. Even her family's chambers became bright with color, for her father often was offered only barter for the small crops he managed to grow. Long before Diana earned a reputation as an inspired weaver, Thymara wore a sweater and scarf made by her clever fingers and the carved chest that held her clothing had been made by Raffles himself. She loved those things not because they were valuable, but because they were daring and new. It was only later that her mother would be able to sell them for prices that amazed them all, but did not console Thymara for their loss.

As always happens, or so her father said, the wealthy patrons of the artists began to frequent the Bird Nests. Not content to purchase merely what the artists made, the patrons began to buy their lifestyles as well. Soon the sons and daughters of the wealthier Rain Wild Trader families were living among them, behaving as if they were artists but creating nothing save noise, traffic, and a wild reputation for the Bird Nests. Their families were able to pay much higher rents than her father could afford. The wealthy folk who had holiday homes among them demanded safer walkways and wider branch roads, and so they were taxed accordingly. Shops and cafés moved into adjacent trees. The artists who had established themselves were delighted. They were becoming wealthy and well known. "But the high rents pushed us right out. We couldn't afford to pay the taxes anymore, let alone eat in the cafés. We had to sell off all the art my father had received as barter, take what coin we could get, and move up again." She craned her head and looked up. A few yellow lights in tiny cottages flickered above. "I suppose the next time we get pushed out we'll end up in the Tops. You get light every day up there, but I hear the rooms rock in the wind almost all the time."

"I don't think I'd like all that swaying," Tats agreed.

"Well, no. But I like it here in the Cricket Cages. We get plenty of rainwater, so we don't have to haul it ourselves or buy it from the water carriers. My mother wove us a bathing hammock when we first moved here, and it's lovely in the summer when the water is naturally warm. Moss grows along the edges, and we get visits from little frogs and butterflies and basking lizards. And it isn't so far to climb to find the flowers that reach for the sunlight. When I can get those, my mother takes them down trunk to sell, in the markets where they hardly ever see the flowers from the Tops.

As if the mention of her had summoned her, her mother's voice, sharp and angry, split the peace of the evening. "Thymara! Come in this minute. Now!"

Thymara flowed to her feet. There was something in her mother's voice, something beyond ordinary irritation. A note of fear or danger that set Thymara's teeth on edge.

"Give me a moment," Tats said and began to untangle himself from the tree limb.

"Thymara!"

"I have to go now!" she exclaimed. She took two swift steps toward him. She heard Tats's gasp as she braced her hands on his shoulders and leaped lightly over him, landed on the still-swaying branch, and then scampered across it to the trunk. Something her father had once said of her came back to her. *You were made for the canopy, Thymara. Never be ashamed of that!* Yet this was the first time she had ever felt a strange pride. Her agility had shocked Tats. His shoulders had been warm when she touched them.

"Can I see you tomorrow?" he called after her.

"Probably!" she replied. "When my chores are done."

She went down the trunk swiftly, ignoring the safety line and the foot notches to dig in her claws and rapidly descend. When she reached the two outstretched branches that supported her family's home, she scuttled along them and then swung down to slip in her bedchamber window. She landed on the fat leaf-stuffed cushion that was her bed; it completely occupied the floor of the chamber. A moment later she was in the main room. "I'm home," she announced breathlessly.

Her mother was sitting cross-legged in the center of the small room. "What are you trying to do to me?" she demanded furiously. "Is this your idea of revenge, after your father all but forbade me to speak about the offer? Do you seek to shame your whole family? What will folk think of us? What will they think of me? Will you be happy when they drive us all away from Trehaug completely? Isn't it bad enough that because of you we have to live as close to the edge as we possibly can? Is that why you think it's fine for you to shame us completely?"

There was a flower in the canopy Tops called an archer bloom. It was lovely and fragrant, but at the slightest touch to the stem, tiny thorns launched to pepper the assailant. Her mother's questions stung her like a storm of thorns, each striking her and giving her no chance to react. When her mother paused for breath, her chest was heaving and her cheeks were pink.

"I did nothing wrong! I did nothing to shame myself or my family!" Thymara was so shocked she could scarcely get the words out.

Her words only woke more outrage in her mother's eyes. They seemed to bulge from their sockets. "What! Will you sit there and lie to me? Shameless! Shameless! I saw you, Thymara! Everyone saw you, sitting up there in plain sight, so cozy with that man. You know it is forbidden to you! How can you let him call on you, how can you let him keep company with you, unchaperoned?"

Thymara's mind scrambled to make sense of her mother's words. Then, "Tats? You mean Tats? He works for Da, sometimes, at the market. You've seen him, you know him!"

"I do indeed! Tattooed across his face like a criminal, and all know him as the son of a thief and a murderer! Bad enough that one such as you allows a man to call on her, but you have to pick the lowest of the low to dally with!"

"Mother! I . . . he is just the boy who helps Father sometimes at the trunk market! Just a friend. That's all. I know that I can never . . . that no one can ever court me. Who would want to? You're being unfair. And foolish. Look at me. Do you really think that Tats came to court me?"

"Why not? Who else would have him? And he is probably thinking that you'll get no better offer, so you'll take what pleasure you can get, with whomever you can get! Do you know what our neighbors would do to us if you became pregnant? Do you know what the Council would decree, for all of us? Oh, I tried to warn your father, from the very beginning, that it would come to this. But no, he never listens to a word I say! What can it come to, I asked him, what kind of life can she have? And he said, 'No, no, I'll look after her, I'll keep her from being a burden, I'll keep her from bringing shame on us.' Well, where is he now? Turned down the offer I had for you, without ever hearing me out, and then off he goes and leaves me here alone to deal with you, while you go flaunting yourself through the byways!"

"Mother, I did nothing wrong. Nothing. We sat and we talked. That was it. Tats was not courting me. We had a conversation, and as you yourself said, we were out in plain sight of everyone. Tats was not courting me, he doesn't think of me that way. No one will ever think of me that way." Thymara's voice had started out low and controlled, but by her final words her throat was so tight that she could scarcely squeeze the words out in a high-pitched whisper. Tears, rare for her and painfully acid, squeezed from the corners of her eyes and stung the scaled edges of her eyelids. She dashed them away angrily. Suddenly, she couldn't stand to be in the same room with the woman who had given birth to her and hated her ever since. "I'm going to go sit outside. Alone."

"Stay where I can see you" was her mother's harsh reply.

Thymara didn't deign to give her a response.

But neither did she defy her. She climbed up onto the branch that was the main support for their home and walked out toward the end. That, she knew, would satisfy her mother. The branch led nowhere, and if her mother truly wanted to be sure she was alone, all she had to do was look out of the window. Thymara went farther out than she usually ventured and then sat down, both legs on the same side of the branch. She swung her feet and looked down, daring herself. If she focused her eyes one way, she became aware of the bright lights that sparkled below her. Each light was a lit window. Some were as bright as lanterns; others were distant stars in the depths of the forest below her.

If she focused her eyes another way, she saw the bars and stripes of darkness that latticed the forest below her. A falling body would not plummet straight down to the distant forest floor. No. Her body would strike and rebound and, despite all her resolves, snatch and cling, however briefly, to every branch she struck on the way down. There was no swift plummet to an instant death there.

She'd learned that when she was eleven. It was strange.

She remembered that day in fragments. It had begun with an encounter at the trunk market. As she recalled it now, it was the last time she had ever brought her mother flowers from the Top to sell at the market and accompanied her there. The trunk markets were the best places to sell. Close to the trunk of the trees, the platforms were large and they were often the crossroads for hanging bridges from other trees. The traffic was good, and of course, the farther down one went, the wealthier the passing customers. The flowers she had gathered were deep purple and brilliant pink, as large as her head and brimming with fragrance. Their petals were thick and waxy, and bright yellow stamen and sepals extended past them. They were bringing a good price and twice her mother had smiled at her as she pocketed silver coins.

Thymara had been squatting beside her mother's trading mat when she noticed that a pair of slipper-shod feet below a blue Trader's robe had remained in front of her, unmoving, for quite a time. She looked up into an old man's face. He scowled at her and took a step back, but his blunt, scolding words were for her mother. "Why did you keep such a girl? Look at her, her nails, her ears — she will never bear! You should have exposed her and tried for another. She eats today but offers us no hope for tomorrow. She is a useless life, a burden upon us all."

"It was her father's will that she live, and he prevailed in it," her mother said briefly. She lowered her eyes in shame before the old man's rebuke. By chance, her gaze met Thymara's. She had been staring up at her, hurt that her mother offered so poor a defense of her. Perhaps her look stabbed a drop of pity from her mother's shriveled heart. "She works hard," she told the old man. "Sometimes she goes with her father to gather some days, and when she does, she brings home almost as much as he does."

"Then she should go out daily to gather," he replied severely. "So that her efforts may replenish the resources she consumes. Everything is dear here in the Rain Wilds. Have you lost sight of that?"

"And a child's life is most dear of all," her father had said, coming up behind the old man. He had come down to meet them at the end of their day's trading. He had just come from the canopy; his clothes were bark smeared and leaf stained from his climbing. Thymara was far too old to be carried, but her father had scooped her up and carried her off with him as he strode away from the market. The carry basket on his other shoulder was half full. Her mother had hastily rolled up her mat with their unsold wares inside it and hurried along the walkway to catch up with them.

"Stupid, sanctimonious old man!" her father growled. "And what, I'd like to know, does he do to be worth what he eats? How could you let him speak of Thymara like that?"

"He was a Trader, Jerup." Her mother glanced back, almost fearfully. "It wouldn't do to offend him or his family."

"Oh, a *Trader*!" Her father's voice was scathing with feigned awe. "A man born to position, wealth, and privilege. He earned his place here exactly as any eldest child did; he was wise enough to be first to grow in the right woman's belly. Is that it?"

Her mother was panting as she tried to keep up with them. Her father was not a large man but he was wiry and strong as were most gatherers. Even carrying her, he crossed the bridges and climbed the winding stairs that circled the trees' big trunks with ease. Her mother, burdened only with her market bag, could scarcely keep pace with his angry stride.

"He saw her claws, Jerup, black and curved like a toad's. She is only eleven, and already she is scaled like a woman of thirty. He saw the webbing of her toes. He knew she had been marked from birth and it offended him that you had — kept her. He isn't the only one, Jerup. He simply happened to be old enough and arrogant enough to speak the truth aloud."

"Arrogant indeed," her father said brusquely, and then he had stepped up his pace again, leaving her mother behind.

On that long ago evening, Thymara had finished her day alone on their tiny veranda, fingering the budding wattles that fringed her jawline. Her knees were drawn up to her chest. Occasionally she flexed her webbed toes, regarding the thick black claws that ended each of her toes. Inside the house, all was silent, the silence that was her mother's most potent anger. Her father had fled it, to do late bartering with what he had brought home. One could argue with words, but her mother's silence denied everything. The silence left plenty of room for the old man's words to echo in her mind.

Around her, the canopy of the rain forest rustled and bustled with life. Leaves stirred in the wind. Iridescent insects crawled on bark or flew from twig to leaf. The subtle colored lizards and the jewel-toned frogs basked or crawled or simply sat still, pulsing with life. All the living beauty of her forest home surrounded her. Thymara looked out past her curved toenails to the shadowed distance of the swamp that floored her world. She could not see the ground. In the thicker, safer branches below them, the sturdy homes of wealthy people clustered, offering their yellow window light to the gathering night. That, too, was a sort of living beauty.

She had tried to imagine living somewhere else, some city where the houses were built on the ground and the bright, hot sunlight touched the earth. A place where the ground was hard and dry, and people grew crops in the earth and rode on horses to travel instead of poling a raft or boat. Bingtown, perhaps, where people kept huge animals to pull wheeled carts for them, and no proper lady would think of climbing a tree, let alone spending most of her life in one. Thymara thought of that fabled city and imagined running away to it, but as swiftly as her smile came at the thought, it faded away. Rain Wilders seldom visited Bingtown. Even those of them who were not marked strongly by the Wilds knew that their appearances would attract stares. If Thymara ever went there, she'd have to go cloaked and veiled at all times. Even so, people would stare at her and wonder what she looked like beneath her shrouds. No. That would not be a life to dream about. Strong as her imagination was, Thymara still could not imagine a beautiful or even an ordinary face and body for herself. She had sighed.

And then, it seemed to her, she had simply leaned forward too far. She remembered that first moment with an odd kind of ecstasy. She had spread out her limbs to the wind's rush past her, and almost, almost recalled flying. But then the first branch slapped her face stingingly, and then another thicker branch slammed into her midsection. She curled around it, gasping for air, but flipped past a hold and fell, back first, onto the next lower branch. It caught her across the small of her back, and she would have screamed if she'd had air in her lungs. The branch gave and then sprang up, flinging her into the air.

Instinct saved her life. Her next plummet was through a swathe of finer branches. She clutched at them, hand and foot, as she passed through them, and they sagged down with her, giving her grasping hands time to clamp tight on them. There she clung, mindless but alive, gasping and then panting, and finally weeping hopelessly. She was too frightened to seek for a better hold, too frightened to open her eyes and look for help or open her mouth and cry out.

A lifetime later, her father had found her. He had roped up to reach her, and when finally he could touch her, he had tied her body to his, and then painstakingly cut the thin branches that she would not let go of. Even when they no longer served any purpose, she had held tight to those handfuls of twigs and continued to clutch them until she fell asleep that night.

At dawn her father had woken her and taken her with him for the day's gathering. That day and every day after, she was always with him. She thought on that now and a chill question rose in her. Had he done so because he thought she had tried to kill herself? Or because he thought her mother had pushed her?

Had her mother pushed her?

She tried to recall that moment before the fall. Had a touch from behind given her momentum? Or was it only her own despair drawing her down? She couldn't decide. She blinked her eyes and ceased trying to recall the truth. The truth didn't matter. It was a thing that had happened to her, years ago. Let it go.

She felt the branches of her perch give and smelled her father's pipe as he ventured out to join her. She spoke without looking at him. "Has she said any more about the offer for me?"

"No. But I visited down branch, and Gedder and Sindy asked me what decision you had made. I had suspected your mother would brag to Sindy before she had even spoken to you and me about it. The offer is a bad one, Thymara. It's not for you, and I'm angry that your mother even considered you for it. It's more than dirty and hard; it's dangerous to the point of no return." Her father was scowling, and his words came faster with his cascading anger. "I'm sure you've heard talk. The Rain Wild Council has long been weary of pouring resources into feeding the dragons. Tintaglia ceased keeping her end of the bargain long ago, and yet here we are, paying taxes to hire hunters or, worse, bring in sheep and cattle to keep the dragons fed. There is no end in sight to it, either, for all have heard tales of the longevity of dragons, and it is obvious to all that these dragons will never be able to feed themselves. When Selden of the Khuprus and Vestrit Traders was present, he kept the Council soothed by promising them that Tintaglia and her new mate must eventually come and help with the problem. And he bullied them a bit by saying that if they neglected the dragons or were deliberately cruel to them, Tintaglia would certainly be angered. Well, Selden has been called away to Bingtown. The Elderlings Reyn and Malta Khuprus have spoken out on the dragons' behalf, but they are not as persuasive as young Selden. The entire city is tired of living with a horde of hungry dragons nearby, and who can blame them?

"But for the first time, the Council heard proposals for dealing with the situation. It was a closed session, but no door is so tight that rumors cannot escape it. One angry member of the Council said that the dragons have no future and that it would be kinder to put them out of their misery. No sooner had Trader Polsk spoken than Trader Lorek rose to denounce him and say that he but hoped to salvage the dragon corpses and sell them off. There have been rumors of the Duke of Chalced offering enormous sums of money for a whole dragon, alive or pickled, it was all one to him, and lesser sums for any part of a dragon. It is well known that Polsk's affairs have suffered lately and that he might be tempted by such offers. There are rumors that already one dragon was lured away from the herd and slaughtered for trophies. All that is known for certain is that one dragon disappeared in the night. One member of the Rain Wild Council claims it was done by Chalcedean spies; others suspect their fellows, but most think the pathetic creature wandered off and died. So Polsk repeated that the dragons seemed in such poor condition that it would be mercy to kill them.

"Trader Lorek asked him if he did not fear that Tintaglia might visit the same sort of 'mercy' on Trehaug. So then another Council member pointed out that we have had offers from wealthy nobles and even cities hoping to buy dragons. Surely, he said, that was better and more sensible than killing valuable creatures. They proposed sending out notices to those considered most likely to be able to purchase a dragon, advertising the colors and genders available and rewarding the highest bidders with the dragons of their choosing.

"Dujiaa, the woman who advises the Council on matters relating to the Tattooed, stood up angrily to protest that. She is among those who can hear the dragons, and so she spoke out strongly saying that creatures that can think and speak as the dragons do are not animals to be sold on an auction block. A few of the other Traders who dispute that the dragons are anything but animals said that she was taking the matter too seriously, that creatures that can only communicate with some people rather than everyone should not be treated as if they are equal to humans. And then, of course, the arguments degenerated. Some demanded to know if that meant speakers of foreign languages were not full humans. Someone else quipped that surely that explained Chalcedeans. That, from what I was told, at least broke the tension, and people began to discuss all sorts of possible solutions to the dragon problem."

Thymara listened raptly. Her father did not often discuss Rain Wild politics with her. She had heard scattered rumors of problems with the dragons, but had not paid much attention to the details before now. "Why cannot we just ignore the dragons, then? If they are dying off, then soon the problem will have solved itself."

"Not soon enough, I fear. Those that remain alive are tough, and some say becoming more vicious and unpredictable every day."

"Seems to me that we can scarcely blame them," Thymara said quietly. She thought back to the shining promise the newly hatched dragons had seemed to offer on that long-ago day and shook her head over what had become of them.

"Blame them or not, the situation cannot go on. The diggers at Cassarick have refused to try to do any more work there while the dragons are loose. They're a hazard. They have no respect for humans. They've had problems with dragons following the workers down into the excavations, and knocking loose the blocking and supports. One worker was chased. Some people say that the dragon wanted to eat him, others that he provoked the dragon, and still others that the dragon was after the food he was carrying. It all comes down to the same thing. The dragons are both a danger and a nuisance to the people who have moved to Cassarick to develop the digs there. And there have been a series of incidents involving the dead. At a recent funeral, a family was committing a grandmother's body to the river. They let the river take the bound corpse, and as they were casting the wreaths and flowers out onto the river, a blue dragon waded out, seized the body, and ran off into the forest with it. The family gave chase, but couldn't catch up with it. None of the dragons will admit it happened, but the family is virtually certain that their grandmother's body was devoured by a dragon. And, of course, the worry is that while they may begin by sating their appetites with our dead, it may not be long before they eat the living."

Thymara sat in shocked silence. Finally she said quietly, "I suppose they are not what I thought dragons would be. It's disappointing to know that they are no more than animals."

Her father shook his head. "Worse than the lowest beasts, my dear, if what we are hearing is true. Dragons can speak and reason. For them to sink to those sorts of things is inexcusable. Unless they are deranged. Or simple."

Thymara unwillingly dragged out her memories of the hatch. "They did not seem healthy when they emerged from their cocoons. Perhaps their minds are as badly formed as their bodies."

"Perhaps." Her father sighed. "Reality is often unkind to legends. Or perhaps, in the distant past, dragons were intelligent and noble. Or perhaps we have looked at the images the Elderlings left us and decided to imagine them as other than they really were. Still, I have to agree with you. I think I am as disappointed as you are, to find them such low beasts."

After a time she asked, "But what does any of this have to do with me?"

"Well, Gedder and Sindy only had the bones of it, but after much debate, the Council has decided on the obvious. The dragons must be moved away from Cassarick. Selden the Elderling has spoken of a place far upriver, a place where dragons and Elderlings once lived side by side, with plentiful hunting and elegant palaces and gardens . . . well . . . it all sounds to me like a tale of a place that might have existed long ago, when both Trehaug and Cassarick were aboveground. Several years ago, he proposed an expedition to search for it. No one rose to the bait at the time. Well, who can say that it is not all sunken and buried in a swamp now? But the Council has chosen to believe it is not; evidently the young dragons have vague memories of it themselves, and some have spoken of it longingly. There are even rumors that it was the capital city of the Elderlings, and that their treasure houses were there. Of course, that has piqued quite a bit of interest. The Council wishes the dragons to leave and go there to live. The dragons have agreed to go, but only if they are accompanied by humans who will hunt for them and assist them on the journey. And so, in their wisdom, the Council has cast about for folk it considers expendable. And that is the 'offer' that has been made for you, for you to be a dragon tender and herd them upriver to a place that possibly no longer exists, and that definitely has never been seen by any Rain Wilder." He snorted. "It will be a thankless, dangerous, and futile task. All know that for days both upriver and down, the area under the great trees is endless swamp, bog, and slough. If there were a great city, our scouts would have found it long ago. I don't know if it's a mirage of riches that greed makes us seek, or exile for the dragons under the pretense of sending them to a refuge."

Her father had become more and more outraged as he spoke. As he did when agitated, he had taken so many puffs on his pipe that Thymara felt she sat in a cloud of sweet tobacco smoke. When he fell silent at last, she turned her head to glance back at him. His eyes were faintly luminescent in the darkness. Her own, she knew, glowed a strong blue, yet another mark of her deformity. She held his gaze as she said quietly, "I think I'd like to go, Father."

"Don't be silly, child! I doubt that any such place still exists. As for making a perilous trip upriver past any charts we have, in the company of hungry dragons and hired hunters and treasure seekers, well, there can be no good end to such an errand. Why would you want to go? Because of things your mother has said? Because no matter what she says about you or to you, I will always—"

"I know, Father." She cut through his rising storm of words. As she spoke, she turned her head to look through the network of foliage at the lights of Trehaug. It was the only home, the only world, she had ever known. "I know that I am always welcome in your home. I know that you love me. You must. You must have always loved me, to salvage my life when I was only a few hours old. I know that. But I think my mother is also right in another way. Perhaps it is time for me to go out and find a life of my own. I am not foolish, Father. I know this can end badly. But I also know I am a survivor. If it looks like the expedition is doomed, I'll come back to you and live out my life here as I always have. But I will have made at least an attempt at one adventure in my life." She cleared her throat and tried to speak lightly as she added, "And if the expedition to move the dragons is successful, if at the least we find a place for them, or if we are wildly successful and actually rediscover this fabled city, think what it could mean for us. For all the Rain Wilders."

Her father finally spoke. "You don't have to prove yourself, Thymara. I know your value. I've never doubted it. You don't have to prove yourself to me, or your mother, or anyone else."

She smiled and again looked over her shoulder at him. "Perhaps not to anyone except myself, Father." She took a deep breath and spoke decisively. "I'm traveling down trunk tomorrow, to the Council Hall. I'm going to accept their offer."

It seemed to take her father a long time to reply. When he spoke, his voice was deeper than usual and his smile seemed almost sickly. "Then I'll go with you. To see you off, my dear."

✦ ✦ ✦

Day the 20th of the Hope Moon

Year the 6th of the Independent Alliance of Traders

From Detozi, Keeper of the Birds, Trehaug
To Erek, Keeper of the Birds, Bingtown

In the sealed scroll case, a message from Trader Mojoin to Trader Pelz. Confidential. Deliver with all seals intact.

Erek,

I note with gratitude that the two cages of Jamaillian king pigeons you shipped to us on the Goldendown *have arrived safely and settled well into their new coop. The size of the adult birds is impressive and I can only hope that their carrying capacity and endurance will match their size. Thank you for sharing this new influx of breeding stock. I hope that Reyall continues to live up to your expectations for him and to make his family proud. His father will be calling upon him soon to meet the family of his Three Ships intended and see if the match is suitable. Please do not advise him of this. His father wishes to see him about his work when he is unaware of a family visit. Again, my thanks for the kings.*

Detozi

✦ ✦ ✦

CHAPTER SEVEN

PROMISES AND THREATS

Because I want to go." She spoke each word crisply and precisely. "Because, five years ago, you promised me I could. The promise was given, in fact, on the same day that you gave me this scroll." Alise leaned across her oversize desk to tap the glass-topped rosewood box lined with silk in which the scroll was displayed and protected. She refrained from handling it as much as possible. Even the necessary work of transcribing it had taken a toll. When she needed to, she consulted the careful copy she had made of the precious work.

"I've scarcely returned home from my travel, my dear. Cannot I have a few days to think on this? Quite honestly, I will admit that I had forgotten I'd promised you such a trip. The Rain Wilds!" He sounded amazed.

Hest's words were not precisely accurate. He had returned from his latest trading expedition to Chalced yesterday afternoon. But Alise had learned, over the years of their marriage, that Hest's return to Bingtown on any given day did not necessarily match his return to the home they shared. As he had so often told her, there were many matters to settle at the tariff docks, merchants to contact immediately to inform them of goods he had secured on his latest venture, and often the sales of those goods took place within hours of their touching the docks. Such transactions necessitated the wine and fine dinner and late-night conversation that smoothed the way for commerce in Bingtown. Yesterday, she had become aware that he had arrived back in town when his traveling trunks were brought up to the house, but when both luncheon and dinner had passed with no sign of him, she had not bothered to wait up. Yesterday had been the fifth anniversary of their wedding. She wondered if he remembered it with the same degree of regret that she did, and then had laughed aloud at the idea that Hest might remember their anniversary at all. That night, she had sought her own bed at her usual late hour, and as they did not share a chamber except on the occasions when he chose to visit hers, she had been unaware of his return home. At breakfast, the only evidence that the master of the house had returned was the presence of his favorite garlic sausages on the sideboard, and the large pot of tea that had joined her favored coffee on the heavy silver service tray. Of Hest himself, there had been no sign.

At midmorning, his secretary Sedric had visited her study, to ask if any vital invitations were still pending, and to inquire if any other important missives had arrived during the master's absence. Sedric had spoken formally, but smiled as he did so, and after a moment his good nature and charm had forced her to return that courtesy. As annoyed as she was with Hest, she would not take it out on his secretary. Sedric had that effect on most people. Although he was only a couple of years younger than Hest and older than Alise, she could not help thinking of him as a boy. It wasn't only that she'd known him since childhood when she and his sister Sophie had been close friends. Even though

he was older than both of them, they had still treated him
as if he were younger, for so he had always seemed to Alise.
There was a gentleness to him that she'd never seen in other
men. He'd always been willing to pause in his day and listen
to their girlish concerns. Such attention from an older boy
had been flattering.

He was, she reflected, still a favorite with her. His at-
tentiveness and interest in her conversation at meals often
eased the sting of Hest's near contempt for her thoughts. Not
only Sedric's manner but his appearance was always charming. His head of gleaming brown curls was perpetually tousled in an artlessly perfect way. His eyes were always bright,
never showing the effects of a late night spent accompanying his master to whatever gambling parlor or theater Hest's
latest merchant partner favored. No matter how short the
notice, Sedric was always able to rise to the occasion, appearing impeccably clad and groomed and yet still retaining
an easy manner that suggested it was effortless for him.

Alise had long since ceased to wonder why Hest made
Sedric his constant companion. In any social situation, the
man was an asset. Born of Trader stock himself, he moved
easily in Bingtown society and with acumen when Hest was
dealing with his trading partners. There had been a flurry of
gossip when Hest had offered Sedric a position as his secretary; it was obviously beneath his perceived social position,
no matter how poor his family had become. Alise had been
a bit startled when Sedric accepted it. But in the years since
then all had come to see that he was far more than a humble
servant. He had proven himself as an excellent secretary to
Hest and certainly as an affable and entertaining comrade
on the long sea trips that Hest had to undertake yearly. He
advised and assisted Hest in matters of dress and grooming. When Hest's sometimes abrupt manner gave offense or
cooled a budding business relationship, Sedric artfully employed his tact and charm to set things to rights.

And when Hest was home, Sedric's affable presence at
her table was something that Alise greatly enjoyed. He ex-
celled at all social occasions from dinners to cards to long
afternoon teas. As she was prone to be a listener rather than

a talker, Sedric enlivened their meals with his jests, wry observations of their latest travel disasters, and gentle harrying of Hest. Sometimes it seemed to her that it was only due to Sedric that she knew her husband at all.

Did she know him at all? She watched Hest now as he smiled distantly at her, so certain that he could postpone this discussion with her. Well they both knew that if he could procrastinate long enough, he'd be off on one of his trading trips again and she'd once more be left behind at home. She firmed her courage and replied to him, "Perhaps *you* have forgotten that you promised me that one day I should visit the Rain Wilds and see dragons for myself. But *I* have not forgotten your promise."

"Nor outgrown your desire for it?" he asked her gently.

She flinched at the barb, wondering, as she frequently did, if he was aware of how often his words stung her. "Outgrown?" she asked him quietly, her voice going wooden.

He came back into the room. He had not entered it in search of her. Rather, he had come in quietly, selected a book from the shelves, and attempted to leave just as covertly. He could walk so softly. If she had not chanced to lift her head, she would never have known he'd been there. Her words had detained him just as he'd stepped outside the door. Now he closed it firmly behind him. The book he'd chosen was still in his hands. It was an expensive one, she noted, bound in the new way. He turned it gently as he mused over her question.

"Well, my dear, you know that times have changed. Dragons were quite fashionable the year we were wed, but that was five years ago. Tintaglia had only recently appeared, and Bingtown was just emerging from the ashes, so to speak. Talk of dragons and Elderlings and new treasure cities as well as our independence from Jamaillia—well, it was a heady mix, was it not? All the ladies in their Elderling cosmetics and every fabric patterned to look like scales! It was no wonder dragons fired your imagination. You'd come of age in a harsh time in Bingtown. You needed to escape reality, and what could be a better fantasy than tales of Elderlings and dragons? Trade was in a shambles with the

New Traders and their slave labor undercutting all our established ways. Your family fortunes were suffering. And then we had a war. If Tintaglia hadn't appeared and come to our aid, well, I think we'd all be speaking Chalcedean now. And then she locked us into that bargain that we'd help her serpents get up the river and tend the new dragons when they hatched. Well, we certainly discovered that the reality of a dragon was far different from any fantasy you might have imagined."

He gave a small snort of disdain. Tucking his book under his arm, he wandered across the room to the windows and looked out over the gardens below. "We were fools," he said quietly. "Thinking we could negotiate with a dragon! Well, she got the best of us, didn't she? We're as close to being at true peace with Chalced now as we've ever been, trade is rebuilding, Bingtown rejuvenating, and Tintaglia has found a mate for herself and hardly ever comes to call. It should be a better life and time for everyone! But the Rain Wilders are still dealing with her errant offspring and the expenses they create. They eat constantly, trample the earth to muck, foul everywhere, and hamper efforts to explore the underground ruins. They are pathetic cripples, unable to hunt or care for themselves. All the Traders must contribute to pay for hunters to keep them fed. With no return for us! No one thought to write an end clause for that agreement. And from what I hear, it will never change. Those sorry creatures will never be able to take care of themselves, and who knows how long they will live? We've waited five years for them to grow up and become independent. They haven't. It would be a mercy to put them down."

"And profitable, too," Alise said coldly. She felt silence growing in her. Sometimes it reminded her of a fast-growing ivy; silence covered her and cloaked her, and she suspected that one day she would smother in the silences Hest could create. It was an effort to break through that strangling quiet, but she did it. "All have heard how much the Duke of Chalced would pay for even one scale of a real dragon. Think how much he'd give for a whole carcass." When she thrust a cutting remark into one of Hest's pauses, it was like

trying to stab a knife into hardwood. It never seemed to
stick and left scarcely a mark.

Now he turned toward her as if startled. "Did I hurt your
feelings, my dear? I didn't mean to. I forgot how sentimental you are about those creatures." He smiled at her dis-
armingly. "Perhaps I'm too much the Trader this day. You
should expect it of me when I've just returned from a trip.
It's all I talked about with anyone for the last two months.
Profitability and tightly written contracts and well-negoti-
ated bargains. I'm afraid that's what fills my mind."

"Of course," she said, looking down at her desk. And, *Of
course,* she said to herself as her anger slipped away from
her. It wasn't gone, only sunken in the bog of uncertainty
that engulfed her life. How could she hold on to her anger
when, in an instant, he could sidestep it in a way that made
her feel it was unjustified? He had been preoccupied, that
was all. He was a busy man, immersed in trade negotiations
and contracts and social details. He undertook those things
for both of them, so that she could live in the quiet social
backwater that she seemed to prefer. She could not expect
him to be perfectly tuned to her life. More than once, he had
gently pointed out to her that she always seemed to put the
worst possible interpretation on his words whenever they
had even the mildest disagreement. More than once, he had
expressed bewilderment that she sometimes resented how
he sheltered her.

A tiny childish part of her stamped and gritted her teeth.
*And he has sidestepped your question as well. Demand an
answer. No. Just tell him you are going. You have the right.
Just tell him that.*

Hest was already drifting toward the door. He stopped
by a tobacco humidor, opened it, and scowled. Evidently the
servants had not replenished it since his return.

"I've planned my journey to the Rain Wilds. I'll be departing at the end of this month." The words leaped out of
her mouth. Lies, every one of them. She'd made no specific
plans, only dreamed.

He turned to look at her, his brows arched in surprise.
"Indeed."

"Yes," she asserted. "It's a good time to travel to the Rain Wilds, or so I'm told."

"Alone?" he asked, sounding scandalized. And a moment later, annoyed as he said, "I've made commitments of my own, my dear. It would be impossible for me to break them. I can't go with you at the end of the month."

"I hadn't given that part much thought," she admitted. *Any thought at all.* "I'm sure I can find an appropriate companion for the journey." She wasn't sure of that at all. It had never occurred to her that she might require such a person. She had thought, somehow, that marriage had put her beyond the need for chaperonage. "I cannot imagine that you could doubt my fidelity to you," she observed. "I am not chaperoned in the months when you are away on your trading journeys. Why should I be chaperoned when I travel?"

"Perhaps we should avoid the topic of 'doubting' anyone's 'fidelity,'" he observed cuttingly. "Or perhaps we should discuss it in terms of presenting a proper appearance. After all, it takes very little for someone to assemble tiny bits of 'evidence' and then see wrongdoing where none exists."

She looked away from him. He seldom missed a chance to remind her of her ill-founded allegations against him. She pushed the stinging memory of that humiliating day away and struggled to think of a sufficiently respectable matron to accompany her as chaperone. "I suppose I could ask Sedric's sister Sophie. But I have heard she is with child and in delicate health, not disposed to visit, let alone travel."

"Ah. Her husband, I see, is far more fortunate than I am in that regard. And your health, Alise?"

"My health is excellent," she replied pointedly.

Hest shook his head in disappointment. He cleared his throat and then asked wryly, "I am to assume, then, that our latest efforts have come to naught?"

"I'm not pregnant," she said bluntly. "I assure you if I were it would be the first piece of news I would give you." She stopped short of asking him how he could possibly imagine she would be pregnant. He'd been away three months, and in the two months he had been home prior to that, he'd visited her bedchamber exactly twice. The infrequency and brevity of his performances were more relief than disappointment now. He visited her, she thought, with the regularity of a man performing a scheduled task, and with all the enthusiasm. Sometimes she wondered if he kept a ledger of his efforts. She imagined him ticking an item on his social calendar. *Attempted impregnation. Results still in doubt.* It humiliated her now to recall her brief and girlish infatuation with him before their wedding.

In the months and then years that had passed since she had realized that neither love nor lust would have a place in her marriage, she had never denied herself anything in her quest for knowledge. To balance that, she had never denied Hest on the occasions when he came to her chambers to assert his marital rights. She had never wept over his lack of romantic interest in her, nor tried to charm him into changing his mind. She had made only two failed and shameful attempts to pique his sexual interest in her. She did not allow herself to dwell on those humiliating memories. They had prompted him to a mocking cruelty that had branded those two nights forever in her memory. No. Better to submit, almost ignore his efforts, for then his services to her remained brief and perfunctory.

After each visit that he paid her, he waited until she had reported the failure of it before he visited her again. Only twice in the five years that they had been married had she announced a pregnancy. Each time, Hest had greeted the event with great excitement, only to express his frustration and annoyance with her when, a few months later, she had miscarried.

So Hest now greeted her blunt dashing of his hopes with only a small sigh. "Then we shall have to try again."

She quietly considered the weapon he had just handed her, and then, coldly, employed it. "Perhaps when I return from the Rain Wilds. To undertake such a journey while pregnant might endanger the birth. So I think we shall wait until I return before we make another attempt."

She saw her target quiver. His voice was stronger, touched with indignation as he demanded, "Do you not think that producing a son and heir is more important than this hare-brained journey of yours?"

"I am not sure that you think so, dear Hest. Certainly, if it were of the highest importance to you, you might make more frequent efforts in that area. And perhaps forgo some of your own journeys and late-night engagements."

He clenched his hands and turned away from her to stare out of the window. "I am only trying to spare your feelings. I am aware that well-bred women do not suffer a man's needs willingly."

"Dear husband, do you infer that I am not 'well-bred'? For I would agree with you. Some women of my acquaintance would think me absolutely 'unbred' were I to share the details of our private life with them." Her heart thundered in her chest. Never before had she dared to speak so pointedly to him. Never before had she voiced anything that might be construed as a criticism of his efforts.

The jab made him turn back to her. The daylight behind him put his features into darkness. She tried to read his voice as he said, "You would not do that." Plea? Threat?

Time to gamble. She suddenly had the feeling that she must risk it all now or concede defeat forever. She smiled at him and kept her voice calmly conversational. "It would be easiest not to do that if I were away from my usual companions. If, for instance, I went off on a journey to the Rain Wilds, to observe the dragons."

There had been a few times in their marriage when they had dueled like this, but not many. Even fewer were the times when she had won. Once, it had been over a particularly expensive scroll she had purchased. She had offered to return it and let the seller know that her husband could not afford it. Then, as now, she had seen him pause, calculate, and then revise his opinion of her and his options. He canted his head as he considered her, and she wished suddenly that she could see his face more clearly. Did he know how uncertain she felt just now? Could he see the timid woman cowering behind her bold bluff?

"Our marriage contract clearly states that you will cooperate in my efforts to create an heir."

Did he think he had her at a disadvantage? Did he think her memory was not as good as his? Foolish man! Anger made her bolder. "Was it worded that way? I don't recall you speaking it aloud in quite those words, but I am sure I can consult the official document if you wish me to. While I am consulting with the Document Keeper, I can also look up the proviso in which you promised I should be allowed to go on a journey to the Rain Wilds to study the dragons. That clause I do recall, quite clearly."

He stiffened. She had gone too far. Her heart began to hammer. Hest had a temper. She'd seen it taken out on in-animate objects and animals. But she did not think that precedent made her safe from it. Doubtless he classified her with both those things. His face reddened and he bared his teeth. She stood stock-still, as if he were a rabid dog. Perhaps that stillness helped him to gather some control of himself. When he spoke, his voice was low and tight. "Then I think you *should* go to the Rain Wilds."

And then he simply left the room, slamming the door so hard that the water leaped in the vase of flowers on her desk. Alise stood trembling and catching her breath. For an in-stant, she wondered if she had won. Then she decided she didn't care. As she tugged the bellpull that would summon her maid, her mind was already busy with what she needed to pack.

"You've ruined this shirt."

Hest looked up from the desk in the corner of his bed-chamber. His pen was still in his hand, his brow furrowed in annoyance at the interruption. "If it's ruined, then it's ruined. I don't want to hear about it. Just throw it away." He dipped his pen again and scratched away furiously at what-ever he was writing. He was in a bad temper. Best to keep quiet and finish his unpacking for him.

Sedric sighed to himself. There were days, he thought, when he could not imagine any better future than continu-ing to serve Hest. But there were also days, like today, when he wondered if he could tolerate the man for even another minute. He looked a moment longer at the scatter of care-

less burns across the blue silk of the sleeve. He knew just
how the shirt had been ruined. A pipe, carelessly knocked
out against the door of a carriage, and the flying sparks had
flown back to burn the sleeve before Hest had drawn his arm
back in. With his fingernail, he scratched at the fabric, and
the small scorches became tiny holes. No. There was no way
to salvage it. A shame.

He well remembered the sunny day and the Chalcedean
market where they had purchased the bolt of silk. It had
been on the very first trading trip he'd made to Chalced with
Hest. Going abroad to trade had been a heady experience for
him. It had enhanced Hest's status in his eyes to see how his
friend and now employer moved so confidently and competently through the clatter and clutter of the foreign market. It
had still been a dangerous venture then, two Bingtown merchants venturing into a market in the Chalcedean capital.
The war was still fresh in everyone's mind, the peace too
new to trust. For every merchant anxious to capture a new
market, there were two Chalcedean soldiers still smarting
at how Bingtown had repelled their invasion and willing to
settle the score with an unwary foreigner. Widows clustered
to beg at the market outskirts routinely spat and cursed at
them. Orphans alternated between begging for coins and
throwing small rocks at them.

For a moment he recalled it all, the hot sun, the narrow
winding streets, the hurrying slave boys in their short tunics
with dusty bare legs, the thick smell of harsh smoking herbs
wafting through the open market, and the women, draped
in lace and silk and ribbons so that they moved like small
ships transporting mounds of fabric rather than people. Best
of all, he recalled Hest at his side, striding along, his mouth
set in a grin, his eyes avid for every exotic sight. He'd darted
from one market stall to the next as if there were a race to
find the most desirable goods. He did not let the awkwardness of his Chalcedean slow the trading process. If a vendor
shook his head or shrugged his shoulders, Hest spoke louder
and gestured more widely until he made himself understood. He'd bought the bolt of blue silk for a careless scattering of coins, and then hastened off, leaving Sedric to finish

the transaction and hurry after him, the roll of azure fabric bouncing on his shoulder. Later that day, they'd visited a tailor's shop near their inn, and Hest had ordered the silk converted to three shirts for each of them. The shirts had been ready and waiting for them on the following morning. "You have to love Chalced!" he'd exclaimed to Sedric when they picked them up. "In Bingtown, I'd have paid three times as much and had to wait a week for them to be finished." And the fit of each shirt had been perfect.

And now, two years later, the last of Hest's blue silk shirts had been spoiled by careless ash. The last shared memento of that first journey together, gone. It was so typical of Hest. He was all passion and no sentiment. All three of Sedric's blue silk shirts were still intact, but he doubted he would wear them again. Sedric gave a small sigh as he folded the shirt a last time and reluctantly consigned it to the discard pile.

"If you've something to say to me, say it. Don't moon about in here, sighing like a lovesick maiden in a bad Jamaillian play." Whatever calculations he had been making had gone badly; Hest thrust the pages away from him, sending several wafting to the floor. "You remind me too much of Alise, with her reproachful glances and secret sighs. The woman is intolerable. I've given her everything, everything! But all she does is mope or suddenly announce she is taking more."

"She mopes only when you mistreat her." The words were out of Sedric's mouth almost before he knew he was going to say them. He met Hest's flinty gaze. There was a quarrel foretold in the lines at the corners of his eyes and the flat disapproval of his thinned lips. Too late for apologies or explanations. Once Hest wore that look the quarrel was inevitable. Might as well have his full say while he had a chance, before Hest riposted with his icy sharp logic and cut his opinion to shreds. "You *did* promise Alise that she might go to see the dragons. It was in your marriage vows. You spoke it aloud and then you signed your name to it. I was there, Hest. You do remember it, and you do know what it means to her. It's not some girlish whim; it's her life's interest. Her study of the creatures and her scholarly pursuit of knowledge about them are really all she has to take pleasure in, Hest. It's wrong of you to deny that to her. It's not fair to her. And it's dishonorable of you to pretend that you don't recall your promise to her. Dishonorable and unworthy of you."

He paused to take a breath. That was his mistake.

"Dishonorable?" Hest's voice was chill, disbelieving. "Dishonorable?" he repeated, and Sedric felt his breathing grow shallower.

Then Hest laughed, the sound like a burst of cold water over Sedric. "You're so naive. No. No, that's not it. You're not naive, you're childishly obsessed with your idea of 'fair.' 'Fair' to her, you say. Well, what about 'fair' to me? We made our bargain, Alise and I. She was to wed me and bear me an heir, and in return, I let her make free with my fortune and my home to follow her obsessive studies. You're privy to my finances, Sedric. Has she deprived herself at all in her pursuit of rare manuscripts and scrolls? I think not. But where is the child I was promised? Where is the heir that will end my mother's carping and my father's rebuking glances?"

"A woman cannot force her body to conceive," Sedric dared to point out quietly. Coward that he was, he did not add, "nor can she conceive a child alone." He knew better than to bring that up to Hest.

But even if he didn't utter the words, Hest seemed to hear them. "Perhaps she cannot force herself to conceive, but all know that there are ways a woman can prevent conception. Or be rid of a child that doesn't suit her fancy."

"I don't think Alise would do that," Sedric asserted quietly. "She seems very lonely to me. I think she would welcome a child into her life. Moreover, she spoke a vow to do all she could to give you an heir. She wouldn't go back on her word. I know Alise."

"Do you?" Hest fairly spat the words. "Then how surprised you would have been had you heard our conversation earlier! She all but refused to do her wifely duties until she had made her trip to the Rain Wilds and returned. She blathered some nonsense about not wishing to travel while she was pregnant. And then put all the blame on me that she is not already pregnant! And threatened to shame me, publicly, for what she deems my failures!" He picked up an ivory pen stand from his desk and slammed it down. Sedric heard the ornament crack and silently flinched. Hest's temper was roused now, and on the morrow, when he recalled how he'd broken the expensive stand, he'd be angry all over again. Hest hissed out a furious sigh. "I will not tolerate that. If my father offers me one more lecture, one more suggestion, about how to get that red cow with calf, I will . . ." He strangled wordlessly on humiliation. Hest's clashes with his father had become more frequent of late, and every one of them put him in a foul temper for days.

"That does not sound like the Alise I know," Sedric said as he tried to divert the conversation. He knew he ventured onto dangerous ground when he did so. Hest was very capable of exaggerating, or slanting, a story to put himself in the right, but he seldom lied outright. If he said that Alise had threatened him, then she had. Yet that seemed at odds with all Sedric knew of her. The Alise he knew was gentle and retiring; yet he had known her to be very obstinate on occasion. Would her obstinacy extend to threatening her husband to force him to live up to his word? He wasn't sure. Hest read his uncertainty in his face. He shook his head at Sedric.

"You persist in thinking of her as some angelic girl-child who befriended you when no one else would. Perhaps she was, at one time, though I doubt it myself. I suspect she was just being kind to someone as friendless and awkward as she was herself. A sort of alliance of misfits. Or kindred spirits, if you would prefer. But she is not that now, my friend, and you should not let those old memories sway you. She is out to get whatever she can from our relationship and at as little cost to herself as she can manage."

Sedric was silent. *Friendless and awkward. Misfits.* The words rattled inside him like sharp little stones. Yes, he had been so.

As always, Hest had told the truth. But he had a knack for studding it with tiny, painful but undeniably true insults. A memory rose, unbidden. A hot summer day in Chalced. He and Hest had been invited to an afternoon's relaxation at a merchant's home. The entertainment had consisted of a wild boar confined in a circular pit. The guests had been given darts and tubes to blow them from. The others had found great amusement in maddening the trapped creature, vying to stick the darts in its most tender places. The culmination of the diversion had been when three large dogs were set on the creature to finish it off. Sedric had tried to rise from his bench and move away. Hest had unobtrusively gripped his wrist and hissed at him, "Stay. Or we'll both be seen as not only weak but rude."

And he had stayed. Even though he'd hated it.

The way Hest now jabbed him with tiny insults reminded him of how he had helped torment the pig. Hest's face then had had that same dispassionate but calculating look that it did now. Going for the tenderest flesh with tiny, sharp words. His sculpted mouth was a flat line, his green eyes were narrowed and cold, catlike as they watched him.

"I wasn't friendless," he said quietly. "Because Alise was my friend. She came to visit my sisters, but she always took time to speak with me. We exchanged favorite books and played cards and walked in the garden." He thought of himself as he had been then, shunned by most of the young men at his school, a source of bafflement to his father, a target for teasing by his sisters. "I had no one else," he said softly, and then hated himself for how much those words betrayed about him. "We helped each other."

But the whispered comment seemed to have touched and softened something in his friend. "I'm sure you did," Hest agreed smoothly. "And the little girl that she was then was probably flattered by the attention of an 'older man.' Perhaps she was even infatuated with you." He smiled at Sedric and said quietly, "How could I blame her? Who wouldn't have been?"

Sedric stared at him, breathing quietly. Hest returned his gaze, unflinching. And now his eyes were the deep green of moss under shade trees. Sedric turned away from him, his heart tight in his chest. Damn him. What gave him such power? How could Hest hurt him so, and a moment later melt his heart?

He looked down at his hands, still holding Hest's blue shirt. "Do you ever wish it were different?" he asked quietly. "I am so tired of the deceptions and trickery. So tired of holding up my end of the pretense."

"What pretense?" Hest asked him.

Sedric looked up at him, startled. Hest returned his gaze blandly. "If I had your wealth," Sedric ventured. "I'd go somewhere else, away from everyone who knows us. And start a new life. On my own terms. Without apologies."

Hest spat out a laugh. "And very quickly there would be no wealth. Sedric, I've told you this before. There is an immense difference between having money and true wealth. My family has wealth. Wealth takes generations. Wealth has roots that stretch far and wide, and branches that reach out and twine through a city. You can take money and run away with it, but when the money is gone, you are poor. And all you have before you is the prospect of long years of very hard work so you can build a foundation for wealth for the next generation.

"And that's something I have absolutely no interest in doing. I like my life, Sedric. I like it the way it is. Very much. And that is why I do *not* like it when Alise proposes to upset it. I dislike it even more when you seem to think that's acceptable behavior on her part. If I fell, what do you think would become of you?"

Sedric found himself looking down at his feet as if shamed as he mustered the last of his courage to take Alise's side. "She needs to go to the Rain Wilds, Hest. Give her that, and I think it will be enough to last her the rest of her life. One chance to be out in the world, doing things, seeing things for herself instead of reading about them in tattered old scrolls. That's all. Let her go to the Rain Wilds. You owe her that. I owe her that, for wasn't I instrumental in bringing her to marriage with you! Give her this small, simple thing. What can it hurt?"

Hest snorted, and when Sedric lifted his eyes to look at him, his face was set in mockery, and his eyes were green ice. Sedric reviewed his own words and saw his mistake. Hest never liked to hear that he owed anyone anything. Hest rose from his desk and paced a turn around the room. "What can it hurt?" he asked, in a voice that mimicked Sedric's. "What can it hurt? Only my wallet. And my reputation! My pride, too, but I suppose that is nothing to you. I should let my wife go traipsing off to the Rain Wilds, unaccompanied, on some crackpot mission to find an Elderling hiding under a rock or to save the poor crippled dragons? It's bad enough that she spends every spare hour of her day immersed in such idiocy; should I let her make her obsession public?"

Sedric kept his voice reasonable. "It's not an obsession, Hest. It's her scholarly interest . . ."

"Scholarly interest! She's a woman, Sedric! And not a particularly well-educated one! Look at the schooling she received, sharing a governess with her sisters! A cheap governess, probably couldn't teach them much more than how to read and do arithmetic and embroider little flowers on scarves. Just enough education to get her into trouble, if you ask me! Just enough to make her give herself airs about being a 'scholar' and think she can buy a passage on a ship and go off on her own, with no thought at all about propriety or her duties to her husband and family. And never a pause, I'm sure, to wonder how much such a frivolous trip will cost her husband!"

"You can well afford it, Hest! Just the other day, I was listening to Braddock talking about how much his wife spends on dresses and little parties for her friends and her constant refurbishing of their home. Alise costs you none of that; she lives as simply as can be, except for the materials she requires for her scholarly pursuits. Really, Hest, don't you feel you owe her that outlet, after all the years she has waited? So let her make her journey. You've plenty of connections up the Rain Wild River. A word from you would probably win her free passage on the *Goldendown* or any other liveship. And I can think of half a dozen Rain Wild Traders who would be delighted to offer her hospitality, no matter how eccentric she might be. They'd do it to gain favor with you and—"

"Favor I'd later have to pay back. And you said it just now, yourself. 'No matter how eccentric she might seem!' There's a fine recommendation for me. I can hear it now. 'Oh, yes, we had Hest Finbok's mad wife come stay with us. Spent all her time nosing about in the ruins and chatting up the dragons. Delightful woman. Her brain is as riddled as a tree full of beetles.'"

Hest was adept at voices and mannerisms. Upset as he was with him, still Sedric had to stifle the impulse to smile as his friend suddenly became a gossipy old woman with a swampy Rain Wild accent. He held his tongue and shook his head at him rebukingly.

Hest spoke decisively. "I don't care what she says or what she has arranged. She can't go. Certainly not alone."

Sedric found a voice. "Then don't send her off alone. See this as the opportunity it is! Go to the Rain Wilds with her. Freshen up your trade contracts there; it must be six years since you last visited—"

"And for very good reasons. Sedric, you cannot imagine how that river smells. Nor the endless gloom of that forest. People living in houses made of paper and sticks, eating lizards and bugs. And half of them are touched by the Rain Wilds in ways that make me shudder just to look at them. I can't help myself. No. Going face-to-face with the Rain Wild Traders would only damage my contacts there, not strengthen them."

Sedric pursed his lips for a moment and then ventured a topic that had been at the back of his mind for some time. "Do you remember what Begasti Cored said to us on our last visit to Chalced? That a merchant who could provide the Duke of Chalced with even the smallest part of a dragon could be a rich man to the end of his days?"

"Begasti Cored. The bald merchant with the horrible breath?"

"The bald, extremely rich merchant with the horrible breath," Sedric corrected him, grinning. "The one who has founded his fortune not on trading vast amounts of anything, but, as he told us, in delivering a small amount of something very rare to the right man at the right time."

Hest gave a martyred sigh. "Sedric, those tales have been circulating for the last year and a half. All know the Duke of Chalced is aging, and perhaps dying. He thrashes about, trying every quackery under the sun in hopes of a cure for death."

"And he has the money to do so. Hest, if you traveled to the Rain Wilds with Alise, you'd have the perfect excuse to get close to the dragons and those who tend them. Alise has contacts with them; I know she does, I've sent off her missives for her and brought dozens of posts back to her. If she goes, you know she'll manage to get to Cassarick, and she'll go directly to the dragon grounds. She'll be as close to the beasts as anyone can get." He found he had lowered his voice as he said, "A few shed scales. A vial of blood. A tooth. Who knows what you might be able to bring back? What we do know is that anything you acquired would be worth, not a small fortune, but a very large one." Sedric let the clothing he had been folding fall from his hands. He sank down onto Hest's bed and said quietly, "With that much money, a man could go anywhere. He could live any way he liked and be above rebuke. Enough money will buy that. Respectability regardless of what you do." He stared through the walls of the chamber into an invisible distance and dreamed.

Hest's voice snapped him back to the here and now. "Do you ever listen to a word I say? I like where I live and how I live now. No one rebukes me. Why would I risk the very comfortable life I have here? Idiocy! I have no desire to traffic in dragon body parts. That is something that I could well be rebuked for."

"We've trafficked in other articles far stranger for less money!" There were words that died in his throat unspoken. What that money could mean to him, to both of them. The life it could buy, far from Bingtown. Hest either could not or refused to consider the possibility.

Hest was unswayed by Sedric's words. "Just now you spoke of respectability. I am respectable now! Will that be so if people see my wife traveling alone to the Rain Wilds? What will they think she is really seeking? Do you think I don't know that people shake their heads and pity us, that she has not yet borne a child? And if she goes trotting off alone to the Rain Wilds, what will the gossip tongues wag then?"

"Oh, for Sa's sake, Hest! She isn't the first Bingtown woman to have trouble conceiving! Why do you think they call this place the Cursed Shores? Hard enough for a family to keep its name alive here, let alone flourish. No one thinks anything about your still being childless, save to offer you sympathy! Look around the town. You're not alone! And as to her traveling by herself, well, I've just shown you the solution: take her yourself. Or find her a companion then, if you will not take the time to escort her yourself. It's easily enough done!"

"Fine, then!" Hest all but spat the words. As quickly as that, he had gone from trying to win Sedric with his antics to giving off sparks of anger. "I shall let her go. I shall let her dash off to the Rain Wilds and content her poor little soul with dithering about dragons and Elderlings. I shall let her spill coins from my purse as if it has no bottom. And you are right, dear, dear Sedric. I shall have no trouble at all finding an appropriate companion for her. You've told me often enough this night what a wonderful friend she has been to you! So, you shall surely enjoy your trip to the Rain Wilds with her. Evidently you've become bored with being secretary to such a dishonorable, selfish man as myself. So serve Alise. Be her secretary. Scribble notes for her and carry her bags. Sniff about in the muck for a dropped dragon scale. It will spare me the bother of having to look at either of you for a month! I have a journey of my own to contemplate. And it seems that I must find some affable companions to share it with me." As if that settled the matter completely, Hest crossed to the room and dropped back into the chair before his writing desk. He took up his pen and studied the pages before him as if Sedric did not exist.

For a moment, Sedric could not speak. Then, "Hest, you cannot mean that!" he gasped.

But the other man ignored him, and Sedric knew with sudden certainty that he did.

✧ ✧ ✧

Day the 17th of the Growing Moon

Year the 6th of the Independent Alliance of Traders

From Erek, Keeper of the Birds, Bingtown
To Detozi, Keeper of the Birds, Trehaug

From the Bingtown Traders' Council to the Rain Wild Traders' Councils at Trehaug and Cassarick. An inquiry into recent rumors and speculations about the health and well-being of the young dragons, and their marketability as stock or as trade items, with references to our original contract with the dragon Tintaglia.

Detozi,

It was delightful to meet your uncle Beydon. He speaks highly of you and is obviously very knowledgeable about pigeons. I have sent with him two sacks of an excellent dried yellow pea. I have found that a regular feeding of it greatly enhances the plumage of my birds. I do hope the rumors that the dragons must be slaughtered due to a disease are false!

Erek

✧ ✧ ✧

CHAPTER EIGHT

INTERVIEWS

Thymara had never felt comfortable meeting new people. Inevitably, they ran their eyes over her and realized that she should not have survived. It was even more uncomfortable to stand alone before a committee of some of the most revered Rain Wild Traders and answer questions about herself. There were eight of them, mostly middle-aged and male, all dressed in their formal Trader robes. They sat in solid chairs made of dark wood in the opulent chamber at a long, heavy table. The floor under her feet was built from thick plank. Even the walls and the ceiling of the room were made of wood. Never before had she been in a structure so heavy and substantial. She and her father had journeyed far down the trunks to reach this place. He was waiting for her outside. It was the Rain Wild Traders' Concourse, a structure so old and so close to the ground that it more resembled a Jamaillian mansion than a Rain Wild house. Only this far down the trunk did such large and imposing constructions exist. She was oddly aware at all times of how massive it was; but instead of making her feel safe, the solidity of the structure seemed to threaten at any moment to crash to the earth below. Even the air seemed trapped and still inside it.

Only two of the committee seemed able to meet her gaze. The others looked aside, or past her, or down at the papers on the long table before them. Of the two who could look at her, one was Trader Mojoin, the head of the committee. He looked her up and down in a way that plainly said what he thought of her before he asked her bluntly, "How is it that you were not exposed at birth?"

She had not expected such a bald question. For a moment, she stood dumbly before him. If she spoke the truth, how much trouble would she bring down on her family? Her father had broken all the rules when he secretly followed the midwife and brought his infant back home instead of leaving her exposed for the animals and weather to finish. She took a breath and hedged. "My defects manifested as I grew. They were not completely obvious at my birth."

Trader Mojoin gave a brief snort of disbelief. One of the other Traders shifted in embarrassment for her. "Do you understand the terms of your employment?" Mojoin asked her bluntly. "Does your family accept that after you leave with the dragons, we will not guarantee your safety or even your return?"

She was surprised at how calm her voice was when she replied. "My parents both signed the papers before you. They understand, and more important, I understand. I am of age to make this commitment." As Mojoin gave a curt nod and leaned back in his seat, she added, "But I would like to know more clearly exactly what my tasks are, and what our final mission is."

He scowled. "Didn't you read the contract you were given, girl? The offer states it plainly. The dragons have requested that humans accompany them up the river to their new home. You'll be assigned a dragon or dragons. You'll assist in moving the dragons upriver to a location more suitable for them, in ways the dragons may request or as you are assigned. You will help provide for your dragon or dragons by hunting or fishing. And you will remain at the dragons' new location until they have established themselves there and are self-sufficient or otherwise no longer need you."

She spoke her next words coolly. "So if my dragon or dragons die, I'm free to return home."

Mojoin sat up straight. "That isn't the sort of attitude we're looking for! We expect you to do all in your power to uphold the contract the Traders signed with the dragon Tintaglia. Your task is to help your dragon or dragons find a better area in which to live, and to become more self-sufficient." He shifted slightly in his seat and added, almost reluctantly, "It's no secret that we are hoping the dragons can lead you to this Elderling city they claim to recall. Kelsingra."

She bit back other words and questions to ask, "Is there a specific location that we are journeying toward? Has anyone scouted it out, so that we might know how long we should expect to travel?"

Mojoin's mouth worked as if he'd tasted something foul and wished he could spit it out. When he spoke, his words were evasive. "The dragons themselves seem to have some inherited memories of where it might be. They will be your best guides in finding an appropriate place where they can establish themselves. While the ancient city may be your eventual destination, it's entirely possible that you will discover a different area better suited to the dragons."

"I see," she responded curtly. And she did. Her father had been right. This was not an emigration, but an exile. A banishment of both the annoying dragons and an assortment of misfits from the population.

"You see? Excellent!" Trader Mojoin's response was instant and relieved. "Then we are in accord." He picked up a seal from the table beside him and stamped the papers. "Once you sign, you are officially hired. When you leave this chamber, you will be given your supply pack and taken down to meet the dragons. You will receive half your wages in advance. You should make your farewells to your family quickly, for you depart as soon as is possible." He pushed a paper across the table to her. "Can you write? Can you sign this?"

She didn't dignify that with an answer. She took up the waiting pen and wrote her name carefully. Then she stood up straight. "That's all, then? You're finished with me?"

"That we are," one of the other men said in a soft voice. Someone else made a noise that might have been an uncomfortable chuckle. She pretended not to notice but inclined her head and stepped forward to receive her stamped copy of the agreement. She was surprised to find that her hands were shaking. It took her a moment to master turning the heavy knob on the large wooden door of the chamber, and then she pushed it too hard and nearly fell out into the antechamber. She caught her balance and then completed her humiliation by shutting the door so firmly that it slammed. The other applicants awaiting their turns looked at her with mild surprise and some disapproval.

"Good luck," she muttered to them, avoiding meeting their gazes, and hurried out of the room. The doors to the outside were even larger and heavier, but this time she was prepared for them. She managed to get through them and out into the air. Even so, it was not the relief she had hoped for. This far down the trunks, so close to the earth and the river, the air seemed thicker and more full of smells. The light was dimmer, too, and she felt as if she could not open her eyes wide enough to see clearly. She spotted her father waiting for her at the edge of the large wooden deck that surrounded the Concourse. She hurried toward him, grasping her contract. At more than arm's length, waiting for her but obviously not with her father, stood Tats.

She spoke in a voice intended to reach them both. "I got it. They stamped it. I'll be part of the expedition to resettle the dragons."

Tats grinned at her, and as their eyes met, he waved his own rolled contract at her. Her father had been leaning with his back to the old-fashioned railing that surrounded the deck. He stood up as she approached and smiled. But her father's voice was grave as he said quietly, "Congratulations.

I know you wanted this. I hope it will be what you think it will be."

"I know it will!" Tats burst out, and her father gave him a look. He hadn't been pleased to see Tats when they arrived, and although he had greeted him politely enough, it had been without the usual warmth he showed the boy. Thymara suspected that her mother had said something to her father about Tats's earlier visit, and she had probably added significance to her report that simply didn't exist. Thymara tried to mend the gulf by moving so that she leaned on the railing between them, linking all three of them into a group. She put her back to the Traders' Concourse and looked out over the river and the swampy land that edged it. It felt odd to be so close to the ground. Behind her, she heard the Concourse door open and shut again. A boy's voice proclaimed, "I'm signed up!" The members of the committee were not taking long to grant their approval stamps. She wondered if they would refuse anyone. She doubted it.

"It's hard to know what it will be, Father. But I know it will be me moving out and standing on my own, and beginning a life that belongs to me. That has to be good, no matter how difficult it is."

"As for me, I can't wait to go see the dragons! They told me that as soon as they've signed up the rest of the group, we'll be heading down there!"

Startled by the stranger's voice, Thymara jerked her head to look at him. He had come to lean on the railing by Tats. She had seen him earlier, when she had been waiting to go in for her interview. He was plainly Rain Wilds born, and marked almost as heavily as she was. Despite that, he was handsome in a strange and feral way. His eyes were the palest blue she had ever seen on a man, his hair thick and gleaming black. His black toe-claws clicked on the wood as he tapped a foot impatiently, jittering with nerves. "It's going to be great!" he assured Tats, grinning widely. He stuck out his hand. "I'm Rapskal."

"They call me Tats," Tats said, shaking his hand, and for the first time Thymara realized that probably wasn't his given name, but something he'd been called since he was small. The stranger was grinning at her now and holding a hand out to her father, who took it, saying, "My name is Jerup. This is my daughter, Thymara."

Rapskal shook her father's hand vigorously, and then asked gracelessly, "So are you going with the dragons, or only her? You look a bit old to be part of this group if you don't mind my saying so. A bit old, and not near strange enough!" He laughed heartily at his own rough jest. Behind him, Tats scowled.

Her father kept his aplomb. "I won't be going. Only Thymara. But like you, I've noticed that most of those going are heavily marked by the Rain Wilds."

"Yes, that you could say!" Rapskal agreed cheerfully. "Either they think it makes us tougher, or they're hoping the dragons and river will do what our parents didn't do when we were born." He swung his gaze to Tats. "Except for you, of course. You don't even look Rain Wilds. Why are you going?" Rapskal seemed to excel at asking questions so directly that they seemed rude.

Tats straightened up, standing half a head taller than the other boy. "Because it pays well. And I like dragons, and I'd like to have a bit of an adventure. And there's nothing keeping me in Trehaug."

The boy nodded cheerily, the light scaling on his cheeks flashing as his lips parted in a smile. His teeth were good, a little too large for his mouth. They showed white in his constant grin. He looked, Thymara thought, like a boy on the verge of a sudden growth spurt. "Yes, yes! That's me, too. Exactly." He leaned over the railing, spat noisily, and then straightened. "Nothing for me in Trehaug for a long time now," he added, and for the first time he looked less than optimistic. But an instant later, the light came back into his pale blue eyes and he declared, "I just got to build something better for myself. That's all. What's past is past. So I'm going to get me a dragon and be best friends with him. We're going to fly together and hunt together and always, always be friends and never angry at each other. That's what I want."

He nodded vigorously at his own fantasy. Tats looked incredulous. Thymara kept her mouth shut, horrified not by his wild dreams but how closely they paralleled her own yearnings. Flying with a dragon, as the Elderlings of old did. How foolish those fancies seemed when he spoke them aloud!

Rapskal didn't notice the strained silence. His eyes sparked suddenly with a new interest. "Look over there! I'll bet that they're looking for us. Time to go get our supply packs. And then down to the dragons! Come on!"

He didn't pause to see if they were following, but darted off to join the group forming about an officious-looking Trader in a yellow robe with a fat scroll in his hand. He was reading off names and handing out chits.

"That Rapskal makes me tired just watching him," Tats said quietly.

"Reminds me of a darter lizard; never still for more than a minute," Thymara agreed. She stared after the stranger, wondering if he were more intriguing or annoying. A strange mixture, she decided. She took a deep breath and added, "But he's right. I think we'd best go find out what we're supposed to do now." She didn't glance at her father as she crossed the deck. She had the oddest feeling of division; she couldn't decide if she wished he would say good-bye now and leave her to whatever came next, or if she wanted him by her side through this process. All of the others seemed to be alone. No parent watched over Tats or Rapskal, and she saw only one other adult lurking at the edge of the clustered youths. For youths they were, for the most part. One or two of the Rain Wilders showing a contract and picking up a chit looked to be in their twenties, but just as many looked to be only fourteen or fifteen.

"Some of them are just children," her father complained. He had followed at her heels.

"And Rapskal was right. All of us are heavily marked. Except for Tats." She did glance at her father now. "And that explains why most of us are young," she said simply. Neither she nor her father needed to be reminded that those who were heavily marked from a young age seldom lived long into their thirties.

Her father caught her wrist. "Like lambs to the slaughter," he said quietly, and she wondered at his strange words and how tightly he held on to her. Then he added, "Thymara, you don't have to do this. Stay home. I know that your mother makes things difficult for you, but I—"

She cut him off before he could say anything more. "Papa, I *do* have to do this! I signed a contract. What do we always say? A Trader is only as good as his word. And I've done more than just given my word, I've signed my name to it." She thought of her dreams of a dragon bonding with her. She would not speak those. Rapskal's extravagant fancy still echoed in her mind. She took a deeper breath and added pragmatically, "And we both know that I do need to do this. Just so I can say that I stepped up and did something with my life. I love being your daughter, but that can't be all I ever am. I need to—" She groped for words. "I need to measure myself against the world. Prove that I can stand up to it and be something."

"You're already something," he insisted, but the strength had gone out of his argument. When she put her hand over his, he released his grip on her wrist. She stopped where she was. Tats, ahead of them, looked back curiously. She shook her head at him slightly and he moved on.

"We should say good-bye here," she said suddenly.

"I can't." Her father seemed horrified at the idea.

"Papa, I have to go. And this is a good time for us to part. I know you'll worry about me. I know I'll miss you. But let's part now, at the beginning of my adventure. Tell me 'good luck' and let me go."

"But—" he said, and then suddenly he hugged her tight. He whispered hoarsely into her ear. "Go on then, Thymara. Go on, and measure yourself. It won't prove anything to me because I already know your measure, and I've never doubted you. But go find out what you have to find out. And then come back to me. Please. Don't let this be the last time I see you."

"Papa, don't be silly. Of course I'll come back," she said, but at his words a prickle of dread had run up her spine. *No, I won't.* The thought was so strong that she couldn't voice it. So she hugged him tightly, and then, as he released her, she pushed her small pouch of money into his hand. "You keep this safe for me, until I come back," she told him. Then, before he could react to that, she turned and darted from his embrace. She wouldn't need the money on their expedition. And perhaps, if she never came back, it would be helpful to him. Let him hold it now and think it meant a promise to return.

"Good luck!" he called after her, and "Thanks!" she called back. She saw Tats look at her father in surprise. He turned as if he, too, would go back to say his farewells, but at that moment, the man with the scroll demanded of him, "Do you want your chit or not? You won't get your supply pack without it!"

"Of course I want it," Tats declared, all but snatching it out of his hand.

The man shook his head at him. "You're a fool," he said quietly. "Look around you, boy. You don't belong with these others."

"You don't know where I belong," Tats told him fiercely. Then he looked past Thymara and asked, "Where did your father go?"

"Home," she said. And she avoided his eyes as she stepped up to the man, showed her contract, and said, "I'll need my supply pack chit now."

THE SUPPLY PACKS were barely worthy of the name. The canvas bags were roughly sewn and treated with some sort of wax to weatherproof them. Inside were an adequate blanket, a water skin, a cheap metal plate and a spoon, a sheath knife, and packets of cracker-bread, dried meat, and dried fruit. "It makes me glad I brought my own supplies from home," Thymara commented thoughtlessly, and then winced at the look on Tats's face.

"Better than nothing," he commented gruffly, and Rapskal, who had attached himself to them like a tick on a monkey, added enthusiastically, "My blanket's blue. My favorite color. How lucky is that?"

"They're all blue," Tats replied, and Rapskal nodded again.

"Like I said. I'm lucky my favorite color is blue."

Thymara tried not to roll her eyes. It was well known that some who were heavily marked by the Rain Wilds had mental problems as well. Rapskal might be a bit simple, or simply have an aggressively optimistic outlook. Right now, his cheerfulness bolstered her courage even as his chattiness grated on her nerves. She was baffled by how easily he had attached himself to her and Tats. She was accustomed to people approaching her with caution and maintaining a distance. Even the customers who regularly sought out her family at the market kept her at arm's length. But here was Rapskal, right at her elbow. Every time she turned to glance at him, he grinned like a twig monkey. His dancing blue eyes seemed to say that they shared a secret.

They squatted in a circle on a patch of bare earth, twelve marked Rain Wilders, most in their teens, and Tats. They'd come all the way down to the ground to receive their supply packs. The contents, they'd been told, should sustain them for the first few days of their journey. They'd be accompanied upriver by a barge that would carry several professional hunters with experience in scouting unfamiliar territory and more supplies both for humans and dragons, but each dragon keeper should attempt to learn to subsist on his own resources as well as maintain his dragon's health as quickly as possible. Thymara was skeptical. As she studied those who would become her companions, she speculated that few of them had ever had to find their own food, let alone consider feeding a dragon. Uneasiness churned in her belly.

"They told us we were to help our dragons find food. But there's nothing in here that's useful for hunting," Tats observed worriedly.

A girl of about twelve edged a bit closer to their group. "I've heard they'll give us fishing tackle and a pole spear before we depart," she said shyly.

Thymara smiled at her. The girl was skinny, with thin hanks of blond hair dangling from a pink-scaled scalp. Her eyes were a coppery brown, probably on the turn to pure copper, and her mouth was nearly lipless. Thymara glanced at her hands. Perfectly ordinary nails. Her heart went out to the girl abruptly; she'd probably seemed almost normal when she was born and had only started to change as she edged into puberty. That happened sometimes. Thymara was grateful that she had always known what she was; she'd never had real dreams of growing up to marry and have children. This child probably had. "I'm Thymara, and this is Tats. He's Rapskal. What's your name?"

"Sylve." The girl eyed Rapskal, who grinned at her. She edged close to Thymara and asked even more quietly, "Are we the only girls in the group?"

"I thought I saw another girl earlier. About fifteen. Blond."

"I think you might have seen my sister. She came with me, to give me courage." She cleared her throat. "And to take the advance on my wages home. Money won't be any good to me where we're going, and my mother is very sick. It might get her the medicines she needs." The girl spoke with unselfconscious pride. Thymara nodded. The thought that she and Sylve might be the only females unnerved her a bit. She covered it by grinning and saying, "Well, at least we'll have each other for intelligent conversation!"

"Hey!" Tats protested, while Rapskal peered at her and said, "What? I don't get it."

"Nothing to get," she reassured him. Then she turned to Sylve and rolled her eyes in Rapskal's direction. The other girl grinned.

Sylve sprang suddenly to her feet. "Look! They're coming for us, to take us to see the dragons."

Thymara came to her feet more slowly. Her pack from home was already on her back. She slung the supply pack they'd issued her over one shoulder. "Well. I guess we should go," she said quietly. Involuntarily, she glanced up the trunk toward the canopy top and home. She was surprised but not shocked to see that her father had lingered and was watching her from the wide staircase that wound up the tree's immense trunk. She waved at him a final time and made a small shooing motion for him to go home.

Tats had followed the direction of her glance. He waved

wildly at her father and then impetuously shouted up to him, "Don't worry, Jerup! I'll watch over her!"

"*You'll* watch over *me*?" she scoffed, uttering the words loud enough that she hoped they'd reach her father's ears. Then, with a final wave, she turned and trooped after the others. They were headed for the river dock, and the boats that would carry them upstream from Trehaug to Cassarick and the dragons' hatching grounds.

"HE DOESN'T FEEL right to me."

Leftrin scratched his cheek. He needed to shave, but lately his skin had begun to scale more on his cheekbones and the angle of his jaw. Scales he could live with, if they'd hurry up and grow in. Whiskers and a beard annoyed him. Unfortunately, trying to shave near scales usually resulted in lots of nasty little cuts.

"He's just not his old self."

The two comments in swift succession was as good as a speech coming from Swarge. Leftrin shrugged at the tillerman. "He's bound to be changed. We knew that going in. *He* knew it and accepted it. It was what he wanted."

"Are you sure of that?"

"Of course I'm sure. Tarman's my ship, the liveship of my family. The bond is there, Swarge. I know what he wants."

"I been on his decks close to fifteen years. No stranger to him myself. He seems, well, anxious. Waiting."

"I think I know what that's about." Leftrin stared out over the ship's wake in the river. Overhead, the stars shone in a wide path of open sky. To either side of them, the tall trees of the Rain Wilds leaned in curiously. It was a peaceful time. From the riverbanks came the usual night sounds of creatures and birds. Water purled past the *Tarman*'s hull as the barge made his way steadily upriver. From the deckhouse, yellow lanternlight shone. The crew was at its evening meal. The clack of crockery, the mutter of conversation, and the smell of fresh coffee drifted out to him. Bellin said something, and Skelly laughed, a warm and gentle sound in the night. Big Eider's chuckle was a deep undercurrent to their merriment.

Leftrin ran his hands slowly over Tarman's railing. He nodded to his tillerman. "He's fine. He knew there would be changes."

"I been having dreams."

Leftrin nodded. "Me, too."

A slow smile spread across the tillerman's face. "Wish I could fly."

"So does he," Leftrin agreed. "So do we."

"WHY DID YOU have to book passage on *this* ship?" Sedric demanded abruptly.

Alise looked at him in surprise. They stood together on the deck, leaning on the railing and watching the thick trunks of the immense Rain Wild trees slip past them in a never-ending parade. Some ancient giants were as big around as watchtowers. Strange, how they made the other behemoths look small. Draperies of vine and curtains of lacy moss hung from their outstretched branches, weaving the trees together in a seemingly impenetrable wall. Beneath the canopy of foliage and moss, the forest floor looked swampy and dismal, a land of endless shadow and secretive light.

She had come out on the deck to enjoy the short span of daylight hours. Although the river flowed through a wide swampy valley, the forest that lined the banks of the Rain Wild River was so tall that the tops of the trees formed a leafy horizon. Above them the stripe of blue sky that showed seemed a narrow ribbon even though Alise knew it as almost as wide as the wandering gray flow of the river.

She had been surprised when Sedric came to join her. She'd scarcely seen him since they left Bingtown. He'd even been taking his meals in his cabin. He had been quiet and withdrawn for most of their journey, more subdued and solemn than she'd ever seen him. Obviously, he was not relishing his duty. For her part, she had been astounded to discover the companion that her husband had arranged for her. It made no sense to her. If he wanted to protect her reputation, why send her off chaperoned by his male secretary? Like many things that Hest arbitrarily decided for her life, he hadn't deigned to explain it to her.

"I'm putting Sedric at your disposal for your Rain Wild folly," he'd announced abruptly on entering the breakfast room the morning after their confrontation. Standing, he had helped himself to food and tea. "Use him however you wish," he'd continued. As Sedric entered, Hest hadn't even glanced at him, and only added, "He's to obey your every command. Protect you. Entertain you. Whatever you wish of him. I'm sure you'll find him delightful." Those last words were uttered with such disdain that she'd flinched.

And then Hest had left the room. As she'd turned toward Sedric in confusion she'd been shocked to see how dejected he appeared. Her efforts at conversation as he picked at his breakfast had faltered and died.

Hest hadn't even waited for her departure date before embarking on another trading jaunt of his own. He'd filled the house with his busyness and invited two of his younger friends to accompany him. In the days before his departure, he'd kept Sedric dashing about on errands, securing papers for passage, picking up a new wardrobe that Hest had ordered, and procuring a stock of excellent wine and viands to accompany him on his journey. Sedric's obvious unhappiness with the situation had made her feel sorry for him, and she had done her best to make her own arrangements for travel, to spare him a bit of time for himself. Yet she could not regret her decision finally to make this journey. And strange as it was that Hest had chosen Sedric to accompany her, she could not have been more delighted with the prospect. The idea of having her old friend to herself for a time while on an adventure to see dragons had filled her with cheery anticipation. She had hoped to find him equally enthused.

But in the weeks before they left, and especially after Hest had departed, Sedric had seemed gloomy, even uncharacteristically snappish with her. He'd obeyed Hest's directive, arriving promptly at breakfast every day to report travel tasks completed and request his duties for the day. They'd spoken, but not had conversations. A few days before their departure, he'd begged some time to himself, to dine with one of Hest's Chalcedean trading partners who had arrived unexpectedly in Bingtown. She'd been glad to let him have the evening to himself, in the hopes it would bolster his spirits. But the next morning, when she asked him if his meeting with Begasti Cored had gone well, he had quickly changed the subject to the details of her own journey, and he found a dozen tasks for himself to do that day.

Once they'd boarded the *Paragon,* she had hoped his spirits would lift. Instead, he'd spent the early days of their journey sequestered in his cabin, pleading seasickness. She'd doubted that excuse; he'd traveled so much with Hest that surely he must have the stomach for it by now. Nonetheless, she'd left him in peace and occupied herself with exploring the liveship and trying to get to know the crew. So she had been cheered when Sedric joined her on deck that day, and pleased that he now spoke to her, even if the question was rueful rather than engaged.

"It was the only ship with room for two passengers that was leaving at the right time," she admitted.

"Ah." He pondered that for a moment. "So when you told Hest you had already booked passage, that was a lie?"

His words were flat, not really an accusation, but they still stung. She retreated but did not surrender. "Not a lie, exactly. I'd made my plans, even if I hadn't yet purchased my tickets." She looked out over the roiled gray water. "If I hadn't said I was going, he'd have ignored me again. Or put me off. I had to do it, Sedric." She turned to face him. Despite his glum expression, he looked rather jaunty in a white shirt and blue coat. The sea wind made his uncovered hair dance on his brow. She smiled at him and offered sincerely, "I'm sorry that you got caught up in my quarrel with Hest. I know this isn't a journey you'd choose."

"No. Nor would I choose a jinxed ship to make it on."

"Jinxed ship? This one?"

"The *Paragon*? Don't look at me like that, Alise. Everyone in Bingtown knows this liveship and his reputation. He rolled and killed his entire crew, what, five times?" Sedric shook his head at her. "And you book us as passengers aboard him for a trip up the Rain Wild River."

Alise turned away from him. She was suddenly very

aware of the railing under her hands. It was made of wizard-wood, as they used to call it, as was a great deal of the ship's hull, and his entire figurehead. The *Paragon* was a wakened liveship, that is, he was self-aware and his figurehead inter-acted with his crew, supercargo, and dock crews just as if he were human. She had heard that liveships were conscious of every word spoken aboard them, and certainly the very light thrumming of the wood beneath her hands made him seem alive. So she spoke her words firmly. "It happened, but I am certain it was not five times. That was long ago, Sedric. From all I have heard, he is a changed ship now, and a much happier one." She shot her companion a look that begged him to either be silent or change the subject. He leaned back from her, raising one well-shaped eyebrow in confusion. She continued quickly, "Knowing what we know now about the so-called wizardwood, I cannot blame him for anything he did. Indeed, to me it is a wonder that the liveships recovered so well from finally grasping exactly what they were and how they had been created. What we Traders did was un-forgivable. In their place, I doubt if I would be so gracious."

"I don't understand. Why should they resent us?"

Alise was feeling more uncomfortable by the instant. She felt as if she were lecturing Sedric for the *Paragon*'s benefit. "Sedric! The Rain Wilders who found the dormant drag-ons in their cases, sometimes incorrectly called cocoons, had no idea what they were. They thought they had found immense logs of very well-seasoned wood, the only sort of wood that seemed impervious to the acid waters of the Rain Wild River. So they sawed that wood up into planks and built ships from it. And if, in the center of those 'logs' they found something that obviously was not part of a tree, they simply discarded it. The half-formed dragons were dumped from their cases, to perish."

"But surely they were dead already, having been so long in the chill and the dark."

"Tintaglia wasn't. All it required for her to hatch was some sunlight and a bit of warmth." She paused, and, un-bidden, a lump rose in her throat. Her words were heart-felt as she said, "If only we had understood earlier, dragons would have been restored to the world so much sooner! As it was, we denied them their true shapes. Instead, we fastened planks made from their flesh into ships. Exposed to enough sunlight and interacting intimately with familiar minds, there was a sort of metamorphosis. And they awoke, not as dragons, but as sailing ships." She fell silent, overcome at what humans, in their ignorance, had done.

"Alise, my old friend, I think you torment yourself needlessly." Sedric's tone was gentle rather than condescending, but she still sensed that he was more puzzled by her reaction than stirred to sympathy for the aborted dragons. She felt surprise at that. He was usually so sensitive that his lack of empathy for either the liveships or the dragons puzzled her.

"Ma'am?"

The man had come up behind her so quietly that she jumped at his voice. She turned to look at the young deckhand. "Hello, Clef. Did you need something?"

Clef nodded, and then tossed his head to flip sandy, weather-baked hair from his eyes. "Yes, ma'am. But not me, not exactly. It's the ship, Paragon. He'd like a word with you, he says."

There was a faint accent to his words that she couldn't quite place. And in her time aboard the ship, she hadn't quite decided what Clef's status was. He'd been introduced to her as a deckhand, but the rest of the crew treated him more like the son of the captain. Captain Trell's wife, Althea, mercilessly and affectionately ordered him about, and the captain's small son who randomly and dangerously roved the ship's deck and rigging regarded Clef as a large, moving toy. As a result, she smiled at him more warmly than she would have toward an ordinary servant as she clarified, "You said the ship wishes to speak to me? Do you mean the ship's figurehead?"

A look of annoyance or something akin to it shadowed his face and was gone. "The ship, ma'am. Paragon asked me to come aft and find you and invite you to come and speak with him."

Sedric had turned and was leaning with his back against

the railing. "The ship's figurehead wishes to speak to a passenger? Isn't that a bit unusual?" There was warm amusement in his voice. He flashed the grin that usually won people over.

Although Clef remained courteous, he didn't bother masking his irritation. "No, sir, not really. Most passengers on a liveship make a bit of time to greet the ship when they come on board. And some of them enjoy chatting with him. Most anyone who's sailed with us more than a time or two counts Paragon as a friend, as they would Captain Trell or Althea."

"But I'd always heard that the *Paragon* was a bit, well . . . not dangerous, perhaps, as he used to be, but . . . distinctly odd." Sedric smiled as he spoke, but his charm failed to win the young sailor over.

"Well, ain't we all?" Clef muttered sharply, and then straightened and spoke directly to Alise. "Ma'am, Paragon's invited you to come and talk with him. If you want me to, I'll tell him you'd rather not." He made the offer stiffly.

"But I'd love to speak with him!" she declared. The words and the enthusiasm came easily, for they were honest. "I've wanted to speak to him since I came on board, but I didn't want to be presumptuous, or get in the crew's way. I'll come right now, if I may! Sedric, you needn't accompany me if it makes you uncomfortable. I'm sure Clef won't mind escorting me."

"Not at all. It will be fascinating, I'm sure." Sedric straightened from leaning on the railing.

"Then let us go, right now."

Clef looked uncomfortable but stubborn as he firmly interjected, "But ma'am, it was *you* the ship wished to speak to. Not him."

She was startled. "Then you think the ship will not wish him to be present?"

Clef rocked his weight from foot to foot, thinking, and then he shrugged. "Don't know. As the man said, our Paragon's a bit odd. Might be offended or might be flattered. Probably only one way to find out."

"Then I'll escort the lady," Sedric responded easily. He

offered his arm and she took it with pleasure. He might have just annoyed her, but it was easy to forgive him.

"I'll just let Paragon know that you're coming," Clef responded quietly. He padded off down the deck, barefoot, swift and silent as a cat. She watched him go and remarked quietly to Sedric, "He's an odd young man. Did you notice the slave tattoo on his face?"

"It looked as if he'd tried to abrade it away. A shame. He'd be handsomer without the scar."

"I suppose in his trade, a scar or two is to be expected. When we came down the docks to board, I noticed that even the figurehead is a bit battered. It looks as if he was carved that way, with a broken nose."

"I didn't really notice," Sedric admitted. A moment later, he added, "I should apologize to you, Alise. I've neglected you shamefully on this voyage. I wasn't in the mood for travel so soon after returning to Bingtown."

She smiled and responded to his polite excuse with honesty. "Sedric, I doubt you would ever be in the mood to travel to the Rain Wilds, no matter how long you'd been at home. And I do apologize that Hest chose to inflict me on you. I truly hadn't expected anything of the sort. I was startled to discover that he thought I'd need a chaperone for the journey, and when he said I must have one, I expected him to choose some respected old hen to cluck and scuttle after me. Not you! I never imagined his sparing your time away from him to escort me."

"Nor did I," Sedric replied drolly, and they both laughed. Alise gave him a genuine smile. This was better, much better. Now he was sounding much more like the Sedric of old.

Without thinking, she squeezed his arm slightly and said, "You know, I've missed our old friendship. You may not enjoy this journey, but I think I'll relish it all the more for your company and conversation."

"Company and conversation," he repeated, and an odd note crept into his voice. "I would think you'd prefer your husband for that."

His comment broke the mood. She was shocked at how

deeply she responded to what probably had been intended as a pleasantry. She very nearly told him how very little company and conversation she'd ever had with Hest. Loyalty tied her tongue, or perhaps shame. She teetered on the unpleasant realization that Hest had so completely silenced her. Even out of his presence, he restricted her words. She had no female confidante to divulge her woes to; she'd never had the intimate friendships that she knew some other women enjoyed. Talking with Sedric, recalling how friendly they'd been in their younger years, had wakened a terrible longing for a friend. Yet he was not her friend, not anymore. He was her husband's secretary, and it would be a double betrayal for her to speak frankly of how desiccated a relationship her marriage to Hest was. It was humiliating enough that he knew she had once suspected Hest of infidelity. It would betray her vows to Hest, and worse, it would put Sedric in an untenable position. No. She couldn't do that to him. Had he noticed her sudden silence? She hoped not. She lifted her hand from his arm and broke free of him, hurrying a little ahead to exclaim inanely, "There is just no end to these immense trees! How they shade the land and water!"

Clef was standing beside the short ladder that led to the foredeck. He offered her his hand, but she waved him off gaily with a confidence she didn't feel. The bulk of her skirts and petticoats pressed against the stanchions as she climbed to the foredeck. At the top, she stepped on the hem of her skirt gaining the upper deck and stumbled forward, narrowly avoiding a fall.

"Ma'am!" Clef exclaimed in alarm behind her, and Alise said, "Oh, I'm quite all right. Just a bit clumsy. That's me!" She patted her hair, smoothed down her skirts, and looked around expectantly. The deck narrowed before her, and there seemed to be an inordinate number of ropes and cleats and things she had no names for. As she advanced to the very point of the bow, she could see the back of Paragon's head below the bowsprit. His hair was dark and curly.

"Please, go on forward to speak to him," Clef urged her. Behind her, she heard Sedric's muttering as he gained the deck. She didn't look back at him, but pushed forward until she leaned on a railing and could look over the side. She had known, but it was still a bit startling to see that the much larger-than-life figurehead was not clothed. His bare tanned back was toward her. His muscular arms were crossed in front of him.

"Good day," she began and then halted, tongue-tied. Was that how one addressed a liveship? Should she call him "sir" or "Paragon"? Treat him as a man or a ship?

At that moment, he twisted his torso and neck to look back at her. "Good day, Alise Kincarron. I'm pleased to finally meet you."

His eyes were a pale blue, startling in his weathered face. She could not look away from him. He had the coloring of a man but the fine grain of his wizardwood showed in his face. It looked as flexible as skin but obviously was not. She realized she was staring and looked aside. "Actually, my name is Alise Finbok," she began, and she then wondered how he had known her maiden name at all. She pushed the unsettling thought aside and decided to be both bold and blunt. "I'm so pleased to speak with you as well. I felt shy about coming forward to meet you; I wasn't quite sure of the protocol. Thank you so much for inviting me."

Paragon had turned away from her, putting his attention back on the river. He shrugged one bare shoulder. "There is no protocol that I know of for speaking to a liveship, other than what each ship makes for himself. Some passengers come and greet me immediately, before they board. A few never speak a word to me. At least, not intentionally." He flashed her a knowing grin over his shoulder, as if amused that his words discomfited her. "And some few passengers intrigue me enough that I invite them to come forward for conversation." He put his gaze back on the river.

Alise's heart was beating faster and her cheeks were warm. She could not decide if she were flattered or frightened. Was the ship implying that he'd been aware of her and Sedric's conversation about dragons? He was "intrigued" by her, a high compliment from a creature that should have been a dragon. Yet beneath that giddy feeling of being recognized by such a magnificent being roiled the uneasiness of what Sedric had forced her to recall. This was the *Paragon*, the mad ship, once better known as the *Pariah*. All sorts of rumors had circulated about him in Bingtown, but that he had killed his entire crew not once but several times was no rumor but undeniable fact. It was only now, speaking to him, watching how he alone seemed to determine his course up the river that she realized how completely in his power she was. It was only now that she realized just how truly alive a liveship was. This was a dangerous creature, to be treated with both caution and respect.

As if he had read her thoughts, Paragon turned his head and bared his white teeth in a smile. It sent a shiver up her spine. She recalled that his original boyish face had been damaged, chopped to pieces; some said by pirates, while others believed his own crew had done it. But someone had recarved the splintered wood into the visage of a handsome if scarred young man. The youthfulness of that human face collided with her mental image of Paragon as a wise and ancient dragon. The contrast unsettled her. As a result, her words were more stiffly formal than she intended when she asked, "Of what did you wish to speak to me?"

He was unruffled. "Of dragons. And liveships. I've heard gossip that you are headed upriver, not just to Trehaug, which is the end of my run, but beyond the deep water and up to Cassarick. Is that true?"

Gossip? she wanted to ask him. Instead she replied, "Yes. That's true. I'm something of a scholar of dragons and Elderlings, and the purpose of my journey is to see the young dragons for myself. I wish to study them. I hope to be able to interview them and ask them what ancestral memories they have of Elderlings." She smiled, pleased with herself as she added, "I'm actually a bit surprised to discover that no one before me has thought to do this."

"They probably have, but discovered it was a waste of time to try to speak to those wretched animals."

"I beg your pardon?" His dismissal of the young dragons shocked her.

"They're no more dragons than I am," Paragon replied carelessly. When he glanced back at her this time, his eyes were storm-cloud gray. "Haven't you heard? They're cripples, one and all. They were badly formed when they emerged from their cases and time has not improved them. The serpents were too long in the sea, far, far too long. And when they did finally migrate, they arrived badly nourished at the wrong time of the year. They should have come up the river in late summer, encased, and had plenty of fat and all of winter to change. Instead they were thin, tired, and old beyond counting. They arrived late and spent too short a time in their cases. More than half of them are already dead from what I hear, and the rest soon to follow. Studying them will teach you nothing about real dragons." He was looking away from her, staring upriver. When he shook his head, his curling black hair danced with the motion. In a lower voice he added, "True dragons would scorn such creatures. Just as they would scorn me."

She could not read the emotion behind his words. It could have been deep sorrow or utter defiance of their judgment. She tried to find words that would answer to either. "That scarcely seems fair. You cannot help what you are, any more than the young dragons can."

"No. That is true. I could not prevent what was done to me, nor can I change what people made of me. But I know what I am and have decided to continue being what I am. That is not the decision a dragon would make. And thus do I know for myself that I am not a dragon."

"Then what are you?" she asked unwillingly. She didn't like the direction the conversation was going in. His words seemed almost an accusation. Did she feel tension emanating from the figurehead or was she imagining it?

"I am a liveship," he replied, and although he spoke without rancor, there was a depth of feeling to his voice that seemed to thrum though the very planking under her feet. A finality filled those words, as if he spoke of an unending, never-changing fate. He did, she realized abruptly.

"How you must hate us for what we did to you." Behind her, she heard Sedric give a small gasp of dismay. She ignored him.

"Hate you?" Paragon slowly digested her words before

he spoke again. He did not turn to look at her, but kept his eyes focused on the river ahead of him as the ship moved steadily against the current. "Why would I waste my time with hate? What was done to me was unforgivable, of course. Completely unforgivable. Those who did it are no longer alive to be punished or to apologize. Even if they were and did, it would not undo what they did. The torments I endured cannot be undone. The stolen future cannot be given back to me. The companionship of my own kind, the chance to hunt and kill, to fight and mate, to live a life in which I am neither servant or master—all those things are forever lost to me."

He did glance back at her now; the blue of his eyes had paled to an icy gray. "Can you think of anything that anyone could do to make up for it? Any sacrifice that could be offered that would be adequate reparation?"

Her heart was beating so hard that there was a ringing in her ears. Was that why he had rolled so many times and taken so many human lives? Did he think that enough humans had died in expiation for that sin against him, or would he demand more?

She hadn't answered his questions. His voice was a bit more penetrating as he nudged her with, "Well? What sacrifice would be adequate?"

"None that I can think of," she replied softly. She tightened her grip on the railing, wondering if he would immediately turn turtle and drown them all.

"Neither can I," he replied. "No vengeance could resolve it. No sacrifice would make reparations for it." He returned his gaze to the river. "And so I have decided to move beyond it. To be what I am now, in this incarnation, as no other is available to me. To have what life I may for as long as the wood of this body lasts me."

She couldn't quite believe what she was hearing. "Then you have forgiven us?"

Paragon gave a quiet snort. "Wrong on two points. I haven't forgiven anything. And I don't believe in the 'us' you think I might take vengeance on. You didn't do this to me. But even if you had, killing you would not undo it."

Behind her, Sedric suddenly spoke. "This is the not the attitude I would have expected from a dragon."

Paragon gave a snort, half contempt, half amusement. "I told you. I am not a dragon. And neither are those creatures that you intend to visit and study. That's why I called you forward. To tell you that. To tell you that there's no point to your journey. Studying those pathetic wretches will not teach you anything about dragons. No more than studying me would."

"How can they not be dragons?"

"In a world where dragons lived, they would not have survived."

"Other dragons would have killed them?"

"Other dragons would have ignored them. They would have died and been eaten. Their memories and knowledge would have been preserved by those who fed upon them."

"It seems cruel."

"Would it have been crueler than enabling them to exist as they are now?"

She took a breath and then tried to speak boldly. "You have chosen to continue as you are. Should not they be given that choice?"

The muscles in his broad back tightened, and she felt a gout of fear. But when he turned back to her, there was a spark of respect in his blue eyes that had not been there before. He gave her a slow nod. "A point. But I still ask you to keep in mind, when you study those things, that they cannot teach you what dragons were. I am told that half of them hatched without the memories of their ancestors. How can they be dragons when they emerge not knowing what a dragon is?"

His comment carried her thoughts on a new current. "But you do. Because despite the shape you now inhabit, your dragon memories would be intact." She gripped the ship's rail tightly as a wild hope filled her. "Oh, Paragon, would you talk about them with me? It would be such an opportunity for me as a scholar of dragons, to hear firsthand what you recall! The very concept that dragons can recall their previous lives is so hard for humans to grasp. I should so dearly love to listen to whatever you wished to tell me, and to make a complete record of all you recall. Such conversations alone would make my journey worthwhile! Oh, please, say that you will!"

A taut quiet followed her words. "Alise," Sedric said warningly, "I think you should come away from the railing."

But she clung there, even though she, too, could feel the wave of uneasiness that swept though the ship. The smoothness went out of his sailing; the deck under her feet shifted subtly. Surely it was her imagination that the wind flowed more chill than it had? Paragon spoke into the roaring silence. "I choose not to remember," he said. Alise felt as if his words broke a spell. Sound and life came suddenly back to the world. It included the sudden thud of feet on the deck behind her. A woman's voice said, without preamble, "I fear you're upsetting my ship. I'll have to ask you to leave the foredeck."

"She's not upsetting me, Althea," Paragon interjected as Alise turned to see the captain's wife advancing on her. Alise had met her when they embarked and had spoken with her several times, but still did not feel at ease with her. She was a small woman who wore her hair in a long black pigtail down her back. She dressed in sailor's garb; it was well tailored and of quality fabric, but for all that, she was a woman in trousers and a jacket. Less feminine garb Alise could not imagine, and yet the very inappropriateness of it seemed to emphasize her female form. Her eyes were very dark, and right now they sparked with either anger or fear. Alise retreated a step and put her hand on Sedric's arm. For his part, he turned his body so that he stood almost between them and said, "I'm sure the lady meant no harm. The ship asked us to come up and speak with him."

"That I did," Paragon confirmed. He twisted to look over his shoulder at all of them. "No harm done, Althea, I assure you. We were speaking of dragons, and quite naturally, she asked me what I recalled of being one. I told her that I chose to recall nothing at all."

"Oh, Ship," the woman said, and Alise felt as if she had disappeared. Althea Trell did not even glance at her as she moved forward to take Alise's place at the bow. She leaned on the railing and stared far ahead up the river as if sharing the ship's thoughts.

"Par'gon!" A child's voice piped suddenly behind them. Alise turned to watch a small boy of three or four clambering onto the raised foredeck. He was bare armed and bare legged and baked dark by the sun. He scampered forward, dropped to his hands and knees, and thrust his head out under the ship's railing. Alise gasped, expecting him to pitch overboard at any moment. Instead he demanded the ship's attention with a strident, "Par'gon? You awright?" His babyish voice was full of concern.

The ship swung his head around to stare at the child. His mouth puckered oddly and then suddenly he smiled, an expression that transformed his face. "I'm fine."

"Catch me!" the boy commanded, and before his mother could even turn to him, he launched himself into the figurehead's waiting hands. "Fly me!" the imp commanded the ship. "Fly me like a dragon!"

And without a word, the ship obeyed him. He cupped the child in his two immense hands and lifted him high and forward. The boy leaned fearlessly against the ship's laced fingers and spread his small arms wide as if they were wings. The figurehead gently wove his hands through the air, swaying the youngster from left to right. A squeal of glee drifted back to them. Abruptly the charge of tension in the air vanished. Alise wondered if Paragon even recalled they were there.

"Let's leave them, shall we?" Althea suggested quietly.

"Is it safe for the child?" Sedric objected in horror.

"It's the safest place the boy can possibly be," Althea replied with certainty. "And for the ship, it's the best place, too. Please." She indicated the ladder that led down to the deck. As they approached it, she added, "Do not take my words the wrong way. But I'd appreciate it if you didn't speak to Paragon again."

"He invited me to come forward!" Alise objected, her cheeks flaming.

"I'm sure he did," Althea replied smoothly. "But all the same, I'd appreciate it if you declined any other invitations."

She paused as if she were finished speaking. Then, as Alise turned and tried to bustle her skirts out of the way to descend the ladder, she added in a quieter voice, "He's a good ship. He has a great heart. But no one ever knows in advance what topics might upset him. Not even him."

"Do you truly believe that he has forgotten his dragon memories?" Alise dared to ask.

Althea pressed her lips tightly for a moment. Then she said, "I choose to believe whatever my ship tells me about himself. If he tells me he has forgotten, then I don't ask him to recall anything about it. Some memories are best left undisturbed. Sometimes, if you forget something, it's because it's better forgotten."

Alise nodded. She was turning to put a foot on the ladder when a man spoke below her.

"Paragon all right?" Captain Trell asked, looking up. Alise blushed. She had very nearly stepped off the deck and onto the ladder. Her skirts would have been right over his head.

"He's fine now," Althea assured him. Then, as she noticed Alise's dilemma, she smoothly suggested, "Brashen, would you offer Trader Finbok some assistance to descend?"

"Of course," he replied, and with his offered hand she was able to descend in a more ladylike manner. In a moment, Sedric had joined her on the deck. He put out his arm and she was glad to take it. The events of the last hour had left her flustered, and for the first time she had serious doubts about the advisability of her journey. It was not just that the ship had told her she could not think of the young dragons as dragons, and implied that they would have no ancestral memories. That was daunting enough, but she suddenly also felt that perhaps she had badly underestimated how intimidating it might be to deal with such creatures. Her conversation with Paragon had rearranged her concept of dragons. She had been, she realized, thinking of them as youngsters. They weren't. Not any more than Tintaglia had been a youngster when she emerged from her case. They might be smaller or crippled, but dragons came out of their cases, usually, as fully formed adults.

The captain had not moved away from her. Now, as his wife, Althea, joined him on the deck, they stood side by side, almost blocking her from moving away. The captain spoke courteously but firmly. "Perhaps in the future, it might be better if one of us accompanied you if you wished to speak with the ship. Sometimes those unfamiliar with liveships or with Paragon himself can find him unnerving. And sometimes he can be a bit . . . excitable."

"The lady had no intention of alarming your ship," Sedric informed Captain Trell, a bit stiffly. He put his hand firmly over Alise's, a protective gesture that she found oddly reassuring. "The ship invited her forward to speak with him. And he was the one who brought up the topic of dragons."

"Did he?" The captain exchanged a glance with his wife. She nodded slightly, and he shifted his feet. Alise felt that he granted them permission to move away. His tone was a bit more kindly as he admitted, "Well, I'm not surprised. We've had troubling news about the hatchlings almost every time we visit Trehaug. I think they weigh on his mind. We encourage Paragon not to dwell on things that he finds upsetting."

"I understand," Alise replied faintly. She wished the conversation were at an end. She did not do well at confrontation with strangers, she abruptly decided. With her own husband, she had barely been able to take a stand and feel courageous about doing so. But out here in the real world and almost on her own, she felt she had not done well at facing her first challenge. Even as she felt grateful for Sedric's support, her gratitude shamed her.

"I think you might warn your passengers before they stumbled into such a circumstance," Sedric said firmly. "Your ship is not the only one that might become alarmed. Neither of us sought conversation with him. On the contrary, he invited us forward."

"So you've said," Captain Trell replied, and his voice warned of patience wearing thin. "You may recall you were told that we do not often take passengers, only cargo. Usually those who ride with us are family or friends. They're well aware of Paragon's quirks. I do recall that Trader

Finbok was quite insistent that she had to book immediate passage."

Alise tightened her grip on Sedric's arm. She wished only to go back to her tiny stateroom. Her vision of herself as an intrepid explorer braving new experiences and acquiring firsthand knowledge of dragons was fading. She felt sure that if Sedric had not been by her side, she would have fled. Or worse, burst into tears. At the thought of it, her eyes began to sting. *No. Oh, no, please, not now.*

Perhaps the threat of breaking down in front of strangers gave her courage. She drew a deep breath, squared her shoulders, and with all her might pretended that she was as brave as she wished she were. "Hatchlings," she said quietly. Then she firmed her voice and spoke with more force. She pushed a smile onto her face as well. "I regret that I upset your ship, sir. But I would be extremely interested if you could share any news you have of the 'hatchlings' as you call them. Paragon said that I should not think of them as dragons. I find that an extraordinary statement. Can you clarify what he meant by it? Have you yourself seen them? What did you think of them?" She stacked her questions one on top of the other as if building a wall to protect herself.

"I haven't," the captain admitted.

"I have," his wife said quietly. She turned and walked slowly away from them all. As Alise stared after her curiously, she turned and silently beckoned for them to follow. She led them to the captain's quarters, invited them inside, and closed the door.

"Would you care to sit down?" she asked them.

Alise nodded silently. The sudden hospitality was a bit confusing, but also welcome. The confined room was a setting more familiar to her than the open deck. She immediately felt more comfortable. The stateroom was not large but was still impressive. It was efficiently designed and simply furnished, but every item in the chamber was of excellent quality. Shining brass and richly gleaming wood welcomed them. A chart table dominated the room. A compass rose inlaid into the tabletop was formed from various shades of wood. Heavy damask draperies curtained off a bed in one corner of the wood-paneled room. Scattered about the room were small artifacts that were obviously of Elderling make. A small mobile of fish hung near a window. As the light touched it, the fish "swam" in the air, changing colors as they did so. A fat green pot with a gleaming copper spout sat in the middle of the table. Alise felt as if she had just stepped into the drawing room of a wealthy Bingtown family rather than a stateroom on a ship. She took her offered seat and waited as the others joined her at the table.

Althea smoothed a few stray strands of hair back from her face. She glanced at her husband. Captain Trell had not joined them at the table, but leaned on the wall by a small window, watching the shore slip by. "Paragon helped escort the serpents up the Rain Wild River. He accompanied them as far as he could and had the highest of hopes for them. He was deeply and bitterly disappointed when they emerged as pitiful shadows of the dragons they should have been. Not one of them was near Tintaglia's size. Since then they have grown, but they still are stunted."

Althea picked up the pot on the table, hefting it to check if it still held water. "Will you have a cup of tea?" she offered as she set it down again, as if they were indeed in a Bingtown drawing room. She stroked an insignia on the side of the kettle, an image that looked rather like a chicken with a crown. Almost immediately, the pot gave a small rumble and steam began to waft from its spout.

"Priceless!" Sedric exclaimed. "I'd heard a few such Elderling kettles have been discovered, but none seemed to come to the Bingtown market. It must be worth a fortune."

"It was a wedding gift, from family," Captain Trell said. "Quite a prize. It requires no fire to heat the water. And of course, on a ship, fire is always a concern." He had visited a sideboard and now brought a tray laden with cups and a teapot to the table. Althea took over the hostess duties. It was odd to watch her shift from her mannish abilities on the deck to the delicate business of measuring tea into a pot and setting out cups all around. Alise abruptly felt that she glimpsed a possible life that she had never known existed. Why, she wondered, had she never even considered making her own way in the world? Why had marriage or spinster-hood seemed her only choices? She only realized she was staring at Althea when the woman returned her a slightly puzzled glance. Alise immediately redirected the conversation with a question.

"But Paragon has never seen the new dragons?"

Althea shot her an odd glance. "Of course not. The river is too shallow to permit him to venture that far. A great deal of effort went into making that part of the river passable for the serpents. It was not as successful as it could have been, and winter storms and floods in the years since then have mostly destroyed those works. The banks of the river, as you have seen, are marshy and difficult to walk on. The forest is dense and unfriendly to creatures of that size. So the dragons have never moved from their hatching place."

"But you went to see them?"

"Yes. At Paragon's request, I went. And also because I wished to visit my niece, Malta."

"Malta Khuprus? The Elderling queen?"

Althea smiled more broadly. "So some name her, though she is not queen of anything. It was a fancy of the Jamaillian Satrap to title Reyn and her as the King and Queen of the Elderlings. In reality, they are both of Trader stock, just as you and I are, and not royalty at all."

"But they are Elderlings!"

Althea started to shake her head, and then shrugged instead. "So Tintaglia the dragon called them. And they have both physically changed over the years to resemble, more and more, the images of Elderlings that we've seen unearthed from the ancient Rain Wild cities. But Malta was born just as human as I am, and Reyn, though marked as many of the Rain Wild Traders are, was not extraordinarily different. That's no longer the case, of course. Our family has watched both of them, and Selden Vestrit, my nephew, change substantially since they encountered Tintaglia. It's my thought that exposure to the dragon was what started their changes. All three have grown taller. Malta is remarkably tall for a woman of my family now. And more beautiful in a way that has nothing to do with human beauty. When she goes uncloaked and unveiled, she reminds me of a jeweled statue come to life. Tintaglia has told them that they may enjoy much longer life spans than ordinary humans. But for all of that, Malta is still Malta." Althea sounded as if she almost regretted that fact. Quietly she added, "And I think she and Reyn would trade away all their Elderling glory for one healthy baby."

"But the dragons?" Sedric interrupted to demand. "Are they really so deformed and mentally deficient? Is it possible that we have come all this way on a useless quest?"

Alise felt doubly annoyed that he had interrupted Althea's revelations about the only living Elderlings and that he sounded so hopeful her expedition would come to nothing. Althea folded her hands on the edge of the table and considered her rough brown knuckles before she spoke.

"They are not like Tintaglia," she said quietly. "None of them can fly. We started up the river escorting one hundred and twenty-nine serpents. Fewer than half successfully cocooned and hatched. And now there are left, what? Fewer than seventeen when last I heard." She glanced up and met Alise's desperate gaze. For a moment, sympathy shone in her eyes. "I wish it had been otherwise, if only for Paragon's sake. It was tremendously important to him that the serpents reach their cocooning grounds. Despite what he said to you, I believe the heart of a dragon still resides in this ship. He longed to restore his kind to the skies; it would have given great meaning to his own fate.

"But the creatures I saw when I visited Cassarick were pathetic, malformed things. It is telling that Tintaglia seems to have completely abandoned them. Dragons do not pity the weak, but let them meet their fates. The Rain Wild folk who live closest to them are rapidly losing all sympathy for them. They are unruly and dangerous, intelligent but unreasonable. But perhaps being unreasonable is the only rational response to leading such miserable lives. They have neither respect nor gratitude for humans. They have yet to attack a human, though I've heard rumors that they've chased a few. And devoured at least one corpse in the midst of the family funeral. I don't know what's to become of them, other than gradual decline and death." She paused, sighed, and said, "I think Paragon has decided they are not dragons because that is less painful for him. He can do nothing to help them. So, by separating himself from them, perhaps his shame for them is a bit less. I really think there is nothing any of us can do for them."

Alise sat very still and silent for three breaths. Then she said quietly, "Little of this has been heard in Bingtown."

Althea smiled, a secret shared between fellow Traders. She poured fragrant tea into the cups. Captain Trell came to the table to accept his cup but immediately returned with it to his post by the window and his watch on the river. "Our Rain Wild brethren have always kept their own affairs quiet. And for generations, those of Bingtown stock have been trained not to gossip about them. It still seems strange to me that the outside world now knows that they exist and wish to visit their cities. For so long we kept them secret, to protect them."

Alise looked directly at Althea and suddenly felt grateful for the woman's bluntness. "Do you think I will be able to speak with the dragons at all? Learn anything from them?"

Althea shifted in her chair. From the corner of her eye, Alise glimpsed Captain Trell regretfully shaking his head. "I don't think so," she said. "From what I saw of them, they are fixated on the basics of life. The only talk I heard from them were demands for food. And complaints about their condition. From what little I know of Tintaglia, I would say that dragons do not deem humans worthy of thoughtful conversation. And the hatchlings at Cassarick disdain us as completely as if they were full-grown and powerful dragons. Combine that with the bitterness they feel . . ." She gave a shrug of her shoulders. "I do not think they will confide their ancestral memories to you. If they have any."

Alise nodded dumbly. She felt empty and sick. She took a sip of her tea to give herself time to think, but no ideas came to her. "I feel so foolish," she said softly. She looked at Sedric and apologized, "I've dragged you all this way, for nothing it seems. I should have listened to Hest." She laced her fingers together on the table in front of her and spoke to Althea past a lump in her throat. "I only booked passage on your ship as far as Trehaug. From there, I planned to travel by one of the cargo barges, the small ones. I didn't buy tickets for our return, because I hoped to stay weeks if not months learning from the dragons." She reached up to massage her own temples. A storm of a headache was brewing in her skull. She tried to keep tears out of her voice as she asked, "Is it possible to arrange to return to Bingtown immediately?"

"You can travel back with us." The captain spoke without moving away from his window. There was sympathy in his voice.

"But you should understand that it takes time for us to unload cargo and take on supplies and more cargo." Althea cautioned her. "And I had planned to visit Malta while we were here. So we will not be immediately returning to Bingtown. You will have to spend a few days in Trehaug while we do so."

"I understand," Alise said faintly. "I am sure we will find things to see in Trehaug until you are ready to begin the journey back to Bingtown."

"Then you don't plan to even visit Cassarick? I can't believe that! Alise, you must go. We've come so far, it would be foolish not to at least visit it."

The apparent disappointment in Sedric's voice startled her. A few minutes ago, he had seemed positively hopeful that their journey had been for naught.

"What would be the point of it?" she asked him dully.

"Well"—he seemed to flounder briefly for a reason—"well, to say that you'd seen what you'd gone to see. Done what you meant to do. You said you wanted to see the young dragons for yourself. Do so." Suddenly he seemed more confident of his words. He leaned across the table and took her hands. He gazed earnestly into her eyes. "Isn't that what you've been telling Hest you wanted, for years now? Simply to see for yourself?" He gave her a twisted smile. "Surely you don't want to go back to Bingtown and admit to him that you came all this way and didn't even look at a dragon?"

She stared at him. Suddenly she could imagine Hest's

delighted grin at such an admission from her. Bile rose in the back of her throat. No. No. Her disappointment was big enough without letting it be his triumph. She blinked back tears, and suddenly felt a wave of gratitude toward Sedric that he had thought of her and spoken out to save her from such shame. "You're right," she said in a shaky voice. She thought of her years of carefully compiled notes, scroll after scroll, page after precisely lettered page. Resolve settled and firmed in her. "You're right, Sedric. I have to go. The least I must do is see them for myself." She drew a deeper breath. "I've committed a grave error, one that too many scholars fall prey to. I've let my expectations and hopes color my opinion. If what I see are deformed and near mindless creatures, then that is what I must observe and document. Just because my studies do not reflect what I hoped to find is no reason to turn aside from them. Thank you, Sedric." She sat up, squaring her shoulders and met Althea's measuring gaze. "I will be journeying on to Cassarick."

Althea slowly nodded. A grim smile of understanding touched her face.

"But we won't be staying long," Sedric hastily added. "I suspect that we will still be traveling downriver with you. In fact, I'd like to secure our passage home right now."

Both Althea and Brashen were looking at Sedric oddly. Alise understood. If she hadn't known the man, she too would have wondered at his weather-vane spinning. He'd gone so quickly from persuading her that she must go to Cassarick to declaring that they would stay only a very brief time. But she knew why. She sat silent as he discussed with the captain the likely dates of their departure for Bingtown. Without a word, she signed the note for funds for their return tickets. All the while, she looked at Sedric, not with new eyes, but with fond remembrance of their old friendship. He hadn't wanted to come to the Rain Wilds. She was certain he didn't want to make the uncomfortable journey by flat-bottom barge to Cassarick. But he would do it, for her sake. He'd help her save face with Hest, no matter the discomfort and inconvenience to himself.

When their business was concluded and she rose from

the table, he offered her his arm, just as he always did. As she took it, she looked up at him and smiled. He smiled back and patted her hand reassuringly. "Thank you, my friend," she said quietly.

"Not at all," he replied.

✦ ✦ ✦

Day the 23rd of the Growing Moon

Year the 6th of the Independent Alliance of Traders

From Detozi, Keeper of the Birds, Trehaug
To Erek, Keeper of the Birds, Bingtown

From the Traders' Councils at Cassarick and Trehaug to the Bingtown Traders' Council, in a sealed scroll case, an accounting of the expected expenses for moving the dragons to a spot more conducive to their good health, with the Bingtown Traders' Council's share of the expenses itemized in detail.

Erek,

You should not listen to silly gossip. The dragons are to be moved, not slaughtered or sold! How rumors do twist as they fly. I have received the peas, and the difference in my birds' plumage is already noticeable. Is this feed expensive? Is it possible you could acquire a hundredweight sack for me, if it is not too dear?

Detozi

✦ ✦ ✦

Chapter Nine

Journey

Leftrin straightened up from slouching against the railing and peered down the dock at the procession headed toward the *Tarman*. Was this what Trell was sending his way? He scratched a whiskery cheek and shook his head to himself. Two dock workers were pushing barrows laden with heavy trunks. Another two followed carrying something the size of a wardrobe. And following behind them came a man dressed more for a tea party in Bingtown than for a trip up the Rain Wild River on a barge. He wore a long dark blue jacket over dove-gray trousers and low black boots and was bareheaded. He looked fit, in the manner of a man who is generally so but has never developed the muscles of a particular trade. He carried nothing save a walking stick. "Never worked a day in his life," Leftrin decided quietly.

The woman on his arm looked as if she had at least tried

to be practical. A brimmed hat shaded her face; Leftrin supposed that the loose netting attached to it was intended to protect her from insects. Her dress was dark green. The fitted bodice and wrist-length sleeves showed off a tidy upper figure, but he estimated there was enough fabric in the skirts that belled out around her to dress half a dozen women her size. Little white gloves protected her hands. He caught a glimpse of a neat black-booted foot as she walked toward his barge.

The runner had reached him just before he ordered his crew to cast off for their trip upriver to Cassarick. "Trell from the *Paragon* says he's got a couple of passengers who want to get to Cassarick fast. They'll pay you well if you'll wait for them to transfer."

"Tell Trell I'll wait half an hour for them. After that, I'm gone," he'd told the boy who had run the message. The lad had bobbed an acknowledgment and scampered off.

Well, he had waited substantially more than half an hour for them. And now that he saw them, he doubted the wisdom of accepting them aboard. He'd expected Rain Wild folk in a hurry to get home, not Bingtowners with a full complement of luggage. He spat over the side. Well, he hoped they'd meant what they'd said about paying him well to wait for them.

"Our cargo is here. Get it loaded," he ordered Hennesey.

"Skelly. Get it done," the mate passed the command onto the young deckhand.

"Sir," the girl acknowledged him and jumped lightly across to the dock. Big Eider moved to help her. Leftrin remained where he was, watching his passengers approach. They reached the end of the dock, and the man visibly recoiled at the sight of the long, low barge that awaited them. Leftrin chuckled quietly as the fellow looked about, obviously hoping there was some other vessel waiting to convey them upriver. Lace. The dandy had lace at the neck of his shirt and showing at the cuffs of his jacket. Then the man looked directly up at Leftrin and he composed his face.

"Is this the *Tarman*?" he asked, almost desperately.

"It is indeed. And I'm Captain Leftrin. I assume you're

my passengers, in need of swift transport to Cassarick. Welcome aboard."

The man once more cast a wild glance about. "But—I thought—" He watched in horror as one of their heavy cases teetered on the *Tarman*'s railing before sliding with a thump to land safely on the deck. He turned to his female companion, "Alise, this isn't wise. This ship isn't a proper place for a lady. We'll just have to wait. It can't hurt for us to take a day or two in Trehaug. I've always been curious about this city, and we've scarcely glimpsed it."

"We've no choice, Sedric. Paragon will stay here at Trehaug for ten days at most. The journey from here to Cassarick will take two days, and we have to allot two more days to travel back and meet Paragon before he sails. That gives us only six days in Cassarick, at most." The woman's voice was calm and throaty, with a hint of sadness in it. The veiling on her hat concealed most of her face, but Leftrin glimpsed a small determined chin and a wide mouth.

"But, well, but Alise, six days should be more than ample, if what Captain Trell told us about the dragons is true. So we can wait here a day, or even two if need be, and find more appropriate transport up the river."

Skelly was not paying any attention to the quibbling passengers. She had her orders from the mate and that was who she obeyed. She was waving to Hennesey who had swung a small cargo derrick over the side. Hennesey released the line and the girl deftly caught the swinging hook and began making it fast to the wardrobe trunk. Eider and Bellin were standing by to bring it aboard. Leftrin's crew was good; they'd have the passengers' luggage loaded while the man was still chewing on his lip. Best find out their intentions now rather than to have to offload it all.

"You can wait," Leftrin told the man. "But I don't think you'll find anything else going upriver in the next few days. Not much traffic between Trehaug and Cassarick right now. And what there is will be a lot smaller than I am. Still, it's your choice. But you'll need to make it quickly. I've already waited longer than I should have. I've appointments of my own to keep."

And that was true. The urgently worded missive from the Traders' Council at Cassarick sounded as if it could mean a nice little profit for him, if he undertook their rather dubious mission. Leftrin grinned. He already knew he'd take on the task. He'd taken on most of the supplies he'd need for the journey here in Trehaug. But leaving the Traders' Council in doubt until the last possible minute was one way to push the price up. By the time he reached Cassarick, they'd be ready to promise him the moon. So delaying for these passengers was not really that much of an annoyance. He leaned on the railing to ask, "You aboard or not?"

He was waiting for the man to respond to his words, so he was surprised when the woman replied to him. She tipped her head back to speak to him, and the sun reached through her gauzy veil to reveal her features. Her stance reminded him of a flower turning its face to the sun. She had large gray eyes set wide apart in a heart-shaped face. She had bundled her hair out of the way, but what he could see of it was dark red and curling. Freckles sprinkled her nose and cheeks generously. Another man might have seen her mouth as too generous for her face, but not Leftrin. The single darting glance she gave him seemed to look not into his eyes but into his heart. And then she looked aside, too proper to meet a strange man's eyes.

". . . no choice, really," she was saying, and he wondered what words he had missed. "We'll be happy to go with you, sir. I'm sure your boat will suit us admirably." A rueful smile twitched at her lips, and as she turned her attention to her companion, Leftrin felt a pang of loss as she tilted her head and apologized to him sweetly. "Sedric, I'm sorry. I'm sorry that you were dragged into this whole mess with me, and I'm ashamed that I must drag you from one boat to the next without even a cup of tea or a few hours on dry land to settle you. But you see how it is. We must go."

"Well, if it's a cup of tea you'd like, that's something I can brew up for you here in the galley. And if it was dry land you were after, well, there's little of that in Trehaug, or anywhere else in the Rain Wilds. So you haven't missed it, it was never there. Come on aboard, and welcome."

That brought her eyes back to his. "Why, Captain Leftrin, how kind of you," she exclaimed, and the sincere relief in her voice warmed him. She lifted the veiling on her hat to look at him directly, and he nearly lost his breath.

He seized the railing and swung over it, dropping lightly to the dock. He sketched a bow to her. Surprised, she took two small steps backward. Young Skelly made a small sound that might have been a giggle. Her captain shot her a glare and she quickly went back to work. Leftrin turned his attention back to the woman.

"Tarman may not look as fancy as some of the other ships you've seen, but he'll carry you safely upriver where few vessels as large as he is can manage to go. Shallow draft, you know. And a crew that knows how to find the best channel when the current takes to wandering. You wouldn't want to wait for one of those little toy boats to carry you. They might look a bit fancier than my Tarman, but they rock like a birdcage in the wind and their crews battle to push them against the current. You'll be far more comfortable with us. May I assist you in boarding, ma'am?" He grinned at her and dared to stick out his arm for her to take. She glanced at it uncertainly, then at her disapproving companion. The man crossed his arms. He was no husband of hers, or Leftrin was certain he would have objected. Better and better.

"Please," Leftrin urged her, and it was only when she set her smooth white glove on the rough, stained fabric of his shirtsleeve that he was recalled to the obvious difference in their stations. She glanced down as he looked at her, and he admired her lashes against her freckled cheeks. "This way," he told her and led her to the rough planks that served as a gangway for the Tarman. The ramp creaked and shifted as they trod it, and she gave a small involuntary gasp and gripped his arm tighter. There was a bit of a jump down from the end of the plank to the barge deck. He wished he dared set his hands to her waist and lift her down. Instead, he offered his arm again for her to steady herself on. She leaned heavily on his arm and then gamely hopped. He saw a flash of white petticoat before she landed safely beside him.

"And here we are," he said genially.

A moment later, the man landed with a thud beside them. He glanced at the trunks that Skelly was lashing down with the other deck cargo. "Here, we'll be needing those brought to our cabins," he exclaimed.

"No private cabins on the *Tarman*, I'm afraid. 'Course, I'll be happy to give up my stateroom to the lady for the trip to Cassarick. You and me will have to bunk with the crew in the deckhouse. Not roomy, but as it's only for a couple of days, I'm sure we can manage."

The Sedric fellow looked absolutely panic-stricken now. "Alise, please reconsider!" he begged her.

"Cast off and let's get under way!" Leftrin told Hennesey.

As the crew scrambled to the mate's commands, Grigsby the ship's cat decided to make an appearance. He sauntered up to the woman, sniffed the hem of her dress boldly, and then abruptly stood up on his hind legs and rested his orange paws on her skirts. "Mrow?" he suggested.

"Get down!" Sedric snapped at the cat.

But Leftrin was unreasonably pleased when the woman crouched down to accept the cat's introduction. Her skirts folded onto the deck around her like a blossom collapsing. She put a hand out to Grigsby, who sniffed it and then bumped his striped head against it. "Oh, he's so sweet!" she exclaimed.

"And so are his fleas," the man muttered in quiet dismay.

But the woman only laughed softly, a quiet chuckle that reminded Leftrin of river water purring past the bow of his ship.

NIGHT HAD FALLEN. The dismal meal eaten on a battered wooden table from tin plates was thankfully over. Sedric sat on the edge of a narrow bunk in the deckhouse and pondered his fate. He was miserable. Miserable but determined.

The deckhouse was exactly as it was named, a low structure built on the deck to house the men. It had three chambers, if one wanted to dignify them with such a word. One was the captain's stateroom, where Alise was now ensconced. The next was the galley, with a woodstove and a cramped table with benches to either side of it. And the third room was this, the crew's quarters. A curtain across the end of it granted some privacy to Swarge and his sturdy wife, Bellin, in the larger bunk they shared there. That was a small mercy, Sedric thought.

He'd avoided his bunk as long as he could, remaining out on the deck with Alise to watch yet more forested bank slip by. The barge moved smoothly and made surprisingly fast time going up the river against the current. The crew who pushed it along made the labor seem effortless. Big Eider and Skelly, Bellin and Hennesey used the stout poles that propelled the barge up the river while Swarge commanded the tiller. The barge moved up the river steadily, avoiding shoals and snags as if bewitched. It was an impressive display of seamanship, and Alise was duly awed by it. Although Sedric could appreciate their skill, he tired of watching and commenting on it long before she did. He left her to her enthusiastic conversation with the barge's grubby captain and wandered aft, searching in vain for a quiet place to rest. He ended up perched on one of his own trunks, shaded somewhat by the wardrobe lashed down next to it. The crew offered no promise of intelligent conversation. One of the deckhands, Eider, was the size of a wardrobe. There was a woman, Bellin, almost as muscled as her husband, Swarge. Hennesey the mate had no time to chat with passengers, for which Sedric was grateful. Skelly shocked him by both her youth and her gender; what sort of a ship expected a young girl to do the full work of a deckhand? After one visit to the smelly deckhouse, he'd given up all thought of taking an afternoon nap to make the endless journey pass more swiftly. As well to nap in a kennel.

But now it was night, and insects swarmed. They'd driven him inside, and weariness had forced him to his bunk. Around him in the thick darkness, the crew slept. Swarge and his wife had retired to their curtained alcove. Skelly and the cat shared a bed, the girl curled around the orange monster. Skelly was the captain's niece; the poor girl was his most likely heir and thus had to learn the trade from the deck up. Hennesey the mate sprawled and overflowed his bunk, one muscular arm draped over the side with his hand braced on the deck. The atmosphere seemed thick with the crew's sweat and the moist snores and occasional grunts they gave off as they shifted in their beds.

There had been four unoccupied bunks for him to choose from; evidently Leftrin had once had a much larger crew on his ship. Sedric had chosen a lower bunk, and Skelly had not been too prickly about removing all the clutter from it so he could use it. She'd even tossed two blankets onto it for him. The bunks were narrow and cramped. He sat on the edge of his and tried not to think of fleas or lice or larger vermin. The neatly folded blanket on it had looked clean enough but he'd only seen it by lamplight. Through the sounds of the sleeping crew, he could hear the purling of the water outside. The river, so gray and wet and acid, seemed closer and more threatening than it had when he was on the tall and stately liveship. The barge sat lower and closer to the water. The ripe green smell of the water and the surrounding jungly forest penetrated the room.

When night fell and darkness flowed like a second river over the water, the crew had poled the barge to the river shallows and then tied it to the trees there. The ropes they had used were thick and heavy, and surely the knots were secure. But the river wanted the barge, and it sucked at it greedily, making the vessel sway gently and tug creakily against the ropes that bound it. Now and then the barge gave an awkward lurch, as if it had dug in its heels and refused to be dragged out into the current. He wondered what would happen if the knots gave way. There was, he reminded himself, a man on watch; Big Eider would stay up half the night, keeping an eye on things before rousing Hennesey to take his turn. And the captain himself had been up on the deck, still smoking his pipe, when Sedric had finally decided that he would have to give in and sleep in the noisome deckhouse. He had briefly entertained the notion of sleeping out on the open deck; the night was mild enough. But then the stinging gnats had begun to hover and hum, and he had hastened to come inside.

He took off his boots and set them by the edge of the

bunk. He folded his jacket and set it reluctantly across the foot of his bed. Then, still clothed, he lay back on top of the thin mattress and blanket. The pillow seemed little more than a larger lump on the bed. It smelled strongly of whoever had last slept in this bunk. He sat up, retrieved his jacket, and put it under his head. "Only for two days," he whispered to himself. He could stand this for two days, couldn't he? Then the barge would dock in Cassarick, they'd disembark, and Alise would, he was confident, find a way to be allowed to study her dragons. And he'd be there, cloaked with her credentials and awaiting his opportunities. They'd stay no longer than six days, ample time as he had already pointed out to her. And then they'd return to Tre-haug, board the *Paragon,* and head back to Bingtown. And his new future.

Home. He missed it badly. Clean sheets and large airy rooms and well-cooked food and freshly laundered clothes. Was that so much to ask of life? Just that things be clean and pleasant? That one's table-mates didn't chew with open mouths, or allow cats to hook bits of meat off the platter? "I just like things to be nice," he said plaintively to the darkness. And then winced at the memory the words conjured.

He recalled it so clearly. He'd squared his shoulders, swallowed hard, and stood his ground. "I don't want to go."

"It will make a man of you!" his father had insisted. "And it's a big opportunity for you, Sedric. It's a chance not just to prove yourself, but to prove yourself to a man who can advance you in Bingtown. I've pulled a few strings to get you this opportunity; half the lads in Bingtown would be willing to jump through hoops to get it. Trader Marley has an opening for a deckhand on his new ship. You won't be alone; there will be other lads of your age living aboard and learning how to work the decks. The friends you'll make there will be friends you keep for life! Work hard, bring yourself to the captain's attention, and it could lead to bigger things for you. Trader Marley's a wealthy man, in daughters as well as ships and money. If he comes to look favorably on you, well, there's no telling what future it might bring you."

"Tracia Marley's a very pretty girl," his mother added helpfully.

He had felt trapped between the hopeful gazes of both his parents. His numerous sisters had already finished their tea and hurried away from the table. They'd be off to the gardens or the music room or visiting their friends. Yet here he sat, hedged in by his parents' dreams for him. Dreams he couldn't share.

"But I don't want to work on a boat," he said carefully. As his father's mouth narrowed and his eyes darkened, he added hastily, "I don't mind working. Really, that's true. But why can't it be in a shop or an office? Somewhere clean and light, with pleasant people." He turned his gaze on his mother and added quickly, "I hate the thought of being away from my family for so long. Ships are gone from Bingtown for months, sometimes years. How could I stand not seeing you for that long?"

His mother pursed her mouth, and her eyes grew moist. Such words might win her over. But his father was not impressed. "It's time you were out on your own for a bit, son. Schooling is fine, and I'm proud to have a son who can read and write and figure accurately. If our fortune had fared better these last few years, perhaps that would be enough. But our holdings haven't prospered, so it's time for you to go out and find something of your own, something to bring back and add to your inheritance. If you work out on the ship, you'll be earning a decent wage. You can set something aside for yourself. This is an opportunity for you, Sedric, one that almost any boy in town would jump at."

He'd gathered his threads of courage. "Father, it just doesn't fit with who I am. I'm sorry. I know that you asked favors to get this opportunity for me. I wish you'd talked to me first. I've been on ships and I've seen how the crews live aboard. It's dirty, smelly, and wet, with boring food, and half your fellows are coarse, illiterate boors. Deck work demands a strong back and tough hands and little more than that. That's not who I want to be, a barefoot sailor pulling on a line on someone else's ship! I do want a future, and I'm willing to work hard. But not like that! I'll work somewhere clean and decent, among nice people. I just like things to be nice. Is that so wrong of me?"

His father leaned back abruptly in his chair. "I don't understand you," he said harshly. "I don't understand you at all. Do you know what it's taken for me to get this offer for you? Do you know how embarrassed I'll be if you turn it down? Can't you appreciate anything I do for you? This is your golden chance, Sedric! And you're going to turn it down because you 'like things to be nice!'"

"Please don't shout," his mother unwisely interjected. "Please, Polon, can't we be calm and polite about this?"

"And 'nice' too, I suppose!" his father had snarled. "I give up. I've tried to do my best by the boy, but all he wants to do is wander about the house and read books or go out with his useless idle friends. Well, their fathers have the money to raise useless idle boys, but I don't! You're my heir, Sedric, but what you'll inherit if you don't take hold soon, I don't know. Don't look at the floor! Meet my eyes, son, when I speak to you!"

"Please, Polon!" his mother had begged. "Sedric just isn't ready for this yet. He's right, you know. You should have discussed this with him before you sought it for him. You didn't even speak of it to me!"

"Because opportunities such as this don't wait! They come along, and the man who seizes it is the man who finds a future in it. But it won't be Sedric, will it? Oh, no. Because he's not ready, and it's not 'nice' enough for him. So, very well. You keep him at home here with you. You've ruined the boy with your indulgence of him. Ruined him!"

Sedric shifted in the narrow bunk, pushing the uncomfortable memory away. It came back in the form of a new question. Did his father still think he was "ruined"? He knew that his sire had felt chagrin when Sedric announced he had taken a position as Hest Finbok's secretary. Even his mother, far more patient and tolerant of Sedric's ways than his father was, had winced at the idea of him being employed in such a position. "It's just not something that you expect the son of a Trader to do, even a younger son. I know that it's an upward path, and even your father has said that perhaps you'll make good connections accompanying Hest on his trading trips. But, don't you know, it just seems as if you could have started your career a bit higher in life than as a secretary."

"Hest treats me well, Mother. And he pays me well, too."

"And I hope you are setting money aside from it. For as handsome as Hest Finbok is and as wealthy as his family is, he has a reputation for being fickle in his pursuits. Don't count on him to be someone you can depend on for the rest of your life, Sedric."

In the dark of the deckhouse, he groaned softly as he recalled her words. At the time they had seemed like her usual nattering worry for him. Now they seemed like a prophecy. Had he been a fool to let himself depend on Hest so deeply? His hand crept up and touched the small locket he wore around his neck. In the darkness, his finger caressed the single word engraved on its case. *ALWAYS*. Had "always" come to an end for him?

He shifted in his bunk, but it was uniformly hard. Sleep would not come to him, only memories and worries. He was being foolish, of course. This was only a minor tiff with Hest. He and Hest had had quarrels before and lived to laugh about them later. There had been that business in the Chalcedean town, where Hest, in a towering rage, had left Sedric behind at the inn and Sedric had had to dash through the streets to reach the ship before it sailed. He'd only ever struck Sedric once, and to be fair, Hest had been drinking and in a black temper even before they had quarreled. Hitting someone was unusual behavior for Hest. He had other ways of expressing his domination and control. Sarcasm and humiliation were more commonly his weapons. Physical force was his last resort, and it meant that his temper had reached a red hot heat.

But his current anger was different. It was cold. In the days after he'd ordered Sedric to accompany Alise on her expedition, Hest had been formal and chill with Sedric. He'd smiled at him each morning as he handed him a long list of tasks. He treated him in an absolutely correct, master-to-servant fashion. Every evening, he listened to Sedric report how his tasks had gone. He didn't seem to care that he'd given Sedric the responsibility for Alise's journey. He'd expected him to fulfill his regular chores as well.

Thus Sedric had been the one to arrange passage for Hest and Wollom Courser and Jaff Secudus on a ship bound for the Pirate Isles. At the last minute, with great deliberation and a cruel smile, he'd had Sedric write an invitation to Redding Cope as well. The joyous acceptance had arrived less than an hour after the post was sent. Hest had had Sedric read it aloud to him, and then had pleasantly commented how enjoyable a companion Redding Cope was, so affable and full of enthusiasm for any new adventure.

The next afternoon, they had departed. Cope had waved a cheerful farewell to Sedric as the ship slowly moved away from the dock. This was Hest's first venture at making trading contacts in the formerly dangerous Pirate Isles. It was also a journey that he and Sedric had been discussing for nearly a year. Hest well knew how Sedric had anticipated such a trip. And he'd not only chosen other companions for it, he'd also directed Sedric to book his passage on a ship that offered its passengers every comfort that a civilized man could cherish. While Sedric listened to men snore and fart in the darkness around him, Hest and his friends were probably sipping good port in a softly lit card parlor on the southbound ship. Sedric shifted uncomfortably and scratched the back of his neck. Then he worried that the tickling had been a bedbug. Or a louse. He felt his neck, but his fingers encountered nothing. Then he surprised himself by yawning.

Well, he was exhausted. Alise had seen to that. He'd packed all their possessions hastily, arranged porters, and then they had all but run from the *Paragon* to the *Tarman*. He'd barely glimpsed the fabled treetop city of Trehaug, let alone had time to wander through any of its bazaars. Trehaug was the prime city in all the Cursed Shores for a Trader to find Elderling goods at a reasonable price, and he'd had to race past it without even a glance because Alise feared she wouldn't get to see her smelly, deformed dragons.

He yawned again in the darkness and resolutely closed

his eyes. He would get what sleep he could in such foul conditions, and try to face the morrow with good graces. If all went well, he'd be with Alise when she wangled an invitation to visit the dragons and attempted to speak with them. She'd as much as said that she'd want him with her, to transcribe conversations and make notes and even to help with the sketches she planned to do. He'd be right there, among them, helping her collect her information. If fortune favored him, that wouldn't be all he'd be collecting. He hugged himself in the dark, and then gingerly pulled the blanket over himself. Nights were chill on the river, he decided, even in summer. Nights were as cold as Hest himself. But he'd show Hest. He'd show him that he didn't plan to live his life as only Hest's secretary. He'd show him that Sedric Meldar could do some bartering of his own, that he did have ambitions and dreams of his own. He'd show them all.

THYMARA SAT ON bare earth and stared at the flames of the cook fire. "Did any of us think we'd be doing this, a month ago? Preparing to meet dragons and escort them up the river? Or even imagine this, sitting around a fire down here on the ground?" she asked of her new circle of friends.

"Not me," muttered Tats, always at her side. Several of the others laughed in assent. Greft, seated to her right, just shook his head. His dark ringlets danced, as did the fleshy growths that fringed his jaw. When he had first joined their group, he'd been veiled. No one had commented. It wasn't uncommon for heavily touched men or women of the Rain Wilds to prefer a veil, especially if they were in the lower levels of Trehaug and might encounter the shocked gapes of someone strange to the city. When, on his second night with the dragon keepers, he'd finally appeared among them unveiled, even Thymara had stared. Greft was more heavily marked than anyone she'd ever seen. In his midtwenties, he had more wattles and growths than she'd seen even on the oldest folk of the Rain Wilds. The nails of his hands and feet were smooth but iridescent, and they curved like claws. His eyes were an unnatural blue and at night they unmistakably glowed. Every part of his exposed skin was heavily scaled.

His mouth was nearly lipless and his tongue was blue. He moved with quiet competence, and his maturity and steadiness were attractive to her. In contrast to the boys in the group, he seemed reliable and more thoughtful.

Tonight Greft was just as quiet as the rest of them. Anticipation warred with nervousness. Another day's travel and they'd finally meet the dragons.

The committee had provided them with sturdy canoes, well sealed against the river's acid wash. They'd given them two guides, a man and a woman who always cooked, ate, and slept separately from their charges. So far, food had been provided for them, and some of the keepers had even found time to try their skills at hunting or scouting for fruit and mushrooms along their journey's path. But they had discovered that their blankets were barely warm enough for sleeping on the ground, and that the mosquitoes and stinging gnats were just as thick at river level as they'd always been told. They'd learned that down here under the trees, nights were darker, starless, and longer than any they'd known in the treetops. They'd already learned to conserve potable water and to gather fresh rainfall at every opportunity. They'd exchanged names and stories.

And somehow, in the few days that they'd been together, they'd become close.

Now Thymara looked around at the circle of faces gleaming in the firelight and wondered at her good fortune. She'd never imagined that there would be so many people who would call her by her name, take food from her hands without flinching at her claws, and speak openly of what it was like to be so deformed by the Rain Wilds that not even one's siblings could look at one easily. They'd come from every layer of the canopy, from Trader families and families that scarcely recalled which Trader bloodline they'd originally sprung from. Some had lived hardscrabble lives and others had known education and meals of red meat and redder wine. She looked from face to face and named them to herself, counting them off as if they were jewels in a treasure box. Her friends.

There was Tats beside her, her oldest friend and still her

closest. Next to him was Rapskal, still chortling at some joke he'd made, and beside him, shaking her head at the boy's endless and unfounded optimism, was Sylve. The young girl almost seemed to be enjoying his attention and endless chatter. Kase and Boxter were next, both copper-eyed and squat. They were cousins and the resemblance was strong. They were inseparable, often nudging each other and laughing uproariously over private jokes.

That was something she was discovering about the boys her age. The pranking and foolish jokes seemed constant. Right now, silver-eyed Alum and swarthy Nortel were laughing helplessly because Warken had farted loudly. Warken, long limbed and tall, seemed to be relishing the mockery rather than being offended by it. Thymara shook her head over that; it made no sense to her that boys found such things so funny, and yet their sniggering brought a smile to her face. Jerd, sitting among the boys, was grinning, too. Thymara did not know Jerd well yet but already admired her skills at fishing. She had at first been shocked when she realized Jerd was female. Nothing about her solidly built frame suggested it. What hair she had on her scaled skull she had cut into a short blond brush. Both Thymara and Sylve had tried to befriend Jerd, and she had been affable enough, but she seemed to prefer male company. Her feet and well-muscled legs were heavily scaled and scarred. Jerd went barefoot, something that few Rain Wilders would ever consider doing on the ground.

Next to Jerd were Harrikin and Lecter. They were not related, but Harrikin's family had taken Lecter in when he was seven and both his parents died. They were as close as brothers, yet the one was long and slim as a lizard while Lecter reminded Thymara of a horny toad, squat and neck-less and spiny with growths. Harrikin was twenty, the oldest in their group, save for Greft. Greft was in his middle twenties. In bearing and manner, he made the rest of them seem like boys. And Greft, with his gleaming blue eyes, closed the circle of her friends. He saw her looking at him and canted his head questioningly. A smile stretched his thin mouth.

"It's strange to look around this circle and realize everyone here is my friend. I've never had friends before," she said quietly.

He ran his blue tongue around the edges of his mouth, and then leaned closer to her. "Honeymoon," he warned her in his raspy voice.

"What do you mean?"

"Happens like this. I've worked as a hunter a lot. You go out with a group of fellows, and by the third day, every one of them is your friend. By the fifth day, things wear a bit thin. And by the seventh day, the group starts to fragment." His eyes roamed over the fire-lit circle. Across from them, Jerd was in a friendly tussle with two of the boys. Warken appeared briefly to win it when he dragged her over to sit on his lap. But an instant later, she shot to her feet, shook her head at him mockingly, and resumed her place in the circle. Greft had narrowed his eyes, watching the rough play, and then said quietly, "Two or three weeks from now, you'll probably hate as many as you love."

She pulled back a bit from him, his cynicism chilling her. He shrugged at her, sensing that he'd almost offended her. "Or maybe not. Maybe it's just for me that things always seem to go that way. I'm not the easiest fellow to get along with."

She smiled at him. "You don't seem hard to get along with."

"I'm not, for the right people," he agreed with her. His smile said she was one of the right people. He extended a hand toward her, palm up, an invitation perhaps. "But I have my boundaries. I know what is mine, and I know that it's my decision whether to share it or not. And there are some things that a man just doesn't share. In a group like this, with so many youngsters, that's going to seem harsh or self-ish sometimes. But I think it's only sensible. Now, if I've hunted and been successful, and I've got enough for myself and some left over, then I don't mind sharing, and I think I've the right to expect the same of others. But you should know I'm not the sort that will short myself for the sake of being nice to someone else. For one thing, I've learned it's seldom appreciated. For another, I know that my ability to hunt is based on my strength. If I weaken myself to be a nice fellow today, perhaps all of us will go hungry tomorrow if I'm too slow or distracted to kill my quarry. So I protect my own interests today, to be in a better position to help everyone tomorrow."

Tats leaned across her lap to speak to Greft. She hadn't even realized he'd been listening to him. "So," he asked conversationally, "how do you tell the difference between today and tomorrow?"

"Beg pardon?" Greft said, sounding annoyed at the interruption. His affability evaporated.

Tats didn't move. He was practically lying in her lap. "How do you tell when it's today and when it's tomorrow, in terms of sharing what you have? At what point do you say to yourself, well, I didn't share yesterday, so I was strong and hunted and got some meat today, so I can share this meat today. Or do you just keep thinking, I better eat it all myself so that I'll be strong again tomorrow?"

"I think you're missing my point," Greft said.

"Am I? Explain it again, then." There was challenge in Tats's voice.

Thymara gave Tats a small nudge to get him to move. He sat up, but somehow he was closer to her. His hip pressed hers now.

"I'll try to explain it to you." Greft seemed amused. "But you may not understand. You're a lot younger than I am, and I suspect you've lived by a different set of rules than we have." He paused and glanced across the fire. Harrikin and Boxter had risen and were in a good-natured shoving match. Hands braced on each other's shoulders, feet dug into the mud, each strained to push the other back. On the sidelines, the other keepers shouted encouragement to the combatants. Greft shook his head, seeming displeased with their light-hearted play. "Life seems different when you haven't had to deal with people thinking that you don't have the right to exist. When I was young, no one thought I was entitled to anything. I begged when I was small, and when I was a bit older, I fought for what I needed. And when I was old enough to provide for myself and perhaps do a bit better than that, some people assumed that they had the right to share in whatever I managed to bring down. They seemed to think I should be grateful that they allowed me anything at all, even to exist. So unless you've lived under rules like that, I don't think you can understand how we feel. I see this expedition as the chance to get away from the old rules and live where I can invent rules for myself."

"Is your first new rule to always take care of yourself first?"

"It might be. But there, I told you that you probably couldn't understand. Of course, to balance that, there's something I don't understand about you. Why don't you explain to us why you're going upriver? Why are you discarding your life in Trehaug to set out with a bunch of rejects and misfits like us?" Greft made his question seem almost friendly.

Across the fire ring, Boxter triumphed. Harrikin crashed to the mud and then rolled away from him. "I give in!" he cried out, to a chorus of laughter. Both came back to take seats by the fire. The laughter died down, and quiet fell as everyone became aware of Tats and Greft staring at each other.

When Tats spoke, his voice was deeper than usual. "Maybe I don't see it that way. And maybe I didn't have the favored life that you imagine I did. Maybe I do understand you wanting to get away from Trehaug to a place where you can change the rules to suit yourself. Maybe most of us here are thinking to do just that. But I don't think the first rule I'll make is 'me first.'"

A silence fell after Tats spoke, a silence that was bigger than the three of them. The fire crackled. Mosquitoes hummed in the darkness around them. The river rushed by as it always did, and somewhere off in the distance, a creature hooted shrilly and then was still. Thymara glanced around the circle and realized that most of the dragon keepers had focused on their conversation. She suddenly felt uncomfortable and trapped sitting between Greft and Tats, as if she represented territory to be won to one side or the other. She shifted her weight slightly away from Tats and felt cooler air touch her where his body had been against hers.

Greft took a breath as if about to reply angrily. Then he

sighed it slowly out. His voice was even, low, and pleasant as
he said, "I was right. You don't understand what I'm saying,
because you haven't been where I've been. Where we've all
been." His voice rose on those last words, including all of
them in on what he was trying to say to Tats. He paused and
smiled at him before adding, "You're just not like us. So I
don't think you can really understand why we're here. Any
more than I can understand why *you're* here." He dropped
his voice a notch, but his words still carried. "The Council
was looking for Rain Wilders like us. The ones they'd like
to be rid of. But I heard they also offered amnesty to certain
others. Criminals, for example. I heard some people were
offered a chance to leave Trehaug rather than face the consequences of what they had done."

Greft let his words hang in the night like the drifting
smoke from the fire. When Tats said, "I don't know what
you're talking about," his words sounded unconvincing.
"I just heard the money was good. And that they wanted
people with no strong ties to Trehaug, people who could
leave the city without leaving obligations behind. And that
described me."

"Did it?" Greft asked politely.

It was Tats's turn to look around at the others watching
him. Some were merely following the conversation, but
several of them were now regarding him with a curiosity
bordering on suspicion. "It did," Tats said harshly. He stood
suddenly. "It does. I've got no ties to bind me anywhere.
And the money is good. I've as much a right to be here as
any of you." He turned away from them. "Gotta piss," he
muttered and stalked off into the surrounding darkness.

Thymara sat still, feeling the empty space where he had
sat. Something had just happened, something bigger than
the verbal sparring between the two young men. She tried to
put a name to it and couldn't. *He's shifted the balance,* she
thought as she glanced over at Greft. He had leaned forward
and was pushing the ends of the firewood into the flames.
*He's made Tats an outsider. And spoken for all of us as if he
had the right to do so.* Abruptly, he seemed a bit less charming than he had a few moments ago.

Greft settled back into his place in the circle. He smiled at her, but her face remained still. In the dancing firelight, other conversations were resuming as the keepers discussed their immediate concerns. They'd have to sleep soon if they were to get an early start tomorrow. Rapskal was already shaking out his blanket. Jerd stood suddenly. "I'm going for green branches. If the fire puts out enough smoke, it will keep some of the mosquitoes away."

"I'll go with you," Boxter offered, and Harrikin was already coming to his feet.

"No. Thank you," she replied. She strode off into the darkening forest in the same direction Tats had gone.

Abruptly, Greft leaned close to Thymara. "I'm sorry. I didn't mean to upset your beau like that. But someone had to tell him how it really is."

"He's not my beau," Thymara blurted out, shocked that Greft would think such a thing. Then she abruptly felt as if she had somehow betrayed Tats with that denial.

But Greft was smiling at her. "He isn't your beau, eh? Well, well. What a surprise." Then, he raised one eyebrow at her and leaned closer to ask with a smirk, "Does he know that?"

"Of course he does! He knows the laws. Girls like me can't be courted or married. We aren't allowed to have children. So there's no sense in having beaus."

Greft looked at her steadily. His eyes, blue on glowing blue, suddenly softened with sympathy. "You've been so well schooled in their rules, haven't you? That's a shame." He pressed his narrow lips together, shook his head, and gave a small sigh. For a time he watched the fire. Then when he looked back at her, his thin mouth stretched in a smile. He leaned closer to her, setting his hand on her thigh to speak right by her ear. His breath was warm on her ear and neck. It sent a shiver down her back. "Where we are going, we can make our own rules. Think about that."

Then, smooth as a snake uncoiling, he rose and left her looking into the flames.

Day the 2nd of the Grain Moon

Year the 6th of the Independent Alliance of Traders

From Kim, Keeper of the Birds, Cassarick
To Erek, Keeper of the Birds, Bingtown and
Detozi, Keeper of the Birds, Trehaug

Keeper Erek and Keeper Detozi,

When this position was given to me I was told firmly that the messenger birds were to be used only for official Council business, although Traders may be allowed to pay for the use of them for private messages. It was emphasized to me that Keepers have no special status that allows them to send messages for free. This, it seems to me, would include appending personal messages to official communications. I have no desire to report you for violating these rules, but if evidence of personal correspondence reaches me again, as it did by chance this time, I shall report you to all three Councils, and I am certain you will be liable for the expenses of all the free messages you have sent.

Respectfully,
Keeper Kim

CHAPTER TEN

CASSARICK

By the time they reached the main dock at Cassarick it was almost too dark to see. Even the mosquitoes had given up for the night. The lanterns hung on each corner of the barge illuminated little more than the preoccupied faces of the polers as they endlessly plodded past her. There was a hypnotic quality to watching their circling dance on the deck. Alise still found it amazing how easy it was for them to propel the barge upstream. When she had spoken of it to Captain Leftrin, he had grinned and said something about a very sophisticated hull design.

Alise had stayed out on the deck, well bundled against both the night chill and the insects that descended with darkness. The stars overhead had been distant and yet brilliant. Her first sight of the lights of the town had made her gasp in awe. Like Trehaug, the newer settlement of Cassarick was strung and strewn through the treetops above the river. The yellow lamplight shone from windows through a lacy network of branches. At first they looked like a scattering of stars caught in a net, but as the barge moved steadily closer, the lights grew larger and brighter.

"Won't be long now," Captain Leftrin told her on one of his frequent visits to her perch. "Ordinarily, we'd have stopped for the night an hour ago. But I know how anxious you are to get here and meet your dragons, so I've pushed my crew a bit today. I'd hoped we would dock while it was still light, but no such luck for us. So I suggest that you spend another night with us here, and make an early start of it tomorrow."

Sedric had come out on deck and joined them. In the dark, neither of them had noticed his soundless approach, and they both jumped when he spoke. "I do not think we are that tired. I think a bit of extra effort to find an inn that offers hot baths, soft beds, and a gentle wine with a warm meal would be worth it."

"You won't find any of that here," Captain Leftrin warned him. "Cassarick's a young settlement yet; most of the folk who work here live here, and visitors are few. There's little call for an inn. Oh, if we'd arrived while the sun was in the sky, we might have found a family that would give you a room for the night. But after dark, well, chances are you'd just go from door to door and find nothing. You'd have to climb a lot of steps in the dark. Or use a basket hoist, if you could find one that was manned and you were willing to pay the fee."

Alise nodded at his reasoning. "There's no sense in packing up all our luggage and setting out in the dark in the hope of finding a hospitable family. One more night aboard the *Tarman* won't hurt us, Sedric. In the morning, you can look for lodgings for us while I speak to the local council about the dragons." It seemed a solid arrangement to her. The boat was not palatial, but it was comfortable enough. The food was plain but nourishing. Captain Leftrin might be a bit rough around the edges, but his efforts at gallantry were flattering in their sincerity. She enjoyed his company even if Sedric obviously found him provincial. Several times that day Sedric had given her long-suffering glances at the captain's extravagant compliments to her, and once he had smothered a laugh over the man's efforts to be charming. She'd been surprised that it offended her when Sedric found the captain a cause for amusement. It seemed unkind and petty of him.

And flattering.

She tried not to dwell on that thought but could not help herself. Leftrin's attentions to her had taken her completely by surprise. They had made her uncomfortable at first, and even suspicious. But in the last day, she had become convinced his admiration of her was sincere. She could not deny the thrill of pleasure that went through her at the thought of this rough, masculine river captain finding her attractive. He was so unlike any other man she had ever met. His company made her feel that she was truly adventurous, even reckless in undertaking this trip. At the same time, his evident strength and competence made her feel safe. She had indulged herself in his company, telling herself that it was only for a short time and that she had no intention of being unfaithful to Hest. She only wished to enjoy, for a time, that a man found her pretty.

Then Sedric had reacted to him in a way that she could only construe as protective. It had shocked her. And stirred to new life her ancient childhood infatuation with him. Even before he had blossomed into such a gloriously handsome man, he had fascinated her. He'd paid attention to her when no other boy would have looked at her, with her wild red hair and thick freckles and flat bosom. He'd been kind. Oh, how she had dreamed of him, her best friend's big brother, being more than kind to her. She'd twined their initials on her lesson papers, and stolen one of his riding gloves. It had smelled like him, and she both blushed and laughed to recall how she had kept it under her pillow and smelled it every evening before she went to sleep. She could not recall now what had become of it, or when she had given up her dream that someday he would turn to her and admit that he loved her, too. Was it possible that he had once cared for her? Was it remotely possible that in some corner of his heart, he still did?

Oh, it was a silly fancy, as silly as her timid flirtation with the captain. Silly and absolutely delicious. And what harm could it be for her to imagine, just for a day or so, that two such different men could find her attractive? Hest had, for years now, made her feel so dowdy and stupid and boring. In the light and warmth of the captain's regard and Sedric's protectiveness, she felt like a flower stirring back to life.

In her brief time on the *Tarman,* Alise felt her adventure had approached what she had imagined it would be. The big scow sat so low in the water that it seemed but a breath above the river; it made the trees tower all the higher above them. The birds and the strange river creatures, both dangerous and mild, were closer to her here. From the barge's deck, she'd had glimpses of what Leftrin called marsh elk and riverpig. One large, toothy gallator had slid from his sunbathing on the mudbank to come and keep pace with the barge for a time until Skelly had given him a good rap with her pole that sent him slashing back to shore. She had seen several varieties of very large water birds; Leftrin had caught her sketching them into her journal and been completely amazed at her great artistic talent. He'd persuaded her to leaf back through her days on the river so that he could exclaim over some of her other efforts. She had blushed with pleasure when he'd recognized Captain Trell from one of her sketches, and when he'd told her the Rain Wild names for some of the exotic plants she'd drawn, she'd pleased him immensely by lettering their names in under her sketches. "So pleased to have been of service to such a scholar, ma'am!" he had told her, with such sincerity that she had blushed.

One insight he had given her had dismayed her. He'd sought her out as she sat in her chair on top of the deckhouse, bundled against the evening chill, with the netting of her hat pinned down against the insects. "Would you mind if I joined you briefly?" His careful formality was at odds with his rough demeanor. "It comes to me that I've a bit of information that you might want to know."

"Of course you may join me! This is your ship, isn't it?" she replied, at once intrigued by his conspiratorial tone.

Without more ado, he'd taken a seat on the deck next to her chair, folding up with an ease that surprised her. "Well, it's like this," he began immediately. "The Council at Cassarick has made a plan about the dragons. The dragons have agreed to it, but for a number of reasons, the word hasn't been spread about much. But seeing as how it's important to you that the dragons be there for you to talk to, I've decided to take you in, confidential-like. The fact is, the Council is getting ready to move the dragons out of there. And the word I've received is that it's to happen soon. Within the month for certain."

"Move them? But how? And to where? Why would they do this?" She was shocked.

"Well, as to how, the only way they can go is under their own power. By foot. And to where? That's something I haven't been fully told yet. Only that it's upriver a way. The why is pretty easy; everyone in the Rain Wilds knows that the dragons have become more than nuisances at Cassarick. They're a real danger to the workers in the buried city, and to the inhabitants. Hungry, bad tempered, and some of them aren't too bright. Not bright enough to know they shouldn't bite off the hand that feeds them, if you take my meaning. I don't know how they've persuaded the dragons to leave, but they have. If they can get a crew together to sort of herd them along, they'll move them out of there as soon as they can."

She'd felt faint. What if she arrived only to find that the dragons had already been sent away? What then? She'd found the voice to put her fear into words. To her surprise, the captain had grinned up at her recklessly. "Well, ma'am, that's what I come to tell you. See, I'm part of that crew they're trying to put together. And near as I can tell, if I say no, well then it's not going to happen. That Council may not know it, but there's no other barge on the river that can go as shallow as my old Tarman. No other barge will take on that contract. Up to now, I've just been talking to myself, figuring out how much money to hold out for. But if it comes down to it, I may put another condition on it, and that's that you'll have a chance to talk to the dragons before they depart. So. What do you think of that?"

She was dumbfounded. "I'm surprised that you'd trust me with such a confidential matter. And I'm even more astonished that you'd do such a thing for a relative stranger." She leaned on the arm of her chair and lifted the netting from her face to look down into his. "Why?" she asked, genuinely puzzled.

He shrugged and his grin became bashful. He looked away from her. "Guess I just like you, ma'am. And I'd like to see you get what you come so far to get. What can it hurt to make them wait a day or three?"

"I don't think it could hurt them at all," she said. Gratitude and relief welled up in her. "Captain Leftrin, I'd be pleased if you'd call me Alise."

He glanced back at her then, a boyish flush of pleasure on his weathered face. "Well, I'd be more than pleased to do that!" Then he'd looked away from her and almost visibly shifted the topic. "Fine night, isn't it?" he'd observed.

She'd let the insect netting fall to shield her own blush. "The finest night I've experienced in a long time," she replied.

When he'd excused himself and left the deckhouse roof, she'd found herself giddy as a girl. He liked her. Liked her so much that he'd put a major contract at risk. She tried to think when any other man had actually said to her, "I like you." She couldn't recall any instances. Had Hest ever said that in his early "courtship" of her? She couldn't recall that he had. And even if he had, from him it would only have meant that she suited his purposes. When Leftrin said it, it meant that, for no other reason, he'd put himself at risk for her. Astonishing.

And when he returned, but a few moments later, with thick sweetened coffee in heavy earthenware mugs, she had thought it the most delicious brew she'd ever shared with anyone.

The rustic conditions of life on the barge had not lost their charm for her. It seemed exotic and a bit dangerous to sleep in the captain's bed with its thick wool blankets and gaily pieced patchwork cover. The room smelled of his tobacco and was littered with the implements of his profession. She woke to sunlight on the cunning fish chimes that hung at his window. And it secretly thrilled her that, at any hour, he might tap on the door and ask permission to enter to retrieve his pipe or a notebook or a fresh shirt.

The barge moved slowly but steadily against the current. It stayed to the shallows at the edge of the river where the flow was less strong. Sometimes the crew manned sweeps and sometimes they used long poles to push it along. It seemed like magic to her as the wide heavy ship prevailed against the river's steady push. On the first morning, the captain had placed a chair on the roof of the deckhouse for her so that she could take in all the sights and sounds of their journey. Sometimes Sedric joined her there, and she took keen pleasure in his company when he did, but Captain Leftrin had actually been more constantly at her side than he was.

Captain Leftrin was full of tales of the river and the ships that traded on it. Rain Wild history had changed in his telling of it, and she fancied that she now better understood how the Rain Wild Traders thought of themselves. She had come to enjoy the picturesque members of the crew, right down to the affectionate Grigsby. She'd never had a cat as a pet, but she was rapidly becoming fond of the beast. She'd wondered what Hest might say to such a request, then suddenly resolved not to make it. She'd simply get herself a cat. That was all. It was strange, she thought, how a little rough living made her feel so much more in control of her life. So capable of making her own decisions.

So Leftrin's suggestion of one more night aboard the *Tarman* pleased her. Sedric had sighed and rolled his eyes. She'd laughed aloud at his doleful expression. "Let me have my adventure while I can, Sedric. Soon enough, too soon for me, it will all be over. We'll both be back in Bingtown, and I don't doubt that I'll have a soft bed, hot meals, and warm baths the rest of my life. And little else in the way of excitement."

"Surely a grand lady like yourself doesn't lead as boring and sedate a life as all that," Captain Leftrin had exclaimed.

"Oh, I fear that I do, sir. I'm a scholar, Captain Leftrin. Most of my days are spent at my desk, reading and translating old scrolls and trying to make sense of what they tell me. This chance to speak to real dragons was to be my one real adventure in life. After what Captain Trell and his wife told me about them, I'm afraid it will be far less rewarding than I thought it would be. But, what is so funny? Are you mocking me?"

For Captain Leftrin had broken into a hearty boom of laughter at her words. "Oh, not at you, my dear, I assure you. It's the idea of Althea Vestrit dismissed as 'Captain Trell's wife' that is a rich jest for me. She's every bit as much a captain as Trell is, not that Paragon needs a captain at all these days. There's a liveship that has decided to be in charge of himself!"

Sedric broke in on their conversation. "Surely there must be some sort of lodging available here? Even a humble one would be welcome."

"None that I'd say was fit for a lady, there isn't. No, Sedric my friend, I'm afraid you'll have to tolerate my hospitality for one more night. Now if you'll excuse me for just a bit, I want to confer with my tillerman. There's a tricky bit of river before Cassarick, where they tried to build those locks for the sea serpents the year they came up the river. Didn't help the poor creatures much at all, and they've been a hazard to navigation every since." And so saying, he left his perch on the railing and descended to the deck. He quickly vanished from sight in the darkness.

Alise looked up at the lights of Cassarick growing closer. Sedric spoke quietly in a sour voice. "I can't wait to be off this stinking tub."

She was startled at the venom in his voice. "Do you truly hate it that much?"

"There's no privacy, the food is primitive, the company one level above socializing with street dogs, and my 'bunk' reeks of whoever last slept in it. I can't bathe, shaving is a challenge, and every piece of clothing I packed for this expedition now smells like their bilge. I didn't expect to be comfortable accompanying you on this journey, but I didn't think we'd descend quite this far into squalor."

Alise was struck dumb by his vehemence. Sedric seemed to take her silence as condemnation, for he seethed on, "Well, you cannot pretend to enjoy it here, even if you've a smelly room all to yourself. That pirate shows you no respect at all. Every time I turn around he's leering at you, or calling you 'my dear' as if you were some tavern wench he was set on impressing. He spends more time perched up here beside you than he does running his ship."

She found her tongue. "And you think this is inappropriate? Or that my behavior is reprehensible in this?"

"Oh, Alise, you know better than that." The sharpness dropped from his voice. "I know you wouldn't do anything dishonorable, let alone with some smelly riverman who thinks a 'clean shirt' is one that he hasn't worn in the last two days. No, I don't fault you. You're a very determined woman, and despite your disappointment about the dragons, you leaped to the practicality of trying to actually see them. I'm wretchedly uncomfortable on board this ship. At the same time, I'm relieved that you've recognized the realities we're dealing with and that our visit to the Rain Wilds will not be as extended as you originally planned."

"Sedric, I'm so sorry! You hadn't said a word. I didn't realize you were so unhappy. Perhaps tomorrow you can find appropriate lodgings for us, yes, and spend some time on a hot bath and a decent meal. You can even take a long rest if you wish it. I'm sure I'll be fine talking to the local council. I'd be very surprised if they didn't offer me a guide for my visit to the dragons. There is no reason that you have to go see the creatures at all. Originally, when I had thought I would have long, detailed conversations, I'd hoped you'd be available to take notes of what was said and do some sketches for me. But now that I know my experience will be little more than a trip to a menagerie, I don't see the sense in tormenting you." She resolutely kept her disappointment from her voice as she offered this. She longed to have him at her side when she met the dragons, and not just for the comfort of a familiar face.

She wanted there to be someone who would witness her there. She imagined them both back at Bingtown, at some stuffy dinner, when perhaps someone would ask her about her time among the dragons. She'd modestly say that it hadn't been much of an adventure, but then Sedric might raise his voice to contradict her pleasantly, and make a witty tale out of her time among them. She visualized herself, in her black boots and canvas trousers that she'd bought just for her encounter, striding across the flats to confront the scaled behemoths. She smiled to herself.

Before she met the dragons, she'd have to visit the local Traders' Council, to introduce herself and get its permission. And there again, she hoped to have his companionship. She had no idea whom she'd meet with when she visited the Council. She'd wanted to enter on Sedric's arm, to be seen as a woman worthy of such a handsome and charming escort. But he'd already made so many sacrifices to come with her. It was time for her to set her vanity aside and think of his comfort.

Sedric sat up straighter. "Alise, I didn't mean that at all! I enjoy your company, and I think I shall enjoy your seeing the dragons as much as you will. I apologize for being so discouraging. Let's get what sleep we can and make an early start of the day. You should come with me to find our lodgings; I'd never just abandon you in a strange town. And regardless of what Captain Leftrin says, we've no idea of how safe or dangerous a place this may be. We'll find our lodgings and, as you say, have a meal and a wash and change our clothes, and then we'll go to the Council together. And then, on to the dragons!"

"Then you don't mind going with me?" She was startled by the sudden change in his attitude. She could not keep the smile from her face.

"Not at all," he insisted. "I'm looking forward to getting close to the dragons as much as you are."

"No, you aren't," Alise said with a laugh. She looked into his face boldly, knowing that in the night she did not need to fear letting her affection for him shine in her eyes. "But it's a very kind lie, Sedric. I know you realize how much this means to me, and you've been awfully good about enduring your exile from Bingtown. When we return, I promise I'll find some way to make it up to you."

Sedric abruptly looked uncomfortable. "Alise, nothing of the kind is necessary. I assure you. Let me walk you to your cabin and then say good night."

She wanted to tell him that she could walk herself to her cabin. But doing that would mean admitting to herself that she did enjoy her quiet chats with the captain, and that she rather hoped that he would join her again that night. But Sedric had already made it clear that he had reservations about such conversations, and she would not put him in the uncomfortable position of having to stay awake to chaperone her. She rose and let him take her arm.

SINTARA AWOKE TO darkness. The blackness jolted her, for she had been dreaming of flying in sunlit blue skies over a glittering city by a wide river of blue and silver. "Kelsingra," she muttered to herself. She closed her eyes to the dark and tried to will herself back into her dream. She recalled the tall map tower at the center of the city, the broad city square, the leaping fountains, and the wide, shallow steps that led into the main buildings. There had been frescoes on the walls, images of both Elderling and dragon queens. Some ancestor of hers recalled sleeping sprawled on those wide steps, baking in the heat from the sun and the stone. How pleasant it had been to doze there, barely aware of the folk who hurried past her on their business. Their voices had been as musical as the distant chuckling of the river.

Sintara opened her eyes again. There was no recapturing the dream, and the memory was a thin and tattered substitute. She could hear the river muttering past the muddy banks, but she also heard the stentorian breathing of a dozen other dragons sleeping close by. There was no comparison between the dream and her reality.

Mercor had set his plan into motion with meticulous precision. He had never voiced his rumor directly to a human.

Always, he had arranged for the dragons to be speaking casually of the wonders of Kelsingra when humans chanced to be nearby. Once, it had been as workers were carrying a beautiful mirror frame out of the buried city. She recognized the material it was made from, a peculiar metal that when stroked, emitted light. Mercor had glanced at it and turned aside to remark to Sestican, "Do you recall the mirrored chamber of the Queen's Palace in Kelsingra? Over seven thousand gems were set in the ceiling mirrors alone. How they flared with light and perfume when she entered!"

Another time, it had been when the hunters had brought them the gamy remains of a stag to eat. As Mercor accepted his pitifully small share, he observed, "There was a statue of an elk in the King's Hall at Kelsingra, was there not? Of ivory overlaid with gold, and his eyes were two immense black jewels. Remember how they shone when they activated him, and how he would paw the earth and toss his head when anyone entered the king's chambers?"

Lies, all lies. If any such treasures had ever existed anywhere, Sintara did not recall them. But each time the humans paused and watched him as he spoke, even if he did not glance in their direction. And before the moon had changed, humans came to them in the darkness, without torches, to whisper questions about Kelsingra. How far away had it been? Was it built on high ground or low? How large a city? Of what were the buildings constructed? And Mercor had lied to them as it suited him, telling them that it was not all that far, that it had been built on high ground, and that all the buildings were built of marble and jade. But more than that, he would not tell them, not landmarks that had been nor how many days' travel it had once been from Cassarick. Nor would he consent to help a human make a map of where it once had been.

"Impossible to tell," he explained affably. "In those days, the river was fed by a hundred tributaries. There was a great lake before one came to Kelsingra. That I recall. But more than that, well, I could not say. I could go there and find it again, I am sure, if I had a mind to do so and a way to feed myself. But, no, it is not a thing I can put into words."

The next evening, there had been other men, asking the same questions, and two nights later, still more. All received the same teasing answers. Finally there had come by daylight half a dozen members of the Cassarick Traders' Council to offer a proposal to the dragons. And with them, incensed and fearful, came Malta the Elderling, dressed all in cloth of gold with a turban of white and scarlet on her head.

Only at Malta's request had all the dragons gathered to hear what the Council proposed. The Council had seemed to think that if they spoke to the largest dragon and gained his assent, they would have a binding agreement. Malta had laughed aloud at that and insisted that all be summoned. Then the head of the Council, a thin man with so little meat to his bones that he wouldn't have been worth the trouble of eating, spoke for a long time. Many unctuous words and promises he uttered, saying that the Council was troubled by the poor conditions the dragons were enduring, and that they hoped to help them return to their former homeland.

Mercor had assured them that they knew the humans were doing their best, and that dragons had no "homeland" but were in their rightful forms Lords of the Three Realms of earth, sea, and sky. He had blandly pretended not to understand the broad hints the Council leader dropped, until finally Malta cut through his foolishness to say bluntly, "They think you can lead them to Kelsingra and that they will find vast treasure there. They seek to persuade you to leave here and go in search of that fabled city. But I, who love all of you, fear that they are merely sending you off to your deaths. You must tell them no."

But Mercor had not heeded her advice. Instead he had said sadly, "Such a journey would be an impossible undertaking. We would starve long before we led you to Kelsingra. Every one of us is willing to undertake such a journey. But there are among us some who are small and weak. We would need hunters to feed them, and attendants to groom us and tend us as the Elderlings used to do. No. I fear it would be impossible. I need not say no because yes would be meaningless."

Then despite Malta's interruptions and pleadings and even her angry shouts, they struck a bargain. The Council would find for them hunters and attendants who would accompany them and hunt for them and tend them in every way. And in return, all the dragons had to do was lead them to Kelsingra or where it once had been.

"To this, we can agree," Mercor had told them gravely.

"They are tricking you!" Malta had objected. "They wish only to be rid of you, so that they can dig up Cassarick more easily and be done with feeding you. Dragons, listen to me, please."

But the deal had been struck. Kalo had pressed his muddy, inky foot to a piece of parchment held up to him, as if such a ridiculous ceremony could bind one dragon, let alone all them. Malta had gritted her teeth and knotted her fists as the Council proclaimed this was, indeed, the best plan. And Sintara had felt a shred of pity for the young Elderling who stood in such firm opposition to what the dragons themselves had manipulated the humans into offering them. She had hoped Mercor would find a way to have a quiet word with her. But either he did not care to do so or he thought it might endanger his plan. When the Council members left, she went with them, still pink cheeked with fury.

"This is not final!" she had warned them. "You need the signatures of every Council member to make this legal! Don't think I'll stand idly by while you do this!"

The glimpse of Malta had made her sad, and no doubt was responsible for her dreams. She was a young Elderling, a human newly changed into that form. She had years of growing and changing ahead of her, if she were to become all that the Elderlings of old had been.

But she would not. Some of the humans looked at her with wonder, but as many regarded her with disdain. She wondered what would become of Malta and Selden and Reyn now that Tintaglia had abandoned the new Elderlings, just as she had abandoned the other dragons. She did not fault Tintaglia for being gone. It was the dragon way to see first to one's own needs. She had found a mate and better hunting grounds, and eventually she would lay eggs and they would hatch into serpents. The dragon cycle, the true dragon cycle, would begin again as those serpents entered the sea.

But in the years until then, Sintara and the other dragons were all that existed in the Rain Wilds. All of them were creatures from another time, reborn into a world that no longer remembered them. And unfortunately they had returned in dwindled forms that were unfit for this world.

Lords of the Three Realms, they had once called themselves. Sea, land, and sky had all belonged to dragons and their kin. No one had been capable of denying anything to them. They had been masters of all.

And now they were masters of nothing, doomed to mud and carrion and, Sintara did not doubt, a slow death by slog up the river. She closed her eyes again. When the time came, she would go. Not because she was bound by Kalo's word, but because there was no future in staying here. If she must die as a crippled, broken thing, she would at least take a small measure of life first.

IT WAS NOT quite dawn when Alise awoke. She doubted that she had been asleep more than a few hours. She opened her eyes at the slight creak of her cabin door being unfastened and held her breath, and only then realized that a soft tap at her door had been what wakened her. "Are you awake?" Captain Leftrin asked quietly.

"I am now," she said and drew the bedcovers up to her chin. Her heart was hammering in her breast. What did the man want, coming to her cabin in the darkness before dawn?

He answered her unspoken question. "Sorry to intrude, but I need to get a clean shirt. The local council wants to talk to me, right away. Apparently they've been watching and waiting for me to dock. A runner came to the ship late last night with a message. Says they need to finalize the contracts for moving the dragons as soon as possible." He shook his head, more to himself than to her. "Something's up. The whole thing smacks of someone trying to beat someone else to a prize. This isn't like the Council at all. They always like to pretend there's all the time in the world and keep me tied

up bargaining until I have to take their terms or run out of
ready cash."

"Move the dragons as soon as possible?" At those words,
her mind had frozen. She sat up in his bunk but kept the
blankets clutched to her. "Where are they moving them so
quickly? Why?"

"I don't know, ma'am. I expect that when I meet with
them, I'll find out. The word they sent was that they wanted
to see me as early as possible. So I have to be on my way."

"I'm going with you." The moment the words were out of
her mouth, she realized how forward they sounded. Nothing
he had said had even hinted he might welcome her company.
And she hadn't asked if she might accompany him, she'd
announced it. Was her newfound ability to make decisions
for herself suddenly going to get her into trouble?

But he only said, "I thought you might want to. Let me
get some things and clear out of the cabin so you can have
your privacy. I'll fry a couple of extra pieces of bread and
set out a coffee mug for you." He moved about the cabin
as he spoke, taking a shirt from a hook and scooping up
the box that held his shaving razor and soap. She could not
help but notice that what Sedric had said was true. The shirt
was one he'd worn several days ago, and she'd never seen it
washed or dried. She found she didn't care.

As soon as the door closed quietly behind him, she
sprang from the bed. Suspecting that her day might involve
climbing a lot of steps if not ladders, she dressed in a split
skirt and boots as if she were going riding. The blouse she
put on was a sensible one of thick cotton. She added a nut-
brown jacket of sturdy duck and belted it securely around
her waist. There. She might cut a rather mannish figure, but
she'd be ready for anything the day handed her. The captain's small mirror showed her that her days on the river
had multiplied and darkened her freckles. And her hair was
baked to orange and near as dry as straw despite the sun
hats she had been wearing. For a moment, the sheer homeli-
ness of her image daunted her. Then she squared her shoulders and straightened her mouth. She hadn't come here to be
admired, but to study the dragons. Her fortune was not and

never had been in her face. It was her mind that counted. She narrowed her eyes at the mirror, thrust her chin forward, snatched up a plain hat of woven straw, and jammed it on her head.

She found Captain Leftrin alone at the galley table. Two steaming mugs of coffee waited there. His back was to her as she entered, and he was frying thick slices of yellow bread on the galley stove. A sticky pot of treacle and two heavy earthenware plates awaited the bread. As Leftrin turned to slide a slice of bread onto each plate, he smiled at her. "Well, that was quick! It always took my sister half a day to get dressed to do anything. But here you are, all ready to go and pretty as a picture to boot!"

She was shocked to feel a blush rose her cheeks. "You are too kind," she managed to say, and disliked how formal a response that seemed. She wished that Sedric had not put it in her head that it was inappropriate for her to encourage the captain's rustic flirting. *It is just his manner,* she told herself firmly. *It's nothing to do with me,* and she took her place at the table.

It seemed they were the only two people astir on the boat. She took a sip of the coffee. It was thick and black and had probably been kept on the ship's stove all night. There was no cream to tame it with so she followed the sailors' previous example and generously ladled treacle into it. It tasted like sweet tar then instead of just tar. She trickled threads of syrup over her fried bread and ate it while it was hot. They breakfasted with more efficiency than manners. Leftrin cleared the table, clattering the plates and mugs into a dish pan. "Shall we go, then?" he invited her, and she responded with a nod.

They left the galley together, and he offered her his hand to disembark from the ship. As they had put out no gangplank, this required a small jump from the scow to the dock. Once she had landed safely, it seemed only natural to accept the arm that he offered her. As they strolled down the docks in the early-morning light, he gestured to the boats they passed, telling her their names and a bit about each one. Tarman was the largest vessel by far. "And the oldest," he told her proudly. "When they built him, they didn't spare the wizardwood. The river has eaten thousands of boats since he was launched, but Tarman takes the river, rocks, and acid flows and snags, and just keeps on splitting the water."

When they left the floating docks, it was to step from them onto a wide path of beaten earth. The ground gave strangely under her feet. "It's a leather road," he told her. "It's an old technique. Layers of tanned hides over logs, and cedar branches and bark in the thick layer over that, then more hides and finally ash, and then a layer of earth over all. The rot process is slowed, and the wood-and-leather layers have some buoyancy. It doesn't last forever, but if they didn't do something, this road would be trodden to mud in a few weeks, and soon after that water would seep up and fill it in. May not look like much, but it cost Cassarick a pretty penny to make it. And here we are at the lift station. Or would you prefer the stairs?"

There at the base of an immense tree was a spiral stair- case that wound up and around the tree's trunk. She craned her head back and saw the lowest level of Cassarick above her. Beside the staircase as an alternative was a flimsy- looking platform with a woven railing around it. A long woven cord with a handle dangled next to it. "You pull the bellpull, and if the operator is at work, he sends down the counterweight to lift you up. It costs a penny or two, but it's faster and easier than the staircase."

"I think I prefer the stairs," Alise decided. But she wasn't even halfway up before she regretted her decision. The climb was steeper than it had looked. The captain gamely accompanied her, grunting softly with each step. When she reached the first landing and looked around her, she sud- denly forgot her aching legs.

A wide platform circled the tree's huge trunk. The vendor stalls that backed up to the trunk were just opening their canvas curtains. From the central platform around the trunk, a spiderweb of suspended boardwalks spread out in various directions toward other trees and the platforms that circled their trunks. Although the boardwalks had railings woven of vines, they sagged in the middle, and there were visible gaps in the planking. "This way to their Traders' Hall," Leftrin told her, and putting her hand on his arm, he guided her out onto one of the walks.

Four steps out, she felt giddy. The planks thunked musically under their feet. Leftrin didn't bother with the flimsy rails and seemed unaware of the gentle swaying of the bridge. She glanced down, gasped at a glimpse of the earth far below her, then looked to the side and felt suddenly ill. The bridge sagged under their weight, and she was stepping down the planking and certain that she was going to fall at any moment. Leftrin put his hand over hers on his arm. "Look ahead to the next platform," he told her in a low, reassuring voice. "Get the rhythm of it, and it's just like climbing stairs. Don't look down and don't worry about what isn't there. Rain Wilders have been building these for over a hundred years now. They're our streets. You can trust them."

He spoke in a matter-of-fact way that wasn't condescending. He didn't think less of her for being afraid; he accepted that she would naturally be apprehensive. Somehow that made it easier to take his advice. She firmed her grip on his arm and matched her stride to his, so that soon they were clomping along in rhythm. Suddenly, it was almost like a dance they were partnered in. They reached the lowest point of the bridge and then they were climbing up the gentle rise, the planks becoming a sloping ladder until they abruptly reached the next platform. She halted there to breathe, and Captain Leftrin paused with her.

"Only three more to go," he told her, and although she felt a bit frightened, she didn't feel daunted by the prospect. Challenged, she thought. Challenged, but not afraid to take up that challenge.

"Well, let's go then," she said.

She nearly lost her courage on the second bridge when they encountered a group of workmen heading in the opposite direction. She and Leftrin had to move closer to the edge to allow them passage, and the rhythm of their strides made the whole structure waggle like a friendly dog being petted. But by the third crossing, she had recovered her sen-

sation of dancing with Leftrin. They reached their final platform with her slightly out of breath but feeling triumphant.

Cassarick had ambition. That was evident from the size
of the Traders' Hall they had built all around the trunk of
the largest tree she had visited yet. The platform that supported and surrounded it served as an esplanade. It circled
both hall and tree, and four staircases wound up from it to
platforms in adjacent trees. Early as it was and dim as the
light was this far below the treetops, sputtering torches still
lit the walkways. Their journey had led them away from the
riverbank, and less light from that open area penetrated the
settlement. Alise felt that she had journeyed into a twilight
city of fantastic people.

She had grown up in Bingtown among the descendants
of the original Trader families who had settled there. She
had always known of their Rain Wild kin and respected the
bonds between the Rain Wilds and Bingtown. Only here in
the Rain Wilds were the magical treasures of the ancient
Elderlings to be unearthed. But living in the Rain Wilds and
working in the buried Elderling cities exacted a toll on the
folk who settled there. Almost all Rain Wilders had some
disfigurement at birth, and it increased with each year of
their lives. Sometimes it was a bit of scaling on the scalp or
lips, or a fringe of wattled growths along the jawline. With
age might come a change in eye color and a thickening of
nails; those were typical of the sorts of things one might
see on a Rain Wilder who visited Bingtown. Even Captain
Leftrin had his share of marks. The skin on the backs of his
hands and on the knobs of his wrist was bluish and lightly
scaled. Behind his brushy eyebrows and on the back of his
neck, she thought she had glimpsed more scaling. It had
been easy to ignore.

Here in Cassarick as in Trehaug, the majority of the Rain
Wilders went unveiled. This was their city and if folk who
visited here did not respect them, such folk were swiftly encouraged to leave. She had tried not to stare at the workmen who had passed them earlier. The backs of their hands
and their elbows had been heavily scaled, and the scales had
not been flesh colored, but blue or green or shocking scar-

let. One man had been completely hairless, scales like fine mail over his bared scalp and outlining his brow and replacing his lips. Another had sported a heavy fringe of fleshy growths along his jaw and some that overshadowed his eyes, thick and floppy like the comb of a rooster. She had averted her eyes from them, grateful that keeping her balance on the galloping bridge demanded all her attention.

But now she was on a solid platform and it was difficult to know where to put her gaze. This early in the day, there were not many folk about but all were unmistakably marked as Rain Wilders. Many cast curious glances her way, and she desperately told herself that it was her attire, so different from what they wore, that drew their eyes. The men had been wearing almost a uniform of heavy blue cotton shirts, thick brown canvas trousers, and loose canvas jackets. The boots they wore were heavy things, still clotted with dried mud from their previous day's work. They'd carried their lunches in canvas sacks. Thick gloves and woolen hats protruded from their trouser pockets. "Diggers," Leftrin had told her as they passed. "Headed off for a long day's work underground. Cold down there, and damp, winter or summer."

Now, as they passed a woman clad in soft leather trousers and a leather vest tufted with fur, Leftrin said, "She's a climber. See how she goes barefoot for a better grip. She'll be headed up into the canopy today, to gather fruit or hunt birds."

Just as she nearly decided that the women of Cassarick led hard, lean lives, two chattering girls passed them going the other direction. They wore morning dresses and were perhaps going off to call on a friend or to visit the early markets. Their flounced skirts were shorter than those currently worn in Bingtown and showed off their soft brown shoes. They wore lacy little shawls, and their hats were designed to look like large, softly folded leaves. She turned her head to look after them, and for a moment a familiar envy flooded up to drown her spirits. They looked so cheery and busy, chattering away together. When they came to a bridge, they linked arms and clattered across it together, whooping like hoydens when they reached the other side.

"What makes you sigh?" Leftrin asked her, and she realized that she was staring after them.

She shook her head, smiling tightly at her own foolishness. "I was just thinking that somehow I skipped being that age, and I'll always regret it. I often feel that I went from being a girl to being a settled woman, with none of that giddiness in between."

"You talk like you're an old woman, with your whole life lived."

A sudden lump rose in her throat. *I am,* she thought. *In a few days, I'll go home and settle down to what I'll be the rest of my life. No adventures ahead, no changes to anticipate. Nothing to anticipate except leading a proper life.* She swallowed and by the time she could speak, she had more appropriate words. "Well, I'm a married woman with a settled life. I suppose what I miss is a sense of uncertainty. Of possibility waiting just around the corner."

"And you're saying you never had that?"

She paused because the truth was somehow humiliating. "No. I don't think I did. I think my life was more or less mapped out from the beginning. Getting married was a surprise for me. I didn't think I'd ever marry. But once I was a married woman, my life settled into a routine that wasn't much different from when I was single."

He was silent for longer than was his wont, and when she glanced over at him, his mouth was strangely puckered as if he strove to keep words in. "Just say it," she suggested, and then wondered if she was brave enough to hear whatever judgment he held back.

He grinned at her. "Well, it's not polite to say, but if I were a man and married to a woman such as you, and she said to another fellow that her life as my wife wasn't much different from her life when she'd been single, well, I'd wonder what I was doing wrong." He raised his eyebrows at her and whispered in a ribald tone, "Or not doing at all!"

"Captain Leftrin!" she exclaimed, genuinely shocked. Then, when he burst out laughing, she was horrified at joining in.

When they both paused for breath, he held up a warning

hand. "No. Don't tell me! Some things a wife should never say about her husband! And here we are, anyway, so our time for chat is over."

They had reached the doors of the Traders' Hall. Each tall door was a single slab of black wood, twice as tall as a man. Leftrin pushed on one and it swung silently open.

The hall had no windows. There was an antechamber, lit with a single branch of candles that smelled like orange blossom. Leftrin didn't pause as he crossed the carpeted floor and went through yet another set of tall doors. Alise followed him and found herself in a circular chamber. Tiers of descending benches circled a wide dais. On the dais was a long table of pale wood, with a dozen heavy chairs behind it. Only half of them were currently occupied. Suspended globes that looked like balls of yellow glass cast a golden light throughout the room. The scattered lights bent the shadows in the room in odd ways. The walls of the room were hung with tapestries. They were either of Elderling origin or very clever imitations. Her eyes snagged on them, and she longed to beg for time to study every aspect of them.

But their abrupt entry had caused a stir among the six Rain Wilders seated at the table. Despite the early hour, they were formally dressed in their Trader robes. Each robe was of a different color and design to indicate which of the original settlement families the Trader represented. Alise did not recognize any of them. The Trader families of Bingtown were different from those of the Rain Wilds, even though there had been substantial intermarriage for years. Close to the center of the seating a woman with a lined face and a stiff gray brush of hair glared at them. "This is a private committee meeting," she announced. "If you are here on Trader business, you will have to make an appointment and come back later."

"I believe we were invited to this meeting," Leftrin responded. His use of "we" was not lost on Alise and her heart leaped. He would do whatever he could to keep her here and privy to what was happening with the dragons. "I'm Captain Leftrin of the scow *Tarman*. When I docked late last night,

I was invited to call here 'as early as possible' this morning. To discuss moving some dragons upriver, I believe. But if I'm wrong—"

He let the word hang and the woman's hands fluttered up in a gesture dismissing her previous protest. But before she could speak, the door behind Alise and Leftrin shut with an audible and angry thump. Alise turned, startled, and gasped in surprise. An Elderling woman, gowned all in silver and blue, stood there. Her eyes gleamed metallic in the golden light and her face looked like anger cast in stone. "This is not a legitimate meeting, Captain Leftrin. As you can see, there are not enough members of the committee seated to authorize any action."

"On the contrary, Malta Khuprus." The woman who had spoken earlier held up a sheaf of paper. "I have letters of authorization to act on the behalf of two members who are too occupied with business to attend today's meeting. I can cast their votes as I see fit. And if all of us here vote the same way, then we are a majority, with or without the others voting."

"But you do not, I'll wager, have such a letter from my brother, Selden Vestrit. And, Trader Polsk, as he represents the interests of the dragon Tintaglia, I do not see how you can make any sort of a binding vote without his presence."

"He is only one vote. Whether he agreed with us or not, his vote would not change the outcome."

"He represents Tintaglia's concerns. He speaks for the dragons. How can you finalize decisions about their fate without consulting him? The simple fact is that you cannot!"

The Elderling woman strode past them as she talked. Alise tried not to stare but could not help it. Everyone knew the story of Malta Vestrit. She had been involved with a failed kidnapping plot against the Satrap of Jamaillia. With him, she had been captured by pirates and ultimately she had been one of the forces to help forge a peace between Jamaillia and the Pirate Kingdom. But that was not what everyone remembered about her. She had been in close contact with the dragon Tintaglia just before she hatched from her case. Some said that was what had precipitated her change from ordinary Bingtown Trader girl to a woman who was obviously changing into an Elderling. Others said it had been a gift from the dragon. Both her fiancé and her brother had been affected as well, and they, too, had been present at the hatching of the dragon. All of them showed similar changes.

"We attempted to include Selden Vestrit in this meeting, but he is not here nor in Trehaug. And we have been told that we cannot expect his return for at least four months. By then, we will be venturing toward foul weather, and another long, wet winter with dragons churning the grounds around Cassarick into a quagmire. We have to act now. We cannot delay any longer simply to hear the opinion of a single member of the committee."

"You are acting now purely because he *is* away from the Rain Wilds and unable to intervene on Tintaglia's behalf."

The gray-haired woman at the table looked beleaguered. Several of her fellows looked uncomfortable, but one at least expressed his annoyance by marching his fingers on the table's edge. A young man with a flash of orange scales on his high cheekbones was obviously angry. He gritted his teeth as if to cage furious words. The head of the committee spoke. "You were with us when we went to speak to the dragons. You heard that they understood what we were proposing. You know that the largest dragon, the black one, agreed to our proposal to move them all to a better place. We even acceded to his demands for extra hunters to accompany the herd. Those hunters will be arriving anytime now, and they will expect to leave immediately. Our meeting this morning is, in fact, to assure that we can meet the dragons' expectations. Captain Leftrin, we summoned you here in the hopes of securing you and your barge to escort the dragons and their hunters up the river."

Alise had to admire how deftly the woman had shifted her conversation from Malta to Leftrin. She was still trying to understand how it all fit together. The dragons were to be moved from Cassarick? Hunters would accompany them? And possibly Captain Leftrin's barge?

"This is very short notice," Captain Leftrin replied. He

took a deep breath, and when he spoke, his words were slow and carefully considered. "Almost impossibly short notice. I need to know exactly what I'm agreeing to before I can give you any sort of an answer."

Alise heard the speculation behind his reserved words. Malta's tirade had revealed to him that he had the Council of Cassarick over a barrel. They had admitted that they had to act swiftly. If what Leftrin had told her about his ship was true, then his barge was the only vessel of any size that could accompany the dragons upriver. They'd have to pay him whatever he asked, or lose their window of opportunity. It was clear to Alise that they wished to have the dragons under way before either winter or Selden Vestrit returned.

The Council woman looked trapped as her eyes darted from Leftrin to Malta. "We do have an offer to make you, Captain Leftrin. We wish to negotiate a charter with you. We'd like to hire your vessel as an escort ship for the dragons and their keepers. The *Tarman* would carry extra provisions for both the keepers and the dragons, and be transport and housing for our hunters. It would be the mother ship that the keepers' smaller boats could tie up to at night, if needed. One of the hunters we have chosen to accompany you is an experienced explorer. In addition to providing meat for the dragons, he will construct a chart of the river and keep a journal of any noteworthy events. He will also represent the Council and is authorized to decide when the dragons have been appropriately settled. When he reaches that decision, he will let you know, and at that point you will turn back toward Cassarick."

Malta interrupted with a sharp question, "If the keepers' boats need to tie up at night to a floating vessel, then where are the dragons at that time, I'd like to know, Trader Polsk?"

The woman shook her head. "The need for a mother ship is a hypothetical need, Malta. We are simply making arrangements for every contingency."

"And the Council representative? Why is one necessary? Will not the dragons know when they are 'appropriately settled' and release their keepers from service?"

A strange light had come into the Elderling woman's eyes. They glowed, Alise realized. The set of her mouth proclaimed her anger, but there were other signs of it as well. The shimmering gold orbs that lit the room slowly began to shift their positions. Whatever had anchored them before gave way as the balls of light began to slowly but purposefully drift toward Malta. One Council member gave a brief huff of uneasiness, but the others kept stony faces of indifference.

The chairwoman tried to speak calmly. "The dragons may not realize when we have reached a point where we have done all we can for them. This is sad, but true. So we have arranged for someone to accompany the dragons and provide an impartial evaluation."

Malta spoke. "Impartial? A Council representative who is 'impartial'? Perhaps a representative for the dragons should be assigned also, to see that the dragons are fairly treated and that our contract is observed. Have you considered arranging to keep your word to the dragon Tintaglia? As per the signed contract we made?" The floating orbs ringed her now, leaving most of the rest of the room in dimness. The light from them glittered and ran over her scaled face and gleaming arms. She shone like a jeweled statue. Her eyes were as hard as faceted gems.

"Has she?" Trader Polsk hissed back at the Elderling. "Tintaglia has vanished and left us with a horde of hungry dragons to care for! What would you have us do? Keep them here on the very doorstep of Cassarick? It is not good for them or for us! Keeping them here will solve nothing. But there is the possibility that if we send them upriver, they may find a better location for themselves. Look how many of them have already died, and those who remain are in poor condition. Now is not the time to flaunt your powers to make us cower. You would better use your time to help us plan the best way to aid them in their evacuation. It is the best we can offer them, Malta. Surely you must see that!"

"I see nothing of the kind," Malta retorted in a low voice, but there was a tattered edge of defeat to it. "I see that there is something here I do not know, something that propels the urgency of this expedition. Do any of you see fit to be honest with me?" The lights around her dimmed, very slightly.

Trader Polsk ignored her words and pushed her advantage. "Have you heard from either your brother or the dragon Tintaglia?"

"My brother is traveling, and all know how irregular the mails are from abroad. And I have not heard Tintaglia nor felt her touch in months. I do not know what her fate is. She could simply be far afield, or some terrible accident may have befallen her. I do not know." She sounded anguished. But her voice firmed as she went on, "But I do know that many Bingtown Traders gave their word to her that they would do all they could to help her offspring in return for her aid. Without her actions during our war with Chalced, Bingtown itself might have perished. She kept the Chalcedean ships from the mouth of the Rain Wild River. When we most needed her help, she was there for us. And now that she is away, will we abandon the young dragons to death, simply because caring for them has become a hardship? Has the word of a Trader come to mean so little to us in these kinder days?" As she spoke, the light globes that surrounded her burned warmer. Light reflected from her, until she seemed the source of it rather than the recipient.

A silence, perhaps one of shame, followed her question. A few of the Council members exchanged glances.

Alise timidly broke the silence. "I was there. I was there the night the dragon came to the Bingtown Traders' Concourse. I was there the night the deal was struck. I heard Tintaglia speak, and young as I was, I was among those who signed our agreement with her." Her voice dropped as she added, "I was even there when Reyn Khuprus spoke out and demanded that Tintaglia help him find Malta, as a condition of that agreement." Her glance went from the startled Elderling to the Council. She drew herself up straight and summoned courage she didn't know she had. She lifted her voice, willing it to fill the hall. "My name is Alise Kincarron Finbok. In addition to signing the agreement with the dragon Tintaglia, and thus having a vested interest in these decisions, I am one of the foremost experts on both dragons and Elderlings that Bingtown has to offer. I have traveled here from Bingtown for the express purpose of speaking with the dragons and learning more of their kind.

"Since Tintaglia first appeared in our midst, I have devoted all my time to the studying and translation of every scroll or tablet regarding dragons and Elderlings that exist in Bingtown. When you speak of breaking an agreement with a dragon who had given you her true name as her binding word on it, I do not think you fully comprehend what you are suggesting. As Bingtown's most knowledgeable authority on dragons, I do."

As she drew breath, she shoved aside her doubt that anyone in Bingtown would agree with her previous statement. No one else from Bingtown was here to contradict her. And she knew her words to be true, and right now that was all that mattered. She spoke on, decisively, listening in amazement to the words coming out of her own mouth. "I do not believe that the Traders' Council of Cassarick has the authority to make this decision regarding—"

"You have studied dragons and Elderlings." It was Malta the Elderling who so precipitously interrupted her. "In all the ancient scrolls you have studied, have you ever found mention of a place called Kelsingra? I believe it was an Elderling city."

Alise felt like a sailing boat that had suddenly lost the wind from its sails. Malta's question was so unexpected that she lost the chain of argument that she had wished to present to the Council. The news that they wished to "evacuate" the dragons immediately had stunned her. From what Leftrin had told her on the boat, she had believed she would at least have her few days with them. Now it appeared that even that short time might be snatched away from her. For an instant, she had been filled with resolve to do or say whatever she must to win those few days back. But at Malta's interruption, she lost the thread of her words and her courage. All her bravado suddenly fled. She glanced at the Council members, expecting them to be annoyed by Malta's question. Instead, they seemed as focused on her answer as Malta herself did. Trader Polsk leaned forward, eyes fixed on her. Alise had all but forgotten the captain at her side, but now he reached over and set a reassuring hand on her forearm. "Go on. Tell them."

It rattled her for a moment; how could he know that she knew about Kelsingra? Then she recalled that yesterday afternoon when he had been telling her tales of river navigation, and how quickly a channel he had used one month could silt in by the next, she, burning to distinguish herself, had nodded wisely and recounted a story from an old scroll that had spoken about how often the passage to the Kelsingra docks had to be dredged. He had replied that he'd never heard of such a city, and she had dismissed it with a shrug, saying that perhaps the river had swallowed it long ago.

She looked at Malta. The Elderling looked poised for flight; she leaned slightly toward Alise, her eyes burning with hope. The light globes that had drifted to surround her had spread again, but she still seemed at the center of all light in the room. How could Alise tell her that Kelsingra was little more than a name in a scroll to her? She glanced helplessly about and her eyes, by fate or chance, snagged on a tapestry to the left of Malta. A strange thrill shot through her. She slowly lifted her hand and pointed at it. "There is Kelsingra." She walked toward it, her heart beating faster with every step. "Give me more light here, please," she said, almost forgetting where she was and to whom she spoke in the excitement of her find.

In response to her request, Malta sent the light globes flocking after her. They followed her, and when she halted, they did. When they gathered around the tapestry, it was almost like looking out a window into a woven world. It was all there. The perspective had been skewed deliberately by the weaver so that more landmarks could be included. "There." She lifted her hand and pointed as she spoke. "That would be the famous map tower of Kelsingra. From what I have read, I believe that map towers were created in several of their larger cities. In each tower there would be a large relief map of the surrounding area, and the encircling windows of the tower looked out on the depicted area.

Sometimes there were symbols for more distant locations. The scrolls imply that somehow the map towers helped people to travel swiftly, but they do not say how. The map tower at Kelsingra is referred to in several scrolls, perhaps indicating that it was of more importance than some of the others."

Distantly she heard her own voice. She had taken on a pedagogic tenor, the tone she had sometimes dreamed that she would employ someday when her scholarship was recognized and people would wish her to share her knowledge. Never had she dreamed she would lecture in a place like Cassarick or that her audience would include an Elderling. Her hand moved and she pointed again. "You can see that the map tower is in the spire of a very impressive building. The decorative frieze on the front shows an Elderling woman plowing behind an ox. The adjacent wall, as you can see, depicts a queen dragon. I speculate that the conjunction of the two is no accident, but shows that the two of them were as important to the city as the two walls that support this main city structure. We can only wonder what was on the other two faces of the building.

"Note the depth and width of the stairs that approach the grand entry doors. Humans, or human-size Elderlings, would have no need of such steps, nor of such immense doors. It's clear to me that this structure, identified in one scroll as the Citadel of Records, welcomed both Elderlings and dragons inside its walls."

"But where is it? Where is Kelsingra?" Malta's low anxious voice cut through Alise's lecture.

Slowly the Bingtown woman turned to look at the Elderling. "I cannot tell you that with any precision. As far as I know, no map of the areas that we now call the Rain Wilds has ever been recovered. But from the written descriptions we have, I can say with certainty that it was substantially upriver of both Trehaug and Cassarick. We do have descriptions of the lush meadowlands that surrounded the city and provided good grazing for both domesticated cattle and wild game. The dragons feasted freely on both, and it was considered their right to do so. But such open rolling meadows do not fit with the jungled Rain Wilds that we know. Nor does the description of the river. According to the scrolls, the river that ran past Kelsingra was deep, and during flood times, it was swift running and treacherous. The illustrations in the scrolls and here on this tapestry clearly show keeled sailing vessels both approaching the city and tying up at its docks. There are trade vessels of considerable size already moored there. Again, these images do not fit with the Rain Wild River as we know it now. So, we can speculate that either the river has changed, a fact that is obviously true given the buried ruins that have been unearthed here, or we can wonder if there existed another, different river, a tributary or one that is perhaps merged now with our Rain Wild River, that originally fronted Kelsingra."

She ran out of breath and words at the same time. She turned away from the tapestry and back to her audience. Malta's face was a mixture of triumph and misery. The brushy-haired Rain Wild woman at the table was nodding her head vigorously. "Excellent!" she exclaimed before anyone else could speak. "We are indebted to you, madam. The black dragon has spoken of this Kelsingra as the best possible destination for the dragons. They have dropped hints to us that it was a major Elderling city. But up to now, we lacked confirmation of its existence. You offer us not only the physical evidence of the tapestry, but your scholarly opinion that such a place did, and possibly still does, exist. We could not ask for better news, any of us!"

"I could," Malta asserted flatly. "I could ask for a map that would clearly show us where the city once existed in relation to the two Elderling cities that we have already located." She flicked her fingers as if in annoyance, and the light globes scattered like startled cats. She moved to one of the tiers of benches and slowly sank down onto it. She suddenly appeared not only merely human but very tired. "We have failed them so badly. We gave a promise to Tintaglia and we began by doing the best we could for them. Slowly we let our standards fall, and the last two years have just been a nightmare. So many of them have died."

"Without our help, all of them would have died. Without

our help, most of them would never have cocooned, let alone hatched." Trader Polsk presented the fact simply.

"Without us cutting them up into planks to build ships, more of them might have survived to hatch during that quake," Malta retorted.

"If there had not been liveships, would you have been there at all?" Alise dared to interject the question. Malta appeared to be mired in despair, but Alise felt a growing excitement. The most wonderful idea she had ever imagined was slowly unfolding in her mind. She hardly dared state it. She teetered on dread that they might refuse her and terror that they might accept her offer. She tried to keep her voice steady as she asked, "How soon must the dragons be moved?"

"The sooner the better," Trader Polsk replied. She ran both her hands through her brush of gray hair, standing it up like a dragon's crest. "Delay can only make it worse for all of us, including the dragons. If it were possible for them to leave tomorrow, that is what I would choose."

"Yet I have come all the way from Bingtown just for the purpose of studying these dragons and possibly conversing with them," Alise objected.

"You will find them little inclined to conversation," Malta said drearily. "Even if you had come months ago, it would have been so. They have ancestral memories of the dragons they should have been. Much as I hate to admit it, Trader Polsk is right. They are and have been miserable where they are. I have done my best to visit them often, and I know the hardships that have been created for those who tried to keep faithfully the terms of our bargain with Tintaglia. I am not blind to those things. I just wish it could have a better ending. I wish that I could go with them and see them safely settled in some better place. But I cannot."

She sounded so defeated that Alise wondered if the Elderling woman were ill. But then she set her hands to her belly in the unmistakable gesture of a woman who is with child and sets that child's well-being above all in her life. It was like the last piece of a puzzle falling into place. The circumstances were exactly right for her; if it was not fate, it was close enough.

"You cannot go, but I can." She spoke the words clearly, offering herself and seizing a chance for herself in the same breath. "I am willing to travel with them, using my knowledge of their kind to aid them in any way I can. I am eager to travel with them, to learn of them all I can, and to observe their kind in, if I dare to admit it, the wild hope that I could be with them if and when Kelsingra is rediscovered. Let me be the one to go."

Silence greeted her words, but it was of a mixed sort. Malta looked at her as if she were a vision of salvation. Trader Polsk looked intrigued. Two of the committee members were regarding her with sick horror. She made an intuitive leap; those two had had some inkling that Kelsingra was real and that valuable Elderling relics might be discovered there. She'd just spoiled some sort of secret scheme without even intending to do so. The thought of that fired her courage. She spoke aloud to Malta. "If Kelsingra is rediscovered and is intact at all, it could be the greatest resource yet for understanding how Elderlings and dragons interacted. The mysteries that have been discovered at Trehaug and Cassarick may be solved at Kelsingra."

"Surely that is a matter for Rain Wild Traders to discuss," one of the men at the table assayed.

"Surely it is a matter for Elderlings and dragons," Malta countered.

"The first step is to find the place. And get the dragons to safety." Leftrin was grinning from ear to ear. He strode across the darkened room to step into the light and stand beside her. "If the lady's willing to go on the trip to continue her study of the dragons, then I'm willing to take her." As the gray-haired committee leader leaned forward as if to object, he added calmly, "In fact, I'm willing to make it one of the conditions for my accepting the charter." He boldly turned to Malta and made a small bow. "Perhaps we should defer to Malta Khuprus. She suggested that the dragons should have a representative. Seems to me that having a dragon expert aboard might be one of the wiser things that we could do."

Malta smiled wearily. Then she looked to the committee table. "I will speak for Tintaglia in this." She swung her gaze to Alise, and that look was compelling. Alise was nodding even before Malta said, "If Alise Finbok is willing to go, I am willing to accept her as an impartial judge to act in the best interest of the dragons."

✧ ✧ ✧

Day the 4th of the Grain Moon

Year the 6th of the Independent Alliance of Traders

From Detozi
To Erek

That sneaking little bastard! He is too low for his own pigeons to shit on! As if the weight of our ink on the tiny corner end of a scroll was an added weight for the pigeons to carry! He is so self-righteous, and always seeking a way to discredit me, because he knows that if I am discharged, then his brother will probably be hired on in my place! I pray you, be cautious of which birds you use if you have added a note for me. Recall that all the birds that home to my coop are banded with red bands. Kim does not even paint his bands, but uses plain leather, the lazy piece of dung.

Detozi

✧ ✧ ✧

CHAPTER ELEVEN

ENCOUNTERS

The muddy banks of the river were drying out. Cracks and fissures had opened up in the flat brown plain. As Sintara waded out of the gray silt-laden water, the wet bank gave unevenly under her feet. She lurched as she walked. Dragons, she reflected, were not intended to be creatures of the ground.

Her blue-scaled hide was still dripping from her attempt at a bath; she left a wet trail behind her. She opened her stunted wings, flapped and shook them in a shower of water droplets, and then refolded them against her sides. She wished in vain for a wide bank of hot sand where she could bask until she was dry, and then polish her claws and scales until she shone. In this lifetime, she'd never had the luxury of a good dust bath, let alone a nice rasp on a sandbank. Dust and sand, she was sure, would have cleansed her of a lot of the tiny sucking insects that infested her and the other dragons. Although she still groomed herself daily, few of the others did. As long as they were infested and she had to live in close quarters with them, there seemed little point to grooming. Yet she refused to give up that ritual. She was a dragon, not a mindless mud salamander.

The forest that backed onto the beach put most of the riverbank in perpetual shade. During the years they had been trapped there, the dragons had enlarged the clearing. Some of the surrounding trees had been killed accidentally by dragons sharpening claws or rubbing scaled shoulders against them in search of relief from the pests that infested them. Several trees had been killed deliberately as the dragons sought to enlarge the area in which they were forced to live. But killing a tree and pushing it down and out of the way were two different tasks. Killing it meant that its foliage dropped and an additional but small amount of light reached them. But despite sporadic efforts, not even several dragons together could push down one of the towering trees.

Sunlight reached the riverbank at the height of the day and lingered there strongly only for a few hours. Sintara surveyed the fourteen dragons spread out before her. Most of them slept or at least drowsed, soaking up light and warmth while they could. There was little else for them to do this afternoon. The larger dragons had claimed the prime spots for sunbathing. The lesser dragons took whatever space they could find. Most of them napped in areas that were shadow dappled; the smallest and least able slept in full shade. Even the best spots were barely adequate for comfort. The river mud dried to a fine sneeze-inducing dust that was annoying to eyes and nostrils. But at least it was warm and there was light. Sintara's skin and bones constantly longed for light and heat almost as much as her belly hungered for meat.

The sunlight sparkled on a few of the better-groomed dragons. Kalo, the largest of their clan, gleamed blue-black as he sprawled in the strongest patch of sunlight. His head rested on his forelegs. His eyes were closed, and his slow breath stirred a small plume of dust each time he exhaled. At rest and folded to his back, his wings looked almost normal. He seldom spread them, but when he did, the flimsy musculature betrayed him.

Beside him, Ranculos shone scarlet in sharp contrast to the dusty shore. His silver eyes were lidded in sleep. He was badly proportioned, as if someone had sculpted parts of three different dragons and then assembled them. His front shoulders and legs were powerful, but he dwindled at his hindquarters and his tail was ridiculous. His wings drooped and refused to stay properly closed. Pathetic.

Sintara narrowed her eyes to see that azure Sestican had sprawled out, wings open, and was occupying her space as well as his own. His long scrawny legs twitched in his sleep. Between her and him, several of the smaller and less able dragons were sleeping. Their dull hides were daubed with mud, and they slept packed together like the toes on a foot.

She paid no attention to them as she thrust her way over and through the sleeping creatures. One squeaked and two gave snorting growls as she trod on them. One rolled under her, throwing her off balance. She lashed her tail to stay upright and flapped her still-drying wings, sprinkling all of them with a shower of cold droplets. A mutter of snarls greeted that, but none of them could be bothered to really challenge her. As she reached her place, she deliberately trod on Sestican's spread blue wing, pinning it to the earth.

He gave a surprised roar and tried to roll free. She pressed down harder on the trapped wing, deliberately bending the delicate bones. "You're in my place," she growled.

"Get off me!" he snarled in return. She lifted her foot just enough for him to drag his bruised wing free of her weight. As he snapped it back tight to his body, she sank down to the bared dust. She was still displeased. It was warm from his body heat, but not hot from baking sunlight as she had fantasized. Nonetheless, she settled into place, pushing ungraciously against Veras to make more room for herself. The dark green female stirred, bared her puny teeth, and then went on sleeping.

"Don't ever sleep in my place again," Sintara warned the big cobalt dragon. She arranged her body, resentfully tucking her tail around her instead of letting it sprawl out as she wished to. But she had no sooner settled her head on her front paws than Sestican abruptly lurched to his feet. She snarled as his shadow fell over her. At the edges of the sleeping swarm of dragons, one of the smaller ones lifted her head and asked stupidly, "Food?"

It was not time for them to be fed. There was a general lifting of heads followed by dragons wallowing and lurching to their feet, trying to see past one another for a view of what was arriving on the beach.

"Is it food?" Fente demanded angrily.

"Depends on how hungry you are," Veras replied. "Small boats full of people. They're pulling their boats up onto the bank now."

"I smell meat!" Kalo announced, and before he had even voiced it, the swarm was moving. Sintara shouldered Veras aside. The nasty green female snapped at her. Sintara gave her a lash of her tail in passing but didn't bother with any further retaliation. Being the first to the food was much more important than any vengeance right now. Sintara gathered her strength and made a springing leap over Fente. Her withered wings opened reflexively but uselessly. Sintara snapped them back close to her sides and continued her lumbering gallop down to the riverbank.

The cluster of young humans on the shore huddled together in fear. One yelled and ran back toward the beached boats. As the dragons advanced, three others joined him. Other people were emerging from the narrow beaten trail that led back into the forest and to the ladders that went up to their tree nests. Sintara caught the familiar scent of one of their hunters. The man raised his voice and shouted at the boat humans. "It's all right. They smell the food, that's all. Stand your ground and meet them. It's why you're here. We've got meat for all of them. Let us feed them first, and then you should move among them and let them greet you. Stand your ground!"

Sintara could smell the fear on them. She noted in passing that the humans from the boats were mostly youngsters. Their voices were raised to one another, piping questions and squeaking warnings. Then the other hunters emerged

from the path, pushing their barrows. Each wooden barrow
was heaped high with meat and fish, a generous pile surpass-
ing what they usually held. Sintara chose the third barrow as
hers and pushed Ranculos aside to claim it. He roared, but
swiftly chose the fourth barrow instead. As they always did,
the barrow pushers quickly left the area to stand well back
in the trees. They'd reclaim their barrows and trundle them
away when every dragon had finished eating.

Sintara sank her muzzle into the heaped carrion. The
meat was still, the blood dried and the muscles stiffened.
The deer in it had probably been killed yesterday or even the
day before. The smell of the offal was rank, but she didn't
care. She seized and gulped, seized and gulped, eating as
swiftly as she could. Even though there was a barrow for
each dragon, it wasn't uncommon to have to fight for the
last pieces of her carrion if some other dragon had already
finished his share.

She overturned her barrow in her haste, spilling the final
pieces of meat. The last piece of river carp was covered in
dust: it stuck in her throat and she had to shake her head to
get it down. It still stuck. Ignoring the others, she went to the
drinking hole. The water that seeped in from the sides and
filled it was less acidic than that in the river itself. She sank
her muzzle into it and drew up a long draft. She lifted her
head skyward, pointed her nose up, and swallowed. The fish
was still caught in her throat. Another long drink and it finally slid down. She belched in relief. She was startled when
someone asked her, "Are you all right now? You looked as
if you were choking."

Sintara slowly turned her gaze downward. Standing at
her shoulder was a thin Rain Wild girl. The faint trace of
scales on her cheekbones glinted silvery in the sunlight.
Sintara said nothing to the human, but rotated her head to
look over the mud plain by the river. Some of the humans
still clustered near their small boats, but several of them had
ventured away from the group to mingle with the dragons.
She gave her attention back to the girl who had spoken to
her. The human barely came to her shoulder. She smelled
of wood smoke and fear. Sintara opened her mouth and

breathed in deeply, taking in the girl's full scent. Then she breathed out and saw the girl flinch as her breath streamed past her. "Why do you ask?" she demanded.

The girl didn't answer the question. Instead, she pointed toward the forest and said, "The day you hatched, I was there. Up in that tree. Watching."

"I didn't 'hatch' here. I emerged from my case. Are you too ignorant of dragon ways to know the difference?"

The skin of the girl's face changed temperature and color as her blood beat more strongly there. "I'm not ignorant. I know that dragons begin their lives as serpents, hatched on a beach far from here. To say that you hatched here was just a manner of speaking."

"A careless use of words," Sintara corrected her.

"I'm sorry," the girl apologized.

"I'M SORRY," THYMARA said hastily. This dragon seemed very testy. Perhaps she had made an error in choosing her. She glanced over at Tats. He was trying to approach a small green female. She didn't seem to be paying any attention to him, other than to hiss threateningly when he stepped too close to her barrow of meat. Rapskal already had his arm around a runty little red dragon. He began scratching her head near her neck fringe and the dragon leaned into him, thrumming with pleasure. An instant later, Thymara realized he was dislodging an entire colony of parasites from her. Leggy little insects were falling in a shower from the dragon as he diligently scratched at her scales.

Most of the other dragon keepers still huddled by the boats, watching them. Greft had announced his claim as soon as the boat touched shore. "The big black one is mine. Everyone stay back and give me a chance to talk to him before you approach the others."

Perhaps some of the others were swayed by Greft's assumption of leadership. Thymara wasn't. She'd already seen the dragon she wanted to care for. The female was a gleaming blue with glittering silver markings on her dwarfed wings. Consecutive scaled frills draped her neck like ruffles on a rich woman's dress. She was one of the better-formed dragons, despite her diminutive wings. A survivor, Thymara had judged her, and she had been so bold as to approach the dragon immediately. Now she wondered if she'd made a poor choice. The blue dragon didn't seem especially friendly, and she was large. If the way she'd devoured the barrow of meat was any indication, keeping up with her appetite was going to be a challenge. No, an impossibility, she realized with dawning dismay. What she had seen as feasible back at Trehaug was now revealed to her as a hopeless task. If she was going to be any dragon's sole feeder, that dragon was going to be hungry a good part of the time.

This dragon's temperament didn't seem very kindly even with a belly full of meat. What would she be like when she was hungry and tired after a day's journey? Thymara reluctantly scanned the other dragons, seeking a better prospect for herself. This one obviously didn't like her at all.

But the other dragon keepers had found their courage and were already fanning out through the herd of dragons. Kase and Boxter were approaching two orange dragons. She wondered briefly if the two cousins always made similar choices. Sylve, hands clasped shyly behind her and head bowed, was talking quietly to a gold male. As Thymara watched, he lifted his head, revealing a blue-white throat. Jerd stood close to a green female with gold stippling. As the other keepers spread out through the herd, Thymara did a quick count. There weren't enough keepers. There would be two extra dragons. That could be trouble.

"Why are you here? What is this invasion about?"

There was irritation in the dragon's tone, as if Thymara had insulted her. The girl was startled. "What? Didn't they tell you we'd be coming?"

"Didn't who tell us?"

"The committee. There was a Rain Wild committee to look into solving the dragon problem. They decided it would be best for all if the dragons were moved upriver to a better place. Somewhere with open meadows, dry ground, and plentiful game for you."

"No." A flat denial by the dragon.

"But—"

"That was not what they decided. No humans decided anything about us. *We* told the humans who tend us that we are leaving this place, and that we required their services. We told them to supply us with hunters and tenders for our journey. We told them that we intend to return to Kelsingra. Have you heard of it, little creature? It was an Elderling city, a place of sunlight and open fields and sandy shores. The Elderlings who lived there were creatures of culture and learning who appreciated dragons. The buildings there were created to accommodate us. The plains teemed with cattle and wild game. That is where we intend to go."

"I have never heard of such a place." She spoke hesitantly, not wishing to offend.

"What you have heard or not heard is of little interest to me." The dragon turned away from her. "That is where we shall be going."

This wasn't going to work. Thymara cast about hopelessly. Two dragons remained unclaimed. They were mud-streaked and dull-eyed creatures, nosing stupidly at the empty barrows. The silver one had a festering infection on his tail. The other one might have had a coppery hide but was so filthy he looked dun colored. He was thin in a bony way; she suspected he suffered from worms. In her cold evaluation, neither would survive the trek up the river. But perhaps that didn't matter. It was apparent to her that her girlish fancy of befriending the dragon that she escorted was little more than that. What a silly dream that had been, of friendship with a powerful and noble creature. She was already revising her estimate of what the expedition would be, and her heart was sinking with the burden of that reality. She'd be feeding and caring for creatures that found her irritating and were large enough to kill her with a casual blow. At least her mother had been slightly shorter than she was. The thought that she might prefer her mother's company to that of an irritable dragon twisted her mouth in a sour smile.

The dragon exhaled a blast of air by her ear. "Well?"

"I didn't say anything." She spoke quietly. She wanted to edge away, but not while the dragon was eyeing her.

"I'm aware of that. So you haven't heard of Kelsingra.

That doesn't mean that it doesn't exist. It seems to me that we are as likely to find it as we are to find your 'open meadows, dry ground, and plentiful game.' For it seems likely to me that if any Rain Wilder had ever heard of such a place, there would already be a Rain Wild settlement there."

"That's true," Thymara agreed reluctantly, and she wondered why she hadn't previously thought about it in such terms. Because the committee, of supposedly older and wiser Rain Wild Traders, had told her that was what she would find. But what did they know? Not a one of them had looked like a hunter or a harvester. Most looked as if they'd never even ventured up to the canopy, let alone explored along the riverbanks. What if there was no such place? What if it was all just a ploy to get the dragons and their tenders to leave Cassarick?

She pushed that thought aside. It frightened her, not just because it might be true but because she suddenly knew that the people she had signed a contract with were perfectly capable of banishing both the dragons and their keepers to an endless trek up the boggy riverbank. "Why are you dragons so certain that Kerlinger exists?" she demanded of the big blue female.

"If you are trying to talk about Kelsingra, then at least name it correctly. You are very careless with your language. I suspect that creatures with brains as small as yours must have a hard time recalling information. As to why we know it exists, we remember it."

"But you've never been away from this beach."

"We have our ancestral memories. Well, at least some of us have some of them. And it is one that several of us do recall. The city on the wide and sunny riverbank. The sweet silver water from the well there. The plazas and the buildings created to accommodate the alliance of Elderlings and dragons. The fine fields full of fat grazing cattle." The dragon's voice had gone dreamy, and for a moment, Thymara almost felt the creature's hunger for fat cows full of warm blood and hot moist meat. And afterward, a wash and then a long nap on the white sandy riverbank. Thymara shook her head to clear it of her imaginings.

"What?" the dragon demanded.

"The only Elderling cities we have ever discovered are buried in mud. The folk who lived there are long dead. The tapestries and paintings they left behind show us a place that is so different from what is here now that our scholars have long argued that they depict an Elderling homeland far to the south rather than being representations of their cities as they once were here."

"Then your scholars are wrong." The dragon spoke decisively. "Our memories may be incomplete, but I can tell you that the Cassarick I recall bordered on a deep, swift flowing river that had a gentler backwater and a wide beach of silver-streaked clay. The river was deep enough for serpents to migrate up it easily. The Elderling ships also could come right up the river to Cassarick and go beyond as well, to other cities that bordered the river. Cassarick itself was not a large city, though it had its share of wonders. It was famed mostly as a secondary place for serpents to come to spin our cocoons, if the beaches at what you call Trehaug were full. That did not happen every migrating year, but some years it did. And so Cassarick had chambers capable of welcoming the dragons who came to tend the cases. There was the Star Chamber, roofed with glass panels. From there the Elderlings were wont to study the night sky. The walls of the long entry hall to the Star Chamber were decorated with a mosaic of jewels that held a light of their own. No windows were built in that hall so that visitors might more easily view the vista that the jewel artists had painted with their tiny dots of light. I recall there was an amusement that the Elderlings had built for themselves, a maze with crystal walls. Time's Labyrinth, they called it. It was all trickery and foolishness, of course, but they seemed fond of it."

"If any room like one of those chambers has been found, I have not heard of it," Thymara said regretfully.

"It little matters," the dragon replied, her voice suddenly harsh. "They are not the only wonders that have vanished. You humans go digging through the wreckage of that time like tunneling dung beetles. You don't understand what you find, and you have no appreciation for it."

"I think I should go," Thymara said quietly. Her disappointment as she turned away gnawed upward in her from her belly. She looked at the other two unclaimed dragons and tried to muster pity for them. But their eyes were vapid and almost unseeing. They were not even watching the other dragons as they began to interact with their keepers. The muddy brown one was absently chewing on the bloody edge of the barrow that had held his food. Still. She hadn't signed a contract that promised her the companionship of an amazing and intelligent creature. She had signed a contract that said she would do her best to accompany a dragon on this doomed expedition and do her best to care for it. Perhaps she'd be wiser to start with one that had no expectations. Perhaps she would have been wisest of all not to have had expectations herself.

All of the other keepers seemed to have met with at least moderate success with their choices. Rapskal and his red seemed happiest with each other. He had led the stumpy little creature over to the forest edge and was cleaning her scales with handfuls of evergreen needles. The small red dragon wriggled happily at his touch. Jerd seemed to have won the trust of her speckled green dragon. The creature had lifted one front foot and was allowing Jerd to examine her claws. Greft kept a respectful distance from the black dragon, but seemed to be deep in conversation with it. Sylve and the golden male had found a sunny place and were sitting peacefully together on the cracked mud plates of the riverbank.

She looked around for Tats and the slender green dragon he'd approached. She didn't see either of them at first, and then spotted them at the water's edge. Tats had his fish spear out and was walking along the bank while the green dragon watched with avid interest. Thymara doubted that he'd find anything large enough to spear if he saw any fish at all, but he'd obviously won his dragon's attention. Unlike her. The dragon hadn't even responded to her last comment.

"Thank you for speaking with me," Thymara replied hopelessly. She turned and walked quietly away. The silver, she decided. The injury on its tail needed to be cleaned and bandaged. Thymara suspected they'd be traveling in or near the river water, and untreated, the acid waters would enlarge and ulcerate the injury. As for the skinny copper dragon, if she could find some ruskin leaves and catch a fish, she'd try worming him. She wondered if ruskin leaves worked to cleanse a dragon's system. Studying him as she walked toward him, she decided that they couldn't hurt. There was no one she could ask for advice for physicking a dragon. If he got any thinner, he'd die soon anyway.

Abruptly she realized there was someone she could ask. She turned back to the blue dragon who was regarding Thymara with ill-concealed hostility. Thymara steeled her courage. "May I ask you a question about dragons and parasites?"

"Where did you learn your manners?" The question was followed with a hiss. None of her breath reached Thymara, but the mist of weak venom that rode her breath was faintly visible.

Thymara was jolted. Cautiously she asked, "Is it rude to ask such a question?" She wanted to take a step back but dared not move.

"How dare you turn your back on me."

On the dragon's long neck, the "frills" of scaled plates were lifting. Thymara hadn't understood their use before, but from all she knew of animals, such a display would indicate aggression. A brilliant yellow underlay was revealed as the scaled flaps rose like the opening petals of a reptilian flower. The dragon's large copper eyes were fixed on her, and as Thymara met that gaze, the eyes appeared to slowly spin. It was like watching twin whirlpools of molten copper. The sight was as breathtakingly beautiful as it was terrifying. "I'm sorry," she apologized hopelessly. "I didn't know it was rude. I thought you wanted me to go away."

SOMETHING WAS WRONG, and Sintara didn't know what. By now, the girl should have been completely infatuated with her, on her knees, begging for the dragon's attention. Instead, she had turned her back on her and started to wander off. Humans were notoriously easy prey for a dragon's glamour. She opened her ruff more widely and gave her head a shake to disperse a mist of charm. "Do you not wish to serve me?" she prompted the girl. "Do you not find me beautiful?"

"Of course you are beautiful!" the human exclaimed, but her stance and the rank scent of fear she gave betrayed that she was frightened, not entranced. "When first I saw you today, I chose you as the dragon that I most wished to care for. But our conversation has been . . ." The girl's words trickled away.

Sintara reached for her thoughts but found only fog. Perhaps that was the problem. Perhaps the girl was too stupid to be charmed by her. She searched her dragon memories and found evidence of such humans. Some were so dense that they could not even understand a dragon's speech. This girl seemed to grasp her words clearly enough. So what ailed her? Sintara decided on a small test of her powers, to see if the girl was susceptible to her at all. "What is your name, small human?"

"Thymara," she replied instantly. But as Sintara began to gloat at her leverage, the girl asked her, "And what is your name?"

"I don't think you've earned the right to my name yet!" Sintara rebuked her and saw her cower. But Thymara stank of true fear with no traces of the despair that such a refusal should have wakened in her. When the human said nothing, did not beg again for the favor of her name, Sintara asked her directly, "Don't you wish you knew my name?"

"It would make it much easier for me to talk to you, yes," the girl said hesitantly.

Sintara chuckled. "But you don't seek it in order to have power over me?" she asked sarcastically.

"What power would your name give me?"

Sintara stared down at her. Could she truly be ignorant of the power of a dragon's name? One who knew a dragon's true name could, if she employed it correctly, compel the dragon to speak truth, to keep a promise, even to grant a favor. If this Thymara was ignorant of such things, Sintara certainly wasn't going to enlighten her. Instead she asked

her, "What would you like to call me, if you were choosing
a name to know me by?"

The girl looked more intrigued than frightened now.
Sintara spun her eyes more slowly, and Thymara actually
came a step closer to her. There. That was better. "Well?"
she prompted her again. "What name would you give me?"

The girl bit her upper lip for a moment, then said, "You
are such a lovely blue. High in the canopy, there is a twining vine that roots in the clefts of trees. It has flowers that
are deep blue with bright yellow centers. It has a wonderful
fragrance that entrances insects and small birds and little
lizards. Even it is not as beautiful as you are, but you remind
me of it. We call the flowers skymaws."

"So you would name me after a flower? Skymaw?" Sintara was not pleased. It seemed a silly, fragile name to her,
but she had asked the girl. Perhaps in this one thing, she
could humor the human. But still, she asked her, "Do you
not think I deserve a name that has more teeth to it?"

The girl looked down at her feet as if the dragon had
caught her in a lie. Quietly, she admitted, "Skymaws are
dangerous to touch. They are beautiful and the fragrance
is alluring, but the nectar inside will dissolve a butterfly instantly and devour a hummingbird in less than an hour."

Sintara stretched her jaws wide in pleasure and concluded, "Then it is not just the color of the flower that makes
you think of me? It is the danger it poses?"

"I suppose. Yes."

"Then you may call me Skymaw. Do you see what the
boy over there is doing to the runty red dragon?"

The girl followed Sintara's glance. Rapskal had pulled
an armful of needled branches from a tree and was energetically scrubbing his dragon's back. Cleansed of mud and
dust, even that stumpy little dragon sparkled like a ruby in
the sunlight. "I don't think he means any harm. I think he's
trying to get some of the parasites off her."

"Exactly. And the wax from the needles is good for the
skin." Graciously, Sintara told her, "You are allowed to perform that service for me."

❖ ❖ ❖

As the *Tarman* slowly nosed its way onto the muddy bank, Alise looked over the fantastic scene before her and felt rankest envy. Sun and heat baked the bare riverbank as the final hours of afternoon dwindled away. Scattered about on the bank were at least a dozen dragons in every imaginable color tended by young Rain Wilders. Some of the dragons were stretched out in peaceful sleep. Two stood by the water, waiting impatiently as a couple of boys holding spears walked slowly up and down the riverbank, looking for fish. On the ebbing edge of a sun-washed mudbank, a long gold dragon sprawled, his blue-white underbelly turned toward the last kiss of the sun. Lying against him slept a little girl, her pink-scaled scalp glittering as brightly as the dragon she tended. At one end of the long bank of mud stood the largest dragon of all, tall and black. The sun struck glittering dark blue sparks from his outstretched wings. A bare-chested young man, almost as heavily scaled as a dragon himself, was grooming the creature's wings. At the opposite end of the beach, as if in counterpoint, a girl with a broom made of cedar boughs was diligently sweeping a sprawled blue dragon. The girl's black braids danced against the back of her neck as she worked. The dragon shifted as Alise watched, stretching out a hind leg so that the girl might groom it.

"I didn't realize the dragons had human tenders. I mean, I knew that they had hunters helping provide for them, but I didn't realize that—"

"They don't. Or they didn't." Leftrin had a knack for interrupting her in a way that was friendly rather than rude. "They're all newcomers. Those are the keepers you heard about, the ones who are going to move the dragons upriver. They can't have been here much longer than a day, at most two."

"But some of them are only children!" Alise protested. It was not her concern for them that sharpened her voice. It was, she thought, simple jealousy. There they were, mere youngsters, doing exactly what she had imagined herself doing. Somehow, she had visualized herself as being the first to befriend a dragon, to touch it with kindness and win its confidence. The way Althea and Brashen had described the dragons, she had thought they would be like reptilian half-wits, awaiting, perhaps, her understanding and patience to unlock their innate intelligence. What she saw on the beach was another broken pane in the dream window; she was not to be the dragons' savior, the only one who understood them.

Leftrin shrugged a heavy shoulder in response to her comment, mistaking it for concern. "Youngsters don't get to be children long in the Rain Wilds, and especially not children like those. Look at them. It's a wonder their parents kept them. You can't tell me those youngsters are all late-changers. You don't get claws unless you were born with them. And that young man there? I'll wager he was born with scales on his head and has never had a bit of hair any-where on his body. No, they're all mistakes, the lot of them. And that's why they were chosen."

His blunt and cold appraisal of the dragons' attendants shocked Alise into silence.

"And are you and the *Tarman* a mistake? Is that why you were chosen for the expedition?" Sedric's voice was as acidic as the river.

But if Leftrin noticed the intended unpleasantness in his tone, he didn't react to it. "No, me and Tarman are hired. And the contract's a good one, tight as a contract can be written. And the terms are good, for Tarman and me." Here he tipped Alise a broad wink, and she almost blushed. He spoke on as if Sedric could not have noticed it. "Not just be-cause no one else would take it, but because the Rain Wild Council knows that no one else can do this job. Tarman and I have been farther up the river than any other large vessel. There may be a few who have gone farther, game scouts in canoes and such. But you can't do what the Council wants done from a canoe."

"And what the Council wants done is the dragons driven away from Cassarick."

"Well, that's putting it a bit harshly, Sedric. But look for yourself. They're obviously not in a good place. They're not healthy, there's no game they can hunt for themselves, and they're killing the trees all around the beach."

"And they're impeding a profitable excavation of the old city."

"Yes, that's true also," Leftrin replied implacably.

Alise gave Sedric a sideways look. His last little remark had been barbed. He was still upset, and she supposed he had every right to be. Her session at the Traders' Hall in Cassarick had gone on much longer than she had expected. Thrashing out the details of Leftrin's contract with the committee had taken most of those hours. Malta the Elderling had remained for the long discussion, but with every passing hour, she looked more like a weary pregnant woman and less like an elegant and powerful Elderling. Alise had observed her unobtrusively but avariciously.

When Alise had first encountered the idea that humans became Elderlings, it had cracked her sense of reality. Elderlings had been the stuff of legend for her when she was a girl. Shadowy, powerful creatures at the edge of tales and myths; those were the Elderlings. Legends spoke of their elegance and beauty, of power sometimes wielded with wisdom and sometimes with casual cruelty. When the original Rain Wild settlers had discovered traces of ancient settlements and then connected those ruins to the near-mythical Elderlings, many had been skeptical. Over the years it had become accepted that they had been real and that perhaps the magical and arcane treasures unearthed in the Rain Wilds were the last remaining traces of their passage on this world. They had been a glorious magical race and now they were vanished forever.

No one had connected the unfortunate and sometimes grotesque disfigurements of the Rain Wild settlers with the ethereal beauty of the Elderlings depicted in scrolls, tapestries, and legends. Scaled skin and glowing eyes were not always lovely to look upon, and in the cases of the Rain Wild offspring afflicted with them, their life spans were greatly shortened, not the near immortals that legend decreed the Elderlings were. Vultures and peacocks might both have feathers and beaks, but one did not confuse the two creatures. Yet Malta and Selden Vestrit of Bingtown and Reyn Khuprus of the Rain Wilds had changed, just as those touched by the Rain Wilds changed, not toward the monstrous but toward the fantastic. Dragon touched, some now called them to distinguish them from the others. Somehow, she suspected, their being present during the emergence of Tintaglia from her case and spending so much time with her afterward had caused their metamorphoses to proceed in a different pattern.

Watching Malta Khuprus had given her much to think about during the long and tedious hours of Leftrin's haggling. He had not seemed to find the delay boring, but had settled into his deal making with the enthusiasm of a pit dog trying to pull down a bull. While he discussed who would pay for food and how much the *Tarman* could carry and if the small boats for the keepers would be his responsibility and who would pay if a dragon did any damage to his vessel and a hundred other variables, Alise covertly studied the Elderling woman and wondered. It was too obvious to ignore that the physical changes a human underwent were that his or her body acquired some of the characteristics of a dragon. Or a reptile, she judiciously added. The scales, the unusual growths, Malta's crest on her brow all spoke of some connection to the dragons. But other parts of the puzzle did not fit. The strange elongation of her bones, for instance.

If the Elderlings had known exactly what precipitated the changes that took them from human to Elderling, they had not written it down, at least not in any scrolls that Alise had ever seen. Then she wondered if Elderlings had ever been a completely separate race from humans. Had humans always changed to become Elderlings, or had Elderlings existed separately but perhaps interbred with humanity? Alise had become so enmeshed in her pondering that when Leftrin abruptly announced, "Well, it's all settled then. I'll depart as soon as you've managed to ferry the supplies down to the dock," she felt jolted out of a dream. She looked around her to see the Council members rising from their chairs and coming to shake Leftrin's hand. A document, evidently written as they settled each term, and signed by all, was being sanded to set and dry the ink. Malta, looking frailer than ever, had signed in her turn and was now gazing at

Alise. The Bingtown woman gathered all her courage and went to present herself.

Yet before she reached Malta, the woman had gracefully but with weariness come to meet her. She took both of Alise's hands in hers and said, "I truly don't know how to thank you. I wish that I myself could be going. Not that I have any great fondness for dragons; they are difficult to deal with, being nearly as stubborn and self-justified as humans."

Alise was astonished. She had expected the Elderling to declare her undying devotion to dragons and to beg Alise to do all she could to protect them. Instead, she continued, "Don't trust them. Don't think of them as especially noble or of a higher morality than humans. They aren't. They're just like us, except they are larger and stronger, with potent memories of always having their own way. So, be careful. And whatever you learn of them, whether you find Kelsingra or not, you must record and bring back to us. Because sooner or later, humanity is going to have to coexist with a substantial population of dragons. We have forgotten all we ever knew about dealing with dragons. But they have forgotten nothing about humans."

"I'll be careful," Alise promised faintly.

"I'll take you at your word." Malta smiled, and her face seemed briefly more human. "You seem to be a Trader who remembers what a promise means. In these times, we could do with more like you. And now, I'm afraid I must go home to rest."

"Do you need any help to get home?" Alise was bold enough to ask. But Malta shook her head. She released Alise's hands and slowly but gracefully climbed the shallow steps to the entry doors. Alise was still looking after her when she felt Leftrin's heavy hand clap her on the shoulder.

"Well, didn't you turn out to be just the ticket for both of us! I wonder if Brashen Trell knew what a bit of luck he was sending my way when he sent you to me! I doubt it, but there it is. Well, my lady luck, the deal is signed, save for your mark, and we're all waiting on that."

In astonishment, she turned to find that it was so. The

Council members were reseated in their places. The pen in
its stand awaited her. As she glanced from it to the Council
leader, Trader Polsk gestured at it impatiently. Alise glanced
back at Leftrin.

"Well, get it done," he urged her. "The day gets no
longer!"

In a sort of daze, she crossed the room. She shouldn't do
this. She couldn't do this. Had she ever before set her signature to a document that bound her? Only when she had set
her hand to her marriage agreement with Hest. She recalled
as a waking nightmare all the particulars of that agreement,
and how she had willingly marked her name on every one. It
was the only time her signature had bound her as a Trader.
Time after time, she had recalled that afternoon. Now when
she thought of how quickly Hest had moved through the ceremony, she saw it not as a bridegroom's eagerness, but as
yet another mark of how he would trivialize their bond. She
had lived to regret binding herself that way. How could she
even think of setting her hand to another document? Her
eyes wandered over the words above her name. Someone
had negotiated a wage for her, a daily payment for each day
she was on the vessel. How peculiar to think that she would
earn money, money of her own, doing this. If she did it. And
then she knew that she would.

Because she wanted to. Because despite being Hest's
wife, she was still of Trader stock, and still capable of
making her own decisions. It was her hand, her familiar
freckled hand that lifted the pen and dipped it. She watched,
oddly distant, as she formed the characters of her name in
her strong sloping penmanship. "There. It's done," she said,
and she heard how small her voice sounded now in that
large room.

"Done," agreed Trader Polsk, and dumped a generous
measure of sand on the paper. Alise watched as the sand
was shaken off, leaving her signature strong and black on
the page. What had she just done?

Captain Leftrin was at her shoulder. His hearty laugh
boomed out, and he took her arm and turned her, leading
her away. "And that's a fine morning's bargaining for both

of us. I'll admit that having your company on this expedition suits me very well indeed. The Council insists that it can have Tarman loaded and ready to sail by late afternoon. Between you and me, that won't be much of a trick. I knew I'd get the contract, and I've already made arrangements for the supplies that I want. Now. We've not far to go for the first stop on our journey. The dragon grounds are an hour past the city docks. But for now, there's a bit of time for us to spend as we wish. I've arranged for a runner to take the news to Hennesey. He's a good mate and I've no worries about him seeing the cargo loaded. So. Shall we take a bit of a tour of Cassarick before we go? You didn't have much of a chance to see Trehaug from what you've told me."

She should have said no. She should have insisted on immediately returning to the boat. But somehow, after the morning's adventure, she couldn't bear to return to being not only rigorously correct but timorously so. Nor could she imagine meeting Sedric's eyes and admitting what she had done. Sedric. Oh, Sa have mercy! No. She couldn't confront that thought yet. She boldly set her hand on Leftrin's arm and said, "I think I'd enjoy seeing Cassarick."

And so he had shown her the "city," though Cassarick scarcely merited the word. It was a lively town, still young and raw and growing. She was sure now that Captain Leftrin had deliberately chosen to give her the most adventurous tour possible. It began with a dizzying ride up in a basket lift. They entered it and shut the flimsy door securely. Then Leftrin tugged on a line and far overhead, she heard the tinkle of a small bell. "Now wait for them to ballast it," he told her, and she stood, heart thumping with excitement. After a wait, the compartment gave a lurch and then rose slowly and steadily into the air. The device they rode up in was built of light yet sturdy materials and was so small that they had to stand with their bodies nearly touching. Alise stood looking out over the rim of the basket but could not help but be aware of Leftrin's stout body just behind hers. Midway in their journey, they met the lift tender coming down in the opposing basket. He stood amid a stack of ballast stone, and by a means she couldn't see, he halted both baskets in midjourney for Leftrin to pay the lift fee. Once the man was satisfied, he continued down while their basket continued to rise. The view was astonishing. They traveled past thick branches with footpaths on top of them, past rows of houses dangling like ornaments from tree limbs, past rickety bridges and little basket trolleys whizzing past them on lines that reminded her of the washing line at home. When they finally arrived at their destination and the lift tender's assistant halted their flight, they were so high in the trees that stray beams of bright yellow sunlight filtered down through the thick foliage. The attendant opened the lift door and Alise stepped out onto a narrow balcony affixed to a heavy tree limb. She looked over the edge, gasped, and then nearly shrieked when Leftrin took a sudden and firm grip on her arm. "That's a good way to get dizzy, your first time up a trunk," he warned her. He guided her along a narrow footpath that ran along the thick branch, back toward the trunk of the tree.

She tried to be casual as she set both her hands to the coarse bark of the trunk. She wanted to hug the tree, but it would have been like trying to hug a wall. The flora and the foliage here in the Rain Wilds were on so immense a scale that they seemed more like geographical features than botanical ones. To Leftrin's credit, he hadn't said a word while she caught her breath and found her dignity. When she turned back to face him, he smiled in a way that was friendly, not teasing, and said, "I believe there's a very nice little tea and cake shop this way."

He led her around the trunk on the sturdy boardwalk. More of the town was awake now, and though the walkways were not nearly as crowded as the streets of Bingtown on a market day, there was still a substantial population in evidence. Watching them go so matter-of-factly about their lives slowly changed her perception of them. Their scaled faces and outlandish clothing had almost begun to seem mundane by the time they reached the tea shop and ordered a small meal. They had talked and laughed and eaten, and for a time, Alise forgot who and where she was.

Captain Leftrin was a rough man, almost coarse. Handsome he was not, nor particularly groomed, nor even educated. He didn't care that he spilled his tea in his saucer, and when he laughed, he threw back his head and roared, and every customer in the shop turned to stare at him. It embarrassed Alise. Yet in his company, she felt more like a woman than she had in years, perhaps in her whole life. And that was the thought that made her realize that she had been behaving as if she were not only single, but not accountable to anyone else but herself. The shock of that thought made her catch her breath, and in the next instant she recalled that this sort of misadventure was exactly why Hest had sent Sedric to chaperone her and protect her good name. His good name, she belatedly thought. This was what Sedric had been trying to warn her about. She hastily finished her tea and then sat almost fidgeting as Leftrin slowly enjoyed his.

"Shall we look about a bit more?" he offered her as they left the shop, his grin confident of her agreement.

"I'm afraid I should get back to Sedric and explain to him the change in plans. I don't think he's going to be happy with it," she said, and suddenly the understatement of that rattled inside her. Sedric had been miserable spending only a few days on the *Tarman*. How would he react to the news that she'd volunteered herself to be part of the expedition, a trip that would certainly take days and possibly weeks? Would he forbid it?

That thought made her cold with dread, and then a worse one came. Could he forbid it to her? Did she have to accept his judgment if he said she must give up her wild plan? What would happen if he did? She'd signed her name to an agreement. No Trader would even consider backing out on such a thing. But what if he disputed her right to do so? Just how much authority did she have to yield to him? After all, he was her chaperone, accompanying her to preserve appearances. He was not her guardian or her father. And Hest had said, quite clearly, that he was hers to command. So, if need be, she could force the issue. Wasn't that why Hest paid him? To do what he was told to do? He was Hest's servant.

And her friend.

Her conscience squirmed uncomfortably. She'd begun to think of him more and more that way lately. Her friend. And she'd enjoyed the attentions and deference he'd been showing her. Today, when she'd left so early without even telling him she was going, she'd dismissed the need to do so. Because as her friend, he'd understand. But as her husband's employee, as her appointed chaperone, would he? Had she put him in a difficult position without thinking about it? She spoke quickly, before she could give in to the temptation to wander through Cassarick with the river captain as her guide. "I'm afraid I must go back right away. I have to tell Sedric what I've—" She faltered suddenly, at a loss for words. What she had decided to do? Could she use such a word and not be humiliated in a few hours when Sedric overturned it? For she was suddenly certain that he would.

"I suppose you're right," Leftrin agreed reluctantly. "You'll be needing to make a list of the supplies you want. I've got good sources here. I'll pick them up for you, and we'll settle up when we return to Trehaug."

"Of course," Alise agreed more faintly. Of course there would be more expenses to extending her trip. Why hadn't she thought of that? And who would have to pay for those expenses? Hest. Oh, he'd be so pleased about that! She was suddenly feeling a lot less competent and independent than she had a few hours ago. It would, she thought, be almost a relief when Sedric forbade it. And now she looked at the sky, or attempted to, only to be thwarted by the solid umbrella of vegetation. Just how much time had passed? How many hours had she lost of the time that she could spend with the dragons? The Council had seemed eager to move them as swiftly as they could. Would she even have a full day of research to show for this impulsive journey to the Rain Wilds? She thought of how Hest would rebuke and mock her for her waste of time and money, and her cheeks burned. No more must be wasted.

So she had gritted her teeth and scuttled back across the swaying bridges with Leftrin. She'd never felt anything like the sensation of her belly floating up behind her teeth as they dropped far too swiftly for her comfort in the flimsy basket. Leftrin had a tendency to stroll, and to chat with every passing acquaintance. She stood impatiently at his side through what seemed like dozens of encounters on their way back to the docks.

To every acquaintance, he introduced her as "the Bingtown dragon expert who will be heading upriver with the dragons to get them settled." The title that at one time would have filled her with elation now agitated her. Her discomfiture was complete when she finally arrived back at the *Tarman* to discover that Sedric was not there.

Hennesey was already occupied with loading a stream of crates and barrels of supplies. He seemed surprised to see her. "Well, we all thought you was just taking some extra sleep. That Sedric fellow said to tell you that he'd gone off to find 'suitable lodgings' for the two of you." The way he parodied Sedric's diction made her fully aware of just how the crew viewed Sedric's aristocratic manners and fastidiousness.

For a time, she stayed on the deck, watching with awe just how much the crew could fit into the *Tarman*'s holds. She went back down to the captain's stateroom and tried to imagine living in it for over a week or possibly as long as a month. It had seemed quaint and nautical, but when she considered it for a longer period, she began to feel claustrophobic. She made an excuse to put her head into the crew's living quarters, and then hastily withdrew. No. She could not imagine Sedric existing there any longer than he already had. She was certain now that he would veto her participation in the expedition. She went back on deck and looked anxiously upriver. Several times Leftrin tried to engage her in conversation about what her own needs might be, and once when she asked in some agitation when she would get to see the dragons, he explained that the dragon beach was less than an hour away by river, but quite a bit more than that if she wished to travel there by reentering the city and using the footbridges and lifts to reach it. She gratefully declined to do that and attempted to find both her patience and her aplomb.

She had caught sight of Sedric before he saw her. He

strode down the dock, his normally pleasant face set in grim
disapproval. When he looked up from the dock and saw her
seated on top of the deckhouse, she saw him take a deep
breath and hold it. Then he clambered aboard and came immediately to her. He didn't greet her at all but demanded,
"What are these ridiculous rumors I'm hearing? I tried to
rent some rooms for us, but the landlady asked whatever I
would need them for, when she had heard that the Bingtown
lady who came to study dragons would be heading upriver
on the *Tarman* before the day was out."

Alise was shocked to find she was trembling. For all his
sly mockery of her, Hest had never raised his voice to her.
And in all her years of knowing Sedric, she had never heard
him speak so severely, with anger so plainly bubbling under
his words. She clenched her hands together in her lap and
tried to force steadiness into her voice. "I'm afraid that, yes,
I did volunteer to go. You see, when I accompanied Captain
Leftrin to a meeting with the Cassarick Traders' Council,
I discovered that they intended to remove all the dragons
from here, transferring them upriver. No one quite knows
exactly where they are to be resettled, but the Council is
quite determined that they must be moved immediately.
Malta the Elderling was there, and was very dejected that
she herself could not accompany the dragons, but when I
said that I could, she was—"

"Impossible." He cut off her flow of words. His face had
gone quite red. "I can't believe what I'm hearing! I can't believe what you've done! You left the boat without my knowledge and went off with that man, and now you've involved
yourself in Rain Wild politics, making offers that we can't
possibly fulfill! You can't go off on some harebrained expedition to an unnamed destination, with no fixed date to
return. Alise, what are you thinking? This isn't some sort
of pretend game. They are talking of going upriver beyond
any settlements, perhaps beyond explored areas. They may
encounter all sorts of dangers, not to mention the discomfort
and primitive conditions of such travel. You are scarcely fit
to endure such things. You cannot even imagine what you
are suggesting. Or perhaps you can, but that 'imagining' is

all that you are doing. You have no concept of the reality. And there is the time factor to consider. Summer does not last forever, and we did not pack the clothing or make any arrangements for an extended stay in the Rain Wilds. You may not have real commitments to return to, but I do! This is ridiculous! And backing out of it will be endlessly embarrassing! Hest has trading partners here in the Rain Wilds. How is it going to look, that his wife agreed to do a thing that she could not possibly do and then backed out of it? What were you thinking?"

Between the time when he began his speech and the moment he finished it, a strange thing happened. The trembling inside Alise stilled, and then hardened. In Sedric's outraged gaze she suddenly saw herself reflected as he saw her. Foolish and sheltered. Living out an imaginary adventure before fleeing home to her lifetime of no "real commitments." Ignorant of the real world in which he and Hest moved so competently.

And perhaps she was, but through no fault of her own. She had never been allowed to gather the experiences she needed to be competent and independent. Never been allowed. That was the thought that burned in her like molten iron and suddenly hardened into cold resolve. She was not going to be "allowed" to do anything. Never again would she submit to being "allowed" or "not allowed." She would follow her resolve if it killed her. For being killed by it would certainly be better than going home and dying of not being allowed to follow her dream.

So when he had asked her, so rhetorically, what she had been thinking, she replied literally. "I was thinking that I would finally study the dragons, as Hest promised me I could. It was one of the conditions for me marrying him, you know. That I would be allowed to come here and study them. If he had kept his word, I would have been here years ago, and all of this would have been much simpler. But as he chose, over and over again, to ignore the terms of our bargain, here we are. And the only way that his promise to me will be fulfilled is if I follow the dragons upriver and study them as we go." She ran out of breath and had to pause.

He was staring at her, his mouth open. She saw him take breath to speak and beat him to it. "So. I have signed an agreement with the Traders' Council. We will be going upriver with the *Tarman* to see the dragons resettled. And we'll be leaving by this afternoon, so Captain Leftrin will need a list from you of what supplies must be picked up for us. I'll see to balancing accounts with him when we return to Trehaug. I'll be earning a wage aboard the vessel, of course, so I'll have money to settle with the captain. And of course I'll be speaking to him about changing the sleeping arrangements so that we can both be more comfortable during the journey."

She tossed the last comment toward him as a peace offering, hoping he would focus on it and simply accept the rest. It didn't work.

"Alise, this is crazy! We aren't prepared—"

"Nor will we be, if you don't go to work promptly and make that list! That is, isn't it, the sort of duty that you perform for Hest? And isn't that what he instructed you to do for me, on this journey? So do it."

And then she had stood up abruptly and walked away from him. Just like that. She had been shocked when he had actually done what she told him to do, and uneasy ever since. She'd avoided him successfully, not an easy feat on a ship. Leftrin had been surprisingly reasonable about changing quarters for them.

"I've already put my mind to that, and the materials are on their way. I don't mind giving up my bunk for a night or two, but much longer than that simply won't work. But you'll see. We can set up some temporary shelters on the deck. I've done it before for cattle, and it won't be much different for passengers. The *Tarman* was built to be versatile. Oh, don't look at me like that! You'll see, I'll make it comfortable enough for even Dapperlad there." And with an outrageous grin, he'd tossed his head toward the sulking Sedric.

Leftrin had been as good as his word. She had not noticed the fittings set into the deck that allowed for walls to be raised. The chambers created were neither large nor elegant, being not much roomier than a large box stall, but they were private, and when hammocks were slung in them and her own luggage set in place, she found she could arrange her boxes to make a cozy little den for herself. She had a place to sit and write, and a lantern for her own use, though Leftrin warned her sternly to be eternally cautious with it. "Spilled oil and flame aboard a ship is never a trivial thing," he warned her. Her quarters shared a wall with Sedric's, and once the walls had been raised, he entered his room and shut the door immediately.

And there he had stayed until the ship had departed the wharf at Cassarick only to put in at the muddy banks of the dragon beach less than an hour later. Sedric looked much better now than he had earlier. Access to his wardrobe for fresh clothes, privacy, a nap, and a solitary meal seemed to have restored his energy if not his charm. He had not said anything directly to Alise about her high-handed ways, but the edge to his tongue let her know that he had not forgiven her. She shook her head to herself and turned away from him. She'd deal with Sedric later. Right now, she wasn't going to let anything ruin her first glimpse of the young dragons.

"They're huge!" Sedric sounded daunted. "You don't intend to go down there and walk among them!"

"Of course I do. Eventually." She didn't want to admit that she felt much safer looking at them from the *Tarman*'s deck.

Down the beach, the golden dragon suddenly lifted his head. The small figure beside him stirred. The dragon looked toward them, flaring his nostrils and audibly blowing. He rolled to his feet and began to lumber toward them.

"Now what does he want?" Leftrin muttered uneasily. He watched the dragon approach the barge. The animal turned his head on his long neck, regarding Tarman curiously with shining black eyes. He came several steps closer, and then stretched out his head to snuff at the barge. Sedric stepped back from the railing. "Alise," he warned her, but the captain had not moved. She chose to stay where she was. A moment later, the dragon gently butted his head against the vessel's planked side. Tarman did not budge, but in an instant, both Swarge and Hennesey were at Leftrin's side. Big Eider hulked up behind them, staring balefully at the dragon. Grigsby, the ship's orange cat, joined them. He leaped to the railing and glared at the dragon, lashing his striped tail and muttering cat curses in his throat. "There's no harm done," Leftrin warned them softly. He set a restraining hand on the angry cat's back.

"Not yet," Hennesey replied sourly.

"Is there danger?" Alise asked.

"I don't know," Leftrin said. Then, as the dragon's girl-keeper caught up with the creature, he added quietly, "I don't think so."

Moments later, the immense creature was following the girl placidly down the beach, back to their sunning spot. Alise let her pent breath out in a sigh. "Look how the sun reflects off him. His markings are so delicate. Such amazing creatures. Even flawed, they're incredibly beautiful. Of course, the queen at the end of the beach is the most glorious, but this is to be expected. The females of this species were always the most flamboyantly colored. My studies suggest that they could be assertive, even arrogant perhaps, but given the level of their intelligence, such 'arrogance' was perhaps the natural attitude that such a superior mind might take. Look at her. The sun soaks right into her and shines back out of her."

The blue dragon and her tender were a good distance away, at least a hundred feet. Alise was sure her voice had not carried that far, and yet the blue female suddenly lifted her head from where she had been stretched out on the hard mud and regarded Alise with whirling copper eyes for a long moment. Then she said, quite clearly, "Were you speaking of me, Bingtown woman?"

Day the 5th of the Grain Moon

Year the 6th the Independent Alliance of Traders

From Detozi, Keeper of the Birds, Trehaug
To Kim, Keeper of the Birds, Cassarick

*Has it escaped your tiny little brain that the message
you received from Erek contained information about a
special feed that may enhance the health and longevity
of the pigeon stocks? Did it never occur to you that by
attaching this information on an official matter to a
bird already carrying a message, he was merely being
more efficient? The idea that he and I share a personal
correspondence is rather laughable, considering that we
have never even met each other. If you wish to draw that
missive to the attention of the Councils, oh, please do! It
will give us all a chance to discuss the sorry state of the
coops at Cassarick, the death of over twenty promising
squabs because a snake was able to enter your coops, and
the rumors that squab has been on your family's menu
with a peculiar frequency since you assumed your post.*

Detozi

CHAPTER TWELVE

AMONG DRAGONS

He couldn't believe she had done it. Just couldn't believe it. This woman was not the Alise Kincarron he had grown up with! She wasn't even the Alise Finbok he'd frequently dined with for the last five years. He wasn't sure where this domineering vixen had come from, but he'd be glad to see her depart. If it hadn't been so important for him to accompany her when she visited the dragons, he never would have allowed her to go this far.

He leaned on the railing beside her. To her left, the disgusting Captain Leftrin matched her posture, so close that he was practically touching her, while she spouted her infatuated nonsense about the dragons. Well, let her have a day or two of it. Angry as he felt toward her right now, he still dreaded the tasks that were before him. He'd go ashore with her and act as her secretary while she "interviewed" the lumbering beasts down there. Soon enough, she'd realize what they were, and that would be the end of it. He thought of her inevitable disillusionment and almost felt sympathy for her. He'd been foolish even to argue with her earlier when she'd proposed her wild dream of accompanying the captain and the dragons on their trek upriver. He just should have nodded and agreed. He'd listened to what Trell and his wife had to say about the dragons. This adventure wasn't going to materialize as Alise had always imagined it. And when she came to him, a night or two hence, crestfallen and disappointed, he'd be ready to comfort her and find passage for the two of them back home. All he had to do was maintain his patience and wait. And not vomit as Leftrin slimed along after her.

He glanced across at them again. She was looking up at Leftrin and smiling. Was she infatuated with that grizzled water rat? It didn't seem possible. Perhaps she construed the man's braying laugh and extravagant compliments as the epitome of rustic charm. After all, Alise had had few opportunities to sample social interchange with a wide variety of men. Maybe his very coarseness appealed to her. He knew her well enough to know that Hest was in no danger of losing her to anyone. Even if she was not happy with her husband, she was far too tightly laced even to consider betraying him. So let her flirt a bit, let her think she was being a woman of the world on this dismal journey. Though why she could possibly want to dally with an old walrus like Leftrin eluded him. How could he compare to the elegant Hest?

At the thought of Hest, his spirits sank again. Where was he now, what was he doing? Who was sharing his table and witty observations? What exotic port had attracted him, what extravagant and unusual cargo had he already purchased? He closed his eyes for a moment and could clearly imagine Hest loading his pipe after a fine meal in excellent accommodations. Would Hest even wonder what Sedric was enduring on his swamp boat journey up a mosquito-infested river? He probably did, and probably chortled with joy each time Sedric came to his mind. It stung even worse to imagine Hest sharing his amusement with Wollom and Jaff and the insidious Redding Cope. He imagined Cope doing one of his infuriating imitations. "This is Sedric, enjoying the mosquitoes." And then that pudgy little excuse for a man would slap himself and leap about and be rewarded with Hest's laughter. Even to imagine it was intolerable. He realized he was grinding his teeth and with an effort calmed his face. This whole misadventure was Hest's doing, and an entirely unreasonable punishment for the sin of simply speaking his mind. All he had wanted was for Hest to be a bit kinder to Alise. And for his troubles, he had not only been exiled by Hest but now was hijacked by Alise to accompany her even deeper into this uncivilized wasteland.

Unmindful of Sedric's displeasure, Alise was chattering away with the goat-man at her left elbow. For a moment, he let his mind follow her words. "Look at her. The sun soaks right into her and shines back out of her. She's magnificent."

Sedric made a mildly agreeable noise and let her dither on. The beach didn't merit the name. It was merely a slope of trampled and sun-baked mud that went down to the river's edge. Soon enough, he'd have to be out there, following Alise about and taking notes for her. Traipsing around the piles of dragon dung and river flotsam. Ruining his boots, most likely. As soon as the men finished tying up or whatever they were doing, Alise would want to go ashore. He'd probably best go into his "room" and see about finding his tools.

"Yes. Yes, I was! You are absolutely glorious!" Alise shouted the words.

Sedric opened his eyes. Alise looked transported by joy. Beneath her multitude of freckles, her cheeks were flushed. She clasped her hands to her bosom as if to hold her thundering heart inside her chest. She turned to him, and he could see in her eyes that, in her excitement, she had completely forgotten their earlier disagreement. Seemingly transfixed, she exclaimed, "Sedric, she spoke to me! The blue dragon. She spoke to me!"

He let his eyes rove over the spectacle of reptilian creatures that sprawled or prowled on the muddy shore. "Which blue one?" he asked her at last.

"The queen. The largest blue queen." She sounded as if she could not get her breath. She lifted her voice again. "May I come ashore and speak with you?"

"Queen? Do dragons have kings and queens?"

"The large blue female." She sounded impatient with him. "That one, there. Next to the girl with the broom."

"Ah. And how do you know she's their queen?"

"Not *their* queen, *a* queen. All female dragons are queens. Just as female cats are queens. Now, please, hush! I can't hear her while you're talking!"

The creature was making a sound like a badly tuned wind instrument, but Alise seemed enchanted by its song. When the dragon ceased its mooing, Captain Leftrin seemed equally fascinated. "Let's get you down there, then," he said.

Alise was already in motion. She glanced back at him as she hurried toward the prow of the barge. "Bring your notebook, please, Sedric. Bring everything you'll need to make a transcript of our conversation. Hurry!"

"Very well. I'll be right along." His own heartbeat jumped a bit at the prospect of finally walking among the dragons. He hurried to the makeshift stall that Leftrin had put together for him. At least it had solved one of his problems. Within the four rough walls, he had a modicum of privacy and access to all his luggage. He opened his wardrobe trunk and then pulled open one of the drawers. He'd prepared everything as carefully as he possibly could, hoping to provide for every contingency. He took out his lap desk and sat down on his bed to open it. The "bed" was little more than a raised plank with some semiclean bedding to soften it, but it was a place to sit, and far better than the canvas sling they had cobbled together for him to sleep in.

He checked the lap desk's contents hastily. There were containers for ink of various colors, some empty and some full. Some quill pens already cut and others whole. His penknife, small and sharp. A generous supply of paper in several weights, and a bound sketchbook. A small box held charcoal sticks and several sketching pencils. He pushed two concealed catches with his thumbs and the bottom of the paper box came loose. He lifted it out. There were his specimen bottles. The larger bottles and the coarse salt were concealed in a different compartment in the base of his wardrobe, but for his first foray, this was enough. Perhaps, if he were extraordinarily lucky, by the time they returned to the barge, he'd have everything he needed.

When he returned to the deck, the others were already gone. How considerate of them! He suppressed his annoyance and went to the side of the barge. A coarse rope ladder was his means of egress from the boat. It was tricky to get down with his lap desk tucked under his arm, but he wasn't about to toss it down onto the baked mud. And of course no one offered to help him in any way. Alise was already a substantial distance down the beach, trotting along by herself. That rogue Leftrin hadn't even seen fit to escort her, had just dropped her off on a beach littered with dragons. How could she stand that man?

He dropped the last few feet to the ground and found the impact harder than he had expected and nearly lost his grip on the precious case. He crouched down to roll up the cuffs of his trousers, scowling at how foolish he'd look, like some sort of a booted stork. Well, better that than spending the rest of the day with his cuffs weighted down with foul-smelling mud.

And it was foul. There was no mistaking the reek of excrement. It combined with the brackish smell of the river and the rank smell of the jungle to make the air a thick soup of stench. Good thing he'd not had an opportunity to eat much today or his stomach would have rebelled completely. "Such a lovely place you've chosen for a stroll, Alise," he muttered sarcastically to himself. "Off you go to frolic among the dragon dung with your river rat."

He heard a noise like a low growl and looked around himself in alarm. No. There were no dragons anywhere near. Yet he had definitely heard the threatening snarl of a rather large creature. Even now, he had the uncomfortable sensation of being watched. Not just watched but stared at, as a cat stares at a mouse. Again he scanned the area near him, then startled as he came face-to-face with two large glaring eyes. His heart slammed against his ribs. An instant later, he realized his error. The eyes looked down at him from the nose of the barge. He'd never noticed them before. It was, he recalled, an old superstition to paint eyes on a ship, to help it find its way. The eyes glared at him with contempt and fury. He gave a shudder and turned away from the hideous thing.

"Sedric! Hurry up! Please!"

He looked up to find Alise looking back at him over her shoulder. Now he saw Captain Leftrin was off to one side, conferring with a delegation of Rain Wilders about something. One had a thick scroll and seemed to be going over a list with him, point by point. The captain nodded and gave his braying laugh. The man with the scroll did not look amused.

Alise had halted just short of the dragons. Now she looked at him like a dog begging for a walk. Anxiety vied with the excitement in her stance. And no wonder. The dragon she had chosen had risen to her feet and was regarding Alise with interest. It was much bigger than it had looked from the deck of the barge. And blue, very blue. The creature's hide sparkled iridescently in the sunlight. The eyes she had turned on Alise were large, much larger than seemed proportionate to the creature's head. They were a coppery brown, with a slit pupil like a cat's, but unlike a cat's eyes the color of the dragon's eyes seemed to melt and swirl around the iris of her eye. It was unsettling. The creature gave a guttural call.

Alise turned her back on him and hastened toward the dragon. "Yes, of course. I apologize for keeping you waiting, beauteous one."

If the dragon had been proportional and perfectly formed, she might have been beautiful, as a prize bull or a stag was beautiful. But she was not. Her tail seemed short compared to her long neck, and her legs were stumpy. The wings that she now lifted and spread seemed ridiculously small and floppy for a creature of her size, and uneven. They reminded Sedric of a parasol that the wind had blown inside out, presenting the same aspect of flimsy ribs and uneven fabric. He stood up, tucked his lap desk under his arm, and set off across the mud in pursuit of Alise.

A commotion off to one side made him halt. A small red dragon with a boy clinging to its back was thudding ponderously along the beach. "Open your wings!" the lad was shouting. "Open your wings and flap them. You got to try, Heeby. Try really hard."

And in response, the misshapen creature spread out wings that were not even well matched. One was larger than the other, but the dragon obediently flapped them as it ran. Its "flight" ended a moment later as it charged directly into the river. The boy yelled in dismay and then shouted, with laughter in his voice, "You got to watch where we're going, Heeby. But that was good for a first try. We just got to keep at it, girl."

He was not the only one who had stopped to stare at the spectacle. Dragons and keepers alike were frozen. Some of the keepers were grinning, and others were horrified. He could not read any expression on the dragons' visages. After all, how would one tell if a cow were amused or offended? Alise, after one moment of staring in shock, turned back to her target and once more hurried off.

His longer legs soon caught him up with Alise despite her dogged trot. She seemed to be talking to the dragon. "You are glorious beyond words. I am so thrilled to finally be here, and to speak with you like this is beyond my wildest dreams!"

The dragon lowed back at her.

For the first time, he really noticed the young girl beside the dragon. She had rested her makeshift pine-bough broom on her shoulder. She didn't look pleased to see them. The scowl on her face and her narrowed eyes made her look even more reptilian. For that was his first impression of her. Lizardlike, he would have said of her scaled face. He had thought her hands were caked with mud, but now he saw that her fingers ended in thick black claws. Her braided black hair looked like woven snakes, and her eyes glittered unnaturally.

"Alise," he said warningly, and when she didn't respond, he raised his voice more commandingly. "Alise, stop a moment! Wait for me."

"Well, hurry then!"

She paused, but he sensed that she would not wait long. In two strides he caught up with her completely. In the guise of taking her arm, he caught hold of her. "Be careful!" he cautioned her in a low voice, pitching his words to carry through the dragon's vocalizing. "You know nothing of the dragon. And the girl looks distinctly unfriendly. Either one or both of them may be dangerous."

"Sedric, let go! Can't you hear her? She says she wishes to speak to me. I think the best way to insult her and anger her is to ignore such a request. And speaking to the dragons is exactly why I came here. And it's why you are here, too! So follow me and please, have your pen ready to record our conversation."

She tried to pull free of him. He kept his grip and leaned down to peer into her face. "Alise, are you serious?"

"Of course I am! Why do you think I came all this way?"

"But . . . the dragon is not speaking. Unless mooing like a cow or barking like a dog conveys some meaning to you. What am I to record?"

She looked at him in confusion that became dismay and then, inexplicably, sympathy. "Oh, Sedric, you cannot understand her at all? Not one word?"

"If she has spoken a word, I haven't understood it. All I've heard are, well, dragon noises."

Almost as if in response to his comment, the dragon released a rumble of sound. Alise swiveled her head to face the dragon. "Please, I beg you, let me have a moment with my friend! He cannot seem to hear you."

When Alise met Sedric's gaze again, she shook her head in woe. "I'd heard that there were some who could not understand clearly what Tintaglia said, and a few who could not even perceive she was speaking at all. But I never thought you would be so afflicted. What are we to do now, Sedric? How will you record our conversations?"

"Conversations?" At first he'd been annoyed at her childish pretense of talking to the dragon. It was the same annoyance he always felt when people greeted dogs as "old man" and asked "how my fine old fellow has been." Women who talked to their cats made him shudder. Alise, as a rule, did neither, and he'd thought her calls to the dragon had been some new and unwelcome Rain Wild affectation. But now, to insist that the dragon was speaking to her and then to offer him her pity—it was too much. "I'll record them just as I would log your conversations with a cow. Or a tree. Alise, this is ridiculous. I'll accept, because I must, that the dragon Tintaglia had the ability to make herself understood. But this creature? Look at it!"

The dragon writhed its lips and made a flat, hissing noise. Alise went scarlet. The young Rain Wilder beside the dragon spoke to him. "She says to tell you that although you may not understand her, she understands every word you say. And that the problem is not in her speaking, nor even in your ears, but in your mind. There have always been humans who cannot hear dragons. And usually they are the most arrogant and ignorant ones."

It was too much. "Keep a civil tongue in your head when you address your elders, girl. Or is that no longer taught here in the Rain Wilds?"

The dragon gave a sudden huff. The force of her exhaled breath blasted him with warmth and the stink of the semi-rotted meat she had just eaten. He turned aside from her with an exclamation of disgust.

Alise gave a gasp of horror and pleaded, "He does not understand! He meant no insult! Please, he meant no insult!" An instant later, Alise had seized him by the arm. "Sedric, are you all right?" she demanded of him.

"That creature belched right in my face!"

Alise gave a strangled laugh. She seemed to be trembling with relief. "A belch? Was that what you thought it? If so, we are fortunate that was all. If her poison glands were mature, you'd be melting right now. Don't you know anything of dragons? Don't you recall what became of the Chalcedean raiders who attacked Bingtown? All Tintaglia had to do was breathe on them. Whatever it was she spat, it ate right through armor. And right through skin and bone as well." She paused, and then added, "You have insulted her without meaning to. I think you should go back to the ship. Right now. Give me time to explain your misunderstanding of her."

The Rain Wild girl spoke again. She had a husky voice, a surprisingly rich contralto. Her silver gaze was both unsettling and compelling. "Skymaw agrees with the Bingtown woman. Whether you're my elder or not, she says you should leave the dragon grounds. Now."

Sedric felt even more affronted. "I don't think that you have the right to tell me what to do at all," he told the girl.

But Alise spoke over his words. "Skymaw? That's her name?"

"It's what I call her." The girl amended. She seemed embarrassed to have to admit it. "She told me that a dragon's true name is a thing to be earned, not given."

"I understand completely," Alise replied. "The true name of a dragon is a very special thing to know. No dragon tells her true name lightly." She treated the dragon's keeper as if she were a charming child who had interrupted an important adult conversation. The "child" did not enjoy that, Sedric noted.

Alise turned back to the hulking reptile. The creature had ventured so close that it now towered over them. Her eyes were like burnished copper, glittering in the sunlight. Her gaze was fixed steadily on him. Alise spoke to the creature. "Great and gracious one, your true name is an honor that I hope one day to win. But in the mean time, I am pleased to give you mine. I am Alise Kincarron Finbok." And she actually curtsied to the creature, bobbing down almost into the mud.

"I have come all the way from Bingtown to see you, and to hear you speak. I hope that we shall have long conversations, and that I shall be able to learn a great deal about you and the wisdom of your kind. Long has it been since humanity was favored with the company of dragons. What little we knew of your kind has, I fear, been forgotten. I would like to remedy that lack." She gestured toward Sedric. "I brought him with me, to be our scribe and record any wisdom you wished to share with me. I am sorry that he cannot hear you, for I am certain that if he could, he would quickly perceive both your intelligence and your wisdom."

The dragon rumbled again. The young keeper looked at

Sedric and said, "Skymaw says that even if you could understand her words, she thinks it likely you would be unable
to comprehend either her intelligence or wisdom, for plainly
you lack both."

Her "translation" was obviously intended to insult. The
girl's eyes, silvery gray, darted toward Alise when she
spoke. If Alise was aware of her animosity, she ignored it.
Instead Alise turned to him and said quietly but firmly, "I'll
see you when I return to the ship, Sedric. If you don't mind,
would you leave your lap desk with me? I may try to write
down some of what we discuss."

"Of course," he said, and managed to keep the bitterness
and the resentment from his voice. Long ago, he thought,
he'd had to learn to speak civilly even after Hest had publicly
flayed him with words. It was not so hard. All he had to do
was discard every bit of his pride. He'd never thought that he
would have to employ that talent with Alise. He thrust the
lap desk at her, and as she took it was almost pleased to see
her surprise at how heavy it was. *Let her deal with carrying
it about,* he thought vengefully. Let her see the sort of work
he'd been willing to do for her. Perhaps she might appreciate
him a bit more. He turned away from her.

Then, with a sudden lurch of heart, he realized there
were things inside that lap desk that he emphatically did
not wish to share with Alise. He turned hastily back to her.
"The entire secretarial desk will be too heavy for you to use
easily. Perhaps I could just leave you some blank paper, and
a pen and ink?"

She looked startled at this sudden kindness, and he suddenly knew that she knew he'd intended to be rude when he'd
burdened her with the whole desk. She looked pathetically
grateful as he took it from her and opened it. The raised lid
kept her from peering inside, but she didn't seem to have any
curiosity about it. As he rummaged inside it for the required
items, she said quietly, "Thank you for your understanding,
Sedric. I know this must be hard for you, to come so far on
such a great adventure, and then to find that fortune has excluded you from the best part of it. I want you to know that I
think no less of you; such a lack could afflict anyone."

"It's fine, Alise," he said, and he tried not to sound brusque. She thought his feelings were hurt because he couldn't communicate with the animal. And she felt sorry for him. The thought almost made him smile, and his heart softened toward her. How many years had he felt sorry for her? It was odd to be on the receiving end of her pity. Odd and strangely touching that she'd care if his feelings were hurt.

"I've plenty of work to do back on the boat. I trust you'll be back for the evening meal?"

"Oh, likely much before then. I shan't stand here in the dark and quiz her, I assure you. Today I'll be happy if we just get to know each other well enough to be comfortable. Thank you. I'll try not to waste your ink."

"You're welcome. Really you are. I'll see you later."

THYMARA WATCHED THE exchange between the well-dressed man and the Bingtown woman and wondered. They seemed very familiar with each other; perhaps they were married. She was reminded of her parents, and how they had always seemed connected and yet distant to each other. These two seemed to get along about as well as her parents did.

She already disliked both of them. The man because he had no respect for Skymaw and was too stupid to understand her, and the woman, because she had seen the dragon and now she coveted her. And she would probably win the dragon, for she seemed to know how to charm her. Couldn't Skymaw see that the Bingtown woman was just trying to flatter her with her flowery phrases and overdone courtesy? She would have thought that the dragon would be angered by such a blatant attempt to win favor with her. Instead, Skymaw seemed delighted with the extravagant compliments the woman showered on her. She fawned on her, openly begging for more.

And in turn, the woman seemed completely infatuated with the dragon. From the first moment they had seen each other, Thymara had almost felt the mutual draw between them. It irritated her.

No. It was more than irritation. It made her seethe with jealousy, she admitted, because it excluded her. *She* was supposed to be Skymaw's keeper, not this ridiculous city woman. This Alise would not be able to feed the dragon or tend her. Would this woman with her soft body and pale skin walk beside the dragon as they wended their way upriver through the shallows and the encroaching forest? Would she kill to feed the dragon and perform the tedious grooming that Skymaw so obviously needed? She thought not! Thymara had spent most of the day scrubbing at Skymaw's hide until every scale gleamed. She'd dug caked mud out of her claws and claw sheaths, picked a legion of nasty little bloodsucking beetles from the edges of the dragon's eyes and nostrils, and even cleared an area of reeking fresh dragon dung so that Skymaw could stretch out for her grooming without becoming soiled again.

But the moment this Bingtown woman threw her a compliment or two, the dragon focused entirely on her as if Thymara had never existed. Would the woman have thought her so "gleamingly beautiful" if she'd seen the dragon five hours ago? Not likely. The dragon was using all Thymara's hard work to attract a better keeper for herself. She'd soon find she'd made a poor choice.

Just like Tats.

The thought ambushed her, and she felt the sudden sting of tears behind her eyes. She pushed all thoughts of Tats and Jerd aside. That night when Tats had left the fireside and Jerd had followed, she'd thought nothing of it. Tats, she thought, had needed time to be alone. But then, when they came back to the fire together, it was obvious to Thymara that he had been anything but alone. He seemed completely recovered from his exchange of comments with Greft. Jerd had been laughing at something he said. At the fire's edge, they'd sat down side by side. She'd overheard Jerd quizzing him about his life, asking the sort of personal questions that Thymara had always avoided for fear of Tats thinking she was too nosy. Jerd had asked them, smiling and tipping her head to look up into his face, and Tats had replied in his deep soft voice. Thymara had sat by the fire and Rapskal supplied an unwelcome distraction as he pelted her with his speculations about the journey and what they would have for breakfast tomorrow and if it was possible to kill a gallator with a sling. Greft had glared at her, Tats, and Rapskal and then had gone stalking off into the forest on his own. Nortel and Boxter had both seemed out of sorts as well, exchanging small barbed comments. Harrikin had suddenly seemed sullen and sulky. None of it made sense to her; she only knew that her earlier sensation of goodwill and friendliness had been more fleeting than the smoke from their campfire.

And that night, Tats had spread out his bedding and gone to sleep near Jerd without even speaking to Thymara to say good night. She'd thought they were friends, good friends. She'd even been stupid enough to think that he'd only signed up as a dragon keeper because he knew that she'd be going, too. Worse, Rapskal had tossed his blankets right down beside hers after she had made her bed for the evening. She couldn't very well get up and move away from him, much as she wished to. He'd slept next to her every night since they left Trehaug. He talked and laughed even in his sleep, and her dreams, when she did find them that night, were uneasy ones of her father looking for her in a mist.

In vain, she tried to recall her mind to the present and focus on the conversation next to her. The Bingtown woman was speaking to Skymaw. "Do you recall, lovely one, your immediate ancestor's experience, your glorious mother's life? Do you know what happened to the world to cause dragons to become nearly extinct and leave humans to mourn in loneliness for so long?" She stood awaiting an answer, her pen poised over her paper. It was sickening.

Worse, Skymaw was wallowing in the praise and answering the woman in dragon riddles while telling her nothing at all. "My 'mother'? Were she here, you would not insult her so lightly! A dragon is never a mother as you know it, little milk-making creature. We never fuss about squealing babies or waste our days in tending to the wants of help-less young. We are never as helpless and stupid as humans are when they are first born, knowing nothing of what or who they are. It is irony, is it not, that you live so short a

time, and waste so much of it being stupid? While we live
for dozens of your lives, aware every instant of what we are
and who our ancestors were. You can see that it is hopeless
for a human to try to understand dragonkind at all."

Thymara turned away abruptly from the dragon and the
Bingtown woman. "I'd best go see if I can kill some food
for you," she announced, not caring that she broke into the
midst of their conversation. It was disgusting anyway. The
woman kept asking Skymaw stupid questions, phrased in
groveling, honeyed compliments. And the dragon kept
evading the questions, refusing her any real answers. Was
that just what any dragon would do? Or was Skymaw trying
to conceal her own ignorance?

Now there was an idea that was almost more disturbing
than the thought that Tats suddenly found Jerd more interesting than she was. And nearly as upsetting that neither the
dragon nor the Bingtown woman seemed to take any notice
of her leaving.

She strode across the mud-baked shore toward their small
boats. She'd left her belongings bundled up with her pack in
one of the boats. She cast a casual glance at the big black
scow at the edge of the shore. The *Tarman*. It was a strange
craft, far more blunt and square than any other boat she'd
ever seen. It had eyes painted on its prow; she'd heard that
was an old custom, older than the Rain Wild settlements. It
was supposed to encourage the boat to look out for itself and
avoid dangers in the river. She liked the boat's eyes. They
looked old and wise, like the eyes of a kindly old man over
his sympathetic smile. She hoped they would actually help
guide the ship as they tried to find a way up the Rain Wild
River. They were going to need all the help they could get to
carry out their mission.

She found her fishing spear and decided to try her luck,
even though it looked as if the other keepers were already
patrolling the shallow bank for any unwary fish. Rapskal
had had a small success. He'd speared a fish the size of his
hand. He did a victory dance with the flopping creature still
stuck on the end of his spear, and then turned to his little red
dragon. She had been toddling along behind Rapskal like

a child's pull toy. "Open up, Heeby!" Rapskal demanded, and the dragon obediently gaped at him. Rapskal tugged the fish off the spear and tossed it into the dragon's maw. The creature just stood there. "Well, eat it! There's food in your mouth; shut your mouth and eat it!" Rapskal advised her. After a moment the dragon complied. Thymara wondered if the creature were too stupid even to eat food put in its mouth, or if the fish had been so small the dragon hadn't noticed it.

She shook her head at them. She doubted that any large river fish would linger there in the sluggish warm water under the open sky. She turned her back on the dragons and her friends and headed toward the far edge of the clearing, where the trees tangled their worn roots right out into the river. Coarse sword-grass grew there, and gray reeds and spearman-grass. The rising and falling of the water level had left fallen branches and dead leaves tangled and dangling from the clawing tree roots that reached out into the river. If she were a fish, that would be where she would take shelter from the sunlight and predators. She'd try her luck there.

Clambering out on the twisting roots was both like and unlike her travels through the canopy. Up there, a fall could mean death, but the layers of branches also offered a hundred chances to grip a limb or liana and regain her life. Down here, there were gaps in the matted tangle of roots under her feet. Below, the river flowed, gray and stinging, at best threatening to give her a rash, at worst eating through skin and flesh down to the bone. There was also the chance of crashing through completely into water over her head, and worse, coming back up under the tangled roots. The trees were still under her feet, as they had always been, but the dangers were different. Somehow that made it hard to remember that she was sure-footed and made for the Rain Wilds.

The third time her booted foot slipped on the roots, she stopped and thought. Then she sat down and carefully unlaced both boots. She knotted the laces together and slung the boots around her neck and went on, digging the claws of her toes into the bark. She found a likely place. The foliage overhead cast a dappling shade over her. A thick twist of root gave sheltering debris a place to cling even as it provided her an opening over the river. The grass and fallen branches filtered the silt-laden river water here, so it was almost translucent. She sat down where her shadow would not fall on the water, poised her fish spear, and waited.

It took time for her eyes to learn to read the water. She could not see fish, but after a time she could see shadows, and then swirls in the sediment that showed a fish had passed. Her shoulder began to ache from holding her spear at the ready; the spear itself seemed to weigh as much as a tree trunk. She pushed the ache out of her mind and focused her whole being on reading the swirls in the sediment. *That would be the tail, so the head would be there, no, too late, it's back under the root. Here it comes, here it comes, here it—no, back under the root. There he is, he's a big one, wait, wait, and—*

She jabbed down with the spear rather than throwing it. She felt it hit the fish and pushed hard and strong to pin it to the riverbed. But the water was deeper than she had thought, and suddenly she had to catch herself on the root to keep from tumbling in while the fish, a very large one, wriggled and jerked on the end of her spear, trying to free itself. She fought to keep her balance while keeping the fish on the spear.

Someone grabbed her from behind.

"Let go!" she roared and pushed the butt of the spear back hard, thudding it solidly into whoever had seized her. She heard a whoosh of exhaled breath and then a faint curse. She didn't turn, for the thud had nearly dislodged her fish. She flipped up the spear end, bracing the butt against her hip and was astounded at the size of the fish she levered out of the river. Thrashing wildly, the fish actually drove the spear deeper and then through its own body. Her prey was nearly half the length of her body and it came sliding down the spear shaft toward her.

"Don't lose him. Keep hold of your spear!" Tats shouted from behind her.

"I've got him," she snarled, irritated that he would think she needed his help. Despite her words, he reached past her shoulder and seized the other end of the spear. Between them, they held it horizontally while the fish struggled wildly. Then Tats produced a knife in his free hand and whacked the fish soundly on the head with the back of the blade. Abruptly it was still. She breathed a sigh of relief. It felt as if her shoulder had nearly been jolted from its socket.

Still gripping her end of the spear, she turned to thank him, and was astonished to find they were not alone. The Bingtown woman's friend was sitting on a hummock of root, his hands clasped over his midsection. His face was red save for where his mouth was pinched tight and white. He gazed at her with narrowed eyes and then spoke in a tight voice. "I was trying to help you. I thought you were going to fall in."

"What are you doing here?" she demanded.

"I saw him going into the forest where you had gone and thought he was following you. So I came to see what he was up to." Tats was the one who answered her question.

"I'm able to take care of myself," she pointed out to him.

Tats refused to take offense. "I know that. I didn't interfere when you thumped him. I only helped you with the fish because I didn't want to see it get away."

She made an impatient noise and focused on the stranger. "Why did you follow me?" Tats gripped the spear to either side of the fish, grinning. She let him take the weight of it but watched closely as he set her catch down on the matted roots.

"You knocked the wind out of me," the stranger complained, and then managed to take a fuller, deeper breath. He uncurled slightly and some of the redness went out of his face. "I only followed you because I wanted to talk to you. I'd seen you with the dragon, the one that Alise is interested in. I wanted to ask you a few things."

"Such as?" A blush betrayed her. He probably thought she was some half-savage Rain Wild primitive. She was starting to think she had misjudged him, but she wasn't going to apologize just yet. Actually, she was beginning to hope she had misjudged him. Earlier she had noticed how polished he was. She had never seen a man dressed so well as this one was. Now that his color was settling, she realized he was extremely handsome. Earlier, when he had been talking with the Bingtown woman, she had thought him stuffy and horribly ignorant of dragons, not to mention arrogant and rude when he spoke to her. His beauty had just seemed a part of the insult, the power that gave him the authority to look down on her. But he'd followed her and actually tried to help her. For which she'd thudded a spear butt into his belly.

But now he made up for many of his sins when he gave her a rueful smile and said, "Look, we got off to a bad start. And I don't suppose I made things better when I startled you. I was insulting when I first spoke to you, but you must admit, you weren't exactly courteous to me. And you are now one up on me for nearly impaling me on the dull end of a fishing spear." He paused, took a deep breath, and his color almost became normal. "Can we begin again, please?"

Before she could reply, he stood, bowed at the waist to her, and said, "How do you do? My name is Sedric Meldar. I'm from Bingtown, and ordinarily my daily work is to be a secretary to Trader Finbok of Bingtown. But for this month, I am accompanying Trader Finbok's wife, Alise, as her chronicler and protector as she seeks to amass new and exciting knowledge about dragons and Elderlings."

Thymara found herself smiling before his speech was halfway out. He spoke so formally yet in a way that let her know he was mocking the formality and the grandness of his work. He was dressed like a prince, with not a hair out of place, and yet his smile and easy ways invited her to feel comfortable with him. As if they were equals, she realized.

"What's a chronicler?" Tats demanded abruptly.

"I write down what she does. Where she goes, the gist of her conversations, and sometimes, when she is doing research, I write down in detail what she learns. Later, she'll be able to look back over what I've written to be sure she is remembering every detail correctly. I'm also a passable artist and intended to do sketches of the dragons, detailed sketches of their eyes, claws, teeth, and well, every part of them. Only today I discovered that I'm not going to be much

use to her for the interviewing part of her work. I seem to
have offended the dragon, which means that I can't be with
Alise while she is studying her. And even if I could be, I
couldn't understand any of the animal's answers to Alise's
questions."

"Skymaw," Thymara supplied helpfully. "The dragon's
name is Skymaw."

"She told you her name?" Tats was astounded.

Thymara was irritated at the interruption. "Skymaw is
what I call her," she amended, giving him a glare. "Everyone
knows that dragons don't tell their real names immediately."

"Yes, that's what my dragon told me, too. Only she didn't
ask me to give her a name to use." He smiled foolishly.
"She's such a beauty, Thymara. Green as emeralds, green
as sunlight through leaves. Her eyes are like, well, I don't
have words. She's a bad-tempered little thing, though. I accidentally stepped on her toe and she threatened to kill and
eat me!"

"Wait, please." It was the stranger's turn to interrupt
them. "Please. Both of you. You are saying that you talk to
the dragons? Just as we are talking right now?"

Only Sedric didn't feel like a stranger to her anymore.
She smiled at him. "Of course we do."

"They move their mouths and the words come out and
you hear them? Just as we are talking together now? Then
why do I hear rumbles and moos and hisses, and you hear
words?"

"Well—" She hesitated, realizing she hadn't thought
about how she "heard" the dragons.

"No, of course not." Tats barged in again. "Their mouths
are all wrong for shaping words like we do. They make
sounds, and somehow I understand what they are saying.
Even though they aren't speaking a human language."

"Did it take you long to learn their language? Did you
study it before you came here?" Sedric asked.

"No." Tats shook his head decisively. "When I first got
here, I picked out my dragon and walked up to her, and I
could understand her. Mine is the green female. She's not
as big as some of the others, but I think she's prettier. Also,

she's fast and other than her wings, I think she's pretty much perfectly formed. She's a bit feisty; she says the others say she's mean and avoid her. She says it's because she's fast enough to get to the food first almost every time. They're jealous."

"Or perhaps they just think she's greedy," Thymara suggested. Time to take control of this conversation. After all, Sedric hadn't followed Tats into the woods to speak to him, even if he now seemed to be hanging on every word the boy spoke. "I've been able to understand the dragons since they hatched," she told the Bingtown man. "I was here that day. And even when they weren't looking at me directly, I could feel what they were thinking, even as they were coming out of their logs. And communicate with them." She smiled. "One of the hatchlings went after my dad. I had to insist that he wasn't food."

"A dragon wanted to eat your father?" Sedric seemed horrified.

"They had just come out of their cases. He was confused." She cast her mind back, remembering. "They were so hungry when they came out. And they weren't as strong as they should have been or as well formed. I think the sea serpents were too old and not as fat as they should have been, and they didn't stay encased long enough. And that's why these dragons aren't healthy and can't fly."

"Can't fly yet," Tats amended. He grinned. "You saw Rapskal. He's determined that his dragon is going to fly. He's crazy, of course. But after I watched them, well, I was looking at my green's wings. They're well shaped, but just small and not very strong. She told me that dragons keep growing for as long as they live. All parts of them grow— necks, legs, tails, and, yes, wings. I'm thinking that if I feed her right and she keeps trying to use them, maybe her wings will grow and she will be able to fly."

Thymara regarded him in astonishment. She had just accepted the dragons as they were; it had not occurred to her that perhaps they might become full dragons as they grew. Now she reconsidered Skymaw's wings. They had seemed floppy when she had cleaned them, and Skymaw

had not been very helpful about unfolding them for grooming. She didn't think Skymaw could move them much. A
surge of envy raced through her; was it possible that Tats's
green dragon might eventually gain flight while Skymaw remained earthbound?

"But you can understand what they say, word for word?"
Sedric seemed intent on dragging them back to his own concern about the dragons. When Thymara nodded, he asked,
"So when you said those things to me, you weren't making
them up? You were actually translating what the dragon was
trying to say to me?"

She suddenly felt a bit abashed by how she had spoken
to him. "I was repeating exactly what Skymaw was saying,"
she excused herself, and felt only slightly guilty for blaming
her rudeness on the dragon.

"So, then. You could translate for me? If I wanted to talk
to her, apologize—"

"No need for that. I mean, you can speak directly to her.
She understands exactly what you say."

"Yes, she did, and that is exactly how I was getting into
trouble with her. But if Alise asks your dragon a question
and your dragon answers, you could translate the answer for
me? Quietly, off to one side, so we don't disturb their conversation."

"Of course. But so could Alise—I mean, the lady. So
could any of the keepers."

"But that would slow down Alise's work. I was thinking
that if someone would interpret for me as the dragon talks,
I could get it all down. I'm a very fast writer. And I suppose
any keeper could do it." He glanced at Tats. "But seeing as
how she is your dragon, I think you would be the logical
choice."

She liked how he kept referring to Skymaw as her
dragon. "I suppose I could."

"Well then—would you?"

"Would I what? Just stand there while they're talking,
only tell you what the dragon is saying?"

"Exactly." He hesitated, and then offered, "I could pay
you, if you wish. For your time."

It was tempting, but her father had raised her to be honest. "I've already been paid for my time, and it belongs to the dragon now. I can't sell my time twice any more than I could sell a plum twice. So I couldn't take your money. And I'd have to ask Skymaw if she would allow you to be near her, and if she would mind if I told you what she was saying."

"Well." He seemed taken aback at the thought she couldn't accept his money. "Would you ask her, then? I'd be indebted to you."

She cocked her head at him. "Actually, I think it would be Alise Finbok who would be indebted to me. After all, she's bought your time, for you to do this work for her. And if I make it so you can do it, well—" Thymara smiled to herself. "Yes, I think actually she'd be the one indebted to me." She rather liked the idea of that.

"So, then, you'll ask the dragon if I can be around her? And if you can interpret for me what she says?"

Thymara bent down and grasped her fishing spear to either side of her prey. She grunted slightly as she lifted the heavy fish. She nodded toward it as she answered him. "Let's ask her right now. I think I have something here that might put her in the mood to say yes."

✧   ✧   ✧

Day the 6th of the Grain Moon

Year the 6th of the Independent Alliance of Traders

Kim to Detozi

I fear you have taken a simple reminder of the rules as if it were a personal rebuke. Detozi, surely we know each other well enough for you to realize that I was only carrying out the tasks of my position when I reminded you of the rules regarding personal messages. I am not the sort of person who would run to the Council with such a trivial complaint. I merely thought that if I reminded you of the rules, I might save you from embarrassment and nuisance if it came to the attention of someone who was petty enough to enforce them. That was all. Sa's mercy, I am shocked at how seriously you have taken all this! I will, for the sake of our friendship, ignore the unfounded accusations and cruel allegations of your last missive.

Kim

✧   ✧   ✧

CHAPTER THIRTEEN

SUSPICIONS

He awoke before dawn, cradled in a warm cocoon of contentment. Life was good. Leftrin lay still in the dark, enjoying it for a few long moments before letting his mind start enumerating the tasks of the day. Tarman was as still as he ever got, nosed up onto the mudbank. Sometimes it seemed to him that his ship grew more thoughtful when it was pulled up on the riverbank, as if he were dreaming of other days and times. He could hear and feel the gentle tug of the river's backwater current on the aft end of the ship, but mostly all was still. It was quieter than when he anchored or tied up in the river, almost as if Tarman himself were dozing on the sunny bank.

The bedding smelled sweet, of the cologne that Alise Finbok wore, but also of Alise herself. He rolled his face into the pillow and breathed deeply of her scent. Then he grinned at his own foolishness. He was as infatuated as a beardless boy who had just discovered that women were wonderfully different from men. The giddiness that had passed him by as a youth now spun him delightfully, infecting every moment of his day. Thinking of her freckled, speckled face made him smile. Her hair, the color of a hummer's breast, turned into tiny curls all around her brow when it escaped from her pins. The times she had reached out and taken his arm when something frightened or alarmed her always made him feel as if he were taller and stronger than he had ever been in his life.

There was no future to it. He knew that in every corner of his yearning, aching heart. When he thought of how it must end, he felt despair. But for now, this morning, on the dawn of carrying her off up the river on a journey that might be weeks or even months long, he was happy and excited. It was a mood that hummed through the ship, infecting the crew as well. Tarman would be very pleased to be under way. Leftrin still considered it a ridiculous mission, a journey to nowhere herding reluctant dragons. Yet the pay the Council had offered was excellent, and the opportunity to take his ship and crew beyond the boundaries of what had been explored was something he'd always dreamed about. To have a woman like Alise not only appear in his life, but suddenly be given him as a companion for the voyage was good fortune beyond his ability to imagine.

He took another deep breath of her fragrance, hugged his pillow, and sat up. Time to face the day. He wanted to make an early start, yet he would wait for the delivery of the supplies he had specially ordered in the hopes of making her more comfortable. He scratched his chest, chose a shirt from the hooks near his bunk, and pulled it on. He still wore his trousers from yesterday. Barefoot, he padded out of his stateroom and into the galley. He stirred the embers in the small stove and put yesterday's coffee to reheat. He wiped out a coffee mug and set it on the table. Outside the small windows of the deckhouse, the world was hesitantly venturing toward day. The deep shadows of the surrounding forest still cloaked the boat and shore in dimness.

He felt a small vibration and then that prickle of awareness. Someone, a stranger to Tarman, was on the deck of
his ship. Leftrin stood silently. From a nearby equipment
box, he picked up the large hardwood fid used for mending
and splicing the heaviest lines. He weighed the heft of it in
his hand, smiled to himself, and moved quietly as the cat to
the door. He eased it open. The cool air of morning flowed
in. In the upper reaches of the forest, birds were calling. In
the lower levels, bats were still heading home to roost. He
stepped out on his deck and began a noiseless patrol of his
vessel.

He found no one, but when he came back to the door of
the deckhouse, a small scroll rested on the deck there. His
heart gave a lurch as he stooped down to pick it up. The
paper of the scroll was soft and thick; it smelled of a foreign
land, bitterly spicy. He carried it back into his stateroom and
shut the door. The wax that sealed it was a plain brown blob;
no signet press betrayed the owner. He flicked it off and un-
rolled the small scroll. He read it by the gray light seeping
in his small window.

*There are no coincidences. I've maneuvered you
into place. Lend your support to the one that I've
arranged to be there. You will know him soon
enough. You know what he seeks. A fortune rides on
this, and the blood of my family. If all goes well, the
fortune will be shared with you. If it does not go well,
my family will not be the only ones to mourn.*

It was not signed, but no signature was needed. Sinad
Arich. Months ago, he had given the foreigner passage to
Trehaug, and almost as soon as the boat had docked, the
Chalcedean merchant had vanished. He hadn't asked for
passage back down the river. Two days later, when the
Tarman was loaded with cargo and Leftrin had heard noth-
ing from or about the man, they had departed. The foreign
trader had left few signs of his passage on the *Tarman*.
There had been a shirt that Leftrin had dropped overboard
and some smoking herbs that he'd appropriated for his own

use. The crew never asked what had become of their passenger, and Leftrin hadn't made much noise about his leaving Trehaug that day. The man's papers had been in order and he'd sold him passage up the river. That was what he intended to say if anyone ever asked him about the merchant. But no one ever had, and Leftrin had hoped he had set that misadventure behind him.

He'd hoped in vain. He wished he'd never heard of that damn Chalcedean merchant, wished he'd found a way to throw him overboard a year ago. Sinad Arich had haunted his nightmares since he'd last seen the man. After all that time, Leftrin had almost believed he'd seen the last of him, that the man had only wanted to use him once and then let him go.

But that was what it was to deal with Chalced or any Chalcedean. Once they knew you had a weakness, a secret spot of any kind, they'd hook into you, exploit you until you were either killed in the process or turned on them and killed them. He gritted his teeth together. Only a few moments ago, he'd been doltishly happy at the prospect of traveling upriver with the object of his fascination. Now he wondered who else would be traveling with him, and how relentless they would be in their threats. He wondered if he would have to kill someone on this journey, and if he did, how he would do it and if he would be able to keep it concealed from Alise.

It saddened him. He suspected that if she knew half the things he'd done in his life, she'd have nothing to do with him. He didn't like that he had to conceal part of what he was to enjoy her companionship, but he would. He'd do whatever he must to have what little time with her that he could. He was already at an immense disadvantage with such a fine lady. Here he was, a Rain Wild riverman with little more than a boat to his name. She couldn't even imagine what a unique and wonderful boat the *Tarman* was. She couldn't possibly see his ship as his fortune. So he didn't know why she seemed to like him. He worked hard and expected he always would. He had no fine home to present to her. His clothes were rags compared with the garments of her dandified escort; he wore no rings. Before she had set foot on his ship, he'd had little more ambition than to continue doing what he'd always done: carrying freight shipments up and down the river, and making enough to pay his crew and to have a good meal when his schedule allowed him to over- night in a town. He'd had his chance to make a fortune sell- ing off that wizardwood. He could have been a wealthy man now, with a palatial home in Jamaillia or Chalced. He didn't regret the decision he'd made; it was the only right thing he could have done.

Yet he wondered at how small a life he'd been willing to settle for. He wished in vain that he'd foreseen that some day such a woman might walk into his life. If he had, perhaps he would have saved the sort of wealth that might impress her. But what could he have acquired that could compare with whatever her rich husband in Bingtown offered her?

He looked at the little scroll again. He wondered if he should have killed the Chalcedean merchant and dropped him over the side before they ever reached Trehaug. He didn't think of it casually; he'd only killed one man, long ago, and that had been over a game of chance gone wrong, with accusations that he was cheating. He hadn't been, and when the fellow and his friends had made it clear that they'd kill him before they let him walk off with his winnings, he'd beaten one man unconscious, killed another, and fled the third. He didn't feel proud that he'd done so, only competent that he'd survived. It was another decision that he refused to regret.

So now as he contemplated retroactive murder, he did it only in a "what if" frame of mind. If he'd killed the mer- chant, he would not be standing here now holding this threatening scroll, he wouldn't have to wonder which of the people who would be accompanying him on his journey was a traitor to the Traders, and he wouldn't have to speculate on whether Sinad Arich had really had a finger in his win- ning this sweet plum of a contract. And, he thought, as he reduced the scroll to shreds of fiber and dropped them out of the window, he wouldn't be worrying if he'd have to do something that might cause Alise to think less of him.

❖ ❖ ❖

"Time to get up!"

"Get up, pack your stuff, rouse your dragons!"

"Get up. Time to get on your way."

Thymara opened her eyes to the gray of distant dawn. She yawned and abruptly wished she had never agreed to any of this. Around her, she heard the grumbles of the other rousted keepers. The ones doing the rousting were the people who had accompanied them from Trehaug to here. Their duties would come to an end today, and apparently they could not wait for them to be over. The sooner the keepers rose, woke their dragons, and began their first day's journey, the sooner the escorts who had brought them here could turn around and go back to their homes.

Thymara yawned again. She supposed she'd better get up if she wanted anything to eat before the day started. She'd never known just how much and how fast boys could eat until she'd had to share a common cook pot with them. She sat up slowly, clutching her blanket to her, but the chill morning air still reached in to touch her.

"You awake?" Rapskal asked her. Ever since they'd left Trehaug, he'd slept as close to her as she would allow him. One morning she'd awakened to find him snuggled up against her back, his arm around her waist and his head pillowed against her. The warmth had been welcome, but not the awakening to sniggers. Kase and Boxter had teased them relentlessly. Rapskal had grinned rakishly but uncertainly; she suspected he wasn't quite sure what the joke was. She'd resolutely ignored them. She told herself that Rapskal's need to be near her had more to do with a kitten's desire to sleep close to something familiar than any amorous intent. There was no attraction between them. Not that she would have acted on it if there had been. What was forbidden was forbidden. She knew that. They all knew that.

But she wondered if they all accepted it as deeply as she did.

Greft had strongly hinted that he did not. He was going to make his own rules, he'd said. So. What about Jerd? Would she keep the rules they had all grown up with?

As Thymara rubbed the sleep from her eyes, she tried not
to notice who slept adjacent to whom, nor to wonder what
any of it meant. After all, everyone had to sleep somewhere.
If Jerd always spread her blankets next to Tats, it could
simply mean that she felt safe sleeping beside him. And if
Greft always found an excuse to try to engage her in talk
when the others were getting ready to sleep, it might mean
only that he thought she was intelligent.

She glanced over at him now. He was, as usual, among
the first to rise and was already folding his bedding. He slept
without a shirt; she'd been surprised to discover that a lot of
the boys did. Jerd, who had brothers, was surprised that she
didn't know that, but Thymara could not recall that she'd
ever seen her father half clothed. She watched Greft as he
scratched his scaled back. She knew that feeling of relentless itching. It meant that the scales were growing thicker
and harder. She watched him bend his spine slightly so that
he could ripple the scales up and scratch beneath them. If he
was self-conscious at all about how heavily the Rain Wilds
had marked him, he didn't show it. This morning it almost
seemed as if he were showing off his body.

Her mind flitted back to his words the night he had all
but driven Tats away. Greft wanted to make his own rules,
he'd said. And he had already begun to do just that. She
was a little surprised at how easily he had made himself the
leader of their group. All he had to do was behave as if he
were. All the younger ones had fallen in with him immediately. Only a few remained outside his spell. Tats was one of
them. She suspected that if Greft had not made his move so
quickly and so definitively labeled Tats as an outsider, Tats
would have moved up to a position of leadership. Tats, she
thought, probably knew that as well. Jerd was another one
who regarded Greft with suspicion, or at least reservation.
It's because we are both female, Thymara thought. *It's because of the way he looks at us, as if he's always evaluating
us.* She'd even seen it the first time he looked at Sylve; she'd
almost seen him dismiss her as too young.

It was oddly flattering yet a bit frightening to have him
look at her. As if he could read her thoughts or feel her gaze,

he suddenly turned his head. She looked down, but it was too late. He knew she'd been staring at him. From the corner of her eye, as he stretched yet again and rolled his shoulders, she saw him smiling at her. She spoke to Rapskal before Greft could start a conversation with her. "Are you awake? We're supposed to start our journey today."

"I'm awake," the boy said. "But why do we have to start so early? The dragons aren't going to like being made to move before the day warms up."

Greft responded before she could. "Because the good people of Cassarick are very much looking forward to us being gone. Once we've moved the dragons out, they'll put docks along the shore here. They'll probably repair or perhaps properly build the locks they attempted to build for the serpents. Done right, it would allow them to bring larger ships here from Trehaug. Improved shipping could mean that they could better exploit whatever they can dig out of the old city. And with the dragons gone, they'll feel safer about coming and going and digging deeper and closer to this place. To answer your question more directly, Rapskal, it's about money. The sooner we take the dragons out of here, the sooner the Traders can stop spending money on dragons and make more money from the buried city."

Rapskal greeted his words with the furrowed brow and slight pout that meant he was thinking hard. "But . . . why do they have to make us wake up so early? Will one morning make that much difference?"

Greft shook his head, muttered something uncomplimentary, and turned away from the boy. A shadow of hurt flickered across Rapskal's face. And Thymara felt a moment of absolute dislike for Greft. It startled her in its intensity.

"Let's get something to eat before we have to get going," Thymara suggested quickly. "This will be the last day that they feed the dragons for us. Beginning tomorrow, we're going to have to provide for them. And hope they can do a bit of providing for themselves."

Rapskal's face brightened at her words. It took so little to make him happy. Her words didn't have to be kind, even, just not cruel. She tried not to wonder what his early life had been like that mere neutrality seemed like friendship to him. She began folding her blankets up with a small sigh. Of course, even neutral comments attracted Rapskal. Talking to him directly had probably earned her a full day of his close and chattering company.

"I've been worrying about how we're going to feed our dragons. I think the dragons can find some food for themselves. Dead stuff should be easy for them, and maybe big fish, too. Or big dead fish, that might be easiest of all for them. My Heeby likes fish, and she doesn't much care if she gets it alive or dead."

"Heeby. Is that her real dragon name?" Tats had suddenly appeared behind Rapskal. He had his pack already loaded and on his back. He'd shaved, too. So he'd been awake for a while. He didn't shave often, only about once a week. Thymara had seen him do it once since they'd left Trehaug. He didn't seem very confident of his technique; he crouched with a small mirror balanced on his knee and scraped carefully with a folding razor. It had surprised her to see him shaving; she had realized then that she still thought of him as more boy than man. She glanced over at Rapskal. She supposed that she thought of all of them as boys still, with the possible exception of Greft. Rapskal, she realized, was probably close to her own age. Not a boy at all, really. Until he spoke.

"No. I don't think Heeby had a name before I got here. But she likes me and she likes the name I gave her, so I think it's going to be all right." Rapskal suddenly halted where he stood. Then he smiled indulgently. "Rats! I thought about her too loud and waked her up. I'd better eat fast and get over there. She's hungry. And I got to tell her again that today is the day we're going up the river. She forgets stuff pretty easy."

He crumpled his blanket up and stuffed it into his pack, then looked around the area where he'd slept. He snatched up his extra shirt, pushed it into the top of his pack, and then said, "Time to eat," and headed off to the main campfire. Tats and Thymara watched him go.

"I think Rapskal and Heeby are pretty well matched,"

Tats observed with a smile. He stooped down and picked up a stray sock Rapskal had dropped. "I wish he weren't so careless," he added more soberly.

"Give it to me. I'll make sure he gets it."

"No, I've got it," Tats replied easily. "I'm headed that way anyway. You're right. We'd better enjoy our last easy meal."

Thymara put her neatly folded blanket into her pack and did a quick check of the campsite. No. She hadn't forgotten anything. All the others were beginning to stir. Greft, she noticed, was first in line by the porridge pot. She'd watched how he ate; he'd be fast and get a second serving before some of the others had even had a first one. His bad manners annoyed her even as she wondered if she were a fool for not copying him. A couple of the boys had started to do so, over the last day or so. Kase and Boxter imitated him in most things, she'd noted. It made her uneasy to see them trail after him now, food bowls brimming. When Greft sat down to eat, they squatted to either side of him. She was surprised to see that Nortel had a black eye and a bruised face. "What happened to him?" she asked.

"Got in a scuffle with one of the other lads," Tats said briefly. "What's going to become of the unclaimed dragons?" Tats's question distracted her from staring at Nortel.

"What?"

"There are two dragons who don't have keepers. You must have noticed."

Food bowls in hand, they fell into line behind Nortel and Sylve. The girl immediately turned to join the conversation. "The silver one and the dirty one," she filled in.

"I think if he were cleaned up a bit, he'd be copper," Thymara mused. She'd noticed them. She'd almost chosen one of them when it looked like Skymaw was going to refuse her. "They're both in bad condition," she added, and then forced herself to voice what she knew they were all thinking. "Without keepers to help them along, they won't last long on this journey. I'm not even sure they'll follow us when we leave. Neither one looks very intelligent."

"You're right about that. I saw the silver snuggling up

to the barge last night, as if it were another dragon. It's not there this morning, so maybe it figured it out. Still. Not very intelligent. But I doubt that the Cassarick Council will allow us to leave any dragons behind," Tats said. "If we did, I suspect they'd both be dead within a week. Somehow I doubt they'd continue feeding them once we were gone."

"That's mean," said Sylve. "They've been stingy and cruel to these dragons for a long time. My poor Mercor says he can't remember a time when dragons were so badly treated by humans or Elderlings."

Nortel nodded wordlessly. The man dishing the porridge glopped a scoop into his bowl. Nortel held his bowl steadily there until the man grudgingly added a bit more. Sylve stepped up to take her place, holding her bowl over the cauldron of porridge. It bobbed as it received its load.

"Well," Tats said reluctantly, "if we just let those two tag along after us and don't do anything for them, we'll be letting them die just as surely as if we left them here to be starved."

"They aren't fit to survive," Alum observed. He was in line behind Tats. "My Arbuc may not be bright, but he's fast and physically healthy. That's why I chose him. I thought he had the best chance of surviving the journey."

"The midwife said I wasn't fit to survive," Thymara said quietly as her bowl was filled with porridge. She trailed after Sylve to a pile of hard bread rolls set out on a clean towel. Each girl chose one and then moved on.

"We live in a hard land. A hard land requires hard rules," Alum said, but he didn't sound quite as certain as he had a few moments before.

"I'll take on the copper one," Tats said quietly. The keepers were settling into a circle to eat. "I'll clean him up a bit and get some of the parasites off him before we leave this morning."

"I'll help you." Thymara hadn't noticed Jerd, but there she was, sitting down carefully next to Tats. She balanced her chunk of bread on one knee, then held her bowl in one hand and her spoon in the other to eat.

"I'll take the silver," Thymara declared recklessly. Somehow she didn't think it would sit well with Skymaw. She suspected the dragon would be jealous of any attention she gave the creature. *Well, let her see how it felt,* she thought, almost vindictively.

"I'll help you get his tail bandaged up," Sylve offered.

"And I can get some fish for him, maybe," Rapskal said as he wedged himself into their circle between Tats and Thymara, blithely unaware that he might be intruding. He dug into his porridge with fervor. "Never got porridge for breakfast at home," he announced suddenly through a full mouth. "Grain was too expensive for my family. We always had soup for breakfast. Or gourdcakes."

Almost all the keepers were present now, all crouched or sitting with bowls and bread. Several nodded.

"Sometimes we had porridge with honey," Sylve said. "But not often," she added, as if embarrassed to admit that her family had been able to afford such things.

"We usually had fruit, whatever my father and I had gathered the day before and hadn't sold," Thymara said, and was ambushed by a wave of homesickness. She looked around herself suddenly. What was she doing here, sitting on the hard ground, eating porridge, and preparing to depart upriver? For a moment, none of it made sense, and the world seemed to rock around her as she realized how far she was from home and family.

"Thymara?"

She nearly dropped her spoon at the man's voice behind her. She turned and found Sedric standing awkwardly at the edge of their circle. He was impeccably groomed and a fragrance almost like perfume floated on the air. "Yes?" she answered him stupidly.

"I don't mean to rush your meal, but we are told that the departure time is imminent. I wondered if you could possibly come now to do some translating for me. Alise is already with the dragon . . ."

He let his words trail off. Probably the look on her face had silenced him. She looked aside and tried to calm the sudden jealousy she felt. Alise was already up and talking with Skymaw? This early in the day? Yesterday, when she

and Sedric had returned, the light was waning. As the day
lost its warmth, the dragons became more lethargic. By the
time Thymara and Sedric reached Alise and Skymaw, the
dragon plainly wished to be left alone to sleep. She had not
been too tired, however, to gulp down the fish they brought
her, Thymara recalled wryly. She had felt a great deal of
satisfaction at Alise's unconcealed astonishment at the size
of the fish, and her awe at how quickly the dragon devoured
it. While Skymaw ate, Thymara had won her grudging permission for Sedric to be present when Alise talked to her.
Afterward, Skymaw had immediately headed for the dragons' sleeping area. Thymara had bid Sedric and Alise good
night and watched them go back to the beached barge.

She had noted how Alise took Sedric's arm, and how
he carried all her supplies for her, and wondered what that
meant. He'd said he was her assistant, but she sensed there
was more between them than that. She wondered if secretly they were lovers. The thought had sent a strange thrill
through her, and then she had felt ashamed of herself. It was
no business of hers if they were. Everyone knew that Bingtown folk lived by their own rules.

"Translating?" Greft stood, coming to his feet with a
smooth and easy motion that was still somehow challenging. It jerked Sedric's attention to him.

The Bingtown man seemed startled at the question. So
was Thymara. "She said she could help me understand what
the dragon was saying so that I could take notes." When
Greft continued to stare at him, Sedric added, "I seem to
have an unusual handicap. When the dragons speak, I don't
understand them. I only hear animal noises. Thymara told
me yesterday she might be able to help me. Or am I taking
her away from other duties?"

It took Thymara a moment to comprehend that Greft's
stance had made Sedric think he controlled her in some
way and that Sedric must ask his permission for her to go
with him. She tucked her unfinished bread in her pocket and
stood with her empty bowl. "I have no other duties at the
moment, Sedric. Let me put my bowl and spoon away and
I'll come now."

"Didn't I just hear you say that you'd take care of the silver? Someone has to bandage his tail and try to form a bond with him."

Greft spoke as if he were her superior, reminding her of a neglected task.

She turned to face him squarely and spoke clearly. "I'll do what I said I'd do, in my own time, Greft. No one put you in charge of me, or of the dragons in general. I didn't hear you volunteer to take on an extra dragon. Only Tats."

She had meant it as a rebuke to him. Too late she saw that she had brought Tats and Greft back into direct confrontation. Tats stood and rolled his shoulders as if loosening them. He might have been sitting still too long, but to Thymara, it looked as if he prepared himself for a possible fight. "That's right. I did. Sylve, if you need help with the silver's tail, let me know. Rapskal, it would be good if you could find him a fish or any extra food. I'm going to go say hello to my green, and then I'll check on the dirty copper one to see what I can do for him. You go with Sedric, Thymara. We can manage without you for now."

She watched Sedric's eyes dart from Greft to Tats, and suddenly knew he was wondering just who was in charge here. Of her. She felt a flush of anger at both of them. It made her sharp. "Thank you, Tats, but I said I'd do it and I will. I don't need anyone's help. Or permission."

The look on his face made her realize she'd spoken more harshly than she intended. She'd only meant to assert that no one was in charge of her except herself. It was made worse by the smug look on Greft's face. She ground her teeth. In less than two days, she'd gone from being mildly infatuated with Greft and flattered by his attention to actively disliking him. She knew he was manipulating the situation, but she could not seem to escape his puppet strings. Now everyone would think she was at odds with Tats, when she wasn't. Or at least, didn't want to be. Jerd was looking at the ground, but Thymara knew she was smiling. Tats was turning aside from her rather stiffly, and there was nothing else to do but follow Sedric. Even he seemed aware of the awkwardness as she walked away with him.

"I didn't mean to cause you any problems," he apologized.

"You didn't," she said shortly. Then she took a breath and shook her head. "I'm sorry. That came out wrong. Honestly, you didn't cause any problem. Greft is the problem, and sometimes Tats. Greft wants to be the leader of the dragon keepers, so he just acts as if he is and hopes everyone will fall into line. And it's so infuriating that some of them do! The truth is, no one was put in charge among us; we're all free to do our own jobs. But Greft is very good at causing discord among those who refuse to concede to him. Like Tats and me."

"I see." He nodded as if he actually did.

"Usually Tats and I get along very well. Then Greft came along, and he just seems to enjoy making trouble. And manipulating people. Sometimes it seems that if he can't make us do what he wants, he focuses on making us as miserable as possible. At first, I thought he liked me. He behaves as if he can't stand for me to have a friend, like it makes him less important. It's almost as if he tries to drive a wedge between Tats and me. Why are some people like that?"

She hadn't expected him to have an answer, but he looked startled, as if she had asked him something of great significance. When he answered, his words came slowly. "Maybe because we let them be that way."

SEDRIC FELT AS if he'd been hit in the back of the head. Twice. First by the glimpse of the extraordinary young man who'd seemed to dispute his right to ask Thymara to translate for him. He'd never seen such a person, at least not unveiled and unhooded. Most people marked as strongly by the Rain Wilds as Greft was went veiled. But Greft didn't. Was that a defiance of custom, or had they traveled far enough up the Rain Wild River that the locals no longer cared what outsiders thought of them?

There had been a definite reptilian cast to his features that somehow only lent power to his presence. His blue eyes had gleamed like polished lapis lazuli beneath his finely scaled brows. The austere lines of his face reminded Sedric of a

sculpture, save that this was no cold stone. He was closer
to an animal than anyone Sedric had ever met. He'd felt he
could almost smell him, as if the dominance Greft sought
to assert were a musk emanating from him. Even his voice
had held an inhuman tenor, a hum that reminded Sedric of a
bow drawn across dark strings. The scales repelled him and
the voice attracted him. No wonder the girl at his side was
so agitated by his presence. Anyone would be.

Even Hest. He and Hest would have collided like ant-
lered bucks battling for territory. Even as that thought occurred to him, the girl had asked that telling question. It had
snapped a stinging realization into his mind. Hest didn't like
him being friends with Alise. Hest didn't want him to have
conversations with her or have opinions about her. She was
supposed to be something he'd surrendered to Hest, a part of
his past he'd given to the man when he suggested that marrying her would put an end to his problem with his parents.
He didn't like thinking of all the implications of that. He
pushed aside the thought of other friendships he'd neglected
for Hest's, even how he'd alienated his father by taking the
position with Hest rather than striking out on his own or following his father into his business.

He forced himself to focus on the business at hand. He
glanced over at the annoyed girl stalking along beside him.
"I'm sorry I created problems for you."

She snorted in amusement. "Oh, you didn't create them.
They came with who I am, and multiplied when I signed a
contract to do this. That's all." She cleared her throat and he
could almost see her wrench the topic to one side. "Why is
Alise awake so early for this?"

"She's eager, I suppose. Once we start to travel, I suspect
she'll have little time for chatting with the dragons." That
wasn't the truth. He'd wakened Alise and suggested to her
that she attempt an interview before the day's travel began.
She'd been very willing, appearing fully dressed only a few
minutes later. He was hoping against hope that they would
both have all they needed before the dragons actually departed. That hope was fading now, but this was his final
chance. If the results of this morning's "interview" were as

lackluster as what she'd recounted to him last night, perhaps he could persuade her that she'd learn more by remaining in Cassarick for a few days and studying the ruins there. If luck favored him, perhaps they'd still find a way to connect with Captain Trell and journey home on the *Paragon*.

"Or it could be that she'll find she has far more time than she can actually fill. I suspect this expedition is going to take a lot longer than they told us it would. I don't think anyone actually knows where we are going, and the folk who aren't going with us don't much care, as long as we take the dragons with us when we leave."

Sedric thought that summed it up nicely, but it hardly seemed kind to say so. He tried to find a way to steer the conversation back to something he'd overheard earlier. When inspiration didn't strike, he simply pushed it there. "So. In addition to the blue dragon, you'll be taking care of a silver one?"

"So I said," she admitted. She sounded as if she regretted it now.

"Tats said the dragon was injured? Something about his tail?"

"I haven't taken a close look at it, but he has some sort of wound there and it looks infected. The dragons are fairly immune to the acidity of the river water, as are the water birds and fish. As long as their hides are intact, they do fine. But the water eats away at open sores. So we need to clean the injury, bandage it well, and somehow make sure he doesn't get his tail in the water if we have to do any wading. And I consider it very likely that we will."

Alise and the blue dragon were walking by the river. The dragon made her seem tiny. Sedric knew that Thymara had spotted them as well, for the girl quickened her pace. He deliberately walked more slowly, holding her back. What he had to say to her was not for Alise's ears. "I've always had an interest in animals and medicine, and dragons in particular. Perhaps I could be of some assistance in helping the poor thing."

Thymara shot him a startled look. "You?"

It rather stung. "Well, why not me?"

"I just . . . well, you can't even understand them when you hear them speak. And you're so, well, particular. Clean, I guess I mean. It's hard for me to imagine you dealing with a muddy dragon with an infected tail."

He put a smile on his face. "You've only just met me, Thymara. I think you'll find there's a lot more to me than meets the eye." That at least was true!

"Well, I suppose if you want to help, you can. But first I'll translate while Alise talks to Skymaw. I don't think that will be for long, for they'll be bringing the dragons' food soon, and I know Skymaw will want to eat just as much as the others. But after they've been fed, I want to check on the silver and see what I can do for him."

"Perfect. I'll gather my equipment and come with you then."

"Equipment?"

"I've some basic medical supplies I brought with us for this journey. Lint and bandages. Sharp knives, if we need them. Alcohol for cleaning wounds." And for preserving specimens. With a bit of luck, he might have a vial of dragon scales before they even left the beach. Sedric smiled at her reassuringly.

IT WAS NOT going well with the dragons. Alise knew it, and the sense of impending failure burdened her. Why had she ever imagined that it would be easy to talk with dragons? Yet in her dreams, when she arrived at the Rain Wilds, the creatures had sensed a kinship with her and opened their hearts and memories to her. Well, that fantasy certainly wasn't coming true.

"Can you share with me any of your ancestral memories?" she asked the dragon. She phrased it that way out of despair. Skymaw, as her keeper called her, had neatly deflected every question she'd asked of her.

"I doubt it. You are only a human and I am a dragon. In all likelihood, it would be impossible for you to ever share the remotest idea of what it is to be a dragon, let alone comprehend any of my memories."

Skymaw dashed her hopes yet again. And she did it with

a well-modulated voice that was treacly with courtesy and kindness. Her lovely eyes spun as she spoke to Alise, and Alise's heart yearned for a bond with this creature. She knew she was falling under the dragon's glamour; she recognized the hopelessness of the unrequited worship she felt for the dragon. Yet she could not help herself. The more the dragon patronized and insulted her, the more she longed to win her regard. It didn't help that she'd read of such things in her old scrolls. One could read about addiction and still fall prey to it.

She made a final desperate attempt. "Do you think you will ever answer any of my questions?"

The dragon regarded her in silence. Without moving, she seemed to come closer to Alise. Alise was flooded with a mawkish love for the creature. If only she could spend all her days in service to the dragon, she would be happy. She had been right to come to the Rain Wilds, and if she did not accompany this dragon up the river, all of her life would have been a meaningless tragedy. Skymaw was her destiny. No other relationship could fulfill her as this one—

As abruptly as a dropped doll hits the floor, Alise jolted back to the summer day on the riverbank. "They're bringing the food," the dragon announced suddenly, and Alise actually felt the creature dismiss her. It had been a glamour. The dragon had been toying with her. She could not deny it, and she should have felt shamed to have fallen under her charm so easily. Instead she felt only a wretched longing to regain Skymaw's attention. It echoed unpleasantly how Hest had once made her feel, and that memory of utter humiliation finally broke the spell. Something hardened in her, and she turned away from the dragon. All that she had longed for was never going to be, not with Hest and her life in Bingtown, and not with her foolish dreams of journeying with the dragons. Abruptly she wished she could give up and go home.

Did the dragon know she had lost her worshipper? It almost seemed that way, for on the way to the barrows of carrion, Skymaw suddenly halted and looked back at her. Alise looked resolutely away. No. She would not fall under her spell again. It was over.

"Oh, dear. It looks as if we're too late."

Sedric's voice startled her. It was even more surprising to discover that he had arrived with Skymaw's keeper in tow. The girl looked as disapproving of her as ever; or perhaps that was an assumption on Alise's part. The way her exposure to the Rain Wilds had disfigured her, it was hard to read the girl's expressions.

"Skymaw was hungry and decided to go and eat rather than answer questions," she explained needlessly. She glanced at the girl, wishing she weren't there, and then spoke anyway. Her words came out stiffly, as if the lump in her throat had squeezed all inflection out of them. "Sedric, I've discovered that you were right. Brashen Trell and his wife were right. Even Hest was right. I'm not making any headway in speaking to the dragon. She delights in thwarting me." She formed the last and most difficult words. "I've put us both through so much to get here. I foolishly signed an agreement to go upriver. And now I wonder if I will gain any real knowledge of dragons at all from this experience. That creature is so, so—"

"Exasperating," Thymara supplied quietly, with a small smile.

"Exactly!" Alise replied. And to her surprise, she found herself smiling back at the girl.

"Well, at least I know that it isn't only me." Thymara cocked her head at Alise and asked shyly, "Does this mean you're giving up and going back to Bingtown?"

Alise could not miss the mixed emotions that flickered across Sedric's face. Hope seemed to be a strong one, but anxiety was there as well. He spoke before she could. "It's perfectly understandable if you've decided not to make the journey, Alise. I can have us packed and unloaded from Leftrin's barge in a very short time. But before we do that, I promised Thymara that I'd assist her with one of the other dragons. An injured one."

"The silver," Thymara said quietly.

Alise looked from Sedric to Thymara and back again, trying to make sense of his words. She had never known him to have any fondness for or interest in animals. Oh, he shared some of her scholastic interest in dragons, but she had never seen him pet a dog or talk to his horse. And now he was going to assist this girl in doctoring a dragon? There was something here, and she felt she stood at the edge of a strange and perhaps dark current. Could he possibly be interested in the girl? She was so young and so peculiar looking. It would be very inappropriate. She spoke without thinking.

"I'll come along. Perhaps it is only Skymaw who is so difficult. You are right, Sedric. I should not give up so easily, especially after I gave my word to the Council. Shall we go right now?"

He looked uncomfortable. "Perhaps later. I don't think we should bother him while he's eating."

"Actually, that might be a good opportunity," the Rain Wild girl suggested. "It may be that while he is distracted with eating, we can look at his injuries."

"But I've heard one should never bother an animal while it is eating!" Sedric protested.

"Ordinary animals, perhaps," Thymara agreed. "But the silver is a dragon. And while he looks very stupid, perhaps there is a kernel of intelligence there. If I'm going to help care for him on the upriver journey, the sooner I get to know something of him, the better."

"Let's go then," Alise agreed.

"Of course," Sedric replied weakly.

✦ ✦ ✦

Day the 6th of the Grain Moon

Year the 6th of the Independent Alliance of Traders

From Detozi, Keeper of the Birds, Trehaug
To Erek, Keeper of the Birds, Bingtown

A copy of the contract between the Rain Wild Council of Cassarick and Captain Leftrin of the liveship *Tarman*, including a binder concerning Alise Kincarron Finbok, Dragon Scholar of Bingtown, with the suggestion that a copy of this document be retained in the Council Records for Alise Kincarron Finbok. A detailed accounting of the expenses involved will follow.

Erek,

In my official capacity of Bird Keeper for Trehaug I am relieved to tell you that the exceptionally ugly bird that was vomiting on itself after eating its own droppings has apparently cured itself. There is no danger of the contagion spreading to either of our flocks. Sa's mercy on us all!

Detozi

✦ ✦ ✦

CHAPTER FOURTEEN

SCALES

Sintara shouldered her way past Veras and seized the swamp-deer carcass the green had been eyeing. The smaller female hissed around the meat that she gripped and made a half-hearted swipe at her. Sintara ignored her. She would not waste time fighting while there was food to be had. The meat that was being dumped from the relay of barrows was the most she had seen in months. All the dragons had converged on it, forming a half circle of large, hungry creatures. She didn't intend to stop eating until every last bit of it was gone. Then she would nap in the sun and digest. Let the humans flutter and squawk that it was time to leave; she'd leave when she was ready and not before.

She was surrounded by the sounds of feeding dragons. Bones crunched, meat tore, and dragons grunted as they raced to consume the most food. The larger dragons had pushed into the central area and claimed the largest pieces. The smaller dragons, shouldered to one side, had to be content with birds, fish, and even rabbits.

It was when she tossed her head back to gulp down the front quarter of the swamp deer that she noticed the cluster of humans around one of the other dragons. The dragon, a malformed silver, was trying to eat. He was ignoring the humans who had seized his tail and drawn it out to its unimpressive length. Apparently he was so hungry that nothing could distract him from his meal. Sintara would have dismissed the sight for a very similar reason if she had not noticed that two of the humans fussing over him belonged to her.

She swallowed and then gave a low rumble of displeasure. She considered interfering, but decided to continue feeding while she thought about it.

To her surprise, she had begun to enjoy the humans' attention. It was flattering to have attendants, even if they were merely humans. They were so ignorant. They did not know how to praise her properly and had not brought her any gifts, but the younger one was acquiring some grooming skills. Last night Sintara had slept deeply, not waking even once to claw bloodsucking parasites from her nostrils and ears. The girl had brought her a fish, too, a large fish and fresh. And the Bingtown woman was at least attempting to address her with proper respect and flattery. Dragons, she reflected, were not so foolish as to be swayed by flattery, but it was pleasant to listen to compliments and endearments, and they did indicate that the human was adopting the proper deference.

It had pleased her, too, to be the only dragon with two attendants hovering around her. Now it seemed that both of them had defected to the mindless silver dragon, a prospect that was very distasteful to her. It had been pleasant to feel the vibrations of jealousy between the two women as they vied for her attention. Thymara had taken great pleasure in bringing her that fish, a pleasure that was rooted not only in serving the dragon but in serving her better than Alise could. Sintara had been looking forward to nudging them into sharper competition. She noted their current cooperation with displeasure and felt insulted that they now seemed as solicitous of the silver dragon as they had been of her. Alise's useless male companion had joined them as well.

Kalo had taken advantage of her distraction to sink his teeth into a goat carcass that had been closer to her than to him. Sintara hissed her displeasure and seized the other end of it. It was no great prize. It was nearly rotten and tore in half before she had even tugged at it. Kalo swallowed the piece he had stolen and observed, "You should teach your tender more respect or you'll lose her."

It was humiliating that he had noticed the girl's defection. Sintara had been on the point of going after her and the other woman. Now her pride prevented her from doing that. "I don't need a keeper," she informed him.

"Of course not. None of us do. Nevertheless, I wouldn't allow anyone to take mine from me. He's very satisfactory. You have noticed, of course, that the leader of the humans has chosen me to tend. He says it is because they have recognized me as the leader of the dragons."

"Have they? How nice for you. What a pity that none of the dragons has!" Quicker than a lizard's blink, she shot her head out, seized a young riverpig carcass that had been right in front of him and dragged it over to her spot. He bristled at her, the half-formed spines of his mane trying to rise. "Pitiful," she commented quietly, as if she hadn't intended him to hear it. She clamped her jaws on the pig, crushed it to a pulp, and swallowed it whole. When it was down, she added, "One of the females who tends me is quite knowledgeable about both dragons and Elderlings, and highly respected in her city. She chose to come with us out of admiration for me. And she knows that when the dragons of the past did acknowledge one as a leader, it was always a queen. Like me."

"A queen like you? So, even then, there were dragons with no wings?"

"I have teeth." She opened her jaws wide, reminding him.

Across the circle from them, Mercor slowly lifted his head. Since he had been cleaned, his gold scaling flashed in the sunlight. On the sides of his neck, a subtle mottling marked where he might have carried false-eyes in his serpent days. He was not as large as either of them, yet when he lifted his head, he radiated command. "No fighting," he said calmly, as if he had the right to regulate them. "Not today. Not when we are so close to leaving this place and beginning our journey back to what we were. To what we are meant to be."

"What do you mean?" she demanded of him. Secretly, she was glad of the distraction. She had no desire to fight, not when there was food to eat.

Mercor met her gaze. His eyes were solid, gleaming black, like obsidian set into his eye sockets. She could read nothing there. "I mean, today we begin our journey back to Kelsingra. Search your memory, and perhaps you will understand."

"Kelsingra," Kalo retorted skeptically. Sintara suspected that he, too, was relieved that Mercor had spoken and diverted them from a fight. But he could not admit that, and so he turned his disdain on the golden male.

"Kelsingra," Mercor agreed and bent his head and snuffed the ground, searching for any remaining scraps of food. The humans had brought more than they usually did, perhaps as a farewell gift or perhaps to be rid of any surplus they'd been holding in reserve. Even so, the dragons had devoured it quickly, and Sintara knew that she was not the only one who remained hungry. She wished she could remember what it felt like to be full; in this life, she'd never known the sensation.

"Kelsingra," Veras suddenly echoed Mercor, and around the circle, other dragons lifted their heads.

"Kelsingra!" Fente suddenly trumpeted and actually leaped, her front two legs leaving the ground. Her wings opened and flapped spasmodically and uselessly. She snapped them back to her body as if shamed.

"Kelsingra!" Both orange dragons chorused a response, as if the word brought them joy.

Mercor lifted his head, looked around at all of them, and then said ponderously, "It is time to leave this place. For too long we have been kept here, corralled as humans corral meat animals. We have slept in the place they have left for us, eaten what they fed us, and accepted that we were doomed to these shadow lives. Dragons do not live like this, and I for one will not die like this. If die I must, I will die as a dragon. Let us go." Then he turned and headed toward the river shallows. For a time, all the dragons just watched him go. Then, without warning, some of the dragons began to follow him.

Sintara found herself trailing after them.

THE GASH IN the silver dragon's tail looked as if it had been made by another dragon's claw. It had never been a clean cut; it looked more like a tear. Thymara wondered if it had been intentional or merely an accident during the daily scramble for food. She also wondered how long ago it had happened. The injury was close to where his tail joined his body and was about as long as her forearm. A raised ridge of flesh along either side of the gaping tear indicated it had tried to close and heal, but had broken open again. It looked bad and smelled worse. Flies, some large and buzzing, others tiny and myriad, swarmed and settled on it.

Alise and Sedric, both her elders, were standing there like timid children, waiting for her to do something about it. The silver seemed to be paying no attention to them; it was at the far end of the crescent of dumped meat and feeding dragons, snatching at what it could reach and then retreating a half step from the others to eat it. She wished she had something larger to feed him, something that would keep him standing still and his mouth occupied. She watched him pick up at large bird, toss it up, catch it, and gulp it down. She had to act soon; when the food was gone, there would be nothing to distract him.

Sedric had fetched his kit of bandages and salves. It lay on the ground, open and ready. Thymara had brought other, more prosaic supplies: a bucket of clean water and a rag. She felt like a messenger who'd forgotten the words he'd been paid to say as they all waited for one of them to begin. She turned away from them and tried to think what she would do if she were here alone, as she had expected to be.

Well, no, she admitted to herself. She'd expected Tats to be here with her, or at least Sylve or Rapskal. She now felt a fool for volunteering to take on the hapless silver dragon. Skymaw was more than enough to deal with. She couldn't possibly care for this dull-witted creature as well. She pushed that thought away and angrily crushed her self-doubt before the two Bingtowners. She set one hand lightly on the silver dragon's dirty hide, well away from the wound on his tail. "Hello?" she said quietly.

He twitched slightly at her touch, but made no reply. She refused to let herself glance at her companions. She didn't need their approval or guidance. She made her hand more firm on his skin. He didn't pull away. "Listen, dragon, I'm here to help take care of you. Soon we'll all be going up the river to look for a better place for you to live. But before we start traveling, I want to look at the injury on your tail. It looks infected. I'd like to clean it and bandage it. It may be a bit painful, but I think it has to be done. Otherwise, the river water will eat at it. Will you let me do that?"

The dragon turned his head to look at her. Half of a dead animal hung from his jaws. She couldn't determine what it had been, but it smelled dreadful and she didn't think he should eat it. But before she could frame that warning, he tipped his head up, opened his jaws, and swallowed it. She felt her gorge rise. Lots of animals ate carrion, she sternly reminded herself. She couldn't let herself be upset by it.

The dragon looked at her again. His eyes were blue, a mingling of sky and periwinkle that swirled slowly as he stared at her. He made a questioning rumble at her, but she received no sense of words. She tried to find some spark of intelligence in his gaze, something more than bovine acceptance of her presence. "Silver dragon, will you let me help you with your injury?" she asked him again.

He lowered his head and rubbed his muzzle against his front leg to clear a strand of intestine that dangled from the side of his mouth. He pawed at his nose, snorting, and with a sinking heart she noticed that his nostrils and ears were infested with tightly clinging parasites. Those would have to go, too. But first, the tail, she reminded herself sternly.

He opened his mouth, revealing a long jaw full of glistening pointed teeth. He seemed so placid, even unaware, but if she hurt him and it angered him, those teeth could end her life.

"I'm going to start now," she told the dragon and her companions. She forced herself to turn to the Bingtowners and add, "Be ready. He's not really responding to anything I say. I don't feel like he's any more intelligent than an ordinary animal. So when I try to look at his tail, there's no telling what he'll do. He may try to attack me. Or all of us."

Sedric looked properly daunted, but Alise actually bared her teeth in determination. "We must do something for him," she said.

Thymara dipped the rag into the water and wrung it out over the gash. Water trickled from the rag into the gash and ran away in a dirty rivulet down the dragon's tail. It carried off a few maggots and disturbed a cloud of insects, large and small, that rose, buzzed, and tried to resettle immediately. It did little more than wash away surface dirt, but at least the dragon had not turned and snapped at her. She mustered her courage and gently pressed the rag to the injury. The dragon rippled his flesh around the area but did not growl. She wiped gently around it, taking off a layer of filth and insects and baring a raw stripe down the center. She plunged the rag into the bucket, rinsed and wrung it out, and applied it more firmly. Crusty scab came away and there was a sudden trickle of stinking liquid from the wound.

The dragon gave a sudden snort and whipped his head around to see what they were doing to him. When he darted his head toward Thymara, she thought she was going to die. She couldn't find breath to shriek.

Instead the dragon nosed at the oozing injury. He pressed his nose flat to the swelling, forcing the pus from it. For a moment he worked at it, starting at the top of the gash and pushing his snout along it. The smell was terrible. Flies buzzed excitedly. She closed her nostrils as much as she could and lifted her hand, pressing the back of her wrist against her nose. "At least he's trying to help us clean it," she said through clenched teeth.

Abruptly, the dragon lost interest and turned back to his feeding. Thymara seized the opportunity to wet the rag again and wipe the pus away from the injury. Three times she rinsed out the rag and cleansed it, until she feared the water in the bucket was as foul as the stuff she was trying to wipe away.

"Here. Use this."

She turned to find a grim-faced Sedric offering her a thin-bladed knife. She stared at it; she'd been expecting him to hold out salve or bandaging. "For what?" she demanded.

"You need to cut away the proud flesh. Then we need to bind it closed. Perhaps even stitch it closed. Otherwise, it's not going to heal well."

"Proud flesh?"

"That swollen, tough-looking stuff at the edges of the wound. You need to cut it away so that you can bandage it, fresh cut to fresh cut. So the flesh can heal together."

"Cut away the dragon's flesh?"

"You have to. Look at it. It's all dried out and thick. It's already dead, really. It can't heal that way."

She looked at it and swallowed sickly. He was right. From the palm of his hand, on a flat fold of clean cloth, he offered her the shining knife.

"I don't know how to do this," she admitted.

"I doubt that any of us do. But we know it has to be done."

She took the proffered knife and tried to grip it firmly. She set her free hand flat on the dragon's tail. "Here I go," she warned them, and she gingerly set the blade to the ridged flesh at the edge of the wound. The knife was very sharp. Almost without effort, it slid into the flesh. She watched her own hand move, carving away the stiffened skin at the edge of the injury. It came away like shriveled rind from a dried-up fruit. It was caked with dirt and scales; the moving knife bared dark red flesh. It oozed blood in slow, bright droplets, but the dragon went on snorting through his food, as if he didn't feel it.

"That's it," Sedric said in a low, excited voice. "That's right. Cut that piece free and I'll get it out of your way."

She did as he bade her, scarcely noticing how he deftly caught it in a gloved hand. Alise had gone silent, either raptly watching or intently not watching. Thymara could not afford to look at her to find out which. She had cleared one edge of the wound of proud flesh. She took a breath, steeled herself again, and set the blade to the other side.

A trembling ran through the dragon. She froze, the razor-sharp blade set in the rubbery edge of his injury. He didn't turn his head toward her. He hissed low. "Fight." The word barely reached her ears; it was spoken with a childish inflection, without force.

Dread edged the word. She wondered if she had imagined it.

"Fight?" Alise asked him gently. "Fight what?"

"What?" Sedric asked, startled.

"Fight—together, fight. No. No."

Thymara stood absolutely still. She had begun to think the silver had no intelligence beyond animal instinct. It was almost a shock to hear him speak.

"No fight?" Alise said as if she were talking to a baby.

"Fight what?" Sedric demanded. "Who's fighting?"

It was an unwelcome distraction. Thymara caught her breath before she could lose her temper and said quietly, "She isn't talking to you. The dragon mumbled something and it's the first time we've been aware of him speaking. Alise is trying to talk to him." She took a breath, recalled her task, and moved the sharp knife steadily through the stiffened flesh at the edges of the wound.

"Concentrate on what you're doing," Sedric suggested, and she found herself grateful for his support.

"What's your name?" Alise said quietly. "Lovely silver one, dragon of the stars' and moon's color, what is your name?" She put cajoling music into her voice. Thymara felt a subtle difference in the dragon. He didn't speak, but it felt as if he were listening.

"What are you doing?" Tats demanded behind Thymara. She jumped but didn't let the twitch reach her hand.

"What I said I would do. Taking care of the silver."

"With a knife?"

"I'm cutting away the proud flesh before we bind it." She felt a small satisfaction in knowing the right term to use. Tats crouched beside her and surveyed her work intently.

"Still a lot of pus there."

She felt a moment of annoyance with him, as if he had criticized her, but then he offered, "Let's clean it again. I'll go get more water."

"Please," she said and felt him leave. She carved carefully, and again, as the ridge of dried flesh and clinging scales fell away, Sedric caught it and whisked it out of her way. As she gave the knife back to him, she realized her hands were trembling. "I don't think we should do anything else until we've washed it a bit more," she suggested.

He was stowing things away in his case, working quickly and carefully, as if that were more important than tending the dragon. She caught a strong smell of vinegar and heard the sound of glass on glass. "Probably not," he agreed.

She had pushed Alise's murmuring voice into the back of her awareness. Now she listened as the woman said, "But you'd like to go somewhere, right? Somewhere nice. Go where, little one? Go where?"

The dragon said something. It wasn't a word, and suddenly Thymara realized that it had never been "words" she had been hearing. Her mind had imposed that reference. The dragon didn't "say" anything to her, but he remembered something strongly. She recalled a flash of hot sunlight beating on her scaled back; the scent of dust and citrus flowers floated in the air on the distant music of drums and a softly droning pipe.

Just as suddenly as it had come, the sensory image faded, leaving her bereft. There was a place, a kindly place of warmth and food and companionship, a place whose name was lost in time.

"Kelsingra."

The silver had not spoken. The name came to her from at least two of the other dragons. But it was like a frame falling around a picture. It captured and contained the images the silver had been trying to convey. Kelsingra. That was the name of the place he longed to be. A shiver ran over him, and when it had passed, he felt different to her. Confirmed. Consoled, almost.

"Kelsingra," Alise repeated in a low and soothing voice. "I know Kelsingra. I know its leaping fountains and spacious city squares. I know its stone steps and the wide doors of its buildings. The river banked with grassy meadows, and the well of silver water. The Elderlings with their flowing robes and golden eyes used to come to greet the dragons as they landed in the river."

Alise's words fed the silver dragon's coalescing awareness. Without thinking about it, Thymara reached to put a hand on the creature's back. For a fleeting moment, she sensed him, like brushing hands with a stranger in a market crowd. They did not speak with words, but shared a longing for a place.

"But not here!" he said plaintively, and Alise murmured, "No, dear, of course not here. Kelsingra. That is where you belong. That is where we have to take you."

"Kelsingra!"

"Kelsingra!"

The shouts of agreement from other dragons took Thymara by surprise. She had been crouching by the silver's tail. She rose to her feet now and became aware that the dragons had finished eating. Another one suddenly stood briefly on his hind legs, roared "Kelsingra!" and came down with a thud.

She glanced at Sedric and realized that once more, he'd only heard half of a conversation. She interpreted hastily. "The dragons want to go to Kelsingra. The place that Alise has been talking about to the silver. It's the name of a city, an Elderling city, that they all seem to recall."

She sensed restlessness in the air and saw another of the dragons fling up his head, turn, and abruptly move toward the river's edge. "They've finished eating. We'd best get this fellow's tail bandaged and gather our gear. I'm sure our barge will give us the signal we're to leave soon. This morning they told us they wanted us to leave as early as possible."

As if her words had sparked it, dragon after dragon was leaving the feeding grounds and striding toward the river.

It was the first time she had seen the dragons move with such concerted purpose. She kept her hand on the silver, as if that could detain him. She saw Tats coming with a bucket of clean water. "Are they just going down to drink?" she asked him, as if he would know the answer. She'd seen the dragons wallow and even drink the river water, something that would have meant eventual death for a human.

But he looked after the departing dragons with the same puzzlement she shared. "Maybe," he said.

But before another word could escape his mouth, the silver dragon lifted his head high. He stared after the others, and Thymara felt a shimmer of excitement from him that infected her whole body. "Kelsingra!" he trumpeted suddenly, a blast of sound and emotion that sent her reeling. Even Sedric recoiled from it, staggering back and lifting his hands to his ears. It was well that he had, for the dragon wheeled away from Thymara's touch and suddenly lurched after his departing fellows. With no regard for the humans, he trampled through them, narrowly missing Tats as he leaped to one side and shouldering Alise as he passed. The Bingtown woman was knocked off her feet and landed heavily on the ground. Thymara expected her to cry out in pain. Instead, she caught her breath and shouted, "His tail! We didn't bandage it up. Sedric, head him off! Don't let him get into the river!"

"Are you mad? I'm not getting in front of a hurrying dragon!" Alise's friend stood clutching his medicine case to his chest.

"Are you all right?" Thymara asked her, hastening to her side. Tats was already there, kneeling by the supine woman. Sedric hastily knelt and opened his case of supplies, and Thymara half expected him to offer bandages, but he appeared to be checking the contents for damage. His face was anxious.

"Sedric, please, go after him. Stop him. The river water will eat into his tail!" Alise commanded him.

He shut the case with a snap and looked after the retreating dragons. "Alise, I don't think anyone can stop that creature. Or any of them. Look at them go. They're like a flock of birds on the wing."

They were not the only ones shocked by the dragons' abrupt departure. Thymara heard the voices of other keepers lifted in alarm and surprise. All up and down the mud-flats, humans trotted after their large charges, shouting to them and to one another. On the barge, a man called a warning to another man on the shore and pointed at the dragons.

Alise sat up with a groan, rubbing her shoulder. "Are you hurt?" Thymara asked her again.

"I'm bruised, but no more than that, I don't think. What got into him? What got into all of them?"

"I don't know."

"They're not stopping," Tats observed in awe. "Look at them."

Thymara had thought that when they reached the river, they would halt there. For so long, their lives had been bordered by the forest at the back of the clearing and the river that flowed past it. But now the lead dragons waded out into the shallows and headed upstream. The smaller and less able ones didn't hesitate, but followed them out into the water. Even the silver and the dirty copper dragon followed the herd out into the murky gray water.

"Help me up!" Alise demanded of Sedric. "We have to follow them."

"Do you think they're leaving here, just like that? Now? With no thought, no preparations?"

"Well, they haven't much to pack," the Bingtown woman said, and laughed at her own feeble jest. She sat up, then gasped and clutched at her shoulder. She caught her breath raggedly and cried out, "Sedric, stop gaping at me. Yes, they're leaving. Couldn't you feel it? 'Kelsingra!' they shouted, and suddenly off they went. They'll leave us behind if we don't hurry."

"Now wouldn't that be tragic," Sedric observed wryly, but he offered Alise his hand and helped her to her feet.

"Do you think they know the way?" Tats asked with interest. "I mean, I've heard the name of the city, but it's like hearing about an imaginary land. People say this or that about it, but no one really knows anything about Kelsingra."

"I do," Alise asserted with quiet confidence. "Quite a bit,

actually, though I won't claim to know the exact location, other than that it's upriver of here, possibly on a tributary of the Rain Wild River. But the dragons will know more than that. They have their ancestral memories to draw on. I suspect they'll be our best guides."

"I'm not sure how much they recall," Tats said quietly. "My little green dragon seems ignorant of a lot of things."

"Such as?" Alise pushed.

Tats shifted uncomfortably under her focus. "Oh, odd things. I was talking with her while I groomed her, but she seemed to have very little to say, so I was chatting about anything at all. I asked her if she remembered being a serpent, and she said no. Then I told her that it had been years since I'd seen the ocean, and she asked me what the ocean was. It was very strange. She knows she hatched from a serpent, but the river seems to be the only body of water she recalls." He halted, as if he dreaded admitting something, and then added, "I don't think she remembers anything except the life she has had here."

"That's . . . disturbing," Alise agreed. She stared after the dragons, frowning.

Thymara shifted restlessly. "We need to follow them."

The man from the barge, Captain Leftrin, came running across the mudflats toward them. "Alise!" he shouted. "Sedric! Get aboard. We need to cast off and follow the dragons as soon as possible. The ship is ready to leave."

"I'll be right there," Alise promised, but Sedric shook his head wearily. "What is the need to hurry? They're going upriver. Seems to me that it would be hard for us to lose track of that many dragons on a riverbank."

"If the Rain Wild River were a single river, that might be true," Thymara said. "But it isn't. There are tributaries that feed into it. Some are seasonal and shallow, but others are rivers in their own right. There's no telling which one the dragons will follow."

Captain Leftrin joined them just as she finished speaking. The riverman was panting from his jog across the mudflats. Thymara had met him only briefly, but she already liked him. He was a man who worked. It showed on his weathered face and capable hands, and even on his worn clothing. He looked at her directly when he spoke to her, and even when he had first met the dragon keepers, he hadn't flinched at the sight of them. It was too soon for her to say she trusted him, but she doubted that he would deliberately deceive anyone. She valued that. He pulled a bright orange kerchief from his pocket and wiped his sweating face before he spoke. "The girl's right. That's been the whole difficulty with this expedition. 'Upriver' from Cassarick can take a man in any of a dozen directions. Unfortunately, no more than three or four of them have been charted, and those charts are unreliable. Channels and waters that were navigable by flatboat one year are sanded in the next."

"But I've seen charts of the Rain Wild River. I've seen them for sale in the bazaars of Chalced. They're very expensive and not offered to all, but they exist."

"Have you?" Leftrin grinned at Sedric and his comment. "I imagine that the same booths will sell you charts to the treasure island of Igrot the Pirate. Or maps of the best harbors in the Spice Islands." He shook his head. "Cheats and fakes, I'm sorry to say. People know there's a market for such things, so what they don't have, they're willing to create. But don't feel bad. I've seen experienced mariners fooled by them."

The Bingtown man looked at him. "Then how do we know where we are going?"

Captain Leftrin's grin widened. "I'd say our best bet is to follow the dragons."

SEDRIC'S HANDS WERE sweating. So far, it had all gone so well. He had inside his case two strips of dragon flesh and hide, with scales attached. One he had pushed into a bottle prepared with vinegar and stoppered it securely. The second piece he had placed in a small wooden box with coarse salt around it and latched the lid tightly. One or the other method, he trusted, would work. Both preservation vessels had been prepared weeks ago, before he had embarked on this journey. Once he had realized that Hest was serious, that he was going to force him to go to the Rain Wilds as

Alise's companion, he had been determined that the journey would provide him with a way to escape a life he had begun to find burdensome. Everyone knew that the desperate Duke of Chalced was willing to pay anyone's asking price for the ingredients that might cure his maladies and extend his life. Sedric had decided he would be the one to furnish them.

And he had succeeded.

Now he was torn between triumph and dismay. He had exactly what he needed to change his fortune. As soon as he returned to Bingtown, he could contact Begasti Cored. The man had been eager to act as a go-between when Sedric had ventured the idea to him. Begasti would arrange his journey and his audience with the Duke of Chalced. It wasn't just the riches that these scraps of flesh would bring him. It was the complete change in his life that he hungered to experience.

For the first time, he would have money, money that was his, earned solely by his own efforts. Not his father's money, not his family's money, not even the inflated wages that Hest paid him for his services. His own money, to spend as he desired. Exactly as he desired. Dreams that had slowly shaped themselves inside his heart for the past four years clamored to be free. With this money, he could take Hest and they could leave Bingtown. They could go south, to Jamaillia, no, beyond Jamaillia, to lands he knew only as exotic names. There were places where two men could live as they wished to live, without questions, without condemnation or scandal. The money these scraps of dragon flesh would bring him would carry the two of them to those places, far from their families and their histories. It would buy them a future without secrets.

He scarcely dared to taste the thought that followed. It would buy him a future in which he and Hest were on an equal footing. For far too long he'd been completely dependent on Hest financially. The inequity had intruded more and more cruelly into their relationship. Hest was no longer merely assertive; he'd become cruelly dominant of late. If Sedric had a fortune of his own, perhaps Hest would give him more respect.

He had what he needed; all that was left to do was to

get his treasure safely back to Bingtown and make contact with Begasti. And the sooner the better. It was a long sea journey to Chalced, but he would not trust these goods to any hand save his own; the swifter he delivered his merchandise, the better. Vinegar and salt were excellent ways to preserve many sorts of vegetables and flesh, but they had never been tested on dragon meat. The stuff that the girl had cut from the dragon wasn't exactly of the best quality, either. He planned, when he had a quiet, private moment, to clean both strips of maggots and tidy them up a bit. He'd pluck the scales free and store them separately from the flesh. But the important thing was to get them back to Bingtown as quickly as possible. An extended wander along a riverbank following a herd of dim-witted dragons did not feature in his plans.

"Alise," he said, and her name came out more sharply than he intended. She turned away from Captain Leftrin, her brows raised quizzically. The others were watching them, but he spoke as if they were alone. "You can't intend to follow through on this wild adventure. Surely by now you've seen that nothing is to be gained by following the dragons. They've scarcely spoken to you, and what they did say wasn't useful. Alise, it's time to admit that you've learned all you can here. We can't get on Captain Leftrin's boat and leave here. Once we do, we're committed to travel for weeks, perhaps months. Neither of us can do that. It's time to admit we've done all we can with these creatures." He let his voice drop into gentleness. "You did what you set out to do. It's not your fault that they aren't what you hoped to find. I'm sorry, Alise. It's time to go home."

She stared at him. She wasn't the only one. Leftrin was looking at him as if he'd taken leave of his senses. The two Rain Wild youngsters exchanged glances, and Tats suddenly said, "I think Thymara and I had best be going after our dragons." It was as awkward an excuse to flee from the site of a quarrel as Sedric had ever heard. But the girl was obviously grateful for it, because she nodded emphatically. The two of them immediately set off at a dogged trot.

Alise was silent for a moment longer, obviously waiting

for them to be out of earshot. Sedric could almost see her putting her objections into polite phrases. They would quarrel, yes, but politely and calmly, as civilized people did.

Leftrin had evidently never been taught such niceties. The color had come up in his face. He took a deep gulp of air, struggled for control, and then blurted, "How can you say such a thing to her? She can't go back now. She's the only one who knows about Kelsingra. Besides, she promised. She signed the contract! She can't go back on her word."

"This doesn't concern you," Sedric said flatly. His voice had risen in spite of himself. He was offended, both that Leftrin had dared to challenge him on this and that he had sided with Alise. It was going to be hard enough to herd her safely back to Bingtown; if she felt she had an ally in Leftrin, it was only going to complicate his task.

"It does," the captain said flatly. "She was there when I made my deal with the Council. Think I would have agreed on this trip if she hadn't said she'd heard of the place and that it did exist? I only took the contract because I thought that she'd be along as a guide, not just to the possible location but to the dragons."

Sedric glanced at Alise, but she seemed content to let Leftrin speak for her. Sedric focused his words on her anyway. "You may have heard of the city, but that doesn't mean you know the way. Come, Alise, be your calm, sensible self about this. You're a scholar, not an adventurer. Even the dragon that can speak to you told you nothing; you said so yourself. And the silver and Tats's dragon don't seem promising sources of information, either. If you are honest, you have to admit that you'd gain more from spending a week in Trehaug, touring the underground city. There is a treasure trove of material there for you to study and translate. Why not return there with me and put your time to something that will not only increase our knowledge of Elderlings and dragons but will gain you the respect you deserve from those who know the most about these creatures?" Even if they had to spend a few days in Trehaug to placate her, that would be better than setting off on a harebrained journey to parts unknown. He knew that once they boarded that barge and departed upriver there would be no easy way for them to return, save on the barge itself. And that stubborn old goat of a captain was not likely to turn back until he'd given the task an honest try. "Alise, it's not safe," he went on desperately. "How can I accompany you on this journey, how can I allow you to go? You've all admitted you don't know where you are going, or how long it will take to get there, or even if the city still exists. This is a ridiculous journey." He firmed his resolve and ended his lecture with, "We aren't going. That's all there is to it."

He had never spoken so firmly to her. For a long moment, she regarded him in silence. Her mouth worked and he feared she would cry. He didn't want to make her weep, only to be sensible. She glanced over at Leftrin. The riverman had folded his arms across his chest; his face was set like stone. Even the stubble on his unshaven cheeks stood out stiffly. He looked, Sedric thought, like an indignant bulldog.

When Alise's gaze came back to him, she was pink all around her freckles. Her voice was low, not shrill. She declared stubbornly, "You may do as you wish, Sedric. As you say, it's a foolish quest. I won't argue with you there, for I can't. You're right. It's insane. But I'm going."

He stood stunned as she turned away from him. She put her hand out as if groping blindly, and suddenly Leftrin was there, offering her his arm. She set her hand on his grubby jacket sleeve and then he was leading her away, leaving Sedric staring after her. He clutched his precious case with the preserved bits of dragon in it and weighed his options. In his anger, he wanted to just do as she had suggested; leave her there and go home himself. Leave her to her own foolish decision and let her find the disaster she was so eagerly courting.

But he couldn't. He couldn't go back to Trehaug, let alone Bingtown, without her. Certainly not back to Hest, not even if he had dragon flesh and scales worth a fortune preserved in his case. It would take time to change those things into money, time and discretion. And returning to Bingtown without Hest's wife would be the most indiscreet thing he could ever do. He'd have no way to explain it. It would focus attention on him, attention he could not afford to attract to himself just now.

He realized abruptly that Alise and Leftrin had nearly reached the barge. Ropes were being untied, and the polemen stood ready to shove the barge back out into the river. He looked up and down the mudflats. The dragons were gone. At the river's edge, the keepers were dragging small boats down to the water. In a very short time, he suspected this area would be deserted. "Alise!" he shouted, but she didn't even turn her head. The sound of the river and the endless wind carried his voice away. He cursed then and began to walk toward the barge as swiftly as he dared. "Alise, wait!" he shouted as he saw her start up the ladder dangling over the barge's stern. And then he began to run.

✧ ✧ ✧

Day the 7th of the Grain Moon

Year the 6th of the Independent Alliance of Traders

From Detozi, Keeper of the Birds, Trehaug
To Erek, Keeper of the Birds, Bingtown

Enclosed in a sealed scroll case, from the Traders' Councils at Trehaug and Cassarick, an accounting of the initial expenses of mounting the expedition to move the dragons, with the Bingtown Council's share of said expenses shown separately.

Erek,

Your missive concerning the cost and availability of a hundredweight sack of peas to improve the health of the flock at Trehaug has still not been delivered to me. Please resend the information.

Detozi

✧ ✧ ✧

CHAPTER FIFTEEN

CURRENTS

The dragons hadn't halted at the river's edge. Some had plunged into the shallows. Others had tried to walk on the flotsam-littered bank until the undergrowth and river debris had forced them out into the water. But all of them moved steadily and doggedly upstream.

The keepers, including Thymara, had hastened to their small boats and followed. She had hoped to be paired with Tats. It had been a selfish hope; he was well muscled and experienced with small boats and she knew he would do his share of the work and perhaps more. Jerd had been waiting at the shore, standing by one of the small boats. She waved cheerily at Tats as they arrived and called out to him, "I've already loaded your rucksack, slowcoach. Let's go! Your green dragon was one of the first ones into the water."

"Sorry, Thymara," Tats had muttered, red-faced.

"Sorry for what?" she'd said, but it was a moment too late for him to hear it. He was already hastening to push Jerd's boat out into the water. Nearly all of the other boats were already loaded and pushing away from the shore, each carrying two or three dragon keepers. Rapskal sat alone and dejected in the sole remaining boat. His face brightened the moment he saw her. "Well, I guess we'll be partners, then," he'd greeted her. And as annoyed as she'd felt with the situation, she still found herself nodding. Tats's "sorry" was still rankling in her breast. He'd known that what he was doing was rude enough to rate an apology to her, but it still hadn't dissuaded him from doing it. The scum-rat.

"Let me get my gear," she'd told Rapskal, and had run back to their deserted campsite. She'd grabbed her pack and returned to the canoe. Rapskal sat in it, paddle poised, as she shoved it out into the river. She'd leaped the water and landed in the narrow boat, making it rock wildly but keeping her feet dry. Seizing her heavily waxed paddle, she pushed them out into deeper water. A spare set of paddles was under her feet. Not for the first time, she wondered how long their paddles would stand up to the river, and how long their boat would last. The river had been mild of late, its water dark gray. Like every child who had grown up in the Rain Wilds, she knew the water was most dangerous when it ran milky white. Then anyone who fell into it might be scalded and blinded from a single dunking. The dark gray water that flowed past her paddle today would do no more than sting, but its touch was still to be avoided.

This was her first time to partner with Rapskal in a boat. To her surprise, he proved to be competent, digging his paddle in rhythm with hers. He guided them deftly around snags and mud bars as she provided most of the power that pushed them along. They kept to the edge of the river and the shade of the leaning trees, moving where the current was slowest, and soon caught up with the others. Greft, she noticed, had joined Boxter and Kase in one of the larger boats. Their paddling was uneven; Greft was using his oar mostly as a tiller. She and Rapskal moved easily alongside them and then passed them. She felt a small thrill of satisfaction at that. Rapskal grinned at her conspiratorially, and she felt an irrational lift to her spirits.

The boats of the other keepers were arranged in a straggling line before them. Sylve and Lecter shared a canoe, as did Warken and Harrikin. Alum and Nortel seemed well matched as paddlers. Tats and Jerd had moved up to lead them all, not that leadership was necessary. The trail the dragons had left was unmistakable, both in the river shallows and on the boggy bank. They had trampled the brush into the mucky shore of the river, and in the shallows, their deep footprints streamed a deeper gray water into the slow current.

"They're moving pretty fast, aren't they?" Rapskal observed enthusiastically.

"Right now they are. I doubt they'll be able to keep it up for long," she replied as she paddled doggedly. The dragons steadily and swiftly increased their lead. She was astonished to see them move so rapidly. She had expected the small swift boats to keep pace with them easily, but every time she glanced up, the dragons were farther away. Even the silver and the copper dragons were lolloping along after the others. She noticed that the silver was holding his tail above the water, and hoped he'd continue to do so. It bothered her that she hadn't finished bandaging his injury. It bothered her even more that Skymaw had left without even speaking to her. Apparently she meant little to the blue queen.

"Did you see your dragon today?" she asked Rapskal. She was settling into the rhythm of paddling again. First, she knew, her muscles would ache. Then they'd ease into the exercise and for a time, all would go smoothly. What she dreaded was when they'd begin to ache again, because no matter how they hurt, they could not stop paddling until they went ashore for the night. A few days of traveling by boat had toughened all of the dragon keepers and taught them the basics of watercraft, but she had a feeling that her body would hurt a lot more before she was completely accustomed to this. She leaned harder into her paddling.

" 'Course I did." Rapskal timed his words to his efforts. "After I ate, I went and groomed Heeby. Then we did our flying exercises. Then I watched Heeby eat. It made me mad. The big dragons take the best food. She doesn't get as much to eat as they do. When we stop tonight, I got to catch her a fish or something. But I think that's going to be a problem. If the dragons go this fast, so we have to paddle all the time to keep up, when are we going to have time to hunt or fish for food for them?"

"There's supposed to be some food on the barge, for us, and some dried meat for the dragons. We don't know how long they'll keep up this pace. Maybe they'll stop in a few hours and we'll have time to hunt." She shook her head. "There's a lot we don't know yet. I guess we'll learn as we go along."

"I saw the hunters get on board the barge back there. They're supposed to help us get meat for the dragons each day."

"I didn't see them. I'm glad they got here before the dragons decided to leave. But if the hunters are on the barge back there, how are they going to hunt anything?"

"That's a very good question. What's that ahead of us?" She squinted against the sunlight bouncing off the river. "Looks like a big snag sticking out into the water, with a lot of driftwood piled up against it."

Rapskal grinned. "We'll have to go out in the current to get around it."

"No. Let's hug the shore. If we have to, we'll portage around it. I don't want to get out in the current."

"Are you scared?" Rapskal sounded delighted at the prospect. When she glanced over her shoulder at him, he turned his wide grin on her. When he smiled, all his strangeness seemed to melt away and he became simply a very handsome Rain Wild youth. She still shook her head at his challenge.

"Yes. I am scared," she replied firmly. "And we are not going out into the current. Not until I'm better at managing this boat."

But suddenly, partnering with Rapskal instead of Tats did not seem such a poor trade.

❖ ❖ ❖

LEFTRIN WAITED UNTIL Alise was aboard the barge before
he started up the ladder. He knew he needed to focus his
mind on the final loading of the barge and shoving the
Tarman back out into the current. No one had expected the
dragons to stampede off like that. The plan had been that
the barge would lead the way, followed by the keepers in
their canoes guiding and encouraging the dragons. Now
the dragons were completely out of sight, and the last of the
canoes would soon vanish around a bend in the wandering
river. And here he sat, on shore still, with cargo of dried
meat, hardtack, salt pork, and pickled breadleaf still being
loaded. If any of the young keepers overturned their canoes,
there would be nothing he could do to help them. And from
what he'd seen of the youngsters, mishaps seemed more
likely than not.

Well, all he could do right now was worry about them
until he had all the stores safely stowed. Then he'd have to
get his barge back out into the water and headed upriver. He
tried to push Alise out of his thoughts. Now was no time to
be wishing that he could sit her down in the galley and offer
her a quiet cup of tea and some talk. He'd been so proud of
her for standing up to Sedric when he tried to bully her into
backing out of her adventure. She'd kept a stone face and a
stern resolve all the way back to the barge. He followed her
up the ladder, wondering if he'd have time to let her know
how impressed he was.

But as he stepped onto his deck, he encountered not
only a heap of unstowed cargo but three strangers lounging against it. Alise had frozen where she was, just off the
ladder, her back to the barge's rail. Instinctively he moved
between her and the men. He sized up their scattered goods
in one glance. Spears and bows, one a heavy bow for distance shooting. A carefully folded net. Several quivers of
arrows. Hunters' gear. These would be the fellows they'd
been waiting for, the hunters hired by the Council. One
turned toward him, grinning, and only then did he recognize Carson. He'd grown a beard. The big man put out a calloused hand to him, saying, "I'll bet you're surprised to see
me here! Or maybe I was exactly what you were expecting.

This is just the sort of misadventure that always finds us, so it's no coincidence we've both signed on for it."

Simple words spoken between old friends, yet they suddenly made Leftrin's heart sink. He desperately hoped there was no meaning layered beneath that greeting, that his use of the words was a true coincidence. He didn't want Carson to be the one whom the note had warned him to expect. Not Carson. He forced an answering grin to his face and asked him, "Now why would I be expecting a drunken sot like you on my clean deck?"

"Because drunk or sober, I'm the best damn hunter this river has ever seen, and I'm exactly what you're going to need to keep those dragons from eating each other or you before this is all over. This is Davvie here, an up-and-coming bowman who still needs his arse kicked from time to time. He's my nephew, but don't let that stop you when it comes to arse-kicking time. And this fellow is Jess, who I only met this morning, but he seems to think he can keep up with me. I'll soon teach him better."

The first was a youngster near fresh faced as a Bingtowner but with the shoulders of a good archer. He bore a strong resemblance to his uncle, with the same unruly brown hair and dark eyes. He shook Leftrin's hand and met his eyes with an honest grin. If Carson was up to something nefarious, Leftrin would wager that Davvie had no knowledge of it. He still gave the boy a serious look and told him firmly, "You see that Skelly? The deckhand with the long black braid down her back? Well, she may look like a girl but she's not. She's my deckhand and my niece. And that means that, to you, she's not a girl."

Davvie looked properly daunted, but Carson just shook his head, a smile twitching the corner of his mouth. "I guarantee you, Leftrin, there will be no problems with Davvie in that department," he said as the lad ducked his head and blushed.

Jess was an older man with graying hair above gray eyes who scowled at Carson's deprecating introduction and offered Leftrin only a curt nod. Leftrin instantly disliked him, and he felt a thrill of distrust go through him as well.

He didn't offer the man his hand, and Jess didn't appear to notice that lack of courtesy.

Carson demanded abruptly, "And aren't you going to introduce me and explain what a fresh flower like this is doing on your stinking old barge?"

It seemed impossible but he had briefly forgotten that Alise was standing there behind him. He glanced at her, then grinned as he confronted Carson. "Stinking barge? Not until you came on board, Carson. Alise Finbok, I'm afraid I have to introduce you to an old friend of mine. Carson Lupskip. Hunter, braggart, and drunk, not necessarily in that order. Carson, this is Alise. She's aboard as our expert on dragons and Elderlings, newly arrived from Bingtown and happily willing to advise and educate us on this voyage."

He'd thought his words would make her smile. Instead, she ducked her head and abruptly declared in a husky voice, "You must excuse me. I've a few things to do before we depart." And before he could say another word, she scuttled away to her quarters and slipped inside, shutting the door firmly behind her. He suspected it would be dark and hot in there, but off she'd gone anyway. And even knowing as little of women as he did, he suspected she sought privacy for weeping. Damn him for a fool. He should have known that the confrontation with Sedric would upset her. He was just as glad the man wasn't going to be accompanying them. She'd get over her doubts a lot faster without him around. He wanted nothing so much as to follow her and reassure her, if she would allow such a thing. But he couldn't, not with this threesome cluttering up his deck with their gear and themselves. When he turned back to Carson, he found his old friend regarding him knowingly.

"Is she expert on more than dragons?" he asked teasingly.

"I wouldn't know," Leftrin snapped back at him. Then, embarrassed, he tried to soften it with, "Welcome aboard, Carson. Maybe tonight we'll find some time to catch up on old news. For now, please, all three of you find yourselves some space in the deckhouse and stow that stuff where it won't be underfoot. Swarge! Did the rest of our cargo come

on board yet? Because at the rate those dragons were traveling, we'd best be after them."

"They won't keep up that pace for long," Carson predicted. "By afternoon—"

The hunter stopped speaking abruptly, staring past
Leftrin. The captain turned to find Sedric awkwardly climbing over the rail of the barge. He gripped his supply case
to his chest with one arm while he struggled. "What do
we have here?" Carson asked quietly. A slow smile spread
across his face.

"Oh, him." Leftrin fought for neutrality in his voice. He
spoke to Carson alone, saying, "He goes where Alise does.
Supposed to look after her."

"That must be inconvenient," Carson muttered quietly.

"Just shut up," Leftrin replied with feeling.

Davvie had darted over to the ladder and attempted to
help Sedric by taking his case for him. The man scowled
at the lad and held tight to it as he clambered awkwardly
over the railing. As he straightened up, he brushed at his
clothing, and then came directly to the captain, demanding,
"Where's Alise?"

"She's gone to her quarters. We launch soon. You'd better
round up your gear if you want it to go ashore with you."
Leftrin kept his voice flat.

The Bingtown man stopped and stared at him. He didn't
quite grind his teeth, but he clenched them for a moment.
"I won't be going ashore," he grated. He turned away from
Leftrin and said meaningfully over his shoulder, "I wouldn't
leave Alise alone on this barge."

With you, Leftrin mentally added to his words, and
fought to keep from grinning. *That slimy little bugger
wanted to say he wouldn't leave Alise alone with me, but he
didn't quite have the spine.* Aloud, he said, "She'd scarcely
be alone, you know. She'd come to no harm with us."

Sedric glanced back at him. "She's my responsibility," he
said flatly. Then he opened the door of his small cabin and
vanished inside it, shutting it nearly as firmly as Alise had
done. Leftrin tried to push aside his disappointment.

"Doesn't bark too loud for a watchdog," Carson observed

slyly. When Leftrin scowled at him, he only grinned wider and added, "I don't think he has his heart in what he's guarding. Appears to me he might have other things on his mind."

"Get your gear off my deck. I don't have time for you now. I got a boat to get back in the water."

"Indeed you do," Carson agreed. "Indeed you do."

IT WAS STUFFY in the cabin and dim. Alise sat on the floor and stared up at the rough ceiling. Lighting a candle was too much trouble, and climbing into her hammock too much of a challenge. The little room that had earlier felt cozy and boldly quaint now seemed like a child's treehouse. And she felt like a child, hiding from discipline that must sooner or later descend on her.

Why had she defied Sedric? Where did those bursts of audacious bravery come from, and why did she keep yielding to them when she knew she could not back up her threats? She'd go without him. Oh, of course she would! Off, up the river, on a ship full of sailors and other rough folk, headed no one knew where. And when she came back, what then? Then Leftrin would discover that Hest would not cover the debts she had run up while defying her chaperone, and even if she'd gained any knowledge, she'd be disgraced in Bingtown and Trehaug. She would no longer have any home to go to. She thought of what Hest would probably do to her study and her papers when he discovered she'd run away. He'd destroy them. She knew how spiteful he could be. He'd sell the valuable old scrolls, probably in Chalced. And he'd burn her translations. No, she suddenly thought bitterly. He'd auction them along with the scrolls. No matter how angry Hest might be, he never passed up the opportunity to make a profit.

She clenched her teeth in frustration, and tears stung her eyes. She wondered if he would find out then how valuable her studies and notes were. Or would some collector just acquire her treasures and hide them away in his library, unaware of what he had? Worse, would someone else claim her work as his own? Use what she had painstakingly learned of Elderlings and dragons for his own profit?

The thought was unbearable. She couldn't let her work come to such an end. She couldn't ruin her life in such a headstrong, childish way. She had to go home. That was all there was to it.

The thought strangled her, and for a time she gave way to wild weeping. She cried as she had not cried in years, letting the deep sobs rise and choke her as they passed through her. The world rocked with her anguish. When finally the fury passed, she felt as if she'd been the victim of a terrible physical mishap, a hard fall or a beating. Sweat had plastered the hair to her head, and her nose was running. Her head spun with dizziness. In the darkness she rose, her body aching. She groped around until she found one of her shirts in the wardrobe, pulled it out, and wiped her face on it, not caring how she soiled it. What did it matter anymore? What did anything matter? She wiped her face again on a dry spot and then sullenly threw the shirt to the floor. She heaved a great sigh. The tears were gone, used up with as little result as they ever had. It was time to surrender.

There was a timid knock at her door. Her hands flew to her face. Reflexively she patted her cheeks and smoothed her hair. She must not be seen like this. She cleared her throat and attempted to sound sleepy. "Who's there?"

"It's Sedric. Alise, may I have a word with you?"

"No. Not now." The refusal was out of her mouth before she thought about it. Her deep sadness blazed up and was suddenly heedless fury again. Another wave of vertigo swept over her. She put out a hand and steadied herself on the desk she would never use. For a time, a frozen silence held outside the door. Then Sedric's voice came again, stiffly correct.

"Alise, I'm afraid I must insist. I'm opening the door now."

"Don't!" she warned him, but he did, pulling it open to admit a slice of afternoon light into the small room. Instinctively she moved beyond its reach and half turned her face away from it. "What do you want?" she demanded, and in the next breath, "I'm packing my clothing back in my wardrobe," she lied. "I'll be ready to leave soon."

He was merciless. He pulled the door open wide. She stooped to pick up the blouse from the floor, contriving to turn her back to him. As she did so, she lost her balance and nearly fell. In two steps he was inside the room, catching her arm and holding her up. She clung to him gratefully, both hands on his arm as she looked over his shoulder. "I'm dizzy," she admitted breathlessly.

"It's just the movement of the barge on the river," he said. In the same moment, she realized that the barge was in motion again. Behind him, she saw the stately parade of immense tree trunks as the ship moved upriver. Her vertigo was suddenly the gentle shifting of the floor under her feet. It passed.

"We're under way," she said in wonder. She found herself clutching his arm and staring over his shoulder at the passing riverbank. She could not quite believe it. She had defied him, and she had won. The barge was carrying her upriver.

"Yes. We are." His response was curt.

"I'm sorry," she said, and then wondered at her words. She wasn't sorry, not at all, and yet she could not keep herself from apologizing. When had it become so ingrained in her to apologize whenever she wanted something for herself?

"That makes two of us," Sedric responded. He took a deep breath, and she was suddenly aware of how close she was standing to him. It was almost an embrace. She could smell him, the spicy scent he wore, the soap he used. She was surprised that she recognized those scents. They brought Hest sharply to mind, and she stepped back. She suddenly wondered if the two men used the same perfumed oils. She frowned, thinking about that.

His voice was deep and regretful as he interrupted her thoughts with, "Alise, this is mad. We've just embarked on a journey with no fixed destination, into territory that has never been successfully mapped. We'll be gone for weeks, if not months! How can you do this? How can you just walk away from your entire life?"

A stillness welled up in her and then a joy as dizzying as the gentle rocking of the barge spun her. He was right.

She'd left it all behind. After a moment, she found her voice. "Walk away from my life, Sedric? I'd run away from what you think is my life if I could. The hours sitting at my desk, scratching away with a pen, living a life based on things that happened centuries ago. Dining alone. Going to bed alone."

Her harshness seemed to shock him. "You don't have to dine alone," he said awkwardly.

Her mouth was dry with bitterness. "I suppose I don't have to go to bed alone, either. Yet, when one weds, one expects one's husband to be her companion for those things. When Hest asked me to marry him, I foolishly thought that I wouldn't have to worry about loneliness again. I thought he would be there, with me."

"Hest is with you when he can be." Sedric sounded uncertain, probably because he knew he was lying. "He's a Trader, Alise. You know that means he must travel. If he doesn't travel, he can't find the special goods that bring in the prices that allow him to provide you with the life you have."

"You don't understand, Sedric." She cut off the spiral of words that she had heard so many times from Hest in the early years of her marriage. The tightening noose of words that inevitably proved how selfish she was to resent being left home alone, night after night, week after week. "It isn't that he's away so much. I don't mind that anymore. I don't pine after him. Do you know what I hate now, Sedric? I hate that I'm glad when he's gone. Not because I like to be alone; I've learned a great tolerance for it. I'm very good at it, actually. I don't think of him when he's gone. I don't wonder who he might be with or how he treats her." She halted abruptly. She'd made a promise to Hest, never to accuse him of lying again, never to pelt him with such suspicions. Sedric had been there and knew of the promise. She pressed her lips tightly closed.

Her words had made him uncomfortable. She felt him shift slightly, as if he wished to move away from her but didn't know how to untangle himself gracefully. With a leap of certainty, she knew her suspicions were well founded. Hest did have someone else now, and Sedric knew about her. Knew about her and felt guilty for shielding Hest. She suddenly decided to free him from that guilt. "Don't worry about it, Sedric. I promised I'd never ask again, and I won't. I don't wonder anymore if other women in Bingtown know how little he cares for our bed. If they like him, they are welcome to him. I'm tired of his hard words, his hard heart, and his hard hands."

She felt his muscles stiffen. "Hard hands?" he said in a strangled voice. "Does he— Alise, he hasn't . . . Has Hest ever struck you?" He sounded horrified.

"No," she admitted in a low voice. "No, he has never struck me. But there are many ways for a man to be hard-handed with a woman that do not involve striking her." She thought of how he would take her arm and grip it when he wished to leave an evening's entertainment and she had not responded immediately to his polite suggestions that it was time for them to go home. She thought of how he sometimes took things from her, not snatching them but removing them from her grip as if she were an errant child. She refused to think of his hands on her shoulders or upper arms, gripping so tight that sometimes she had bruises, as if she might flee him even though she had never shown any resistance to his attempts to impregnate her.

Sedric cleared his throat and moved away from her. "I've known Hest a long time," he said stiffly. "He's not a bad person, Alise. He's just—" He halted and she saw him searching for a word.

"He's just Hest," she finished for him. "He's a hard man. Hardhanded. Hard-hearted. He doesn't strike me. He doesn't have to. He has a hard, cruel mouth when he's crossed. He can humiliate me with a glance. He can pound me with words and smile while he's doing it, as if he doesn't realize what he's doing. But he does. I'm ready to admit that to myself now. He does know just exactly how much he hurts me and how often."

She turned away from his shocked gaze but kept her eyes on the moving riverbank. "I'm not sorry," she finally said. "I'm not sorry I defied you and I'm not sorry that we're headed up the river. I know it's foolish and dangerous. I'm scared. I'm scared of going and I'm scared of what I'll have to face when I return home. But I'm not sorry to be doing it. I'm not walking away from my life, Sedric. I'm running toward the chance to have a little bit of a life of my own, for a little time.

"I *am* sorry to drag you along, Sedric. I know it's not the sort of thing you'd choose to do. I wish Hest hadn't inflicted me on you. But I'll admit that I'm glad you came back to the barge and you're here. If I'm going to do a foolish thing like this, I can't think of a better companion to have along with me."

She sensed him fumbling for some sort of a reply. She had told him things that had made him uncomfortable, things he probably should never have heard about his employer. She tried to regret it and couldn't. She only hoped it would not sever whatever it was between them. Almost she hoped that he would gather her into his arms and hold her, even if it was only for a moment, as a friend. She tried to recall the last time anyone had embraced her with affection. She recalled her mother's quick hug of farewell. When had a man held her?

Never.

He took her hands in both of his, giving them a gentle squeeze before he released them. Then he made an awkward attempt at levity as he stepped clear of her touch. "Well, I suppose that should be a comfort to me. But it's not."

His words were harsh, but the rueful smile she looked up to see was not. It faded quickly from his face however, as if he did not have the strength to sustain it there. He shook his head at her and then said, "I'd best go get things settled in my room. It looks as if I may be living there longer than I thought."

HE LEFT HER as quickly as he decently could and walked briskly back to his compartment, trying not to appear to be fleeing from her. Even though he was.

He shut the door of the tiny room behind him. Earlier, he had opened the ventilation slots in the upper wall. He refused to think of them as windows. They were too high and too narrow to provide any sort of a view. But they did let in a flow of air, even if it was tinged with the river smell, and admitted a murky light in his room. A reflection of the river rippled on the ceiling of the small cabin. He sat down on his trunk and stared at the closed door. His case with its precious cargo was on the floor. A fortune in dragon parts, and he was headed upriver with them. Away from all profit, and away from every reason he had for dreaming of making a profit. He hoped the salt and the vinegar would preserve the tattered flesh. They represented his last, best chance for an honest life. He lowered his face into his hands and retreated into stillness.

Hest. Oh, Hest. What have we done to her? What cruelty have I been a party to?

Hest's hard hands.

He didn't want to think about it yet he could not stop himself from thinking about it. He didn't want to envision Hest's hands on Alise. He knew that Hest must be with her, that he must do his best to father a child with her. He'd chosen never to think of the mechanics of that, never to wonder if Hest was tender and passionate with her. He didn't want to know, didn't want his feelings stirred about such things. What would it matter? It had nothing to do with Hest and him.

But he'd never imagined Hest would be harsh with her, or rough. But of course he would be. That was Hest. The man had strong hands, with long fingers and short, well-groomed nails. Sedric didn't want to think of those hands gripping her shoulders and the nails sinking into her flesh. They'd leave little half-moon dents there that would be small bruises by morning. Sedric knew. Unbidden, his hands left his face to touch and then grip his own shoulders. It had been weeks since Hest had left small bruises on him. He missed them.

He wondered in desolation if Hest missed him at all. Probably not. He'd spurned Sedric relentlessly in their last days together. At the same time, he had been sure that his secretary handled all the details of whom Hest would invite to accompany him on his latest trading venture. Hest wasn't alone right now, and almost definitely, he wasn't thinking of Sedric. Redding. That damn Redding, always so obvious

in his interest in Hest. Redding with his plump little mouth
always quirking, and his little hands always patting his curly
hair back into place. Redding was with him.

A thick choking lump rose in his throat. It would have
been a comfort to weep, but he couldn't. What he felt right
now went beyond weeping. *Hest. Hest.* "Hest." He said the
man's name aloud, and it was a comfort that cut like a knife.
He was the only one who truly knew Sedric, the only one
who understood him. And he'd set him aside, sent him off
on this ridiculous errand with the wife he didn't love. The
wife he gripped with his hard hands, the same powerful
hands that had held him by the shoulders and pulled him
close in that first squirming and desperate embrace.

Sedric hadn't been much more than a boy, barely shaving, desperately unhappy, at odds with his father, unable to
confide in his mother or his sisters anymore. Unable to confide in anyone. Bitterly, he now reflected on how successful
Hest had been in returning him to that isolation, the isolation that Hest had once shattered for him. Was that what
he'd wanted to prove to Sedric? That he could put him right
back where he'd been, all those years ago?

Their first encounter had happened at a Trader gathering,
at a winter wedding. The bride had been seventeen, and the
young husband-to-be had been his friend Prittus, an older
neighbor who had tutored him in the Chalcedean language
that his father had insisted he must learn. He had always
been kind and patient with Sedric, their lessons much more
social and enjoyable than the ciphering and history and basic
navigation lessons that he received from his other tutor. The
other tutor was a shared master, hired by a group of Trader
families to instruct their sons. That man was an ogre, and
his fellow students alternated between coarse mockery of
one another and sarcastic comments on Sedric's precise
recitations and reports. He hated attending those classes,
dreaded the snubbing and mockery of the other pupils. It
was a wonder he had learned anything there. But Prittus
had been different. He'd been a teacher who cared, one who
found readings for his pupil that interested him. He'd treasured his hours with Prittus.

So he'd watched Prittus make his wedding promises in a sullen gloom of disappointment. He'd have no time to tutor Sedric now; he'd be following his father into the spice trade and he'd have all the concerns of a young man with his own household. Sedric's sole island of company was sinking back into his sea of isolation.

Prittus had stood tall in his simple green Trader robe, the candlelight waking glints in his gleaming black hair. The vows spoken, he turned to the girl at his side and looked down into her face with that smile that Sedric had come to know so well. The girl's face lit with a rosy blush of joy. He put his hands out and the girl set her small fingers in his; Sedric had to turn aside, choking with jealousy over all he could never hope to possess. The couple turned to face their guests and the applause washed around them like the breaking waves of a gentle sea.

Sedric had not clapped. When the applause ended, he'd finished the glass of sparkling wine he held and set the glass down on the edge of one of the laden feast tables. The room swirled with smiling, talking people, all eager to wish the young couple well. Close to the door, a handful of young men were speaking in deep good-humored voices to one another. He caught a leering reference to the night that awaited Prittus, and the round of bawdy chuckles that followed it. He'd made an excuse as he pushed past them to the door and left the crowded Traders' Concourse to go outside for some air. He didn't even bother with his coat; he wanted to feel the wind on his face. He wanted to be cold. It would match his mood.

A storm was threatening, one that couldn't make up its mind between icy rain and wet, driven flakes of snow. The wind gusted and died, and then spat sleet again. The thick clouds were making late afternoon into early evening. He didn't care. He'd left the shelter of the large porch of the Concourse, strolled past the line of waiting carriages and well-bundled drivers. He'd gone walking in the deepening twilight on the meticulously groomed grounds that surrounded the Concourse.

The gardens were desolate and deserted this time of

year. Most of the trees had lost their leaves, and the unimpeded wind blew sharply. Fallen leaves littered the gravel paths. There was a stand of evergreens at the edge of an herb garden that had gone to seed. He headed instinctively toward the protection of the grove. In the circle of their shelter, the wind could barely find him. He turned his eyes up to the cold winter sky and tried to find a single star through the overcast. He couldn't. He lowered his face and wiped rain from his cheeks.

"Weeping at a wedding? What a sentimental fool you are."

He'd turned in shock. He hadn't imagined anyone else would be out in this weather. It was even more of a shock to realize that the man was Hest, and that he must have followed him. He'd been a part of the group of men by the door. Sedric knew his name and his reputation, but little more than that. The wealthy and popular young Trader moved in a social circle several notches higher than Sedric's orbit. He wondered why he had followed him out into the night. His long deep-blue cloak was nearly black in the dimming light. The collar was turned up high, framing his face.

"It's just rain. I came outside to clear my head of a little too much wine."

Hest listened to him silently, head cocked mockingly. He raised his sculpted brows in a rebuke for his lie.

"I'm not weeping," Sedric added defensively.

"Aren't you?" Hest came toward Sedric through the wet snow. It was definitely snow now. Big flakes of it spangled the tall man's dark hair. "I saw you watching the happy couple and thought to myself, now there's a spurned lover, watching his dreams stroll off without him."

Sedric watched his approach warily. "I hardly know her," he said. "Prittus was my tutor. I'm just here to wish him well."

"As we all are," Hest agreed smoothly. "Our dear friend Prittus enters a new stage of his life now. He takes on the duties of a husbandman. And his loving friends, though we wish him well, will see far less of him now." The light was waning from the sky, and the shadows of the evergreens made the winter afternoon even darker. The fading light took the colors with it; Hest's face was a study of planes and shadows. He was smiling. His narrow lips were chiseled into a fine smile as he asked him, "And what did Prittus tutor you in?"

"Chalcedean. My father says that every Trader needs to speak Chalcedean well, without an accent. Prittus speaks it like a native; he had a Chalcedean tutor."

Hest stopped, not even an arm's length away. "Chalcedean?" His smile grew wider, baring even teeth. "Yes. I agree with your father. Every Trader should know Chalcedean. Some say they will always be our enemies. I say, that is a good reason to learn as much as we can about them. Not just their language, but their customs. Ancient enemies or not, they will be our partners as we buy and sell goods. They'll cheat the man who is vulnerable to them. But you'll need more than just the language. A man can speak the language of a place, but if he lacks knowledge of the customs, he will always betray himself as a foreigner. And thus not be accepted. Don't you agree?"

"I suppose. Yes." The tall Trader was drunk, Sedric decided. He had come close enough that Sedric could smell the spirits on his breath.

His dark eyes roved over Sedric's face in a disconcerting way. He licked his lips and said, "So. Let me hear your accent. Say something in Chalcedean."

"What?"

"That's not Chalcedean." Hest grinned. "Try again."

"What would you like me to say?" Sedric felt trapped. Was the man mocking him or trying to make his acquaintance? His conversation walked a knife's edge between taunting and friendliness.

"That would be good. Yes. Say, 'Please, sir, what would you like?'"

It took him a moment to parse it in his mind. When he spoke, the words came smoothly, but Hest shook his head and made a sad mouth. "Oh, dear. Not like that. You need to open your mouth more. They're a very voluble people."

"What?"

"Say it again, but open your mouth more. Purse your lips out."

It was mockery. Sedric was certain of it now. He made his words brisk. "I'm cold. I'm going back to the Traders' Concourse now."

But as he strode past him, Hest's hand had shot out suddenly and gripped Sedric's left shoulder. He'd tugged him sharply, spinning the smaller man so that Sedric almost collided with him. "Say it again," he urged him pleasantly. "In any language you like. Say, 'Please, sir, what would you like?'"

His fingers were biting into Sedric's shoulder right though the formal Trader's robe he'd donned for the occasion. He tried to squirm away. "Let go! What do you want?" Sedric demanded, but Hest had responded by seizing his other shoulder. He gave a sudden jerk that nearly pulled Sedric off his feet. They were suddenly chest to chest, with Hest staring down into his face.

"What do I want? Hmm. Not quite the same as asking me what I would *like,* but it will do. You should be asking what you want for yourself, Sedric. I wonder if you've ever dared to ask that question, let alone answer it. Because the answer is very plain to me. You want this." One of his hands suddenly grabbed a fistful of Sedric's robe right below his throat. The other shifted to a grip on the hair on the top of his head. Hest bent his head, and his mouth was hard on Sedric's, his lips moving as if he would devour him, his hard hands pulling him closer. Sedric had been too astonished to struggle, even as Hest shifted his grip and pulled Sedric's body tight against his own. A sudden heat rushed through him, a lust he could not conceal or deny. Hest's mouth tasted of liquor, and his cheek, though shaven, rasped against Sedric's when Sedric tried to pull away from him. Sedric gasped for breath, smothered between the kiss and the truth of how badly he wanted this. He put his hands against Hest's chest and pushed but could put no strength into the rejection. Hest held him easily, and his deep, quiet chuckle at Sedric's feeble struggle vibrated through them, chest to chest. Hest finally broke the kiss but continued to press himself tightly against Sedric. He spoke by his ear. "Don't worry. Struggle as much as you think you should, or need to. I won't let you win. It's going to happen to you. Just as you always dreamed it would. Someone just needs to take a firm hand with you."

"Let me go, man! Are you mad or drunk?" Sedric's voice wavered uncertainly. The wind blew harder, but he scarcely felt it.

Hest effortlessly pinned his arms to his side. He was taller and stronger, and he lifted Sedric, not quite off his feet but in a way that let him know he could. He pressed his body against him and spoke through clenched teeth. "Neither mad nor drunk, Sedric. Just more honest than you are. I don't have to ask 'what do you want, please, sir?' It was written all over your face as you stared at the happy couple. It wasn't the bride you were lusting after. It was Prittus. Well, who wouldn't? Such a handsome fellow. But you'll never have him now and neither will I. So perhaps we should settle for what we can have."

"I didn't," Sedric started to lie. "I don't know . . ." Then Hest's mouth descended again, kissing him deeply and roughly, bruising his lips until Sedric gave in and opened them to him. He'd made a small, involuntary noise, and Hest had laughed into his open mouth. Then suddenly, he'd broken the embrace and stepped back from Sedric. He'd nearly fallen then. He'd stumbled back from Hest, and the night grove of trees had seemed to swing around him in a wide circle dance. Sedric had lifted the back of his hand to his mouth, tasted the salt of blood from his stinging lips. "I don't understand," he said faintly.

"Don't you?" Hest had smiled again. "I think you do. All of this will be easier when you admit you do." He stepped closer to him, and Sedric hadn't retreated. He reached for Sedric again, and Sedric hadn't fled. Hest's hands had been hard and strong and knowing as he seized him and pulled him close.

Sedric had shut his eyes tight then, and again as he recalled it. Every moment of that wild night under the cold and stormy sky was clear in his memory. It was etched into him, defining him. Hest had been right. It had been easier when he'd admitted what he wanted.

Hest had been merciless. He'd teased him, and hurt him, then soothed and smoothed him. He'd been rough and then gentle, harshly demanding and then sweetly urging. The storm swept around them, making the trees bow and dance, but the cold couldn't reach them. The deep bed of needles in the darkness beneath the low-swooping evergreen branches had smelled sweet when they were crushed beneath their weight. Hest's cloak had covered them both. Time and family and the expectations of the rest of the world were blown away by the storm's breath.

Shortly before dawn, Hest had left him at the end of the carriageway to his family home. He'd limped home in mud-died and torn garments, his hair wild, his mouth bruised. He'd slept as late as his father would allow him. Later that day, standing before his father in his study, he told a long lie about drunkenness and a tumble down a creek bank in the dark and a long walk home. He'd ached in every muscle, and his lips had been puffy and swollen. For three agonizing days, he'd moved quietly about his father's house. Mostly he kept to his room, seething with shame whenever he wasn't staring into the darkness and reliving every moment. Regret and lust warred in him.

On the morning of the fourth day, Hest's written invita-tion to a riding party had arrived. The large dove-gray en-velope with his name written on it in a bold hand contained a note in Hest's hand on a lighter piece of gray paper. His father had been astonished and pleased that he'd made such a socially uplifting connection. His mother had been sent scampering to be sure his jacket and breeches were present-able. His father had loaned him his horse, the only respect-able mount the family had. Just before Sedric had left, his father had warned him not to be the first to depart from the gathering, and he urged him to linger if Hest seemed conge-nial to the idea.

Hest had, indeed, been congenial to the idea of him lingering. Sedric had been the only other member of the "riding party" and they'd gone only as far as a small, de-

serted farmstead owned by Hest's family. All the rooms in
the rickety little house had been dusty and unkempt, save for
a lushly appointed bedchamber and a sidebar well stocked
with spirits.

In the weeks that followed, he'd quickly learned that all
of Hest's "riding parties" had little to do with horses. For a
time, Hest became his entire world. Light, colors, and sound
all seemed more brilliant in his presence. Hest plunged
him into a world of temptation and satiation, stripped him
of fears and inhibitions, and taught him new hungers to replace the half-formed longings he'd never dared to confront.
Sedric found himself smiling fondly as he recalled those
days. There had been dinners together, and then evenings
out with Hest's friends. Hest's friends—now there had been
an education for him! Wealthy Traders, some young, some
older, some single, some married, but all of them committed
to a life that included the greatest pleasures that money could
buy for them. He'd been astonished at their self-indulgence
and scandalized at their headlong pursuit of all manner of
pleasures. When he'd expressed his reservations about them
to Hest, the other man had laughed. "We're Traders, Sedric,
born and bred. We make our livings by discovering what
other men want most and getting the best prices for it. So
of course we discover what is most desirable, and want it
for ourselves. And with the money we make, we acquire it.
That's the whole point of all that we do: to make money, and
then use it. What is wrong with that? Why do we work so
hard if not to enjoy ourselves with what we earn?"

He'd had no answer to that.

Hest had remade Sedric, telling him how to comb his
hair, what colors to wear and what cut of jacket, and where
to buy his boots. When Sedric's modest budget could not
keep pace with Hest's tastes, Hest had first gifted him with
the required clothing, and then, when Sedric's father had
looked askance at such largesse, Hest had eventually invented employment for him that required Sedric to live with
him. Hest had transformed Sedric's life; no, he had transformed Sedric himself. He had not only learned the pleasures of fine wine and a well-prepared joint of meat, but had

come to expect such things at table. A badly cut jacket was not to be tolerated. And now what would become of him? If upon his return, he discovered that Hest had replaced him, what then? Sedric closed his eyes tight and tried to imagine life without Hest. Life without Hest's fortune and lifestyle, yes, that he could imagine. But life without Hest's touch?

The barge wallowed unevenly in the current. Sedric let himself become aware of the boat. The crew members were at their sweeps. Possibly they had put up the sail if the wind was favorable. The barge and how it moved was a mystery to him; it seemed impossible that such a large object could be rowed up a river, and yet they were moving steadily along.

As Sedric must.

He would not give up. He'd take Alise's stubbornness for an example and build on it. She intended to be remorseless about seizing this opportunity for herself. Well, so could he. Let Hest wonder where they were and why they did not return as scheduled. It would do the man good to have some doubt and discomfort in his life. And Sedric didn't doubt that Hest's life would be much less comfortable without a wife and a secretary to manage any unpleasant detail he wished to avoid.

As for his own ambitions, well, those could be better fulfilled, too. If he was forced to keep company with the dragon keepers and their charges, he would find opportunities to collect more merchandise. He sat up slowly and then moved to the floor. At the base of his wardrobe trunk, there was a concealed drawer. Hest had had the trunk made especially, so that exceptionally valuable merchandise and their cash would travel safely. He never would have imagined the use to which Sedric now put it.

He pulled it open and peered at the two glass containers he had filled today. In the dim light he could not tell much about them. In the drawer awaited other glass and pottery containers, some empty, some with preservative fluids and salts already in them. He had planned this meticulously from the first moment that he had realized he could turn Hest's punishment of him to his own advantage.

There was even a neatly lettered checklist of the various

specimens he hoped to acquire and estimates of their worth.
Blood. Teeth. Nail. Scales. Liver. Spleen. Heart. He thought
of how queasy he'd felt watching the girl cut the tissue from
the dragon's wound. He'd have to get over that. If one of the
animals was injured or died, he'd have to find a way to be
close to it quickly. His banishment might prove the foundation of his fortune.

He stored his specimens carefully away and shut the
drawer. No regrets, he told himself again. No regrets and
no hesitation.

SINTARA HAD FOLLOWED the other dragons down to the
banks of the river, and waded right in behind them. Mercor
led them. She was surprised that all of the dragons seemed
to accept his leadership, but especially Kalo. Hadn't he been
claiming the role by virtue of his size only hours ago? The
excitement that had infected them seemed strong enough to
inspire them all to action. For now.

They walked all morning in the shallows at the edge of
the river. Here the current was gentler and the water offered
less resistance. She would have preferred to stay on the
shore, but the thick vegetation of the Rain Wild Forest came
right to the river's edge and sometimes ventured into the
water in the form of straggling roots or fallen trees. For the
most part, the dragons were large enough and strong enough
to push past such impediments, but in midafternoon, they
had to wade out into deeper water to go around one immense snag that projected into the river.

The trunk of the tree was immense, so large that she
couldn't even see over it. The acid waters of the river were
already devouring the fallen giant, but going around it still
meant wading out so deep that the water tried to lift her
off her feet. That was a disconcerting feeling. The first time
it happened, she paddled and floundered, splashing wildly.
One of the smaller green dragons, Fente, shrilly trumpeted
her distress. The current caught Fente and for a moment she
flailed wildly before successfully passing the fallen tree.
She hastened for the shallows in a panicky gallop. When
she resumed her steady plodding up the river, her breath

still came in loud snorts. Sintara was glad she was taller and stronger than Fente. The river had not lifted her. Dragons could swim, but only by necessity.

She thought about swimming, and sluggish memories stirred. One was of a terrifying accident; a cliff's edge had given way and a dragon had fallen into a deep, cold fjord. She had had to swim, and the steep cliffs that surrounded the fjord had defied her attempts to clamber out. By the time she had found a place wide enough to emerge from the water, she had been so chilled that she had barely been able to open her wings and flap them dry before flying away.

There were other memories of being underwater, and with a mental hitch and jerk, she connected them with Kelsingra. She pondered that for a moment, trying to put the pieces together. There had been the city on the bank, a beautiful city that sparkled in the sun, and before it, the wide, deep river. The current's press against her chest seemed to help her remember. Yes. One flew over the city and circled it, once, twice, thrice. It was not just for show, though swooping low or turning a slow roll in flight might win shouts of admiration from the Elderlings who peopled the city. It was to notify everyone, dragon and Elderling, of one's intent to arrive. It gave the small fishing boats notice to get out of the way. For the best way to land at Kelsingra was to come in low over the water and then clap one's wings tight, extend the neck, and plunge beneath the surface of the water. The river cushioned the landing. Once in the water, the dragons did not swim, but waded to the bank, up and out, scaled hides glistening and gleaming. Once out of the water, pleasure awaited. There were always Elderlings waiting to greet the dragons, people whose duty it was to—

She stumbled as a large rock in the riverbed turned under her foot, and the fragile thread of memory snapped. She groped desperately after it. It had been such a sweet thing, something wonderful to recall, and now it was gone. All around her, the other dragons waded on, huffing and grunting with the effort of moving against the current. Closer to the bank, the water was shallower and slower, but the mud at the bottom made it hard going. She decided the sticky footing was less annoying than the deeper water. She waded past several of the others and then deliberately increased her speed until she had passed every dragon except Mercor and Ranculos.

The golden dragon was toiling steadfastly along. He was not as big as Kalo and Sestican, but here in the river he seemed longer. Perhaps it was how he strode along, his neck straining, his long tail lifted above the water. "Mercor!" she called to him. She knew he heard her, but he didn't turn his head or slacken his pace. Scarlet Ranculos was only a pace or two behind him.

"Mercor!" she called again, and despite how he ignored her, she demanded, "What do you remember about the Elderlings greeting us when we reached Kelsingra? I know that we circled the city three times, to let them know that we were arriving—"

"I remember how they would sound trumpets from the city towers when they saw us. Trumpets of silver and horns of brass, to warn the fishing vessels to clear the depths of the river." This came not from Mercor, but from Ranculos. The red dragon's silvery eyes spun with sudden pleasure. "That just now came to me, when you spoke of circling the city three times."

"I remember that!" Veras surged through the water suddenly, struggling to catch up with them. The gold stippling on her green body, so often obscured by mud and dust, shone now.

"I didn't," Sintara admitted quietly. "But I remember landing in the river, and going down into the water until it was dark. The bottom was sandy. And I remember wading out, up onto the bank. There were always some Elderlings waiting for us when we arrived."

She halted, hoping someone else would say something. But no one did, and Mercor trudged stoically on.

"I remember that something pleasant came next. Some special welcome . . ." She let the thought trail away invitingly. No one spoke. The only sounds were the eternal hiss of the river's motion, and the splashes of the dragons and their heavy breathing as they moved against it. Another snag, not quite as large as the first, loomed ahead of them. Sintara knew a moment of deep discouragement. She was already tired.

Suddenly Mercor lifted his head. His nostrils flared, and then he halted in midstride. He looked all around himself, surveying the wide expanse of river to his right and the dense forest to his left. Then he gave a sudden huff of breath. An abbreviated ruff of toxic quills around his neck stood out, blue white against the gold of his body.

"What is it?" Veras demanded. Then she, too, halted and looked around.

"Riverpig," Sestican said. "I smell riverpig dung."

As if by naming them he had summoned them, the creatures suddenly burst from the water. Their hides were gray as the river water, their hair long and straggling as roots. They had been clustered in the lee of the snag, their hairy, rounded backs in the sun, sheltered from the current's push by the fallen trunk.

Sintara made no conscious decision. Some other dragon, ancient beyond reckoning, prompted her. Her head shot out on the end of her neck, mouth wide. She'd targeted the largest one she could reach. The riverpig reacted an instant before her teeth sank into him. He tried to dive under the water. Her teeth sank into him and her jaws latched shut, but she had not bitten him as deeply as she'd meant to. A correct bite would have sent her teeth sinking into his vertebrae, paralyzing him. Instead, she gripped a layer of fat, thick hide, and hair. The heady succulence of fresh, hot blood in her mouth nearly dazed her.

Then the riverpig in her jaws erupted in a savage struggle for his life.

All around her, other dragons were similarly engaged. Some still pursued pigs, trumpeting as they darted their heads after the squealing prey. Fast in the water, the round-bellied creatures were less agile in the shallows and up on the foliage-tangled riverbank. Dragons slammed against her as they sought prey of their own, and she was nearly knocked off her feet when three riverpigs rammed into her, trying to get past her to deeper water.

Those events barely registered on her mind. Never before
had she gripped live prey in her jaws. Her ancestral memories of hunting were mostly of diving onto cattle or other
prey, slamming them to the earth so they were half stunned
when she darted her head in for the killing bite. The creature in her jaws was desperate, very alive, and in his home
element. He struggled madly so that her head whipped side
to side on the end of her long neck. The weight of his body
dragged her head into the water. She instinctively closed her
nostrils and lidded her eyes. She braced her front feet in the
mucky river bottom and struggled to lift her prey out of the
water. For an instant, she succeeded. He dangled from her
jaws, squealing wildly, his sharp cloven hooves striking out
wildly at her. He waved his head with its diminutive tusks at
her, but couldn't reach her. She caught a breath.

But she could barely hold him up.

She should have been stronger. Her neck should have
been thick with the developed muscles of a hunting predator, her shoulders heavy. Instead, she thought with disgust,
she was as slack-muscled as a grain-fed cow. She should not
have any problem with prey of this size. But if she opened
her jaws for a better grip, he would break free of her, and
while she gripped him as she did, he was battering her with
his struggles. She needed to stun him. He pulled her head
under the river's surface, and she was not quick enough to
close her nostrils. She snorted in water.

Reflexively, she found the strength to snatch him up out
of the water. It was part accident, part intent that when her
strength failed her, she managed to dash him against the
fallen log in the river. For an instant, he hung loose in her
grip. When he suddenly began to struggle and squeal again,
she slammed him against the snag hard. She braced his mo-
mentarily still body against the log, and in the fraction of
a second she gained opened her jaws wide and then closed
them again. He gave one final spasm and then her kill hung
limp from her jaws.

She'd killed! She'd made her first kill!

She pinned the meat against the snag with one front foot
while she tore into it. She had never tasted anything so deli-

cious. The blood was liquid and warm, the meat flopping fresh. She gulped and tore mouthfuls of guts, and crunched bones. When pieces of the pig dropped into the river, she plunged her head in to retrieve them.

It was only when every last bit of the animal had been devoured that she became cognizant of the scene around her. Many of the dragons had caught prey. Veras had pursued her pig up onto the bank and killed it there. Two of the smallest dragons had a squealing pig stretched between them, tugging at it until the creature's body suddenly gave way. Kalo was gulping the last of one pig while he had another pinned under his great clawed foot. That sight sent her looking for more pigs.

"The herd scattered," Mercor said quietly. She found the golden dragon cleaning his claws. He licked them and then nibbled a scrap of meat from under one. He had obviously hunted successfully. As she had. The memory rocked her again. She had killed! She, Sintara, had killed her own meat. And eaten it. How could she not have known how important it was to do this? It suddenly changed everything. She looked around at the river and the other dragons. Why was she mindlessly following the others, like a cow in a herd? This was not what dragons did. Dragons didn't have keepers or depend on humans to kill for them. Dragons hunted alone and killed for themselves!

Instinctively she flexed her shoulders and raised her wings. The drive to fly away from here, to return to hunting, to make another kill and devour it and then find a sunny hillside or a good rocky ledge and take a long nap filled her. It wasn't the meat that had awakened this in her, though the meat had been very good. It had been the struggle to kill, and above all, the triumph of killing and eating the riverpig. She couldn't wait to do it again.

But her spread wings were pathetic things that slapped wetly against her back. There was no strength in them. Angrily, she recalled how hard it had been to battle even such stupid prey as a riverpig. Killing it hadn't felt the way it should have, hadn't matched any of her dragon memories of a kill. She was a weakling, not fit to live. She'd been kept like a cow in a pen. It was time to end that life.

"And that," said Mercor, as calmly as if he had heard and followed all her thoughts, "is exactly why we had to leave that place. It is why we have to travel together, upriver to find Kelsingra. So that we can become dragons along the way. Or die trying."

He lifted his head and gave a trumpeting cry. "Time to move on!" Then, without waiting to see if the others followed him or not, he moved out into the depths of the river and around the long snag.

Sintara followed him.

$$\diamondsuit \quad \diamondsuit \quad \diamondsuit$$

Day the 7th of the Grain Moon

Year the 6th of the Independent Alliance of Traders

From Detozi, Keeper of the Birds, Trehaug
To Erek, Keeper of the Birds, Bingtown

Enclosed, in a doubly sealed scroll case dipped in wax, a missive from Jess to Merchants Begasti Cored and Sinad Arich at the Sailpoint Inn, Bingtown. Fees paid for prompt and confidential delivery, with a bonus to be paid if the message is delivered in less than four days from the sending date.

Erek,

I have chosen Kingsly for this task! If any bird can earn us the bonus money, he can!

Detozi

P.S. Any chance of a squab or two from Kingsly's line? I would trade you some of my Speckle's offspring. She is not as fast as Kingsly, but has flown through many a storm for me.

$$\diamondsuit \quad \diamondsuit \quad \diamondsuit$$

CHAPTER SIXTEEN

COMMUNITY

Nightfall found all the keepers sleeping in a row on the deck of the *Tarman*. Thymara had chosen a spot by the ship's railing. She pillowed her head on her arms and stared toward the riverbank. Except for their dying campfire on shore and the single light from the barge window, the darkness was absolute and hard to get used to. Every time they stopped for the night, it was the same. They had left Cassarick far behind them. There were no friendly lights from a tree-built city to pierce the blackness of night under the great trees, no sounds from neighboring houses. Thymara skirted the edges of sleep but could not seem to enter. Too much had happened too fast in the last few days. She swatted at a mosquito buzzing near her ear and asked the darkness, "Why are we doing this? It's crazy. We don't know where we're going or what to expect. There's no end in sight. Why are we doing this?"

"For money," Jerd whispered back. She sighed contentedly and rolled over in her blanket. "To be doing something
new."

" 'Cause we haven't got anything better to do?" Rapskal
asked from the dimness on her left. "And because it's the
best time I ever had in my life." He sounded deeply satisfied
with his day.

"To get away from everything else and start something
new," Greft asserted grandly. Thymara gritted her teeth.

"I need to sleep!" Tats complained. "Could you all keep
it down?" Tonight, he had thrown his blanket down on the
deck next to Rapskal. He'd seemed in a foul temper about
something.

Someone, possibly Harrikin, chuckled. Silence fell
again. The river lapped at the barge. On the shore, one of the
dragons grunted loudly in its sleep and then was still again.
Thymara pulled her blanket up over her head to block out
the mosquitoes and stared into a smaller darkness.

Nothing was as Thymara had expected it to be. There
was no grand adventure to this journey. So quickly the days
had settled into a routine. They woke early and the keepers breakfasted together, usually on ship's bread and dried
fish or porridge. They refilled their water bottles from the
sand wells they'd dug the night before. The hunters left
camp before dawn each day, paddling upriver. They needed
to go before the dragons' noise and activity frightened all
the game. The dragons went next, as soon as they roused;
then the keepers set out in their small boats, followed by
the barge.

The others traded off partners in their boats, but no one
else ever offered to partner with Rapskal. Several of the
other keepers had expressed interest in sharing a boat with
her. Warken had asked her, and Harrikin. Sylve had suggested twice that they might travel together the next day.
But each morning, there was Rapskal, sitting expectantly
in the boat by the shore, waiting for her. She had thought
of partnering with someone else, knowing that if she did
someone would be forced to share a boat with him. But so
far, she hadn't. Part of it was that they moved a boat very

well together. And part of it was that his good nature and optimism were cheering to her at a time when she felt very much alone. Conversations with him might be odd and wandering, but he was not the lackwit that some of the others seemed to think he was. He simply came at life from a different angle. That was all.

And he was, after all, rather pleasant to look at.

Her body was becoming more accustomed to a full day of paddling the boat, but she still ached each night. The blisters on her hands were turning into calluses. The sunlight glinting on the water no longer seemed as harsh as it first had to her canopy-trained eyes. Her hair felt more like straw each day, and she had the uneasy sensation that her scaling was progressing faster than it had when she lived in the trees. But that was to be expected. Rain Wilders always seemed to scale more as they aged. Those things she could accept, but the physical monotony of paddling, day after day, was beginning to tell on her spirits.

Today had provided no exception. The morning had passed slowly, with little change in the endless foliage along the riverbank. In early afternoon, the keepers had been dismayed to hear wild trumpeting from the dragons ahead. When they caught up to them, some sort of disaster seemed to have befallen them, for the dragons were splashing wildly and sometimes immersing themselves completely in the water.

After several near disastrous accidents among the keepers in their canoes, they had made the discovery that the dragons had simply intercepted a thick run of fish and had made the most of their chance to gorge. Shortly after that, the dragons had hauled themselves out onto a long, low, reedy bank and promptly gone to sleep. By the time the keepers caught up with them there had still been plenty of daylight left. They could have traveled farther upstream, but the sleeping dragons refused to be prodded along. Their keepers had had little choice save to pull their small boats up into the shallows and stop for the rest of the day.

Skymaw had plainly got her share of the fish. Her belly bulged with it, and her somnolence was that of a sated predator. She had not wanted to be bothered by cleaning and grooming. Not only had she refused to awaken, but she had growled in her sleep, baring teeth that looked longer and sharper for the fresh blood on her muzzle.

Fente was the only dragon social enough to tell them about it. She was very excited and insisted on telling the tale over and over as Tats groomed her. She made the process more exciting for him as she became caught up in her bragging, and she acted out how she had darted in her head, seized a huge fish, and broke his spine with a single snap. "And I ate him, gulping him down whole. Now you see that I am a dragon to reckon with, not a penned cow to be fattened with bad meat. I can kill. I have killed a riverpig, and I have eaten a hundred fish of my own catching. Now you see that I am a dragon, and I do not need to be kept by any human!"

Thymara and several of the others had clustered around to hear her words and watch Tats attempt to groom the lively little green. The small dragon had smears of blood on her face, and several long threads of sticky guts stuck to her jaw and throat. Tats energetically scrubbed at her scaled face, smiling indulgently at her brags and her insistence that dragons had no need of human intervention. He was obviously infatuated with her. Thymara knew of the reputation the dragons had for charisma; she did not doubt that the ever pragmatic Tats was more than a little under the glamour of the creature.

She suspected that even she herself was under Skymaw's spell. It had hurt her feelings more than a little that Skymaw had not even wakened enough to tell her of her triumphant kill. She felt excluded from her dragon's life, and a bit jealous of Tats. At the same time, there was a tickling of unease at the back of her mind, as a perception she was reluctant to recognize became clearer for her. No matter how Tats might smile as he washed the blood and guts from Fente's face, she was not a cute or even remotely masterable creature. She was a dragon, and even if her boasting sounded childish, she was swiftly discovering what it meant to be a dragon. Her declarations that she had no need for humans were not idle brags. The dragons tolerated the keepers and their attentions for now, but perhaps not for always.

Somehow, she had expected all dragons to be somewhat alike. In her early fancies about her new career, she had imagined them as noble and intelligent with generous natures. Well, perhaps Sylve's golden could live up to that concept, but the others were as diverse as their keepers. Tats's green was a nasty bit of work when she wished to be. Nortel's lavender dragon was shy, until one approached too close and then he might take a snap. Good-natured Lecter and the large blue male he had befriended seemed well matched, right down to the spikes both were growing on their necks. The cousins Kase and Boxter's orange dragons seemed as like-minded as their keepers.

Ever since she had witnessed the hatching, Thymara had seen the dragons as creatures that needed humans to survive. That perception of them had blinded her to how lethal they could be. She had, of course, always known that any of them were large enough to kill a human easily. Some were quick and clever enough that if they desired to become man-eaters, they'd be deadly and cunning enemies. Their disdain for humanity and sense of superiority had, until today, seemed an annoying but merely dragonish trait. Now her gaze wandered from the lively and occasionally good-natured Fente past her own sleeping Skymaw to Kalo.

The largest and most aggressive of the dragons had made himself a rough nest in the coarse reeds. His large claws had raked up damp earth and the reeds that had grown there to make a sleeping place. He dozed there, his massive head cushioned on his front feet, his wings folded against his back in sleep. Like all the dragons, he lacked the ability to fly, but in every other way, he looked fully formed. When she focused both her gaze and her thoughts on him, it seemed to her that he seethed with anger and frustration, as if his immense blue-black body concealed a simmering cauldron of rage. Greft, his keeper, sat on the ground not far from Kalo. The great dragon was clean, his scales gleaming. Thymara had wondered if his keeper had done that, or if Kalo had cleaned himself. Greft's eyes were almost closed.

He looked, she thought, like a man warming himself at a fire. For a moment, she had a sense of Greft enjoying the simmering heat of Kalo's aggression and anger. Even as the image came to her, Greft opened his eyes. She caught a flash of gleaming blue in them and cast her gaze aside, trying to seem as if she had been staring past him. She felt uncomfortable that he should know she had been watching him.

Nonetheless, he smiled and made a small gesture, beckoning her to come closer. She pretended not to notice it. In response, his grin widened. He put out a hand to caress his sleeping dragon. His hand moved slowly, sensually over the dragon's shoulder, as if he would point out to her how strong the creature was. The whole show unsettled her; she turned her head quickly as if she had been distracted by something Rapskal had said. Greft might have chuckled.

It was actually Sylve's comment that caught her attention. "I am glad they had some luck hunting for themselves. At least they've had some food. Hadn't we best try to do some hunting or fishing here now, for ourselves? Because I think they've settled for the night."

She was right, of course. The boat carried some provisions, but fresh meat was always welcome. The hunters had been doing a good job so far of making daily kills. Every day there was some fresh meat for the dragons, even if it was not enough to fill them. The keepers had not been as successful. They spent most of their short hours of shore time each evening in grooming the dragons or doing what fishing they could. Today they'd have part of an afternoon as well as an early evening. Thymara saw that realization settle over the others. Most of them chose to try for fish; Thymara guessed that the rushes and reeds of this section of bank would offer habitat to lots of fish, but she doubted that any would be large enough to be truly useful in feeding a dragon. And she was tired of the water and the muddy riverbanks. She needed time alone in her forest and up in the trees.

She equipped herself with her bow and a quiver of arrows, a knife, and some rope and headed off into the gloom under the immense trees. She did not move randomly, nor did she stay long on the ground. She paralleled the river for a short way, looking for game trails. When she struck one, she studied it briefly. The paw marks of some of the smaller denizens of the forest had been trodden over by the deeper imprints of cloven hooves. Most of the tracks were small; she knew they belonged to what the Rain Wilders called dancer deer. Small and light-footed, they were creatures that moved quickly and silently through the forest, taking advantage of low browse and whatever dry land they could find under the trees. Some had been seen to scramble up low branches and actually run along them. One of them would not make much of a dent in a dragon's appetite, and they were so wary that even if she found a group of them drowsing, she would not be able to kill more than one before the others had fled.

But a few of the tracks were larger and deeper, the cloven hooves splayed wider. Marsh elk would be traveling alone this time of year. If she had the great good fortune to kill one, she'd be able to carry maybe a quarter of it back to camp. But perhaps Tats would help her fetch the rest back in return for a share. Today, he had shared a boat with Warken instead of Jerd. Perhaps that meant that tonight he'd have time to do something besides sit and listen to Jerd talk. Thymara shook her head to banish thoughts of him. He'd made his choice for companionship. There was no reason it should bother her.

She set her hopes for an elk even as she was resigned to the fact that she'd be fortunate even to get a dancer. It was more likely that she'd encounter one of the pawed omnivores that lived along the riverbank. Their meat was edible, though not something she relished, but she doubted that Skymaw would turn her nose up at it.

As soon as she found an opportunity, Thymara left the ground and moved up into the lower branches of the trees. Here, her clawed feet helped her move efficiently and quietly. She did not travel directly above the game trail, but to the side of it where she could watch it while, she hoped, not alerting any creatures to her presence.

Light dimmed as she moved away from the open spaces along the river's edge. The sounds of the forest changed too, as the rushing of the river was hushed by the intervening of the layers of foliage. Birds called to one another, and up above her, she heard the rustling passage of squirrels, monkeys, and other small creatures. Something very much like peace settled over her. Her father had always been right; this was what she was made for. She smiled at the familiar sounds of the tree creatures and moved deeper into the forest. She would travel only so far into the woods as she deemed she could carry a kill back; if at that point she'd still had no luck, she'd turn her deadly skills on the little animals she could see and hear and hope to take back a game sack full of them. Meat was meat whether it came in a large or small packet.

She had almost reached that turning point when she first smelled and then heard the elk. He was an old fellow, energetically and noisily enjoying scratching his hump against an overhanging branch. Like most of his kind, he was not accustomed to looking up for danger; he was a large animal, and most creatures that could threaten him would be land-bound as he was. Thymara felt almost sorry for him as she silently maneuvered her way from tree to tree until she was directly above him. She shifted, moving silently, until she had a vantage with a clear shot at him. She drew the arrow back, took a breath and held it, and then let it fly. She shot her arrow directly down, aiming for a place just behind his humped shoulders, hoping it would penetrate his rib cage and hit his lungs if not his heart. Her missile struck solidly with a sound like someone hitting a thick drum skin.

Her prey gave a sudden jerk and shuddered, as if the blow were no more than a fly landing on his coat. Then as the pain blasted through him, he fled in a staggering run down the game trail toward the river. She grinned harshly; at least he was moving in the right direction! And she followed him, keeping to the trees. She wouldn't drop down to his level until she was sure he was dead or nearly so.

He ran more and more clumsily and fell once, his front legs folding under him. She thought he was done then, but he staggered up and moved on, blowing blood from his nose and mouth as he huffed out his pain. The second time he went down, he stayed down. Knife drawn, she moved closer and then went down to him. His large brown eyes regarded her malevolently. "I'll end it," she told him. It took all her strength to drive her knife into the hollow behind the angle of his jaw. The blade punched through thick hide and muscle, but when she jerked it out, she was rewarded with leaping gouts of blood. The elk closed his eyes; each burst of blood was less than the one before, and when it slowed to a trickle, she knew he was gone. She had a moment of regret that she pushed aside. Death fed life. He was meat now, and all hers.

Skymaw would be pleased with her. But only if she got the meat back to the dragon; there was no bringing Skymaw to this kill. The thick forest and undergrowth were impenetrable for a creature the size of a dragon. The only way to get the meat back to her would be for Thymara to pack it out. She sized up the animal. She could probably drag a front leg and shoulder back on her own. Then she'd find Tats and they'd come back to cut up the rest and drag it back. Tats could take a share for Fente, and they'd have meat to share at the campfire with the other keepers. She felt a surge of pride at that thought. She doubted that anyone else would have fared as well at the hunt as she had.

The marsh elk's hide was thicker than she had bargained on. Her knife seemed small in comparison to the task and it dulled fast. Twice she had to stop and sharpen it, and each time she thought of the daylight passing. It was already dim back here in the rain forest. If she didn't get back and reclaim the rest of the meat before dark, it would be hopeless trying to find it at night. And by morning, scavengers would have reduced it to bones. Ants and buzzing insects were already trooping to the feast.

When she had finally sliced all around the tough hide and cut the meat down to the bone, she had to use every bit of strength she had to wrestle her blade into the animal's shoulder socket to get the front leg free of the carcass. It finally came loose with a suddenness that made her sit down flat on the ground, the leg half on top of her. She wiped her knife on her trouser leg and sheathed it, and then wiped her hands. She pushed sweaty hair back from her scaled brow. The scales felt tighter and more complete; they were growing. In a few months, she might not even sweat there anymore. For a moment, she wondered what she looked like, and then pushed that concern aside. There was nothing she could do to change how she looked; best not to think about it.

She pushed the leg to one side and stood up, groaning at how much her back ached. She didn't look forward to the trudge back to the riverbank through the underbrush. She glanced again at her kill. "One leg down, three to go," she said wryly.

"And the head. Don't forget the head." Greft's words warned her only a fraction of a second before he dropped down beside her, landing as lightly as a lizard. He looked at her kill and hissed in astonishment. When he lifted his eyes to her, they gleamed with admiration. "You weren't bragging when you said you were a hunter. I congratulate you, Thymara! If anyone had asked me, I would have said this was an impossible task for a girl like you."

"Thank you," she replied uncertainly. Was he complimenting her or suggesting this was a fluke? A bit testily, she added, "A bow doesn't know who pulls the string. Anyone who is strong enough and can shoot straight can bring down an animal."

"True. Undoubtedly true, as the evidence lies right here before us. All I'm saying is that I never thought of you that way before." He licked his narrow lips, and his eyes gleamed blue as he smiled. His glance was approving, but it wandered over her in a way she found unsettling. His voice was both warm and wistful. "Thymara, you have every right to be proud of this kill." He gestured at his hip. Tail feathers protruded from the game bag he carried. "I wish I could say I had fared as well as you had. But the day is winding to a close and two birds are all I have to show for it."

"We have a few hours of light left," Thymara replied. "And I'd best use them or I'll lose the meat. I'll see you back at the camp, Greft." She knelt and put a hasty wrap of line around the elk's leg just above the hoof, and then knotted it in a loop big enough to fit over her shoulder. All the while she felt him standing there, watching her silently. She thrust her arm through the loop of rope as she stood. "See you back at camp," she repeated.

But she hadn't gone two strides before he asked, "You're just leaving all the rest of the meat?"

She didn't want to look back at him, but she didn't want him to know that she felt slightly afraid of him. He was bigger than she was and heavily muscled. He had never threatened her, but the weight of his attention made her uneasy. She found that she wasn't comfortable being alone with him. The worst of it was that beneath her fear there was a darker current of attraction to him. He was handsome in a Rain Wilds–touched way. The gleam of his eyes and how even dim light shifted over his scaled countenance made her want to look at him. But how he returned her look always spoke of forbidden things. His presence stirred her in a way that was dangerous for her. Best to get away from him.

She tried to let none of that show in her eyes or sound in her voice as she said casually, "Tats and I will be coming back for it."

Greft straightened slightly and glanced quickly about the surrounding forest. "Tats is hunting with you? Where is he?"

"Tats is probably still back at the river." She shouldn't have answered his question, she thought, for it suddenly made her feel more alone. "When I tell him I've got meat, he'll come and help me with it."

Greft smiled, relaxing, but his expression only made her more tense. "Why bother? I can help you with it now. I don't mind helping you."

"I NEED TO talk to Thymara's dragon."

Alise snapped her head around, startled and annoyed at the interruption. It was so hard to get Skymaw talking. Things had been going so well, with Skymaw telling a story of someone in Kelsingra creating a fountain around a life-size sculpture of three dragons. To keep her talking, Alise had been standing beside her while the dragon rested her head on her front paws, carefully grooming the scales around her eyes. Fishing in the silty river splashed water into the dragon's eyes and ears, and when it dried, fine dust remained near her eyes. It was careful, ticklish work to remove it, one better done by human fingers than the dragon's own claws. "I beg your pardon?"

The dragon keeper stared at her for a moment. *Rapskal,* she thought. That was his name. She'd spoken to him twice before, and each time found the experience a bit unsettling. His eyes were a very light blue, and sometimes when he blinked, as he did now, the color and the faint light that came from them seemed to be one and the same. He was very handsome, in a Rain Wild way, and would be an extraordinary man. Right now, his face had that unfinished look of a youth venturing toward manhood. The jaw was shaping into firmness. His wild hair, she realized, made him look more boyish than he truly was.

Sedric spoke to the boy's silence. "Why do you need to speak to Skymaw? She was in the midst of giving Alise some very important details about Kelsingra."

"Got to find Thymara. She's going to miss out on the food."

"She's not here," Sedric said, almost patiently. He looked at the pen he was holding. He was sitting on the crate that he'd hauled down from the *Tarman* with his lap desk on his knees. The sheet of heavy paper in front of him was almost covered in his fine handwriting. Even with her having to stop to translate every word the dragon said, the session had been going well; in fact, it had been the best they had ever had. Sedric dipped his pen again and finished the sentence he'd been on. He looked up at her expectantly.

Impatience scratched at her nerves as she told the young man, "I don't know where Thymara is. Have you looked all around the encampment?"

He cocked his head at her as if she were a bit stupid. "Did that before I came here. Skymaw, please tell me where Thymara is?"

The dragon replied with a single word. "Hunting. We are busy here." She canted her head very slightly, to remind

Alise that she had been tending her. Alise went back to work on her.

"Hunting where?" Rapskal persisted.

"In the forest. Go away."

"It's a big forest." Rapskal didn't seem to have the sense not to annoy the blue dragon. Alise felt the dragon flex and knew her claws were digging into the wet mud. She distracted her. "Loose scale right here by the corner of your eye. Don't blink while I lift it away." To her surprise, Skymaw obeyed. Alise held it up on the tip of her finger, marveling at it. It was like both a fish scale and a feather. There were lines on in, possibly indicating how it had grown, but at the edge of it, it feathered into fine tendrils. It was a deep, deep blue, deeper than the best sapphire she had ever seen. She leaned forward, looking at the place it had come from, suddenly seeing how the feathered edges interlocked into a smooth surface with the following scales. "This is incredible," she breathed in awe. "Sedric, can you draw this for me?"

"I'd love to!" he replied with enthusiasm. She was startled to find that he'd set down his desk and come to stand at her shoulder. "But, to do it justice, I'd want a steady surface, a bright lamp, and my colored inks. I have all that back on the *Tarman*. Let me put it in a safe place."

He had reached out his hand for it when Skymaw's head suddenly lifted. Her tongue, long and forked just like a lizard's, was of a size commensurate with her body, and when it flicked out, it was like having a large, fleshy whip crack in the air right between Alise and Sedric. It happened so swiftly that suddenly the scale was gone, lifted deftly away from Alise's fingertip with an accuracy that astonished her.

"No!" cried Sedric, aghast.

"What is a part of me is mine." The dragon spoke sternly.

"Oh, Skymaw," Alise cried sorrowfully. "We only wanted to draw it. Part of the knowledge that I seek to collect is knowledge of your physical body. You let Sedric draw your claw yesterday." She sighed. "I would have loved to have an accurate, to size drawing of a scale."

"Scale?" Rapskal said. Alise was a bit surprised to find

he was still standing there. "Maybe I have one . . . here."
He'd bent down to brush at the rough fabric of his trousers.
When he straightened up, he was offering her a gleaming
ruby. It was substantially larger than Skymaw's blue eye-
scale, the size of a large rose petal, but no rose had ever
gleamed so scarlet. She caught her breath at the sight of it.
When she took in her hand the treasure so casually offered,
she was surprised at the heft of it. Despite the scale's size,
it was less than a small coin's weight. The growth rings and
the feathering were much more obvious than on Skymaw's
scale.

"It fell off Heeby when I was riding her today during her
flying practice. I guess my knee rubbed it off, but she said
it didn't hurt."

"Riding her? You were on a dragon's back?" She was astounded.

"That's disgusting!" Skymaw was outraged. She drew
her head up high, and for an instant Alise feared she would
strike one of them. She saw Sedric reflexively wince away.

Rapskal was unfazed. "Heeby doesn't mind. She's going
to fly pretty soon, and she doesn't want to leave me behind.
We practice every night, and I sort of watch out for rocks
and logs so she can concentrate on running and flapping."

"You are both idiots. Dragons do not run as a prelude to
flying, and we do not allow anyone to ride us. It's humiliating even to think that she does. She's a disgrace to all of us.
You are a moron and she is a half-witted lizard!"

"What did she say?" Sedric demanded.

Rapskal knotted his fists and stepped up to the dragon.
"You take that back! You can't talk about Heeby that way!
She's beautiful and smart, and she's going to fly. Because
she's brave enough to try and smart enough to know I'm
helping her because I love her."

"What is going on?" Sedric demanded in a shaky voice.

"Skymaw! Please! Restrain your wrath, beautiful queen!
He is only a foolish boy, not even worthy of your anger!"
Alise was surprised at how calm her own voice sounded as
she deliberately stepped between the incensed dragon and
her target. She had closed her fist around the precious scale,

and as she spoke, she stuffed it into her bag without looking. She kept her eyes on the dragon. Skymaw's eyes blazed
scarlet and copper like a seething kettle of molten ore. Her
immense head wove back and forth over them, reminding
her of a snake deciding whether to strike. How could she
have forgotten how huge an animal Skymaw was? One snap
of her jaws would sever the boy in two. She spoke over her
shoulder to him. "Rapskal. You should leave *now*. Thymara
isn't here. Thank you for loaning me the scale. I will be certain that it is returned to Heeby after Sedric has finished
sketching it."

"But . . ." Sedric began.

She pushed her words past him, speaking with all the
authority of an older sister. "Rapskal. Go now! If I see Thymara, I'll tell her you are looking for her. For now, do not
bother the lovely, the gracious, the most powerful and awe-
some Skymaw."

Perhaps the severity of her tone finally made him realize the danger he was in. "I'll go," he said sullenly. He
turned on his heel and strode away. But at a safe distance
he stopped and flung back at Skymaw, "Heeby is going to
fly a long time before you ever get your big blue powerful and gracious arse off the ground, Skymaw! She'll be a
real dragon long before you are, queen stick-up-your-bum!"
Then he turned and wisely ran as Skymaw hissed a furious
but venomless mist at him.

SOMEHOW, GREFT HAD moved closer to her. He stared at
her and she found herself meeting his gaze. There were blue
Rain Wild lights behind his eyes, just like her own. Something changed in his smile and in his eyes as he said in a
quieter voice, "I'd like to help you, Thymara."

"Oh, I'll just ask Tats. But thank you for offering." She
turned hastily away from him, uncomfortable with her refusal but certain that accepting his offer would make her
even more uncomfortable. She didn't want to be out here
alone with him.

He refused her dismissal of him. "It will make no difference to you or your dragon who helps you," he pointed out,

his voice hardening as he spoke to her back. "I'm here, right now. I'm stronger than Tats. Together, we can get this meat back to the dragons much more swiftly than if you go there, get him, come back here, and then start hauling it. It only makes sense that two hunters such as ourselves should help each other. Why do you prefer him to me?"

She didn't have to answer him. She didn't *want* to answer him, but the words came out anyway. "Tats and I have been friends for a long time. He used to work for my father sometimes."

"I see. You feel loyalty to him based on a shared past." A lecturing note had come into his voice. She didn't like his smile. It seemed cruel somehow. She didn't like how he assumed he had the right to talk to her in such a tone, to keep her standing here when she wanted to leave. "You and he had a bond in the past. And you think that bond still binds you. But from what I've seen going on, he doesn't feel the same. This life you are entering into now is not your past, and is nothing like your past. You are moving toward your future, Thymara. Sometimes I think you don't comprehend your own freedom now."

He moved a few steps closer to her. "You can break free of everything you've always taken for granted. You can put aside rules that bound you and kept you from thinking for yourself, rules that kept you from doing what you wanted, rules that actually kept you from doing what was best for yourself. Tats was someone your father chose, Thymara. I'm sure he's a very nice fellow in his own way, but he's not one of us and never will be. It was kind of your father to take him on and give him work after his criminal mother abandoned him. It probably kept him from becoming a thief himself. But all of that is in the past, Thymara. I am sure your father is a good man. But you are under no obligation to continue his kindness to Tats. Surely your family has already done enough for him? If he cannot take care of himself by now, then your putting more effort into him is a waste of your time. You've left your old life behind, Thymara, with your father's blessing."

He edged closer to her as he spoke. She stepped back.

He halted where he was, considering her. He looked into her face, at the set, flat line of her mouth and her narrowed eyes and turned his head slightly, as if he would cajole her. Then he smiled and shook his head slowly. "Not yet, perhaps, Thymara, but eventually. You'll see that you and I are more alike than any of the others. I'll let you take your time to discover that. We have a lot of time ahead of us."

Then he dropped down on one knee beside her fallen elk and drew his knife. Without asking her permission, he began to work on cutting free a meaty hindquarter. He kept speaking to her as he worked, his voice deep and sometimes deeper with the effort of cutting. Her anger began to build, but he didn't look at her and his words continued, his voice so reasonable. "You've struck out on your own, to build something new for yourself. As we all have! You are not established with a home and possessions like your family was. You are making your own way in the world. You are making your own future. You will need, eventually, a partner who can pull his own share. You won't always be able to waste your time with half-wits and outsiders. You cannot afford to drag deadweight with you into that new future. I know you're angry now about what I'm telling you. But I don't have to prove it to you. The Rain Wilds will do that. All I have to do is wait."

She pushed out her words and they came more forcefully than she intended. "That is my kill and my meat. Get away from it."

His knife didn't stop moving. "Thymara, haven't you heard a word I said? We need to move into the future, not cling to a past that doesn't apply to us anymore. Ask yourself honestly. Why are you so intent on running back to Tats and having him help you with this?"

"I like him. He's helped me in the past. He's my friend. If he made a kill like this, he would share it with me."

He was still sawing away with his knife. She could tell it was dulling on the thick elk hide. He glanced up at her for a moment; there was no anger in his face, only interest. "Would he? Or would he share it with Jerd? Open your eyes. You have a choice here. You could like *me*. I could help you, a lot more than Tats could, because ultimately you and I are far more alike than you and he could ever be. I could be your friend. I could be more than your friend." He lifted his eyes to meet hers. His voice went deeper and softer on the last words.

Thymara hated how she reacted, how her belly clenched and a shiver went up her back. A handsome, older man had just as much as said that he wanted her. A man, not a boy. A powerful man, one who was assuming a leadership role among the keepers. "Tats is my friend," she managed to assert. She turned, refusing to see if he would listen to her. "And that is my meat. Stay away from it." She refused to think about his words, about any of his words. *Jerd? Was there something Greft knew about Tats and Jerd that she did not? Push that thought away.* Gripping her hunting weapons in one hand, she settled the loop of rope over her shoulder and trudged away from him. He let her go with no further words. She could not move swiftly; she had to push her way through low-growing bushes and dangling branches. She tried to move from hummock to hummock, avoiding the swampiest ground. It wasn't easy.

After a short time, the rope began to chafe on her shoulder. The meat she dragged seemed to snag on every stump or root tangle she passed, and she had to give a strong jerk to break it free. By the time she saw the lighter foliage that indicated she was nearly at the river, she was sweaty, scratched, and bitten by insects. She emerged into the swale of tall, coarse river grass and pushed on toward where she had left Skymaw sleeping. She'd give her dragon the meat first, and then go find Tats to help her bring the rest back. She smiled to herself, imagining Skymaw's surprise at a second hearty meal in one day.

But when she spotted her dragon, she wasn't alone. Skymaw was awake, though she still sprawled comfortably on the deep grass. Seated near her head on a wooden box was the Bingtown woman, dressed in loose trousers and a sensible cotton blouse. Next to her Sedric perched uncomfortably on a wooden crate labeled SALT FISH. His lap desk was on his knees. Paper and ink bottle were before him; his

pen was moving swiftly over the paper. His trimly fitting
jacket was the color of a bluefly. The white shirt he wore
was open at his neck. He'd folded the cuffs of it back over
his jacket cuffs, leaving his lean wrists and capable hands
free to work. A single line marred his smooth brow. His
mouth was pursed slightly, his brows knit in concentration.
Alise was apparently dictating the next phrase. Thymara
heard ". . . crushing or severing the spine to kill it quickly."

As she scented the meat, Skymaw's head turned and
she lunged to her feet. That motion caused both Sedric and
Alise to turn toward Thymara. Skymaw gave her no greeting but simply took three strides and then fell onto the meat
and began feeding. Alise's mouth went into an "O" of surprise and then she laughed merrily, as if watching a favorite
child indulge in a sweet. "She's hungry again!" she called to
Thymara, as if expecting the girl to share her pleasure.

"She's always hungry," Thymara replied, trying not
to sound sour. She felt an echo of assent from the feeding
dragon. Sedric, at least, looked happy to see her. His eyes lit,
and his pursed lips became a welcoming smile.

"I'm so glad you're finally here. I looked everywhere for
you earlier. This process will go a lot faster if you translate."

She hated to disappoint him. "I can't. I mean, I only
brought part of the meat back with me. I have to find Tats
and have him help me with the rest before scavengers take
it." She tried not to imagine that a two-legged scavenger was
already hacking off parts of her kill. *He wouldn't dare,* she
told herself. They were too small a company for anyone to
steal openly from another. No one would tolerate it.

Would they?

Sedric had said something else. He was looking at her
expectantly, waiting for a reply. The twist of anxiety in her
belly made her suddenly dismiss him and his concerns. "I
have to find Tats and go back for the rest of the meat," she
said hastily, and she refused even to wonder if that answered
his question at all. She left them and headed toward the
shore and the other dragons.

Behind her, Alise called out to her, "Rapskal is looking
for you!"

Thymara nodded and kept on going.

Tats was not with Fente. The small green dragon was still dozing, and when Thymara tried to rouse her to ask if she knew where Tats was, the creature made a sincere snap in her direction. Thymara jumped back uninjured and left her quickly. She wondered uneasily if the dragon would have eaten her if she'd drawn blood. She knew from Skymaw that the green queen had a reputation for being vicious when provoked. It was something she should talk to Tats about. If she could find him.

She found him and Sylve with the little silver dragon. Guilt tinged with annoyance suffused Thymara. She'd said she would care for the silver and Sylve had said she'd help. She'd only spoken out because Tats and Jerd had said they'd team up on the copper one. But she'd done little more than to check him for parasites around his eyes and nostrils each night. She hadn't even thought to offer him some of the meat she'd brought back. Sylve was fussing over his tail. Nearby, a little fire smoldered reluctantly on a tussock of grass. A pot of foul-smelling soup had been set on it.

"How is he?" she asked uncomfortably as she approached.

"It's as we feared," Sylve said. "It looks like he let his tail dip below the surface of the river water, and more than once by the look of it. The cut is inflamed." She opened the cloth she'd been trying to wrap around the injury, and Thymara winced. She wondered if her earlier ministrations hadn't done him more harm than good. It must have been painful when the raw flesh met the acid river. She frowned: she couldn't recall hearing him cry out. On a positive note, the dragon was sleeping heavily; from the scraps of gut under his front claws, he had evidently got at least a share of the fish run.

"I wish there were a way to seal the bandaging around his tail to keep the water out," she said hopelessly.

Tats grinned at her. "Maybe there is. I asked Captain Leftrin for some tar or pitch, and he gave me a little pot of it. It's heating now. He gave us canvas, too." His grin grew wider. "I think Captain Leftrin likes that Bingtown woman.

When I was asking for the stuff, I thought he was going to tell me to shove off. But that woman, that Alise, got all fluttery about the 'poor little dragon' and the captain came up with a solution pretty fast."

"Oh," she said. Sylve was nodding approvingly at what Tats said.

"The captain said we should wrap it well, and then tar over the canvas and over his scales to either side. We're hoping that it will stick to his scales well enough to make a watertight bond."

The sheer strangeness of such a patch drove, for a moment, all other concerns out of her head. She stared at Tats. "Do you think it will work?"

He shrugged and grinned. "Nothing to lose by trying. I think the tar is warm enough. I don't want to burn him. In fact, I hope to do this without waking him up."

"How did you get involved in this?"

Sylve answered. "I asked him." Despite the scaling on her face, a blush rosed her cheeks. "I had to," she added defensively. "I couldn't find you, and I didn't know what to do for him." She looked down at the dragon's injured tail. "So I went to find Tats."

As plainly as if she had spoken the words aloud, Thymara saw that the girl was infatuated with the tattooed boy. It almost made her laugh, except that it was so disturbing. Sylve could not have been more than twelve, even if her pink-scaled scalp and copper eyes made her seem older. Didn't she know how hopeless it was for a girl like her to have a crush on someone like Tats? She could never have him; she could never have anyone, any more than Thymara could. What was she thinking?

But Thymara knew the answer to that, too. She wasn't thinking at all. Only yearning after a handsome young man who'd shown her kindness and made nothing of her differences. Thymara couldn't fault her. Hadn't she felt the same, sometimes?

Didn't she now?

She must have been looking at him strangely, because Tats suddenly flushed and said, "I wanted to help. There wasn't much I could do for the little copper one anyway. So I decided to put my time here."

"What's wrong with the copper?"

The grin had faded from Tats's face. "The same things that have been wrong with him since he hatched. He's dull-witted. And his body doesn't work very well. I cleared a load of parasites from around his eyes and nose and, uh, other places. He didn't even stir. I think he's just exhausted from trying to keep up with the others today. I can't even find out if he's hungry. He's that dead tired."

The words echoed through her like a prophecy. "I killed an elk," she blurted out.

In the shocked silence that followed her words, she quickly added, "I need help to bring the meat back. There would be some for each of our dragons, and some for us keepers, too. But we'd have to leave soon if we want to get back to camp before dark. It's going to take us several trips back and forth to get it here."

Tats looked at the tar pot and then at Sylve's face. "We've got to finish this first," he decided. "Then maybe Sylve and some of the others would help us go for the meat. That way we'd only have to make one trip."

"The more people, the less meat for each dragon," she pointed out bluntly.

Tats looked surprised that she'd think of it that way. She was surprised that he'd think of it any other way. For a long moment, the silence held. Then Sylve said quietly, "I can do the silver's tail alone. You can go get your meat."

Thymara relented. "Let's just get it done and then we'll all go."

Sylve kept her eyes down and her child's voice thickened as she said, "Thank you. Mercor made a kill today and he didn't complain of hunger, but I don't think it really satis-fied him. I tried to fish, but the boys had the best places all staked out. When Captain Leftrin said that there would be a serving of meat portioned out to each dragon tomorrow morning, I hoped it would be enough for him."

"Well, let's get this dragon patched up and then we'll go fetch meat for the others," Thymara surrendered.

The heat had loosened the tar. Sylve and Thymara held the bandage firm around the silver dragon's tail while Tats daubed the tar on with a stick. He worked carefully, and to Thymara it seemed that it took an age before the entire bandage was well covered with tar and sealed to the dragon's thick tail. The silver, thank Sa, hadn't even fluttered an eyelid. That thought gave her a moment's concern. The two least-capable dragons seemed more exhausted every day. How long could they keep up this pace? What would happen to them when they could not? She had no answer to that. She forced her mind back to today's problem.

Tats could almost keep up with her as she led them through the forest, moving through the trees rather than on the ground. Sylve trailed him, but not by much. It was easy to find the way back; she just watched for the trail she had made dragging the meat back to Skymaw. She judged they were about halfway there when she heard voices below her. She moved down the tree trunk, her heart sinking. Her worst fears were realized. Greft was below her. He was dragging a hindquarter of her elk. Behind him came Boxter and Kase. Boxter had the other front leg of the elk, and Kase had taken part of a hind leg but not the full quarter. They were chattering about something to one another, their voices full of triumph when she dropped out of her tree and into the path before them. Greft stopped short in front of her.

She didn't mince words. "What do you think you're doing with my kill?"

She heard Tats coming quickly down the tree. So did Greft. He looked up to watch Tats's descent, his face deceptively mild. "I'm taking it back to the dragons. Isn't that what you intended?" He managed to put a mild rebuke into his voice.

"I intended to take it back to *my* dragon. Not yours."

He didn't reply right away. He gave time for Tats to reach the ground and take a stance behind Thymara. There was a shower of twigs, a brief shriek, and then a thud as Sylve half fell and half slid the rest of the way down. Once she was there, Greft glanced up at the tree, as if to assure himself that this was the whole of their party. Behind him,

Boxter and Kase had halted. Boxter looked confused, Kase defiant.

Greft's eyes roved over them. He seemed to be making a mental tally of who they were and how each could best be played, as if he were studying a game board. When he spoke, his voice was calm, his words reasonable. "You took a quarter of the kill for your dragon and left the rest here. You told me you were going to go get Tats. But I knew from looking at it that there was more than you and Tats could haul back in a single trip. Even recruiting Sylve doesn't change that! So I went back, got Boxter and Kase, and started in on the work. I don't understand why you seem to be upset, Thymara. Isn't this what Tats advocated, quite some time back? Surely that is what you told me, that you'd give a share to those who helped bring the meat back. It seemed fair to me."

She stood her ground. "That isn't what I said. I said I intended to get Tats, and that he and I would haul *my* kill back to our dragons. I intended to keep back some of the meat for the other keepers to eat tonight. But I didn't offer to share my kill with you, or with your friends."

Greft looked surprised, almost hurt. "But surely we're all friends here, Thymara! We are too small a company not to be. You told me yourself, at the campfire one evening, that you'd never before had friends such as you had now! I thought you meant it."

Tats was silent behind her. She didn't want to look back at him; he'd think she was seeking his guidance. Nor did she want to see Sylve's face right now. Surely they could see how Greft was twisting everything? Wanting to take care of her friends first was not selfishness. Speak plainly and all would be right. She took a breath. "I killed that elk by myself, Greft. And I decide who I'll share the meat with. I chose Tats. And Sylve, because she helped me. I didn't choose you, or Boxter, or Kase. And you can't have the meat."

Greft made a show of looking at the sky. He couldn't see it through the canopy, but all of them knew that evening would soon plunge them into darkness. "You'd rather let the meat rot or be eaten by scavengers than let us have some of it? There's still more than half an elk there, Thymara, more than you three can haul back in one trip, I'll wager. And you haven't time to make another trip. Be sensible, not selfish. It hurts you nothing to share this. Boxter's dragon didn't make a kill today, and Kase's got a fish, but not a big one. They're hungry."

She knew she should choose her words carefully, but she was so angry at how he was making it seem. "Then they should go hunting for meat for their dragons, just as I did! Not wait and take mine! I've a dragon to feed, too, you know. In fact, I've two dragons to feed."

"And both of them were sleeping with bulging bellies when last I saw them," Greft replied smoothly.

"Mine isn't!" Sylve blurted out suddenly. "Mercor has fed, but not well, even though he is too brave and noble to complain. And Tats's little copper fellow probably got nothing at all. He needs meat, not this argument! Please, can't we just take the meat back to the camp and settle it there?"

"That seems wisest to me," Greft abruptly agreed. He glanced back at Kase and Boxter. "Do you both agree?"

Boxter nodded. Kase, his copper eyes gleaming in the gathering gloom, hunched his shoulders. Greft turned back to Thymara. "Then it's all settled. We'll see you when you get back to the river."

"It's not all settled!" Thymara snarled, but Tats put a warm hand on her shoulder. She felt the weight of it, but she wondered if he was reassuring her that he was with her or holding her back from what he regarded as foolishness. He spoke past her to Greft.

"It will be all settled when we get back to the river. We all know night is coming on and we can't waste time in arguing right now. But it's not all settled, Greft. I agree that meat should be shared, but not the way you're doing it."

Greft's narrow lips moved. It might have been a smile or a sneer. "Of course, Tats. Of course. We'll see you back at the river." He suddenly leaned into the load he was pulling, and Thymara found herself stepping aside, back into the pressing brush behind her, to allow him to pass. Boxter and Kase came behind him, and both of them were plainly grinning. Kase spoke in a low voice as he passed her. "Only fair to get a share of meat if you've done work for it," he observed.

"No one asked you to do any work!" she growled after him. He kept walking. "It's like paying a thief because he worked hard to rob your house!" She raised her voice to hurl the words after him.

"No! It's like giving your workers a share of the harvest!" he shouted back. She drew breath to point out that merely taking the harvest was not working for it when Tats spoke again. She realized then that he'd never let go of her shoulder, for he tightened his grip on her as he said, "Not now, Thymara. Focus on the most important thing. We need to get that meat back to the river before nightfall. And before the insects get any worse."

"Parasites!" she snarled after them, and then turned away. "The meat is this way. Or what's left of it!" She strode angrily through the forest.

Tats was right. The stinging little pests had already begun to swarm around them. Biting insects were never absent in the Rain Wilds, but the evening always brought them out in droves. Well, at least the thieves had broken a better trail for them to follow. She wanted to rant and rave as she thudded along but saved her breath.

When they reached the carcass, she heard the small sounds of several little scavengers scampering away. The smallest ones, the ants and beetles, had already flocked to the feast and were undeterred by the arrival of the humans. They swarmed over the elk's body, congregating in black, shimmering masses wherever the raw flesh was exposed.

Tats had thought to bring a small hatchet. It was messy, for the blade flung blood and bits of meat on every swing, but between it and her knife they cut the rest of the elk into manageable hunks much faster than she could have done alone. She grumbled as she did so. Greft and his cohorts had taken the most manageable parts of the elk. They cut the head and neck free, and then divided the trunk into the rib cage and haunches. It stank as they cut through the torso. The guts would spill and string; there was nothing they could do about it. They could have left them, but Thymara knew that to the dragons they were a delicacy.

Tats had brought more rope as well. It was almost annoying to think of how well prepared he always seemed to be. They spoke little, working swiftly. Thymara tried to focus on what she was doing rather than let her simmering anger interfere. Tats was his quiet, competent self, limiting his words to conversation about the task at hand. Sylve hung back on the edges of the operation, stepping in to help whenever she was asked, but keeping silent in a way that began to bother Thymara. She wondered if the blood and stink bothered the girl.

"Sylve, are you all right? You know, some people just can't do this kind of thing. It makes them sick. If you need to step back from it, just say so."

She saw Sylve give her head a shake, sending her hanks of hair flying wildly around her pink scalp. She had a strange look on her face, as if she didn't want to be there but couldn't bring herself to leave.

"I think," Tats said, between grunts as he fastened rope harnesses to each chunk of meat, "that Greft's arguments . . . made Sylve uncomfortable. She's wondering—hold that while I tie this knot, would you?—if you resent her taking a share of the meat."

The girl turned her face aside abruptly, her hurt so obvious that it smote Thymara. "Sylve! Of course not! I invited you to come and help with this, and of course you deserve some of the meat. I said I'd take care of the silver, and instead that task fell to you. Even if you hadn't come, if you told me that your dragon needed meat, I'd help you. You know that."

Sylve lifted bloodstained hands to wipe her cheeks before turning back to Thymara. Thymara winced. She knew that when you were that far along in being scale-faced, it hurt when you cried. Sylve sniffed. "You said they were thieves," she said thickly. "Well, how am I different?"

"It's different because you didn't take it without asking! It's different because you were helping me with the silver dragon for no other reason than that is how you are. It's different because you put in before you take out. Those three don't care anything about any dragons but their own."

Sylve lifted the front edge of her tunic to dab at her messy face. She spoke from its shelter. "How is that different from us? We're only talking about feeding our own dragons."

"But that was the deal!" Thymara almost exploded. "That was the agreement that each of us signed. Each of us said we'd be responsible for a dragon. And here we are, *we* each have *two* to worry about. Without some ignorant louts coming in and poaching our hard-earned meat. Well, they're not going to get away with it!" As she'd spoken, Thymara had slid her arms into the makeshift harness that Tats had created. She had the front end of the carcass with the rib cage. Tats had taken the heavy hindquarter for himself. Without saying a word, they'd agreed that little Sylve could drag the head and neck back. It was lighter than what they were hauling, but still not an easy load to get back to the river through all the brush and swamp.

"Actually, I think it's likely they will." Tats spoke as he leaned into his load and followed her. Sylve came last of all, getting the advantage of the broken trail through the brush.

"Will what?"

"Will get away with it. What we were just talking about. Greft and Kase and Boxter will get away with taking your meat."

"No, they won't! Not when I tell everyone!"

"By the time we get back, they will have told everyone the story their way. And it will seem to everyone who didn't get a kill for their dragon today that it would only be sensible for you to share with everyone." He added something else in a softer voice.

"What?" she demanded, halting to look back at him.

"I said," he said defiantly, his ears turning a bit pink, "that in some ways it would be only sensible."

"What? What are you saying? That I should do all the work of hunting and making a kill, and then just give it away to everyone else?"

"Keep pulling. Night's coming on. Yes, that *is* what I'm saying. Because you're a good hunter, probably the best we have. If you were free to hunt, and everyone else had to do the butchering and hauling the meat, you'd be able to get a lot more prey. And all the dragons would have a better chance of a real meal."

"But Skymaw would get less! A lot less. She should have had almost half an elk today. Your way, she'd get one-fifteenth. She'd starve on that!"

"She'd get one-fifteenth of what everyone caught. I think you may be our best hunter, but you're not our only one. Think about it, Thymara. There is you, and the three professional hunters, and some of the rest of us are not too bad at fishing and small game. Each dragon would be almost certain of getting at least something to eat every night."

She was sweating now as she dragged the meat through the forest. It was getting dark, and the mosquitoes and gnats had found her. She swiped angrily at her brow and then slapped the back of her neck, crushing half a dozen of the persistent bloodsuckers. "I can't believe you're taking Greft's side," she observed bitterly.

"I'm not. I'm taking my side. Basically, it's the deal you were ready to offer me, only expanded to include everyone."

She went on silently pulling her load, pushing her way past leaning branches and gritting her teeth every time she missed her footing and plunged ankle deep in muck. She was stingingly aware that Sylve could hear every word. She couldn't just say to Tats that it was different, that he was her friend and her ally and she didn't mind sharing with him. Not that she minded sharing with Sylve tonight; the girl had done her best to take care of the injured silver dragon. In a way, Thymara supposed that she was her partner now, since they'd both agreed to do what they could for the creature. In another moment, she became uncomfortably aware that she knew Sylve had only the smallest chance of keeping even one dragon alive, let alone volunteering to help with the silver, too. Maybe she owed the girl her help. She didn't like the way that idea jabbed her. She didn't want anyone depending on her, let alone have someone that she owed help to. And what about Rapskal? If he asked her for meat for his runty little Heeby, would she say no? He partnered with her every day in her boat, and he always did at least half the work there. So what did she owe him? Tats spoke at just the wrong moment.

"You want me to take the lead for a while?"

"No," she replied curtly. No, she didn't want anyone doing anything for her. Because who knew what she would owe them then?

He should have known better than to say anything more. But a few moments later, he asked in a low voice, "So, what are you going to do when we get back to camp?"

She'd been pondering that question herself. Having him poke her with it didn't help her indecision. "What if I did nothing? Would that make me a coward?"

He was quiet for a time. She slapped mosquitoes on the back of her neck and brushed her hands wildly over her ears, trying to drive them and their persistent buzzing away. "I think you'd be doing the sensible thing," he said quietly.

It surprised Thymara when Sylve spoke. "He'll make you look selfish if you say anything. Turn everyone against you. Like he did with Tats that night. Saying he wasn't one of us." The girl was huffing and puffing. Her words came in short bursts. Thymara was rapidly realizing that Sylve was not the little girl she had thought she was. She was younger, but she listened and she thought about what she heard. "Ouch! Stupid branch!" she complained abruptly and then went on, "Greft is like that. He can seem so nice, but there's a mean part of him. He talks like he wants good things for everyone. Changes, he says. But then he has those other times. And you see that he has a mean part of him. He scares me. He talked to me once, for a long time, and, well, sometimes I think that if I stay away from him, that's the safest thing to do. Other times I think that if I don't find a way to be one of his friends, that will be the most dangerous thing."

Silence fell except for their breathing, the sounds of their loads bumping and dragging, and the normal night sounds of the forest. Insects buzzed all around Thymara's head, almost as maddening as the thoughts buzzing inside her head. Thymara wondered just what Greft had said to Sylve in their "talk." She feared she knew, and she felt fresh outrage. Tats broke their mutual reverie. "I'm scared of him for the same reasons. And one other. He has plans. He's not just a fellow taking on a bad job for money or because it looks like an adventure. He's thinking something about all this."

Thymara nodded. "He says he wants to make a place where he can change the rules."

For a time, they plodded on in silence, each pondering this. At last Tats said softly, "Rules exist for a reason."

"We don't have any rules," Sylve interjected.

"Of course we do!" Thymara objected.

"No, we don't. Back home, there were our parents. And the Rain Wild Council, and the Traders, each with a vote to say what got done or didn't happen. But we left all that behind. We signed contracts, but who is really in charge? Not Captain Leftrin. He's only in charge of the boat, not us or the dragons. So who says what the rules are? Who enforces them?"

"The rules are what they've always been," Thymara replied doggedly, but she had an uneasy feeling that the girl was seeing things more clearly than she was. When Greft spoke of making changes, what could he be talking about except changing the rules they'd accepted all their lives? But he couldn't do that. Could he?

There was light breaking through the trees ahead of them, the fading evening light of the Rain Wild Forest. Somehow her legs found the strength to pick up their pace.

"Hey! Hey! Where have you been? I was starting to get worried about you all! The hunters came in and brought a whole load of riverpigs. You should see, Thymara! There's a whole one cooking on a spit for all to share, and the dragons got half a pig each. Hey! What you dragging? Did you kill something?"

It was Rapskal, jumping and hopping as if he were a boy half his age. He stopped dead when he reached Thymara, staring at the meat she was dragging. "What was that thing?"

"An elk," she replied shortly.

"An elk. That's big! You were lucky, I guess. Greft got one, too. He said he brought the meat back to share with

everyone, but it was all dirty and beat up and then the hunters brought the riverpig and started building a big fire, so
Greft's elk got fed to one of the dragons. Oh, you should
come and see Heeby! She ate so much today, she looks like
a stomach with a dragon wrapped around it. She snores
when she's full. You got to hear her to believe it!" Rapskal
laughed joyously. He clapped Thymara on the shoulder.
"Glad you're back, because I'm starving. I didn't want to eat
until I found you and made sure you got a share, too!"

They had emerged from the forest onto the muddy bank
of tall reeds. Well, they had been tall when Thymara had
last left. The activities of the dragons and their keepers had
trampled most of them flat now. From where they stood, the
barge with its welcoming lamps was easily visible. A campfire was burning; silhouetted against the flames was a large
spit threaded with chunks of riverpig. Tats sniffed apprecia-
tively and as if in response his stomach rumbled. They all
laughed. The knot of Thymara's anger loosened. She wondered if she could just let it go. If she did, would that mean
Greft had won something from her?

"Let's go and eat!" Rapskal urged them.

"Soon," Thymara promised him. "First, this meat needs
to go to any dragon who is still hungry. And we should check
on Tats's copper dragon. He said he wasn't eating much."

"Well, I'm going to head down to the fire. I only left it to
come and find you all. Hey, one of the hunters plays harp,
that Carson, and there's a woman from the barge who plays
a pipe, and earlier they were playing some music together.
So we might have music after we eat, too. Even dancing, if
the mud lets us." He stopped suddenly, and a slow wide grin
spread across his face. "Isn't this just the best time ever in
your life?"

"Go enjoy it, Rapskal," Tats urged him.

Rapskal looked at Thymara. "I'm starving," he admitted,
but then asked, "You're coming soon, aren't you?"

"Of course I am. Go and eat."

He needed no other prompting. He left them at a run.
Thymara watched his fleeing shadow as he rejoined the
keepers clustered around the fire. She heard a shout of laugh-

ter go up at someone's comment. A chunk of driftwood was thrown on the fire and a dazzling fountain of sparks flew up into the darkening sky.

"It could be a wonderful time," Sylve said quietly. "Tonight, with talk and food and music."

Thymara sighed and surrendered. "I won't ruin it, Sylve. I'm not going to say anything to anyone about the elk meat and Greft tonight. I'd just sound argumentative and selfish. Here we are tonight, our first night with plenty of food and music. My quarrel with Greft will wait for another time."

"That isn't what I meant," the girl said hastily.

But when she didn't say what she had meant, Tats filled in with, "Let's take this meat to the dragons and go join the others by the fire."

Skymaw was sleeping soundly, her belly distended. Fente roused, claimed the meat that Tats had brought, but then fell asleep with her chin on top of it. Mercor was awake. The gold dragon was standing alone, staring toward the fire and the keepers when they found him. He seemed pleased that Sylve had brought him meat. He thanked her for it, something that astonished Thymara, and then satisfied them all by immediately devouring the head and neck portion of the elk. His great jaws and sharp teeth made nothing of the animal's skull. He closed his mouth on it and the elk's head gave with a wet crushing sound. They left him chewing and went off in search of the copper dragon.

They found him not far from the silver one. The silver was sleeping, his bandaged tail curled around a distended belly. The copper sprawled near him. But his posture didn't look right to Thymara. Tats voiced it. "He looks like he just fell down rather than curled up to sleep." Alone of the dragons, he looked thin and empty. His head was cushioned on his front feet. He was breathing huskily, his eyes half closed. "Hey, Copper," Tats said softly. The dragon didn't react to him. He put his hand on the dragon's head and scratched gently around his earholes. "He seemed to like this earlier," Tats explained. The dragon made a small huffing sound but didn't budge.

Thymara dragged the elk section around and halted with

it right in front of the copper. "You hungry?" she asked the small dragon and found herself deliberately pushing the thought at him. "There's meat here. All for you. Elk. Smell it? Smell the blood?"

He took a deeper breath. His eyes opened wider. He licked timidly at the meat, and then lifted his head. "There you go. Meat for you," Tats encouraged him. Thymara thought she felt an echo of response from him. Tats knelt by the elk and drew his belt knife. He scored the meat several times. Finally, he sheathed his knife and reached up inside the rib cage of the elk. He pulled at the guts and then smeared his bloody hand across the dragon's snout. "There. You smell that? That's meat for you. Eat it."

The dragon's tongue moved, cleaning his muzzle. Then a shudder ran over him. Tats pulled his hand back just in time as the dragon darted his head in to seize a mouthful of the dangling entrails. He made small snorting sounds as he ate, and he seemed to gain strength with each mouthful. By the time they left him, he had his front feet braced on the elk carcass and was tearing free mouthfuls of meat and bone. He appeared to be gulping them down whole.

"Well, at least he's eating now," Thymara commented as they walked away from him toward the fire. The smell of the roasting meat was making her mouth water. She was suddenly extremely hungry and very tired.

"You don't think he's going to survive, do you?" Tats accused her.

"I don't know. I don't know about any of the dragons."

"My Mercor is going to live," Sylve declared earnestly. "He's come too far and through too much to die on the journey."

"I hope you're right," Thymara agreed comfortingly.

"I know I am," Sylve insisted. "He told me so."

"I wish my dragon talked to me like that," Thymara said enviously.

Before Sylve could respond, Rapskal appeared out of the darkness. His face shone with grease, and a thick slab of meat was in his hands. "I brought this for you, Thymara. You have to try this! It's so good!"

"We're coming," Tats assured him.

"Captain Leftrin says we all get to sleep on his deck to-night, too!" Rapskal told them. "Dry bed, hot food—what could make this night better?"

At the circle around the fire, music as sudden and bright as sparks suddenly burst up into the night.

✧ ✧ ✧

Day the 2nd of the Prayer Moon

Year the 6th of the Independent Alliance of Traders

From Erek, Keeper of the Birds, Bingtown
To Detozi, Keeper of the Birds, Trehaug

Detozi,

Apologies for any difficulties you've experienced recently. Am sending a hundredweight sack of the yellow peas. Keep them from damp, as once wet, they spoil quickly. Always feed them dry to your birds. In the same shipment, I am sending two well-fledged youngsters, both of Kingsly's line, a male and a female.

Erek

✧ ✧ ✧

CHAPTER SEVENTEEN

DECISIONS

For three days, their journey upriver had gone better than Leftrin could ever have hoped. Their start had been a bit rough, true, but things had smoothed out soon enough. The dragons had made their own first kill, and that had certainly wrought a change in the beasts. They were still dependent on what the hunters and their keepers killed for them, but now that the dragons knew that they could kill, they attempted to hunt every day. Their successes were uneven, but any food they caught and killed for themselves lessened the burden on their human companions. Their young keepers praised them lavishly for each kill, and the dragons basked in the adulation.

He leaned on Tarman's railing, listening to his ship and the river that caressed it. His rough hands cradled a heavy mug of morning tea. From the small sounds his keen ears picked up from Alise's compartment, he knew she was awake and dressing. He would not let his mind dwell on the details of that process. No sense in tormenting himself. Soon enough, he hoped, she would emerge. They were both early risers, and he cherished these dawn moments almost more than he enjoyed their evenings of companionable conversation. Evenings were wonderful, with food and laughter and music, but he always had to share her with the hunters and the ever-present Sedric. When Bellin played her pipes and Carson the harp, Alise had eyes only for the two of them. Jess, much to Carson's chagrin, had proven himself to be every bit as good a hunter as Leftrin's old friend. He also, it seemed to Leftrin, had an eye for Alise. The fellow was a wonderful storyteller, for his dour expression concealed an ability to make himself the butt of every tale, and to win laughter from everyone, even sour Sedric. The evenings were made pleasant with song and story, but he had to share Alise's attention.

In the mornings he had her to himself, for his crew had already learned to avoid any but the most pressing of questions during those hours. He took a short breath, sighed, and found himself smiling. Truth be told, he even enjoyed the anticipation of waiting for her.

Last night's campsite had not been as wet as the previous ones, and he'd felt no qualms about suggesting that the keepers could sleep ashore with their dragons. In some wild flood rage years ago the river had swept gravel and sand into a compact beach. Tall grass and young trees grew there, creating an unusually sunny woodland for the keepers and their dragons to enjoy. As the years passed, the trees would grow taller until this was just another part of the rain forest. *Or,* he thought, *the next storm flood might sweep it away completely.* For now, he looked out on a grassy sward that was just slightly above the level of the river. The dragons sprawled there, sleeping heavily. Their keepers were scattered among them, rolled in their blue blankets. The remnants of last night's driftwood cook fire sent a thin tendril of bluish smoke toward a deep blue sky. As of yet, none of them was stirring.

Both dragons and keepers had changed mightily in the short time he had known them. The keepers had stopped being a mismatched conglomeration and were starting to form a cohesive community. Most of the time they were exuberant, the boys brash and wild. They splashed one another, challenged one another, laughed and shouted as only boys teetering on the edge of manhood do. Even in the short time of their journey the boys were building muscle from the daily paddling. The girls were less noisy and exhibitionist about the changes they were going through, but the signs were there all the same. The boys vied for their attention, and sometimes the rivalries grew rough indeed. And the girls seemed, like the dragons, to bask in the boys' attention. They preened and flirted, albeit in very different ways.

Sylve was still little more than a child. She'd obviously set her heart on winning Tats's attention. She trailed behind him like a toy on a string. Yesterday, she'd braided flowers into her hair, as if their scarlet glory could hide her pink-scaled scalp. Leftrin gave the young man credit. He was kind to her, but kept her at a proper arm's length, as he should with a girl so young.

In contrast, Jerd seemed to hourly change her mind as to which young man she fancied. Greft courted her in a desultory way. Leftrin had watched him draw his boat alongside hers and endeavor to win her attention with conversation. But during the day's passage Jerd seemed focused not only on making good time to keep up with the dragons that preceded them, but in filling her small boat with as many fish as she could catch. She was dedicated to Veras, grooming her each evening until the small green dragon's gold stippling looked like a sparkling of nuggets on a dark green cloth. In the evenings, when the herders gathered around a riverbank fire, Jerd sat with the other girls and let the young men compete to see who could take the spot next to her. It made Leftrin smile to watch them, even as he wondered uneasily where it might lead.

He had never had much to do with folk born so heavily touched by the Rain Wilds. Most of them were given back to the forest on the day of their birth, for the Rain Wild

Traders had long recognized that those who were born so
deformed would either break their parents' hearts with their
early deaths, or give rise to a second generation of deformed
children who never survived. The Rain Wilds were a harsh
place. It was better to let go of an infant immediately and try
for a new pregnancy than to pour love and food into a child
who would never live long enough to carry on the family
line. The recent influx of the Tattooed folk had brought fresh
life to the Rain Wild population, but for decades before that,
their birth rates had only marginally exceeded their death
rates.

Alise had still not appeared. On the riverbank, Lecter
had arisen. Cloaked in his blanket, he'd wandered over
to the coals of the fire and was feeding it the ends of last
night's wood. A tiny flame leaped up and the boy crouched,
holding out his hands to it. Warken came to join him, rubbing his eyes and scratching at his scaled neck. His skin
had taken on a coppery glint over the last few days, as if
he would complement his red dragon. He greeted Lecter
warmly. Lecter said something that made Warken laugh, a
hearty boy's laugh that came clearly to Leftrin's ears.

As Leftrin watched the youths who should have been
discarded as infants, he almost doubted the wisdom of the
old ways. They seemed vigorous enough, if strange to look
upon. He wished them well, boys and girls alike, and yet he
hoped he would not see romance blossom. Allowing such
folk to breed would go against every Rain Wild tradition.
So far, he had seen no indication that any of the girls would
allow such a transgression. He hoped it would remain so,
even as he uneasily wondered if he had any responsibility
to enforce the Rain Wild rules against them mating. "Well,
Tarman, no one told me that was part of the contract. I
know it's everyone's duty to honor the rules that keep us
alive. But my grandpa used to tell me that everyone's job
was nobody's job. So maybe I won't be blamed if I don't
take that task on."

There was no response from his ship. He hadn't expected
one. The sun was warm and the river gentle here. Tarman
seemed to be enjoying the brief respite as much as his cap-

tain was. Leftrin glanced again toward Alise's compartment. Patience. Patience. She was a lady, and a lady took her
time readying herself every morning before she emerged to
face the day. The effect was worth it.

He heard a sound behind him and turned to wish her
good morning. The welcoming words died on his lips.
Sedric, polished as ever, was pacing quietly over the deck
toward him. Leftrin watched him come, caught between
envy and loathing. Sedric's hair was impeccably combed,
his shirt white, his trousers brushed, and his boots clean. He
was freshly shaven and a faint spicy scent rode the morning
air. He was the worst sort of rival that a man could imagine. Not only was he immaculately groomed every day, his
manners were impeccable. Compared with him, Leftrin felt
swinish and ignorant. And hence the loathing he felt for
him. Whenever they were both in Alise's presence, she must
compare the two of them, and Leftrin must always be lacking in her gaze. That alone was enough reason to hate the
man. But there was more.

Sedric's unfailing courtesy to Leftrin and his men could
not camouflage the contempt he held them in. Leftrin had
seen it before; every ship rat had. There would always be
certain people who saw a sailor and immediately tarred him
with the poor reputation that seamen traditionally had. After
all, weren't all sailors drunken, ignorant louts? Once aboard
the vessel, that disdain often broke down, as the passenger
realized that Leftrin and his men, though rough and unedu-
cated in some ways, were savvy and competent in what they
did. Passengers came to see the sort of brotherhood that existed on a ship, and often their initial disdain turned to envy
before the voyage was over.

But he could already tell that Sedric would not be one
of those. The man clung to his superior position and poor
opinion of Leftrin as if it were the only piece of wreckage
floating after a storm. But the stiff expression and cold gaze
he offered Leftrin now were not based on his generalized
opinion of sailors. Leftrin set his jaw. This dandy looked determined to have a word with him, man to man. The captain
took another mouthful of his coffee and stared out at the

shore. More and more of the keepers were beginning to stir. Soon it would be time to get under way. He'd get no private conversation with Alise today, only more words with Sedric than he'd enjoy.

He'd found his way to the railing. "Good morning, Captain." His tone said that he doubted it.

"Morning, Sedric. Sleep well?"

"Actually, no, I didn't."

Leftrin suppressed a sigh. He should have known that the man would seize on any pleasantry and use it as a pry bar to open a way for his complaint. Leftrin responded, "That so?" and took another drink from his coffee. It was still a bit too hot, but he suddenly decided to finish it as rapidly as he could and then use getting a refill as an excuse for walking away from the man.

"Yes, that is so," Sedric replied, almost mockingly, adding an aristocratic enunciation to the words.

Leftrin took another gulp of his coffee and decided to attack. He was certain he'd regret it, but not as much as he'd regret just standing here and taking Sedric's guff. "You ought to try hard work. Helps a man sleep."

"Perhaps you should try having a clean conscience. But perhaps you slept well despite lacking one."

"I've got nothing on my conscience," Leftrin lied.

Sedric looked like a cat about to spit. He'd huffed up his shoulders. "Then ignoring a woman's marriage vows doesn't bother you?"

He couldn't let those words go unanswered. He turned to face Sedric, feeling his own shoulders and neck begin to swell. Sedric didn't step back, but he saw him shift his weight, to be ready to move quickly. Leftrin forced himself to speak calmly. "You are insulting a lady who doesn't deserve your contempt. Alise hasn't done anything to violate her marriage vows. I haven't tried to persuade her to do anything wrong. So I think you'd best rethink what you just said. Words like that can do big damage."

Sedric narrowed his eyes but spoke calmly. "My words are based on what I've seen. I've a deep affection for Alise, based on a lengthy friendship. I don't say such things lightly.

You might both be innocent, but it no longer appears that way. Early-morning meetings and late-night conversations alone — is that how a married woman should comport herself? I've been cursed with being a light sleeper with very keen hearing. I know that after Alise and I bid you good night and sought our separate quarters, she went out again and met you. I could hear you talking together."

"Did she take a vow she wouldn't talk after midnight?" Leftrin asked sarcastically. "Because if she did, then I admit, she broke it, and I helped her."

Sedric glared at him. Leftrin drank more coffee, looking at him over the rim of the mug. Sedric looked like a man trying to contain himself. When he finally spoke, the eternal courtesy in his voice seemed strained. "For a lady like Alise, married to a prominent and wealthy Bingtown Trader, appearances can be as important as realities. If I know that she arose from her bed to seek out your company late last night, then I'll wager that others aboard this vessel also know. Even a rumor of that sort of behavior released into Bingtown could compromise her reputation."

Sedric finished his speech and turned his gaze out over the riverbank. More of the keepers were waking up. Some were clustered around the fire, warming themselves from the night's chill and heating food. Others were around the shallow sand well they'd dug the night before, taking the earth-filtered water for washing and cooking. The dragons, Leftrin noted, weren't stirring yet. They were creatures that loved the sun and warmth and would sleep as long as their keepers allowed them to, rising at noon if they were left to their own devices. He stared at them and wished his life were as simple as theirs. It wasn't.

Leftrin forced himself to loosen his hold on the mug's handle before he broke it. "I'll speak plain to you, Sedric. Nothing happened. She came up on deck, and I was making my night rounds. So we talked a bit. She walked my rounds of the ship with me. We checked the tie-up lines and the anchor. I showed her some constellations and explained how a sailor can use the stars to know where he's headed. I told her the names of some of the night birds she heard. If any of that offends your morality, it's your problem. Not mine and not Alise's. I've done nothing I'm ashamed of."

He spoke righteously, but guilt coiled inside him like a snake. He thought of the moments when her hands had been under his as he showed her how to tie the bowline. He'd put his hands on her warm shoulders and turned her to face Sa's Plough in the southern sky. And very late or rather early, depending on how one reckoned it, when she had bid him good night and sought her compartment, he'd leaned on the railing outside her door and looked out over the river and pondered all the things that might have been. From there, he'd allowed himself to think of things that still could be, if he had the courage to propose them and she felt the passion to accept them. Under his hands, the railing had thrummed with the sweep of the river's current and the response of his ship to it. It had seemed to him then that he was a sort of river and Alise might be a ship that had ventured into his current. Was he strong enough to carry her off with him?

Sedric spoke, and the gentler tone of his voice took Leftrin off guard. "Look, man. I'm not blind. If there's a man on board this ship who is unaware of your infatuation with her, well, then he's a man with no senses and no heart. Your crew knows, your hunter friends know. Knowing Alise as well as I do, I can also see that she is venturing onto dangerous ground. You're a man of the world, out and about, meeting all sorts of women. But perhaps you've never met someone as sheltered as Alise has been. She went from her father's house to her husband's. He was her first and only beau. In some ways, she and Hest are well matched. He's wealthy, he provides for all her needs, and that includes giving her the materials and the time for her precious studies. She had never met a man like you. To a Bingtown lady, you probably seem a bit larger than life. If your admiration for her tempts her to step outside the bounds of society, she will be the one to pay the cost, not you. To her, the shame and the shunning. Possibly the divorce that will send her, irrevocably shamed, back to her father's household. He's not a wealthy man. If you continue to pursue her, even if she doesn't fall as your conquest, people will hear of it. You could ruin her life, send her back to live in reduced circumstances without the scholarly pursuits she has come to love. I don't mean to sound harsh, man, but are you worth it? Will you continue this dalliance, to her ruin? You'll walk away; forgive me if I say that all know the way of sailors in these matters. But she will be crushed."

Sedric spoke his piece and turned away from Leftrin, as if giving him a chance to think. Two of the dragons were awake now and lumbering down to the water. Sedric stared at them as if fascinated, as if he'd forgotten the man beside him.

Anger vied with horror inside Leftrin's chest. His face had first flushed and then drained of blood. He was not a man who was faint of heart or body, but Sedric's words sickened him. Was he right? Was there any way this would not end in disaster for her? He mastered his emotions and spoke.

"I doubt there's any man aboard this ship who is bound for Bingtown, let alone prone to gossip about a lady. The only exception is you, and if you're her friend, as you claim to be, you won't say ugly, untrue things about her. I have no intention of disgracing the lady. And I think you wrong her when you suspect she would betray her husband." That last he felt was true, but oh, how he longed that she would at least consider it.

"I am Alise's friend. If I weren't, I'd have kept to my words and left her on this ship while I went back to Bingtown. But I knew that if I did, she'd be ruined. The only reason I'm here is to safeguard her reputation. You can't imagine that I'm enjoying this little misadventure! No. The only reason I'm here is for Alise. I want to protect her. Her husband is a close friend as well as my employer. So you might, for a moment, consider what an untenable position you are forcing me into. Do I respect Alise's dignity and refrain from reprimanding her? Or do I respect my employer's dignity and challenge you?"

"Challenge me?" Leftrin was shocked.

Sedric spoke quickly. "That's not what I'm doing, of course. I don't think I need to. Now that I've come to you

and explained the situation in civil terms, I'm sure you'll see
that there is only one solution."

He paused, as if he expected Leftrin to fill in his silence.
He tried. Despite his efforts at control, his voice went deep
with fury and despair. "You want me to stop speaking to
her, don't you?"

Sedric tucked his chin and widened his eyes, surprised
that Leftrin didn't see the obvious. "I'm afraid that, at this
stage and in these close quarters, that would be inadequate.
You need to order one of your hunters to take one of the
keeper's small boats and transport Alise and me back down
the river to Trehaug."

"We are nearly thirty days upriver of Cassarick," Leftrin
pointed out. "And one of those small boats wouldn't hold
half your luggage, let alone you and Alise and all your trap-
pings."

"I'm aware of both those things," Sedric replied briskly.
Leftrin was watching his face. He thought the corner of his
mouth almost twitched into a smile. "Traveling downriver,
with the current, the little boats go much faster. I heard the
hunters talking about it yesterday. I suspect that Alise and I
would have to spend a dozen nights camping out before we
reached Cassarick. From there, we could make proper travel
arrangements to reach Trehaug and then home. As for our
belongings, well, they'll have to remain on board for now.
We'd travel light, and rely on you to ship our things to us in
Bingtown when you finally return to Trehaug. I'm sure we
could trust you to do that."

Leftrin just stared at him.

"You know it's the right thing to do," Sedric urged him
quietly, and then added, like a twist of the knife, "For
Alise's sake."

A long wailing cry of anguish from the shore rose to
crack the sky.

"HE WAS BETTER last night!" Sylve insisted. Red-tinged
tears were streaming down her cheeks. Thymara winced at
the sight of them, knowing well how much such tears hurt.
Perhaps the fear of that pain was the only thing keeping

her own eyes dry. She knelt by the little copper dragon. He had eaten last night, the first really large meal he'd taken since they'd fed him the elk meat a couple of nights ago. But unlike the other dragons, who had put on flesh and gained muscle since their trek began, the copper one had remained thin. His belly still bulged from what he had eaten last night, but Thymara could have counted his ribs. At the top of his shoulders and along his spine, some of his scales looked as if they were slipping loose from his hide.

Tats stood up from examining the dragon's muzzle. He put a comforting arm across Sylve's shoulders. "He's not dead," he told her, laying her fear to rest. But in the next breath, he took that comfort from her. "But I think he will be dead before the day is out. It's not your fault!" he added hastily as a Sylve drew in a sobbing breath. "I think you just came into his life too late. Sylve, he didn't have much of a chance from the start. Look how disproportionate his legs are to the rest of him! And I caught him eating rocks and mud the other night. I think he has worms in his gut; look how swollen his belly is while the rest of him is skinny. Parasites will do that to an animal."

Sylve made a choking noise. She shrugged off Tats's touch and walked away from the group. Other keepers were coming to join them, forming a circle around the downed dragon. Thymara bit her lips tight to keep from speaking. Some callous part of her wanted to ask Tats where Jerd was. After all, she was the one who had volunteered to help him with this dragon. Sylve had promised to help with the silver, but the soft-hearted girl had ended up involved with both failing dragons. And if this copper died, it would devastate her.

"What's wrong with him?" Lecter asked as he hurried up.

"Parasites," Rapskal responded wisely. "Eating him up from the inside, so he gets no good from his food."

Thymara was a bit surprised by the coherency of his remark. Rapskal saw her looking at him and came to stand beside her. "What are we going to do?" he asked her, as if it were up to her.

"I don't know," she said quietly. "What can we do?"

"I think we should make the best of it, and go on," Greft said. His voice was not loud, but his words carried to everyone. Thymara glared at him. She still had not forgiven him for the elk. She hadn't raised a public fuss about it, but she had avoided speaking to him or Kase or Boxter. She watched them, watched how Greft assumed leadership and tended to push the other keepers around, but hadn't said anything openly. Now she lifted her head and squared her shoulders, preparing to take him on.

Sylve abruptly turned back to face them all. Her tears had stopped, but they'd left red tracks down her face. "The best of it?" she said thickly. "What is that supposed to mean? What can be 'best' about this?"

Silence thick as a blanket had fallen over the gathering. Sylve stood, her shoulders lifted and her small fists knotted. All waited to hear what Greft would say. For the first time since Thymara had met him, she saw him hesitant. He surveyed his listeners. It was strange to see his human tongue dart out to lick his narrow scaled lips. What was he looking for? Thymara wondered. Acceptance of his leadership? Willingness to follow him as he made "new rules" for them?

"He's going to die," he said quietly. Thymara saw a scream gather on Sylve's face; she held it in.

"And when he dies, his body shouldn't go to waste."

"'Course not," Rapskal said, breaking the silence that the others held by tacit consent. His matter-of-fact boyish voice in contrast to Greft's controlled and mature speech made him sound foolish as he voiced what everyone else was thinking. "The dragons will eat him to get his memories. And for food. Everyone knows that." Rapskal looked around at the other keepers, nodding and smiling. Slowly the smile faded from his face; he seemed puzzled at their stillness. Thymara concentrated her attention on Greft again; he had an exasperated look on his face, as if what Rapskal proposed should seem obviously foolish to all of them. But when he spoke, there was a note of caution to his words, as if he hoped someone else would speak for him.

"There may be a better use for his body," he said, and

waited. Thymara held her breath. What was he talking about? He looked around at all of them, daring himself to speak. "There has been talk of offers for—"

"Dragon flesh belongs to dragons." It was not a human who spoke. Despite his great size, the golden dragon could move quietly. He towered above them, his head lifted high to look down on Greft. The keepers were parting to let him advance as if they were reeds giving way to the river's flow. Mercor strode majestically past them. He looked, Thymara thought, magnificent. Since their journey had begun, he had put on weight and muscle. He was beginning to look the way a dragon was supposed to look. With the muscling, his legs looked more proportionate. His tail seemed to have grown. Only his broken-kite wings betrayed him. They were still too small and frail-looking to lift even a part of him.

He bent his long neck to sniff at the copper dragon's body. Then he swiveled his head to stare at Greft. "She's not dead," he told him coldly. "It's a bit early to plan to sell her flesh."

"She?" Tats asked in consternation.

"Sell her flesh?" Rapskal sounded horrified.

But Mercor didn't reply to either comment or the murmur of words among the keepers that followed them. He had lowered his head to sniff again at the copper. He nudged her hard. She did not respond. As the dragon slowly swung his head to study all the keepers, his scales flashed in the sun. His eyes, gleaming black, were unreadable to Thymara. "Sylve. Stay beside me. The rest of you, go away. This does not concern you. It does not concern humans at all."

Thymara could almost see the girl drawn to the dragon. His voice was compelling, deep as darkness and rich as cream. Sylve walked to him and leaned against him as if taking comfort and strength from him. She spoke shyly. "May Tats and Thymara stay? They have helped me care for Copper."

"And me," Rapskal announced, reckless as ever. "I should stay, too. I'm their friend."

"Not now," the dragon announced with finality. "There is nothing for them to do here. You stay to be with me. I'll watch over this dragon."

There was a subtle force to his words; Thymara felt not just dismissed but pushed, as if she were a child being ushered out of a sickroom. Without deciding to do so, she turned and found herself walking away. "I have to check on Skymaw," she explained to Tats, as if to excuse her departure.

"I felt it, too," he whispered.

"Sintara." Behind her, Mercor spoke the name. A shiver ran down Thymara's spine, a sudden knowing she couldn't deny. His rich voice vibrated through her. "The dragon you serve is named Sintara. I know her true name, and I know she owes it to you. So have it."

Thymara had halted in her tracks. Beside her, Tats paused, looking at her with a puzzled face. She felt as if her ears were blocked, her eyes dimmed. A storm raged somewhere, just beyond her senses. Sintara was not pleased with what Mercor had done, and she was letting him know it.

Mercor laughed humorlessly. "You can't have it both ways, Sintara. The rest of us realized that right away. None of us has held back our names, save those poor souls who cannot remember that they have proper dragon names."

Rash as always, Rapskal spoke into the pause. "Does Heeby have a dragon name?"

To Thymara's surprise, the great gold dragon took the boy's query seriously. "Heeby is now Heeby. She had made the name hers as you gave it to her. It remains to see if she will grow into it, or find herself limited by it."

Thymara desperately wanted to ask about the injured silver dragon, but did not have the courage. Sometimes, she reflected, it might be easier to be Rapskal, without the sense to be frightened of anything.

Mercor had lowered his nose to the copper dragon. He gave her a nudge, then a stronger push. The copper didn't move. Mercor lifted his head and regarded the fallen dragon with his bright black eyes. "We will have to remain here until she either rises or dies," he announced. He looked around himself gravely and let his gaze stop on Greft. "Leave her alone here. I will be back shortly." Then, "Come, Sylve," he beckoned her and strode off toward the water. His heavy clawed feet left deep tracks. Soon water would seep up to fill them.

MORNING HAD COME and grown strong. Alise could tell by the squares of sunlight that fell in her small chamber from the tiny windows set high in the wall. She tried again to muster her courage to leave her room, and once again sat down at her little desk instead. She had to go outside soon. She was hungry and thirsty and she needed to empty her chamber pot. Instead, she folded her arms on the desk in front of her and then rested her forehead on them. She stared into the small darkness her arms enclosed. "What am I going to do?" she asked herself.

No easy answer came to her. Outside, the deckhands would soon be casting loose and pushing the barge off the muddy bank. Doubtless by now the dragons had set out and their keepers in their flotilla of small boats would be following. Another day of travel up the river awaited her. Ahead of her were vistas of open river, tall trees, and the slice of sky overhead that sometimes seemed like a different sort of river. Every day was a new adventure for her. There would be new flowers perfumed with unfamiliar fragrances, strange animals that came down to the river's edge or rose from its depths to leap glittering into the sunlight. Never had she imagined that the Rain Wilds would be so rich with life. When she had heard of the river and how it could sometimes run white with acid, she had expected the lands to either side of it to be deserted wastelands. To the contrary, she found herself encountering all sorts of trees, plants, and animals that she had never imagined existed. The fish and creatures in the water that had adapted to its varying acidity astounded her. Of the birds alone, there were hundreds. And by sight or song, Leftrin seemed to know them all . . .

And again, her errant thoughts had circled back to him, to the very man who was at the root of all her problems.

No. That wasn't fair. She couldn't blame him. It was her own fault she was so taken with him. Oh, she knew he was infatuated with her; he was an honest soul. He hid nothing from her. His affection for her and interest in her were conveyed in every glance, in every word he spoke to her. An accidental touch of his hand against hers was like a leap of lightning from earth to sky. Feelings, physical sensations she had thought long vanished from her life, were awakening violently and rolling through her like ground-shaking thunder.

Last night, when he had been showing her how to refasten the bowline, she had feigned incompetence at the simple knot. It was a schoolgirl's trick, but the poor, honest man had been completely deceived. He'd stood behind her, with her in the circle of his arms and taken her hands in his to guide them through the easy motions. Heat had flushed through her, and her knees had actually trembled at his closeness. A wave of dizziness had washed through her; she had wanted to collapse to the deck and pull him down on top of her. She'd gone still in his loose embrace, praying to every god she'd ever heard of that he would know what she so hotly desired and act on it. This, this was what she was supposed to feel about the man she was joined to, and had never felt at all!

"Do you understand it now?" he'd asked her huskily. His hands on hers pulled the knot firm.

"I do," she'd replied. "I understand it completely now." She hadn't been speaking of knots at all. She'd dared herself to take half a step backward and press her body to his. She dared herself to turn in the circle of his arms and look up into his whiskery beloved face. Cowardice paralyzed her. She could not even form words. For a time that was infinitely brief and forever, he stood there, enclosing her in a warm, safe place. All around her, the night sounds of the Rain Wilds made a soft music of water and bird and insect calls. She could smell him, a male musky smell, "sweaty" as Sedric would have mocked it, but incredibly masculine and attractive to her. Enclosed by his embrace, she felt a part of his world. The deck under her feet, the railing of the ship, the night sky above her, and the man at her back connected her to something big and wonderful, something that was untamed and yet home to her.

Then he had dropped his arms and stepped back from her. The night was warm and muggy, the insects chirred and buzzed, and she heard the night call of a gnat-chaser. But it had all seemed separate from her then. Last night, as now, she knew herself for the mousy, scholarly little Bingtown woman that she undoubtedly was. She'd sold herself to Hest, prostituted out her ability to bear a child for the security and position that he had offered. She'd made the deal and signed on it. A Trader was only as good as his word, so the saying went. She'd given her word. What was it worth?

Even if she took it back now, even if she broke it faithlessly, she'd still be a mousy, little Bingtown woman, not what she longed to be. She could scarcely bear to consider what she longed to be, not only because it was so far beyond her but because it seemed such a childishly extravagant dream. In the dark circle of her arms, she closed her eyes and thought of Althea, wife to the captain of the *Paragon*. She'd seen that woman dashing about the deck barefoot, wearing loose trousers like a man. She'd seen her standing up by her ship's figurehead, the wind stirring her hair and a smile curving her lips as she exchanged some jest with the ship's boy. And then Captain Trell had bounded up the short ladder to the foredeck to join them there. She and the captain had moved without even looking at each other, like a needle drawn to a magnet, their arms lifting as if they were the halves of the god Sa becoming whole again. She'd thought her heart would break with envy.

What would it be like, she wondered, to have a man who had to embrace you when he saw you, even if you'd just risen from a shared bed a few hours earlier? She tried to imagine herself as free as that Althea woman, running barefoot on the decks of the *Tarman*. Could she ever lean on a railing in a way that said she completely owned and trusted the ship? She thought of Leftrin and tried to see him dispassionately. He was uncouth and unschooled. He told jokes at the table, and she'd seen him laugh so hard that the tea spewed from his mouth, at a coarse jest from one of his sailors. He didn't shave every day, nor wash as often as a gentleman should. The elbows of his shirts and the knees of his trousers were scuffed with work. The short nails of his wide hands were broken and rough. Where Hest was tall and lean and elegant, Leftrin was perhaps an inch taller than she was, wide shouldered and thick bodied. Her female friends in Bingtown would turn aside if a man like that spoke to them on the street.

Then she thought of his gray eyes, gray as the river he loved, and her heart melted. She thought of the ruddy tops of his unshaven cheeks, and how his lips seemed redder and fuller than Hest's sophisticated smile. She longed to kiss that mouth, and to feel those calloused hands clasp her close. She missed sleeping in his bunk, missed the smell of him in the room and on the bedding. She wanted him as she'd never wanted anything or anyone before. At the thought of him, her body warmed even as tears filled her eyes.

She sat up straight and dashed the useless water from her eyes. "Take what you can have, for the short time you can have it," she counseled herself sternly. She wondered briefly why the ship hadn't left the beach yet. She dried her eyes more thoroughly, smoothed her wayward hair, and then stepped to the door. She would not break her word to Hest. They had made an agreement to be faithful to each other. She would honor it.

The brightness of full day was dazzling after the dimness of her room. She came out onto the deck and was surprised to see Sedric standing at the railing with Leftrin. They were both staring toward the shore. "I'm going to see what's going on," Leftrin announced and headed toward the bow. Alise hurried over to join Sedric.

"What is the matter?" she asked him.

"I don't know. Some sort of ruckus among the keepers. The captain has gone to see what it is about. How are you this morning, Alise?"

"Well enough, thank you." On the shore, voices were raised in alarm. She saw some of the young keepers running. Sleepy dragons were lifting their heads and turning them toward the disturbance. "I think I'd best go see what that is about," she said, excusing herself. She started down the deck after Leftrin. He hadn't seen her arrive. As she watched, he climbed over the bow railing and started down the rope ladder to the shore.

"I think it would be better if you didn't," Sedric suggested strongly.

She halted reluctantly and turned back to face him. She studied his face for a moment and then asked him, "Is something wrong?"

His gaze met hers, studying her face. "I'm not sure," he said quietly. "I hope there isn't." He glanced away from her, and for a moment they shared an uncomfortable silence. On the shore, the keepers seemed to be gathering around the small copper dragon. She knew he hadn't been well lately and felt a sudden clutch of fear. "You don't have to protect me, Sedric. If the dragon has died, he has died. I know the others will eat him. And, believe it or not, I feel that I need to witness that. There will be parts of dragon behavior that men will find distasteful, but that doesn't mean that I should avoid learning about them."

She turned to go, but his voice halted her again. "That's not at all what I'm concerned about. Alise, I feel I must speak bluntly. And confidentially. Please, come back here where we can discuss this quietly."

She didn't want to. "Discuss what?"

"You," he said in a soft voice. "You and Captain Leftrin."

For a time, she stood frozen. There was a hubbub of voices on the shore. She glanced that way and saw Leftrin hastening toward the group. Then she turned back and, wearing her calmest expression, walked back toward Sedric. "I don't understand," she offered him, trying to sound puzzled. Trying to keep breathing, to keep the blood from rushing to her face.

He wasn't fooled. "Alise, you do. We've known each other too well for too long for you to be able to hide it from me. You're infatuated with that man. Why, I can't imagine. I compare him to Hest, to what you already have and—"

"Shut up." The harshness of her own voice shocked her, as did the bluntness of her words. She couldn't recall that she'd ever spoken to anyone like that. It didn't matter. It had worked to silence him. He stared at her, his mouth slightly ajar. The words tumbled from her lips, boulders carried on a torrent. "What I already have, Sedric, is nothing. It's a sham of Hest's devising, one I agreed to because I could not imagine that there would ever be anything better. Our marriage is a travesty. But I'm aware that I agreed to it. I took his damn bargain; we shook hands on it, like good Traders, and I've lived up to my end of it. Far more than he has, I might add. And I will continue to live up to my word. But don't, *do not,* ever, compare Leftrin to Hest. Never."

The vehemence in her voice rasped her throat. She'd thought she'd had more to say, but the shocked look on his face drained her words and thoughts from her. The uselessness of ranting against her fate to anyone suddenly exhausted her. "I'm sorry I spoke so roughly to you, Sedric. You don't deserve it." She turned to walk away from him.

"Alise, we still need to talk. Come back here." His voice shook, making his words more a plea than a command.

She halted, not looking back at him. "There's nothing to talk about, Sedric. We've just said it all. I'm imprisoned in a marriage to a man I don't like, let alone love. I know he feels the same way about me. I'm infatuated with Captain Leftrin. I am reveling in the attention of a man who thinks I'm beautiful and desirable. But that's all. I won't act on it. What else is there you want to know?"

"I've told Leftrin that we have to leave. Today. I've asked him to find one of the hunters who will volunteer to take one of the small boats and escort us back to Trehaug. We'll be traveling with the current, so it shouldn't take us long. We may have to camp for a few nights, but we'd manage it."

His words turned her back to him. Her heart leaped against the ribs that encaged it. Despair rose in her. "What? Why would we do that?"

"To remove you from a temptation before you fall to it. To remove a temptation from the captain before he yields to his urges. Forgive me, Alise, but you don't know much about men. You so blithely admit that you are infatuated but assure me that you won't act on it. Captain Leftrin knows how you feel. Can you truly say that if he pressed you, you'd be able to say no to him?"

"He wouldn't do that." Her voice grated low. No matter how much she longed for him to, he wouldn't press her. She knew that.

"Alise, you cannot take a chance. By staying here, you invite ruin, not just on yourself but on Leftrin as well. Your dalliance is still innocent. But people see you and people will talk. You cannot be so selfish as to think only of yourself. Consider how such a rumor would shame your father and distress your mother! And what would it mean to Hest, to wear the horns of a cuckold? He could not let it pass! A man in his position has to be seen as shrewd and powerful, not as a duped fool. I do not know what it would lead to . . . would he demand satisfaction of Leftrin? And then, even if you did not consummate this ill-advised romance, what good would it do you? Alise, you must see that my solution, dangerous as it is, is the only one. We should leave today, before we get any farther away from Trehaug."

She sounded calm, even to herself. "And Leftrin has already agreed to this?"

Sedric set his lips and then sighed. "Agree or not, it must happen. I think he was on the point of agreeing when he heard some sort of outcry from the keepers and went to check on them."

She knew he was lying. Leftrin hadn't been on the point of agreeing to anything. The current that had caught them was sweeping them together, not apart. She seized the opportunity to change the subject. "What was the outcry about?"

"I don't know. The keepers looked as if they were all gathering . . ."

"I'm going to go and see," she announced and turned away from him in midspeech. She was halfway to the bow before he overcame his astonishment.

"Alise!"

She ignored him.

"ALISE!" HE PUT every bit of command into the shout that he could muster. He saw her shoulders twitch. She'd heard him. He watched her seize the bow railing in both hands and swing a leg over it. Her walking skirts wrapped and tangled. Patiently, she shook them out and then clambered over the railing and down the rope ladder to the muddy shore.

She vanished from his view, and then in a few moments he saw her hurrying across the trampled grass and patches of mud toward the clustered keepers. A dragon was moving slowly to join them. Sedric's breath caught for a moment in his chest. Would it be able to tell?

He watched them gather; he could hear the sounds of their voices but couldn't make out the words. His anxiety built, and he suddenly turned from the railing and hurried to his crude cabin. He opened the door, stepped into the dim, close chamber, and shut the door firmly behind him. He fastened the simple hook that was the only way to secure the door and then dropped to his knees. The "secret" drawer in the bottom of his wardrobe suddenly looked pathetically obvious. He unlatched it and dragged it open, all the while listening for the sound of footfalls on the deck outside. Was there a better place to hide his trove? Should he keep it all together or scatter it among his possessions? He bit his lip, debating.

Last night, he had added two items to his store. He held up to the dim light in the cabin a glass flask. The dragon blood filled it, smoky red and swirling when he held it to the light. Last night, he'd thought he'd imagined that motion, but he hadn't. The stuff in the flask was still rich red, liquid and moving as if it were itself alive.

For several days, he had been watching the small brown dragon and daring himself to act. Each morning, the hunters departed before dawn, leading the way up the river in the hope of bagging game before the dragons could frighten it away. When the sun was higher and the day warmer, the dragons awoke. Usually the golden one was the first one to seek the water's edge. The others soon trailed after him. The keepers followed in their small boats and behind them all came the barge.

Yesterday and the day before, the little brown dragon had lagged badly. He had not kept up with the other dragons but had waded alone between them and the keepers who followed them. Yesterday, even the keepers had passed him. The brown had barely stayed ahead of the barge. Sedric's attention had been attracted to it when he found Alise and

Leftrin on the bow, looking down on it and commiserating with each other over how pitiable it was. He joined them there, leaning on the bow rail and watching the stunted dragon slog drearily against the river's pale flow. For a moment, the color of the water caught his attention. It was not nearly as white as it had been during the *Paragon*'s up-river journey. It looked almost like ordinary river water. The captain had made some comment to Alise; Sedric heard only her response.

"It *is* harder for him. Look at how short his legs are. The other dragons are wading but he's nearly swimming."

Leftrin had nodded agreement. "Poor thing never had a chance, really. He was doomed from the day he hatched. Still, I hate to see him die this way."

"Better that he die trying to make something of his life than that he die in the mud near Cassarick." Alise had spoken with such passion that Sedric had turned to look at her. It was then that he realized with some alarm the depth of her attraction to Leftrin. It was not difficult to see how her words applied to her own life. *She is daring herself to act on her urges,* he'd realized in awe. Given all he knew of Alise, it would be a matter of when, not if, she would give herself to Leftrin. The thought of how Hest would react to that sent a finger of cold tracing his spine. Hest might not be in love with Alise, but he regarded her as he did all his possessions, with jealous ownership. If Leftrin "took" her, Hest would be infuriated. And he would blame Sedric almost as much as he'd blame her.

The discomfort he'd felt that every passing day took them deeper into wilderness and farther away from home suddenly became pressing. It was time to get Alise and himself out of here and back to Bingtown.

Then he thought of his paltry collection of dragon bits and scowled. He'd been checking them daily. They didn't look like anything he'd be willing to include in a medicine or tonic. The flesh that Thymara had carved away from the silver dragon's injury had been half putrefied to begin with. Despite his efforts at preservation, the samples smelled foul and looked as one would expect any sort of decayed meat to look. The last time he had looked at them, he had very nearly thrown them away. Instead, he had resolved only to keep them until he had the opportunity to replace them with something better, something specific from the list of dragon items that he knew he could sell.

Somehow, that thought had surfaced again in his mind as he stared down on the feeble brown dragon struggling to stay ahead of them. And suddenly he had known that he would never have a better chance than that night.

It had not been that hard to slip away from the ship at night. Each evening, Leftrin nosed the *Tarman* onto the muddy banks of the river as close as he could get to wherever the dragons were sleeping. Some nights the keepers slept on board; sometimes they bedded down near their dragon wards. He had been fortunate. The dragons had settled for the night on a grassy shore and their keepers had decided to collect driftwood and sleep near them. Leftrin himself had taken the watch. Alise had been his unwitting accomplice for she had distracted the captain so completely that Sedric had no problem in stealthily leaving the ship.

The dying glow of the keepers' bonfire and the nearly full moon had been enough to light his way. He'd slogged over trampled grass and through puddles as best he could, resigned that his boots and trousers would be sodden and caked with mud by the time he returned. He'd taken care earlier in the evening to watch the dragons as they settled, so he knew approximately where the exhausted brown was sleeping. It had been late and both the keepers and their dragons had been sleeping soundly as he moved cautiously among and then past them. The sickly dragon slept alone on the outskirts of the group. It hadn't stirred as he'd drawn near it. At first, he'd thought it was already dead. He could detect no movement and heard no sign of it breathing. He'd forced himself to boldness, and cautiously set a hand to the creature's filthy shoulder. It made no response. He gave it a slight push, and then a harder shove. It made a wheezing sound but did not move. Sedric had taken out his knife.

His first ambition had been to claim a few scales. The shoulder was perfect; he'd put his opportunity to observe the dragons while Alise attempted to talk to them to good use. He knew that the larger scales were usually on their shoulders, hips, and the broadest parts of their tails. By the moonlight's feeble gleam, he had slipped the edge of his knife under a scale, pinched it hard against the blade with his thumb, and jerked. The scale did not come out easily; it was rather like pulling a plate from the bottom of a stack. But it came, edged with gleaming blood. The dragon gave a twitch but slept on, apparently too feeble to care.

He'd extracted three more scales from the creature, each about the size of the palm of his hand, wrapped them carefully in a kerchief, and tucked them into the breast of his shirt. He'd nearly returned to the barge then, for he knew that even one of the scales should bring him a rich price. But while a rich price might be enough to win their freedom, he doubted it would long keep Hest at his side. No. He had taken the risk already. He would either gain enough from this gamble to live like a king or he'd not bother. He'd be a fool to stop now when he was so close to making his fortune.

He'd chosen his tools carefully. The little knife he took out now was a butcher's tool, one used for sticking a pig and draining off the fresh blood for pudding. He'd been surprised to find that such a tool existed, but the moment he'd seen one, he'd bought it. It was short and sharp, with a fuller that passed through a tunnel in the knife's hardwood handle and acted as a passage for the flow of blood.

He had moved to a fresh spot on the dragon's body, on the neck just behind the jaw. He slapped at the mosquitoes that had found him and were now buzzing hungrily about his own ears and neck. "Just a very big mosquito," he suggested to the comatose dragon. He lifted one of the heavy scales on its neck, took a firm grip on his tool, and punched it into its flesh.

The tool was as sharp as a grindstone could make it. Even so, it didn't go in easily. The dragon gave a squeak in its sleep, a comical sound from so large a creature. Its clawed feet twitched against the muddy ground and Sedric knew a moment's terror and very nearly fled. Instead, hands shaking, he'd taken a glass flask from his small pack and drawn the glass stopper out of it. He waited. After a moment, the blood began to fall, drop by shining drop. He maneuvered his flask's mouth under the falling drops and caught them, one by one.

His hands were shaking too much. He'd never done this sort of thing and found it much more distressing than he had imagined. A drop of blood missed the mouth of the flask and ran greasily over his fingers. He grimaced and then braced the neck of the flask against the end of the knife. In that instant, the drips became a trickle and then a sudden flow of blood. "Merciful Sa!" he exclaimed in terror and delight. The flask grew heavy in his hand and then suddenly overflowed. He snatched it away. He had to pour out some of the blood before it would admit the stopper, and he wished in vain that he had brought a second flask. He wiped his bloody hands on his trousers and then carefully stowed the flask in his pack. A quick tug freed the knife from the drag-on's flesh and he added it to the pack.

But the blood had continued to run.

The smell of it, reptilian and strangely rich, filled his nostrils. The insects that had been buzzing around his head forsook him for this flowing feast. They clustered around the wound, feeding greedily. The trickle of blood became a scarlet rivulet down the dragon's shoulder. It dripped from the animal onto the trampled ground. A small puddle started to form. In the moonlight, it was black, and then as he stared at the deepening pool, it reddened. It gleamed scarlet and crimson, the two reds swirling like dyes stirred into water, separated only by silver edging. He felt drawn to it and crouched by the puddle, entranced by the color.

His gaze lifted to the thin stream of falling blood that fed the puddle. He put his hand out, touched two fingers to the flow. The stream parted and ran over his fingers like silken thread. He pulled his fingers back, watching the unimpeded flow and then set his bloody fingers to his mouth and licked them.

He recoiled from the touch of dragon's blood on his tongue, shocked that he had obeyed an impulse he couldn't even recall having. The taste of the blood flooded his mouth and filled his senses. He smelled it everywhere, not just in his nose but in the back of his throat and in the roof of his mouth. His ears rang with the scent, and his tongue tingled and stung. He tried to shake the remaining blood from his fingers, then wiped his hand down his shirt front. He was covered in blood and mud now. And still the dragon bled.

He stooped and cupped a handful of mud-and-blood. It was both warm and cold in his hand, and he felt as if it squirmed there, a liquid serpent coiling and uncoiling within his hand. He plastered it over the injury. When he lifted his hand, the tiny trickle of red burst forth afresh. Another handful of mud and another one, and the last one he held hard against the dragon's throat, panting through his mouth both in fear and with the effort. He tasted and smelled only dragon, he felt dragon inside his mouth and down his throat. He *was* a dragon. There were scales down his neck and back, his claws were sunken in mud, his wings would not unfold and what was a dragon who could not fly? He rocked on his feet dizzily, and when he staggered back from the dragon, the flow of blood had finally ceased.

For a time he had stood there, his hands braced just above his knees, breathing the night air and trying to recover. When his head had cleared a bit, he straightened and felt instead of dizziness, a rush of horror at how badly he had managed this. What had happened to his stealth and his "leave no sign" intentions? He was covered in mud and blood, and the dragon was lying in a pool of blood. How subtle!

He kicked mud over the blood, tore marsh grass loose and spread it there, and then kicked more mud over it. It seemed to take him hours. By moonlight, he could not tell if any red showed through his efforts on the ground or on the dragon's neck. The creature slept on. At least it would have no recall of him.

He went back to the barge and attempted to reboard it. He spent an agonized near hour in the shadow of the bow. Above him, Leftrin and Alise talked softly about knots, of all things. When finally they moved away, he clambered up

the rope ladder and fled to his cabin. There he had changed
hastily into clean clothing and hidden his precious blood
and scales in his case. It had taken him three furtive attempts before he was able to clean his muddy, bloody tracks
from the deck of the barge. Leftrin and Alise had nearly
caught him in the act of throwing his soiled clothing and
ruined boots overboard. If they had not been so completely
engrossed in each other, they would surely have discovered
him.

But they had not. They had not, and the vial of blood that
he now held in his hand was his prize for all he had gone
through. He stared at it, at the slow shifting and tangling of
the trapped red stuff inside it. *Like serpents twining round
one another,* he thought, and a ghostly image of sea serpents
wrapping one another in the dim blue of an undersea world
invaded his thoughts. He shook his head clear of the fancy,
and he resisted the sudden urge to uncap the flask and smell
the contents. He had sealing wax in his case. He should melt
some over the neck of the flask to seal it securely. He should.
He'd do it later.

The sight of his treasure left him oddly calmed. He put
the flask back into the secret drawer and took up a small
shallow box made from cedar. He opened the sliding lid
and looked inside. The scales rested there on a shallow bed
of salt. They were slightly iridescent in the dim light of
the cabin. He closed the lid, replaced the box in the secret
drawer, and shut and locked it. They'd probably find the
brown dragon dead. They wouldn't suspect him, he suddenly knew. He'd covered his tracks well. He'd smeared the
blood away, and the wound from his knife was so tiny that
no one would find it. He hadn't killed the beast, not really.
Everyone saw that it was nearly ready to die anyway. If his
bleeding of the dragon had hastened its death, well, that
didn't mean he'd killed it. It was only an animal anyway,
despite how Alise might moon over it. A dragon was only an
animal, just like a cow or a chicken, to be used by a man in
any way he saw fit.

Exactly the opposite, really.

The intrusion of that thought was so sudden and foreign

that it shocked him. The opposite? That man was to be exploited by dragons as they saw fit? Preposterous. Where had such a silly idea come from?

He straightened his jacket, unlatched his door, and stepped out onto the *Tarman*'s deck.

✦ ✦ ✦

Day the 5th of the Prayer Moon

Year the 6th of the Independent Alliance of Traders

From Erek, Keeper of the Birds, Bingtown
To Detozi, Keeper of the Birds, Trehaug

A missive from Trader Kincarron to the Councils of Trehaug and Cassarick, expressing confusion and concern about the Councils' contract with his daughter Alise Kincarron Finbok and asking for clarification. A speedy reply is requested.

Detozi,

When Trader Kincarron dropped this off, he promised a handsome bonus if both his query and a response traveled quickly. If you can prod anyone at the Council there to send a response before the day is out, and use your swiftest pigeon, I would consider the debt settled for the peas.

Erek

✦ ✦ ✦

Read on for a glimpse at the third installment
of Robin Hobb's spellbinding series

CITY OF DRAGONS

Volume Three of the Rain Wilds Chronicles

Available now in hardcover
from Harper Voyager

DRAGON BATTLE

T he sun had broken through the clouds. The mist that cloaked the hillside meadow by the swift-flowing river was beginning to burn off. Sintara lifted her head to stare at the distant burning orb. Light fell on her scaled hide, but little warmth came with it. As the mist rose in trailing tendrils and vanished at the sun's touch, the cruel wind was driving in thick gray clouds from the west. It would be another day of rain. In distant lands, the delightfully coarse sand would be baking under a hot sun. An ancestral memory of wallowing in that sand and scouring one's scales until they shone intruded into her mind. She and her fellow dragons should have migrated. They should have risen in a glittering storm of flashing wings and lashing tails and flown to the far southern deserts months ago. Hunting in the rocky uplands that walled the desert was always good. If they were there now, it would be a time to hunt, to eat to satiation, to sleep long in the heat-soaked afternoon and then to rise into

the bright blue sky, coasting on the hot air currents. Given
the right winds, a dragon could hang effortlessly above the
land. A queen might do that, might shift her wings and glide
and watch the heavier males do battle in the air below her.
She imagined herself there, looking down on them as they
clashed and spat, as they soared and collided and gripped
talons with one another.

At the end of such a battle, a single drake would prevail.
His vanquished rivals would return to the sands to bask and
sulk, or perhaps flee to the game-rich hills to take out their
frustration in a wild killing spree. The lone drake would
rise, beating his wings to achieve an altitude equal to the
circling, watching females, and single out the one he sought
to court. Then a different sort of a battle would begin.

Sintara's gleaming copper eyes were half lidded, her
head lifted on her long and powerful neck, her face turned
to the distant sun. A reflex opened her useless blue wings.
There were stirrings of longing in her. She felt the mating
flush warm the scales of her belly and throat and smelled the
scent of her own desire wafting from the glands under her
wings. She opened her eyes and lowered her head, feeling
almost shame. A true queen worthy of mating would have
powerful wings that could lift her above the clouds that now
threatened to drench her. Her flight would spread the scent
of her musk and inflame every drake for miles with lust.
But a true dragon queen would not be marooned here on
this sodden riverbank, companioned only by inept flightless
males and even more useless human keepers.

She pushed dreams of glorious battles and mating flights
away from her. A low rumble of displeasure vibrated her
flanks. She was hungry. Where was her Thymara, her keeper?
She was supposed to hunt for her, to bring her freshly killed
game. Where was the useless girl?

She felt a sudden violent stir of wind and caught a
powerful whiff of drake. Just in time, she closed her half-
opened wings.

His clawed feet met the earth and he slid wildly toward
her, stopping just short of crashing into her. Sintara reared
onto her hind legs and arched her glistening blue neck,

straining to her full height. Even so, Kalo still towered over her. She saw his whirling eyes light with pleasure as he realized her disadvantage. The big male had grown and gained muscle and strength since they'd arrived at Kelsingra. "My longest flight yet," he told her as he shook his wide, dark-blue wings, freeing them of rain and spattering her in the process, then carefully folded and groomed them to his back. "My wings grow longer and stronger every day. Soon I shall again be a lord of the skies. What of you, queen? When will you take to the air?"

"When I please," she retorted and turned away. He reeked of lust; the wild freedom of flight was not his focus, but what might occur during a flight. She would not even consider it. "And I do not call that flight. You ran down the hill and leapt into the air. Gliding is not flying." Her criticism was not strictly fair. Kalo had been aloft for at least five wing beats before he had landed. Shame vied with fury as she recalled her first flight effort: the keepers had cheered as she leaped and glided. But her wings had lacked the strength to lift her; she had gone down, crashing into the river. She had been tumbled and battered in the current and emerged streaming muddy water and covered with bruises. *Don't recall that ignominy. But never let anyone see you fail again.*

A fresh gust of wind brought the rain down. She had come down to the river only to drink; she would return to the feeble shelter of the trees now.

But as she started away from him, Kalo's head shot out. He clamped his jaws firmly on her neck, just behind her head, where she could not turn to bite him or to spit acid at him. She lifted a front foot to claw at him, but his neck was longer and more powerful than hers. He held her away from his body; her claws slashed fruitlessly at empty air. She trumpeted her fury and he released her, springing back so that her second attack was as useless as her first.

Kalo lifted his wings and opened them wide, ready to bat her aside if she charged at him. His eyes, silver with tendrils of green, whirled with infuriating amusement.

"You should be trying to fly, Sintara! You need to become a true queen again, ruler of sea and land and sky.

Leave these earthbound worms behind and soar with me.
We will hunt and kill and fly far away from this cold rain
and deep meadows, to the far deserts of the south. Touch
your ancestral memories and remember what we are to
become!"

Her neck stung where his teeth had scored her flesh, but
her pride stung more sharply. Heedless of the danger, she
charged at him again, mouth wide and poison sacs working,
but with a roar of delight at her response, he leapt over her.
As she spun to confront him, she became aware of scarlet
Ranculos and azure Sestican lumbering toward them. Dragons were not meant for ground travel. They lolloped along
like fat cattle. Sestican's orange-filigreed mane stood out
on the back of his neck. As Ranculos raced toward them,
gleaming wings half spread, he bellowed aggressively.
"Leave her be, Kalo!"

"I don't need your help," she trumpeted back as she
turned and stalked away from the converging males. Satisfaction that they would fight over her warred with a sense
of humiliation that she was not worth their battle. She could
not take to the skies in a show of grace and speed; she could
not challenge whoever won this foolish brawl with her own
agility and fearlessness. A thousand ancestral memories
of other courtship battles and mating flights hovered at
the edge of her thoughts. She pushed them away. She did
not look back at the roars and the sound of furiously slapping wings. "I have no need to fly," she called disdainfully
over her shoulder. "There is no drake here worth a mating
flight."

A roar of pain and fury from Ranculos was the only
response. All around her, the rainy afternoon erupted into
shouts of dismay and shrieked questions from running
humans as the dragon keepers poured from their scattered
cottages and converged on the battling males. Idiots. They'd
be trampled, or worse, if they interfered. These were not
matters for humans to intervene in. It galled her when the
keepers treated them as if they were cattle to be managed
rather than dragons to be served. Her own keeper, trying
to hold a ragged cloak closed around her lumpy back and

shoulders, ran toward her shouting, "Sintara, are you all right? Are you hurt?"

She tossed her head high and half-opened her wings. "Do you think I cannot defend myself?" she demanded of Thymara. "Do you think that I am weak and—"

"Get clear!" A human shouted the warning, and Thymara obeyed it, hunching down and covering the back of her head with her hands.

Sintara snorted in amusement as golden Mercor hurtled past them, wings spread wide, clawed feet throwing up tufts of muddy grass as he barely skimmed the earth. Thymara's hands could not have protected her if the dragon's barbed wing had so much as brushed her. The mere wind of his passage knocked Thymara to the ground and sent her rolling through the wet meadow grass.

Human shrieks and dragon roars culminated in a full-throated trumpeting from Mercor as he crashed into the knot of struggling males.

Sestican went down, bowled over by the impact. His spread wing bent dangerously as he rolled on it, and she heard his huff of pain and dismay. Ranculos was trapped under the flailing Kalo. Kalo attempted to roll and meet Mercor with the longer claws of his powerful hind legs. But Mercor had reared onto his hind legs on top of the heap of struggling dragons. Suddenly he leapt forward and pinned Kalo's widespread wings to the ground with his hind legs. A wild slash from the trapped dragon's talons scored a gash down Mercor's ribs, but before he could add another stripe of injury, Mercor shifted his stance higher. Kalo's head and long neck lashed like a whip, but Mercor clearly had the advantage. Trapped beneath the two larger dragons, Sestican roared in helpless fury. A thick stench of male dragon musk rose from the struggle.

A horde of frightened and angry keepers ringed the struggling dragons, shrieking and shouting the names of the combatants or attempting to keep other gawking dragons from joining the fray. The smaller females, Fente and Veras, had arrived and were craning their necks and ignoring their keepers as they ventured dangerously close. Baliper, scarlet tail lashing, prowled the outer edges of the conflict, sending keepers darting for safety, squeaking indignantly at the danger he presented.

The struggle ended almost as abruptly as it had begun. Mercor flung back his golden head and then snapped it forward, jaws wide. Screams from the keepers and startled roars from the watching dragons predicted Kalo's death by acid spray. Instead, at the last moment, Mercor snapped his jaws shut. He darted his head down and spat, not a mist or a stream, but only a single blot of acid onto Kalo's vulnerable throat. The blue-black dragon screamed in agony and fury. With three powerful beats of his wings, Mercor lifted off him and alighted a ship's length away. Blood was running freely from the long gash on his ribs, sheeting down his gold-scaled side. He was breathing heavily, his nostrils flared wide. Color rippled through his scales, and the protective crests around his eyes stood tall. He lashed his tail, and the smell of his challenge filled the air.

The moment Mercor had lifted his weight off him, Kalo had rolled to his feet. Snarling his frustration and humiliation, he headed immediately toward the river to wash the acid from his flesh before it could eat any deeper. Carson, Spit's keeper, ran beside Kalo, shouting at him to stop and let him look at the injury. The black dragon ignored him. Bruised and shaken but not much injured, Ranculos scrambled to his feet and staggered upright. He shook his wings out and then folded them slowly as if they were painful. Then, with what dignity he could muster, he limped away from the trampled earth of the combat site.

Mercor roared after the retreating Kalo. "Don't forget that I could have killed you! Don't ever forget it, Kalo!"

"Lizard spawn!" the dark dragon roared back at him but did not slow his retreat toward the icy waters of the river.

Sintara turned away from them. It was over. She was surprised it had lasted as long as it had. Battle, like mating, was something that dragons did on the wing. Had the males been able to take flight, the contest might have gone on for hours, perhaps the entire day, and left all of them acid seared and bloodied. For a moment, her ancestral memories of such trials seized her mind and she felt her heart race with excitement. The males would have battled for her regard, and in the end, when only one was the victor, still he would have had to match her in flight and meet her challenge before he could claim the right to mate with her. They would have soared through air, going higher and higher as the drake sought to match her loops and dives and powerful climbs. And if he had succeeded, if he had managed to come close enough to match her flight, he would have locked his body to hers, and as their wings synchronized . . .

"SINTARA!"

Mercor's bellow startled her out of her reflection. She was not the only one who turned to see what the gold drake wanted of her. Every dragon and keeper on the meadow was staring at him. And at her.

The great golden dragon lifted his head and then snapped open his wings with an audible crack. A fresh wave of his scent went out on the wind. "You should not provoke what you cannot complete," he rebuked her.

She stared at him, feeling anger flush her colors brighter. "It had nothing to do with you, Mercor. Perhaps you should not intrude into things that do not concern you."

He spread his wings wider still and lifted his body tall on his powerful hind legs. "I will fly." He did not roar the words, but even so they still carried clearly through the wind and rain. "As will you. And when the time comes for mating battles, I will win. And I will mate you."

She stared at him, more shocked than she had thought she could be. Unthinkable for a male to make such a blatant claim. She tried not to be flattered that he had said she would fly. When the silence grew too long, when she became aware that everyone was watching her, expecting a response, she felt anger. "So say you," she retorted lamely. She did not need to hear Fente's snort of disdain to know that her feeble response had impressed no one.

Turning away from them all, she began stalking back to the forest and the thin shelter of the trees. She didn't care.

She didn't care what Mercor had said nor that Fente had mocked her. There was none among them worth impressing. "Scarcely a proper battle at all," she sneered quietly.

"Was a 'proper battle' what you were trying to provoke?" Her snippy little keeper, Thymara, was abruptly beside her, trotting to keep up. Her black hair hung in fuzzy, tattered braids, a few still adorned with wooden charms. Her roll down the hill had coated her ragged cloak with dead grass. Her feet were bound up in mismatched rags, the makeshift shoes soled with crudely tanned deerskin. She had grown thinner of late, and taller. The bones of her face stood out more. The wings that Sintara had gifted her with bounced lightly beneath her cloak as she jogged. Despite the rudeness of her first query, Thymara sounded concerned as she added,

"Stop a moment. Crouch down. Let me see your neck where he bit you."

"He didn't draw blood." Sintara could scarcely believe she was answering such an impudent demand from a mere human.

"I want to look at it. It looks as if several scales are loosened."

"I did nothing to provoke that silly squabble." Sintara halted abruptly and lowered her head so that Thymara could inspect her neck. She resented doing it, feeling that she had somehow given way to the human's domineering manner. Anger simmered in her. Briefly she considered "accidentally" knocking Thymara off her feet with a swipe of her head. But as she felt the girl's strong hands gently easing her misaligned neck scales back into smoothness, she relented. Her keeper and her clever hands had their uses.

"None of the scales are torn all the way free, though you may shed some of them sooner rather than later."

Sintara sensed her keeper's annoyance as she set her scales to rights. Despite Thymara's frequent rudeness to Sintara, the dragon knew the girl took pride in her health and appearance. Any insult to Sintara rankled Thymara as well. And she would be aware of her dragon's mood, too.

As she focused more on the girl, she knew that they shared more than annoyance. The frustration was there as well. "Males!" the girl exclaimed suddenly. "I suppose it takes no more to provoke a male dragon to stupidity than it does a human male."

Sintara's curiosity was stirred by the comment, though she would not let Thymara know that. She reviewed what she knew of Thymara's most recent upsets and divined the source of her sour mood. "The decision is yours, not theirs. How foolishly you are behaving! Just mate with both of them. Or neither. Show them that you are a queen, not a cow to be bred at the bull's rutting."

"I chose neither," Thymara told her, answering the question that the dragon hadn't asked.

Her scales smoothed, Sintara lifted her head and resumed her trek to the forest's edge. Thymara hurried to stay beside her, musing as she jogged. "I just want to let it alone, to leave things as they've always been. But neither of them seems willing to let that happen." She shook her head, her braids flying with the motion. "Tats is my oldest friend. I knew him back in Trehaug, before we became dragon keepers. He's part of my past, part of home. But when he pushes me to bed with him, I don't know if it's because he loves me or simply because I've refused him. I worry that if we become lovers and it doesn't work out, I'll lose him completely."

"Then bed Rapskal and be done with it," the dragon suggested. Thymara was boring her. How could humans seriously believe that a dragon could be interested in the details of their lives? As well worry about a moth or a fish.

The keeper took the dragon's comment as an excuse to keep talking. "Rapskal? I can't. If I take him as a mate, I know that would ruin my friendship with Tats. Rapskal is handsome, and funny . . . and a bit strange. But it's a sort of strange that I like. And I think he truly cares about me, that when he pushes me to sleep with him, it's not just for the pleasure." She shook her head. "But I don't want it, with either of them. Well, I do. If I could just have the physical part of it and not have it make everything else complicated.

But I don't want to take the chance of catching a child, and I don't really want to have to make some momentous decision. If I choose one, have I lost the other? I don't know what—"

"You're boring me," Sintara warned her. "And there are more important things you should be doing right now. Have you hunted for me today? Do you have meat to bring me?"

Thymara bridled at the sudden change of topic. She replied grudgingly, "Not yet. When the rain lets up, I'll go. There's no game moving right now." A pause, and then she broached another dangerous subject. "Mercor said you would fly. Were you trying? Have you exercised your wings today, Sintara? Working on the muscles is the only way that you will ever—"

"I have no desire to flap around on the beach like a gull with a broken wing. No desire to make myself an object of mockery." Even less desire to fail and fall into the icy, swift-flowing river and drown. Or overestimate her skills and plummet into the trees as Baliper had done. His wings were so swollen that he could not close them, and he'd torn a claw from his left front foot.

"No one mocks you! Exercising your wings is a necessity, Sintara. You must learn to fly; all of the dragons must. You all have grown since we left Cassarick, and it is becoming impossible for me to kill enough game to keep you well fed, even with the larger game that we've found here. You will have to hunt for your own food, and to do that, you must be able to fly. Would not you rather be one of the first dragons to leave the ground than one of the last ones?"

That thought stung. The idea that the smaller females such as Veras or Fente might gain the air before she did was intolerable. It might actually be easier for such stunted and scrawny creatures to fly. Anger warmed her blood and she knew the liquid copper of her eyes would be swirling with emotion. She'd have to kill them, that was all. Kill them before either one could humiliate her.

"Or you could take flight before they did," Thymara suggested steadily.

Sintara snapped her head around to stare at the girl. Sometimes she was able to overhear the dragon's thoughts.

Sometimes she was even impudent enough to answer them.

"I'm tired of the rain. I want to go back under the trees."

Thymara nodded, and as Sintara stalked off, she followed docilely. The dragon looked back only once.

Down by the river, other keepers were stridently discussing which dragon had started the melee. Carson the hunter had his arms crossed and stood in stubborn confrontation with Kalo. The black dragon was dripping; he'd rinsed Mercor's acid from his throat. Carson's small silver dragon, Spit, was watching them sullenly from a distance. The man was stupid, Sintara thought. The big blue-black male was not fond of humans to start with: provoked, Kalo might simply snap Carson in two.

Tats was helping Sylve examine the long injury down Mercor's ribs while his own dragon, Fente, jealously clawed at the mud and muttered vague threats. Ranculos was holding one wing half-opened for his keeper's inspection. It was likely badly bruised at the very least. Sestican, covered in mud, was dispiritedly bellowing for his keeper, but Lecter was nowhere in sight. The squabble was over. For one moment, they had been dragons, vying for the attention of a female. Now they were back to behaving like large cattle. Sintara despised them, and she loathed herself. They weren't worth her time to provoke. They only made her think of all they were not. All she was not.

If only, she thought, and traced her misfortune back, happenstance after happenstance. If only the dragons had emerged from the metamorphosis fully formed and healthy. If only they had been in better condition when they cocooned to make the transition from sea serpent to dragon. If only they had migrated home decades ago. If only the Elderlings had not died off, if only the mountain had never erupted and put an end to the world they had once known. She should have been so much more than she was. Dragons were supposed to emerge from their cocoons capable of flight and take wing to make that first rejuvenating kill. But none of them had. She was like a bright chip of glass, fallen from a gorgeous mosaic of Elderlings and turreted cities and dragons on the wing, to lie in the dirt, broken away from all that had once been her destiny. She was meaningless without that world.

She had tried to fly, more than once. Thymara need never know of her many private and humiliating failures. It was infuriating that dimwitted Heeby was able to take flight and hunt for herself. Every day, the red female grew larger and stronger, and her keeper, Rapskal, never tired of singing the praises of his "great, glorious girl" of a dragon. He'd made up a stupid song, more doggerel than poetry, and loudly sang it to her every morning as he groomed her. It made Sintara want to bite his head off. Heeby could preen all she liked when her keeper sang to her. She was still dumber than a cow.

"The best vengeance might be to learn to fly," Thymara suggested again, privy to the feeling rather than the thought.

"Why don't you try that yourself?" Sintara retorted bitterly.

Thymara was silent, a silence that simmered.

The idea came to Sintara slowly. She was startled. "What? You have, haven't you? You've tried to fly?"

Thymara kept her face turned away from the dragon as they trudged through the wild meadow and up toward the tree line. Scattered throughout the meadow were small stone cottages, some little more than broken walls and collapsed roofs while others had been restored by the dragon keepers. Once there had been a village here, a place for human artisans to live. They'd plied their trades here, the servant and merchant classes of the Elderlings who had lived in the gleaming city on the far side of the swift-flowing river. She wondered if Thymara knew that. Probably not.

"You made these wings grow on me," Thymara finally replied. "If I have to have them, if I have to put up with something that makes it impossible to wear an ordinary shirt, something that lifts my cloak up off my back so that every breeze chills me, then I might as well make them useful. Yes, I've tried to fly. Rapskal was helping me. He insists I'll be able to, one day. But so far all I've done is skin my knees and scrape the palms of my hands when I fall. I've had no success. Does that please you?"

"It doesn't surprise me." It did please her. No human

should fly when dragons could not! Let her skin her knees and bruise herself a thousand times. If Thymara took flight before she did, the dragon would eat her! Her hunger stirred at the thought, and she became sensible. There was no sense in making the girl aware of that, at least not until she'd done her day's hunting.

"I'm going to keep trying," Thymara said in a low voice. "And so should you."

"Do as you please and I'll do the same," the dragon replied. "And what should please you right now is that you go hunting. I'm hungry." She gave the girl a mental push.

Thymara narrowed her eyes, aware that the dragon had used her glamour on her. It didn't matter. She would still be nagged with an urgent desire to go hunting. Being aware of the source of that suggestion would not make her immune to it.

The winter rains had prompted an explosion of greenery. The tall wet grasses slapped against her legs as they waded through it. They had climbed the slope of the meadow, and now the open forest of the hillside beckoned. Beneath the trees, there would be some shelter from the rain, although many of the trees here had lost their foliage. The forest seemed both peculiar and familiar to Sintara. Her own life's experience had been limited to the dense and impenetrable forest that bordered the Rain Wild River. Yet her ancestral memories echoed the familiarity of woods such as this. The names of the trees—oak and hickam and birch, alder and ash and goldleaf—came to her mind. Dragons had known these trees, this sort of forest and even this particular place. But they had seldom lingered here in the chill rains of winter. No. For this miserable season, dragons would have flown off to bask in the heat of the deserts. Or they would have taken shelter in the places that the Elderlings created for them, crystal domes with heated floors and pools of steaming water. She turned and looked across the river to fabled Kelsingra. They had come so far, and yet asylum remained out of reach. The swift-flowing river was deep and treacherous. No dragon could swim it. True flight was the only way home.

The ancient Elderling city stood, mostly intact, just as her ancestral memories had recalled it. Even under the overcast sky, even through the gray onslaught of rain, the towering buildings of black and silver stone gleamed and beckoned. Once, lovely scaled Elderlings had resided there. Friends and servants of dragons, they had dressed in bright robes and adorned themselves with gold and silver and gleaming copper. The wide avenues of Kelsingra and the gracious buildings had all been constructed to welcome dragons as well as Elderlings. There had been a statuary plaza, where the flagstones radiated heat in the winter, though that area of the city appeared to have vanished into the giant chasm that now cleft its ancient roads and towers. There had been baths, steaming vats of hot water where Elderlings and dragons alike had taken refuge from foul weather. Her ancestors had soaked there, not just in hot water, but in copper vats of simmering oils that had sheened their scales and hardened their claws.

And there had been . . . something else. Something she could not quite recall clearly. Water, she thought, but not water. Something delightful, something that even now sparkled and gleamed and called to her through her dim recollection of it.

"What are you looking at?" Thymara asked her.

Sintara hadn't realized that she had halted to stare across the river. "Nothing. The city," she said and resumed her walk.

"If you could fly, you could get across the river to Kelsingra."

"If you could think, you would know when to be quiet," the dragon retorted. Did the stupid girl not realize how often she thought of that? Daily. Hourly. The Elderling magic of heated tiles might still work. Even if it did not, the standing buildings would provide shelter from the incessant rain. Perhaps in Kelsingra she would feel like a real dragon again rather than a footed serpent.

They reached the edge of the trees. A gust of wind rattled them, sending water spattering down through the sheltering branches. Sintara rumbled her displeasure. "Go hunt," she told the girl, and she strengthened her mental push.

Offended, her keeper turned away and trudged back down the hill. Sintara didn't bother to watch her go. Thymara would obey. It was what keepers did. It was really all they were good for.

THE CRITICALLY ACCLAIMED
SOLDIER SON TRILOGY FROM
NEW YORK TIMES BESTSELLING AUTHOR

ROBIN HOBB

SHAMAN'S CROSSING
978-0-06-075828-8

Nevare Burvelle was destined from birth to be a soldier in
service of the King of Gernia. Now he must face a forest-
dwelling folk who will not submit easily to a king's tyranny
and they possess a powerful sorcery that threatens to claim
Nevare Burvelle's soul and devastate his world.

FOREST MAGE
978-0-06-075829-5

Freed from the Speck magic that infected him, Nevare Burvelle
is journeying home to Widevale, anticipating a tender reunion
with his fiancée, Carsina. But his nights are haunted by grim
visions of treachery, and his days are tormented by a strange
side-effect of the plague that shames his family and repulses
the lady of his heart.

RENEGADE'S MAGIC
978-0-06-075830-1

Nevare Burvelle stands wrongly accused of unspeakable
crimes, including murder. Suddenly an outcast and a fugi-
tive, he remains hostage to the Speck magic that shackles
him to a savage alter ego who would destroy everything
Nevare holds dear.

HOB 0211